IXTH GENERATION

VOLUME ONE

TOP COW
PRODUCTIONS, INC.®

Published by Top Cow Productions, Inc.
Los Angeles

IXTH
GENERATION

VOLUME ONE

MATT HAWKINS
writer

STJEPAN SEJIC
artist

TROY PETERI
letterer

STJEPAN SEJIC
Cover Art

BETSY GONIA
Editor

TRICIA RAMOS
Production

Want more info? Check out: **www.topcow.com**
for news & exclusive Top Cow merchandise!

IMAGE COMICS, INC.
Robert Kirkman – Chief Operating Officer
Erik Larsen – Chief Financial Officer
Todd McFarlane – President
Marc Silvestri – Chief Executive Officer
Jim Valentino – Vice-President
Eric Stephenson – Publisher
Corey Murphy – Director of Sales
Jeremy Sullivan – Director of Digital Sales
Kat Salazar – Director of PR & Marketing
Emily Miller – Director of Operations
Branwyn Bigglestone – Senior Accounts Manager
Sarah Mello – Accounts Manager
Drew Gill – Art Director
Jonathan Chan – Production Manager
Meredith Wallace – Print Manager
Randy Okamura – Marketing Production Designer
David Brothers – Branding Manager
Ally Power – Content Manager
Addison Duke – Production Artist
Vincent Kukua – Production Artist
Sasha Head – Production Artist
Tricia Ramos – Production Artist
Emilio Bautista – Sales Assistant
Chloe Ramos-Peterson – Administrative Assistant
IMAGECOMICS.COM

IXth GENERATION, VOLUME 1. FIRST PRINTING. AUGUST 2015. Copyright © 2015
Top Cow Productions, Inc. All rights reserved. Published by Image Comics, Inc. Office of
publication: 2001 Center Street, Sixth Floor, Berkeley, CA 94704. Originally published
in single magazine form as IXth GENERATION #1-4 & IXth GENERATION: HIDDEN FILES
#1, by Image Comics. "IXth Generation," its logos, and the likenesses of all characters
herein are trademarks of Top Cow Productions, Inc, unless otherwise noted. "Image"
and the Image Comics logos are registered trademarks of Image Comics, Inc. No part
of this publication may be reproduced or transmitted, in any form or by any means
(except for short excerpts for journalistic or review purposes), without the express
written permission of Top Cow Productions, Inc. All names, characters, events, and
locales in this publication are entirely fictional. Any resemblance to actual persons
(living or dead), events, or places, without satiric intent, is coincidental. Printed in
the USA. For information regarding the CPSIA on this printed material call: 203-
595-3636 and provide reference #RICH-628883. For international rights, contact:
foreignlicensing@imagecomics.com. ISBN: 978-1-63215-323-4

For Top Cow Productions, Inc.

Marc Silvestri - *CEO*
Matt Hawkins - *President and COO*
Betsy Gonia – *Managing Editor*
Bryan Hill – *Story Editor*
Elena Salcedo – *Operations Manager*
Ryan Cady - *Editorial Assistant*
Vincent Valentine – *Production Assistant*

www.topcow.com

"Utopia was here at last:
its novelty had not yet
been assailed by the
supreme enemy of all
Utopias - boredom."

Arthur C. Clarke,
"Childhood's End"

CHAPTER ONE

The Aphrodite Protocol
was initiated in the late
20th Century in an attempt
to save humanity from a
predicted extinction level
event that became reality in
the year 2102 AD.

The Protocol successfully
engineered and evolved
humans into new species
that survived in this new
world via technological
singularity and genetic
enhancement.

The architect of the
Protocol created nine
heirs to rule over this
new world. They were
placed in hibernation for
seven hundred years to be
activated in what became
known as the ASCENSION; the
year 2802, when the self-
proclaimed Gods of the IXth
Generation took control.

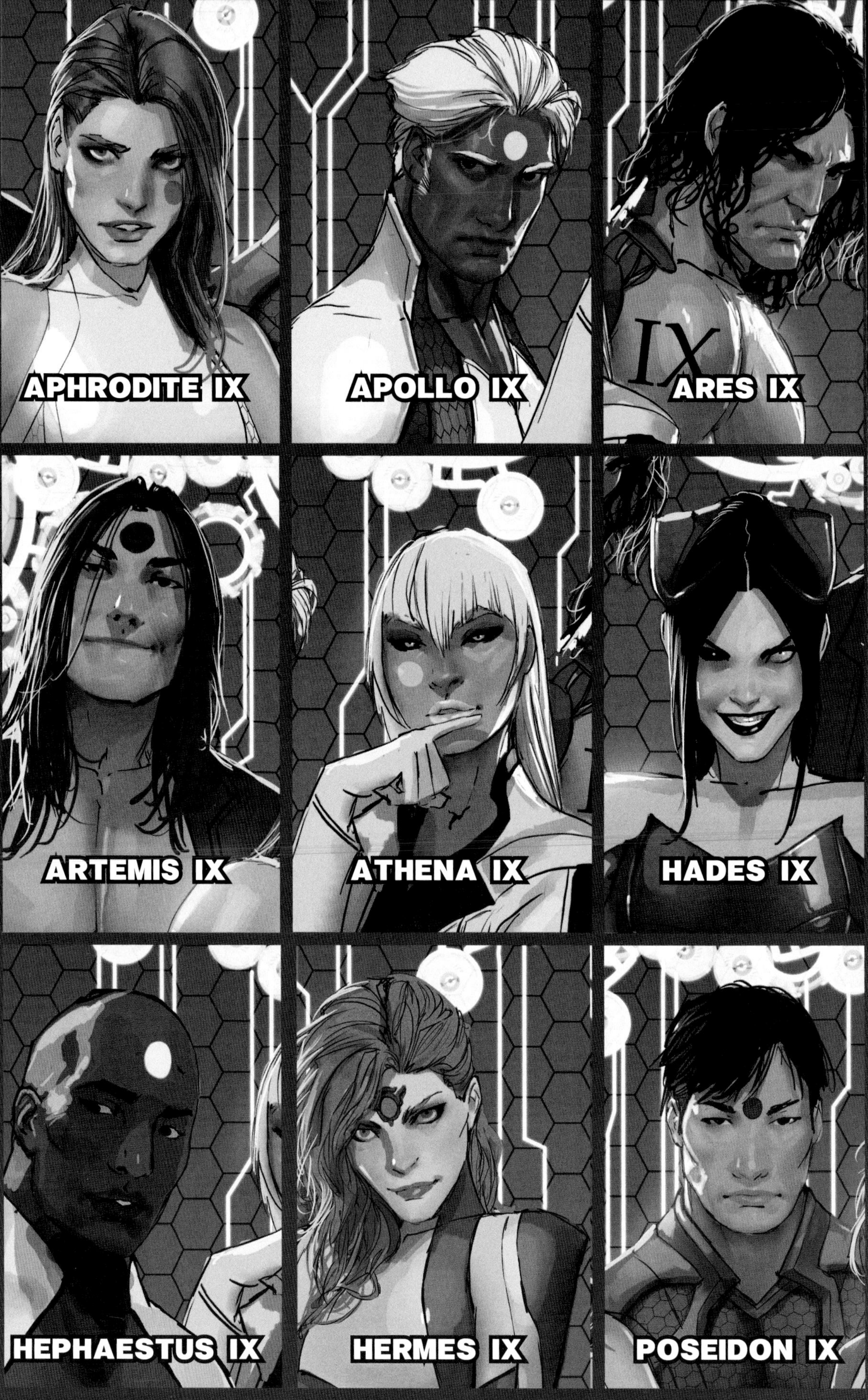
APHRODITE IX
APOLLO IX
IX
ARES IX
ARTEMIS IX
ATHENA IX
HADES IX
HEPHAESTUS IX
HERMES IX
POSEIDON IX

TWENTY-FIVE YEARS AGO THIS WAS SPEROS CITY, THE CAPITAL CITY OF A CYBORG RACE, WHOSE POPULATION WAS REDISTRIBUTED INTO NINE UNIQUE CITY-STATES, RULED OVER BY THEIR NEW IXTH GENERATION OVERLORDS.

THE ONCE-PROUD CYBORGS HAD BEEN RELEGATED TO A *WORKER* CASTE KEPT IN LINE BY THE *WARRIOR* CASTE OF SYNTHETIC XVs, WHO CARRIED THE LIKENESS OF THEIR MASTERS.

SHINK

THE NINE FIEFDOMS GREW AND DEVELOPED A PERSONALITY MODELED AND NAMED AFTER THEIR IX. I CHOSE THE NORTHERNMOST ONE FOR A VARIETY OF REASONS, AND TRIED TO MAKE THE SOMEWHAT ISOLATED *"APHRODITE"* A HARMONIOUS, PEACEFUL LAND.

THE FIRST DECADE WAS QUIET, AND I WAS HOPEFUL FOR OUR BURGEONING UTOPIA. ULTIMATELY IT WAS ONLY *IDEAL* FOR THE NINE OF US IN POWER.

DURING THE SECOND DECADE A FEW SKIRMISHES BROKE OUT, BUT IN THE LAST FIVE YEARS IT'S BEEN ENDLESS WAR BETWEEN THEM ALL.

HAHAHAHAHA!

ALLIANCES SHIFTED BETWEEN THE VARIOUS IXS. ALWAYS FOUR-ON-FOUR. I WAS THE ONLY ONE WHO ABSTAINED FROM ALL THE NONSENSE. A LUXURY PERHAPS OF MY CHOOSING A SECLUDED REGION NO ONE ELSE DESIRED.

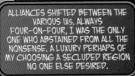

IT WAS ALL A GAME TO THEM. IF ONE OF THEM DIED, THEIR CONSCIOUSNESS AND MEMORIES WOULD BE DOWNLOADED INTO A CLONED BODY, AND THEY WOULD ENTER THE FRAY ANEW.

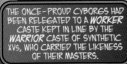

DEATH HAD LOST ITS STING.

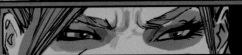

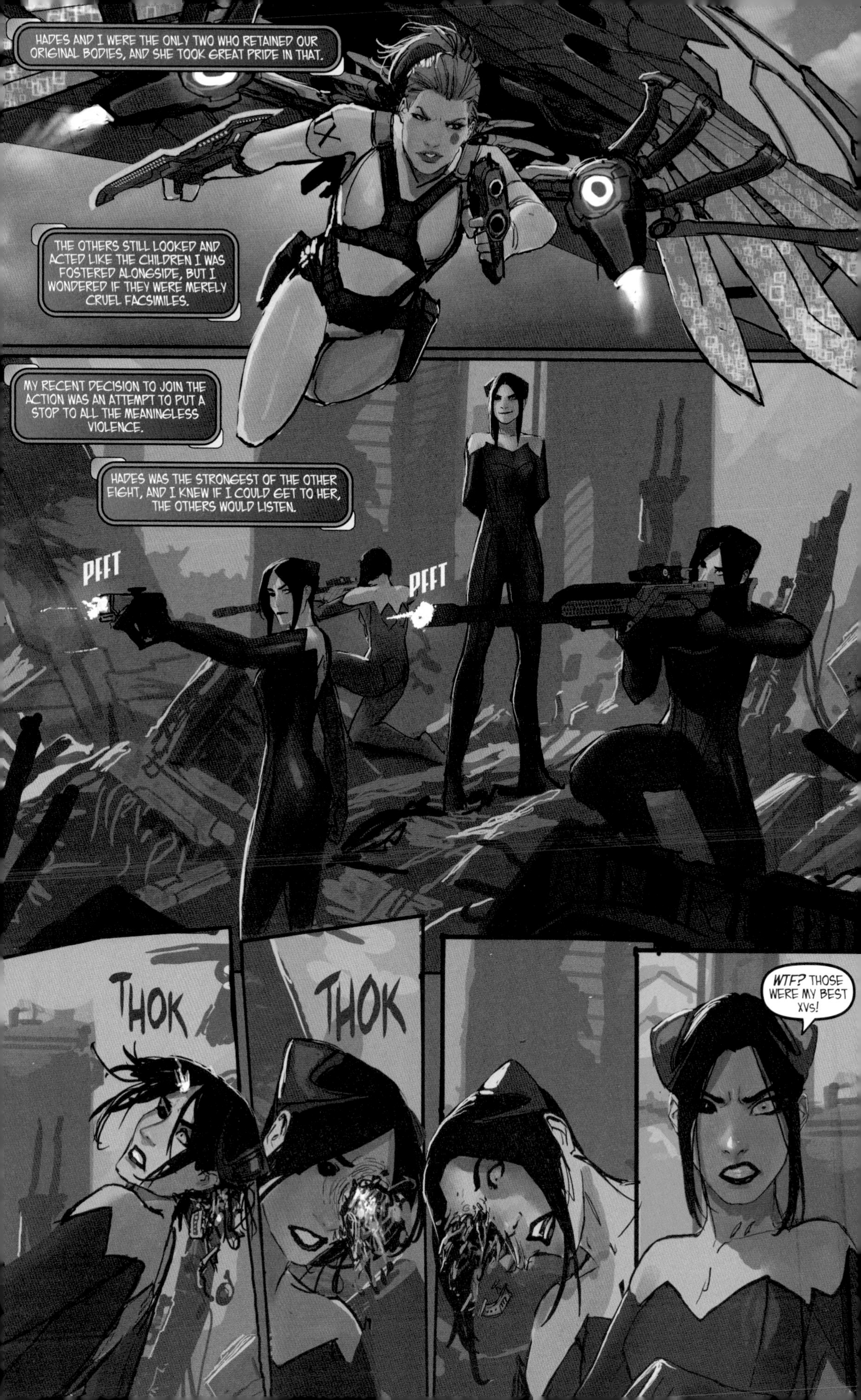
HADES AND I WERE THE ONLY TWO WHO RETAINED OUR ORIGINAL BODIES, AND SHE TOOK GREAT PRIDE IN THAT.
THE OTHERS STILL LOOKED AND ACTED LIKE THE CHILDREN I WAS FOSTERED ALONGSIDE, BUT I WONDERED IF THEY WERE MERELY CRUEL FACSIMILES.
MY RECENT DECISION TO JOIN THE ACTION WAS AN ATTEMPT TO PUT A STOP TO ALL THE MEANINGLESS VIOLENCE.
HADES WAS THE STRONGEST OF THE OTHER EIGHT, AND I KNEW IF I COULD GET TO HER, THE OTHERS WOULD LISTEN.
PFFT
PFFT
THOK
THOK
WTF? THOSE WERE MY BEST XVS!

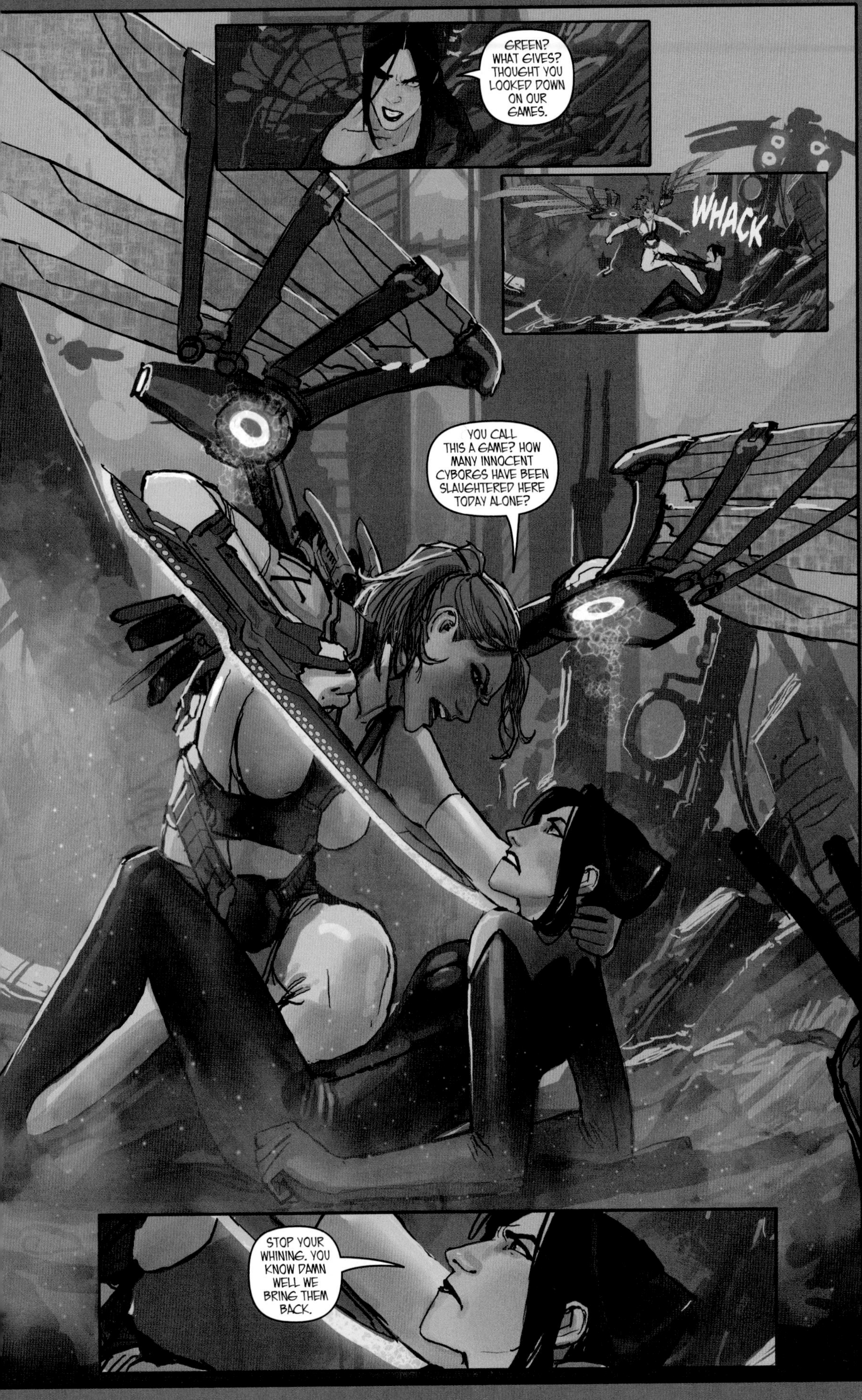
GREEN? WHAT GIVES? THOUGHT YOU LOOKED DOWN ON OUR GAMES.
WHACK
YOU CALL THIS A GAME? HOW MANY INNOCENT CYBORGS HAVE BEEN SLAUGHTERED HERE TODAY ALONE?
STOP YOUR WHINING. YOU KNOW DAMN WELL WE BRING THEM BACK.

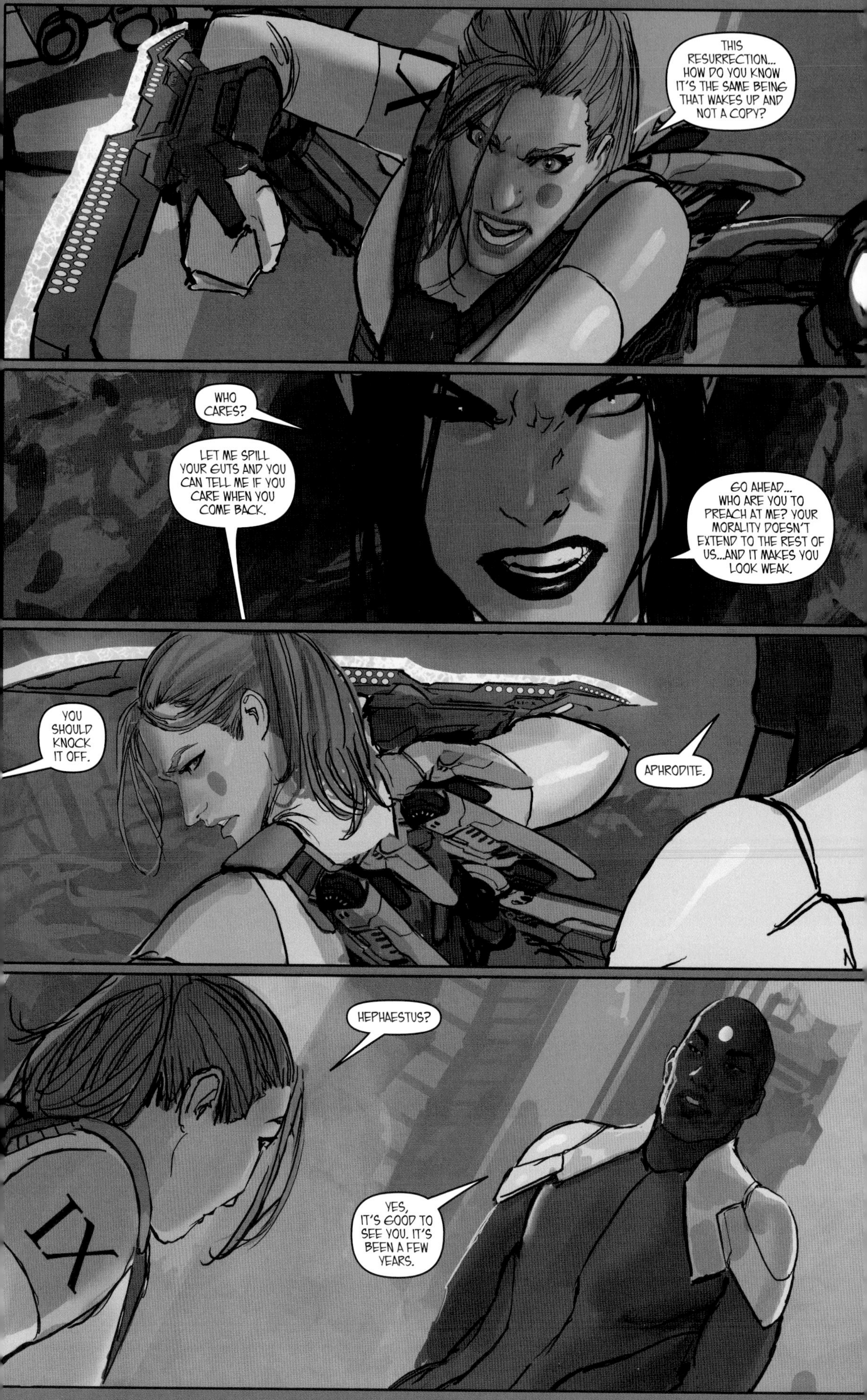
THIS RESURRECTION... HOW DO YOU KNOW IT'S THE SAME BEING THAT WAKES UP AND NOT A COPY?
WHO CARES?
LET ME SPILL YOUR GUTS AND YOU CAN TELL ME IF YOU CARE WHEN YOU COME BACK.
GO AHEAD... WHO ARE YOU TO PREACH AT ME? YOUR MORALITY DOESN'T EXTEND TO THE REST OF US...AND IT MAKES YOU LOOK WEAK.
YOU SHOULD KNOCK IT OFF.
APHRODITE.
HEPHAESTUS?
YES, IT'S GOOD TO SEE YOU. IT'S BEEN A FEW YEARS.
IX

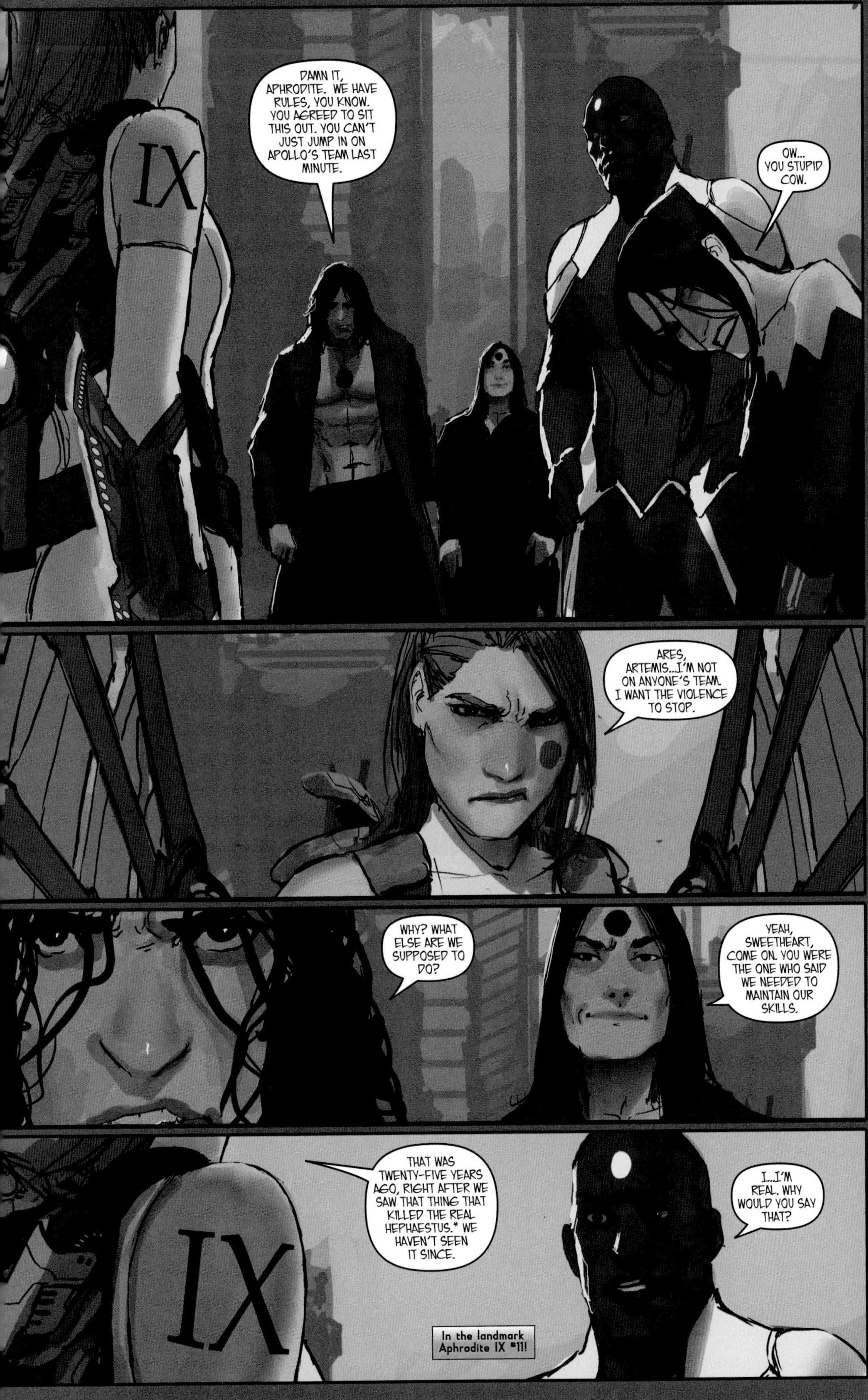
DAMN IT, APHRODITE. WE HAVE RULES, YOU KNOW. YOU AGREED TO SIT THIS OUT. YOU CAN'T JUST JUMP IN ON APOLLO'S TEAM LAST MINUTE.
OW... YOU STUPID COW.
ARES, ARTEMIS...I'M NOT ON ANYONE'S TEAM. I WANT THE VIOLENCE TO STOP.
WHY? WHAT ELSE ARE WE SUPPOSED TO DO?
YEAH, SWEETHEART, COME ON. YOU WERE THE ONE WHO SAID WE NEEDED TO MAINTAIN OUR SKILLS.
THAT WAS TWENTY-FIVE YEARS AGO, RIGHT AFTER WE SAW THAT THING THAT KILLED THE REAL HEPHAESTUS.* WE HAVEN'T SEEN IT SINCE.
I...I'M REAL. WHY WOULD YOU SAY THAT?
In the landmark Aphrodite IX #11!

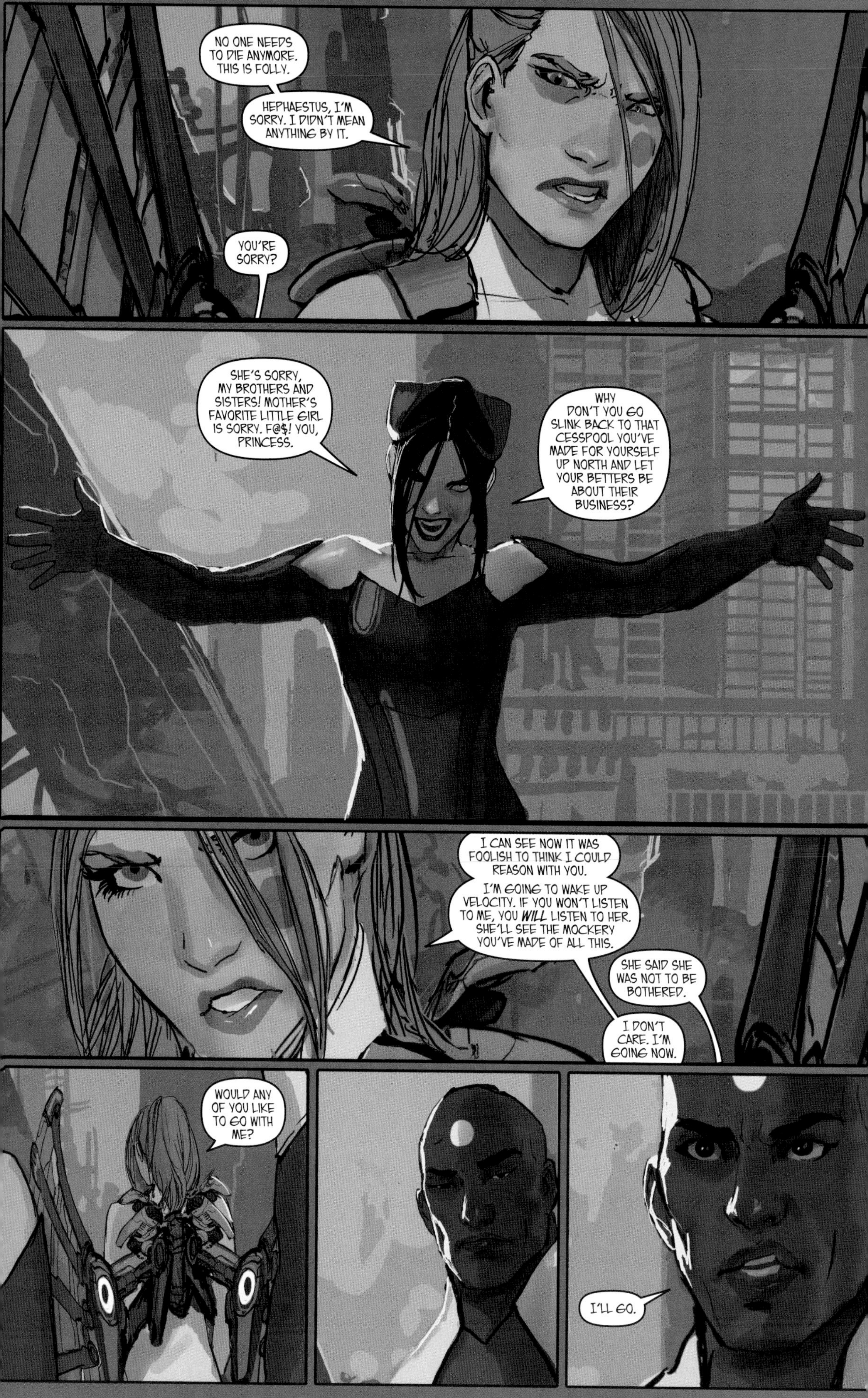
NO ONE NEEDS TO DIE ANYMORE. THIS IS FOLLY.
HEPHAESTUS, I'M SORRY. I DIDN'T MEAN ANYTHING BY IT.
YOU'RE SORRY?
SHE'S SORRY, MY BROTHERS AND SISTERS! MOTHER'S FAVORITE LITTLE GIRL IS SORRY. F@$! YOU, PRINCESS.
WHY DON'T YOU GO SLINK BACK TO THAT CESSPOOL YOU'VE MADE FOR YOURSELF UP NORTH AND LET YOUR BETTERS BE ABOUT THEIR BUSINESS?
I CAN SEE NOW IT WAS FOOLISH TO THINK I COULD REASON WITH YOU.
I'M GOING TO WAKE UP VELOCITY. IF YOU WON'T LISTEN TO ME, YOU ***WILL*** LISTEN TO HER. SHE'LL SEE THE MOCKERY YOU'VE MADE OF ALL THIS.
SHE SAID SHE WAS NOT TO BE BOTHERED.
I DON'T CARE. I'M GOING NOW.
WOULD ANY OF YOU LIKE TO GO WITH ME?
I'LL GO.

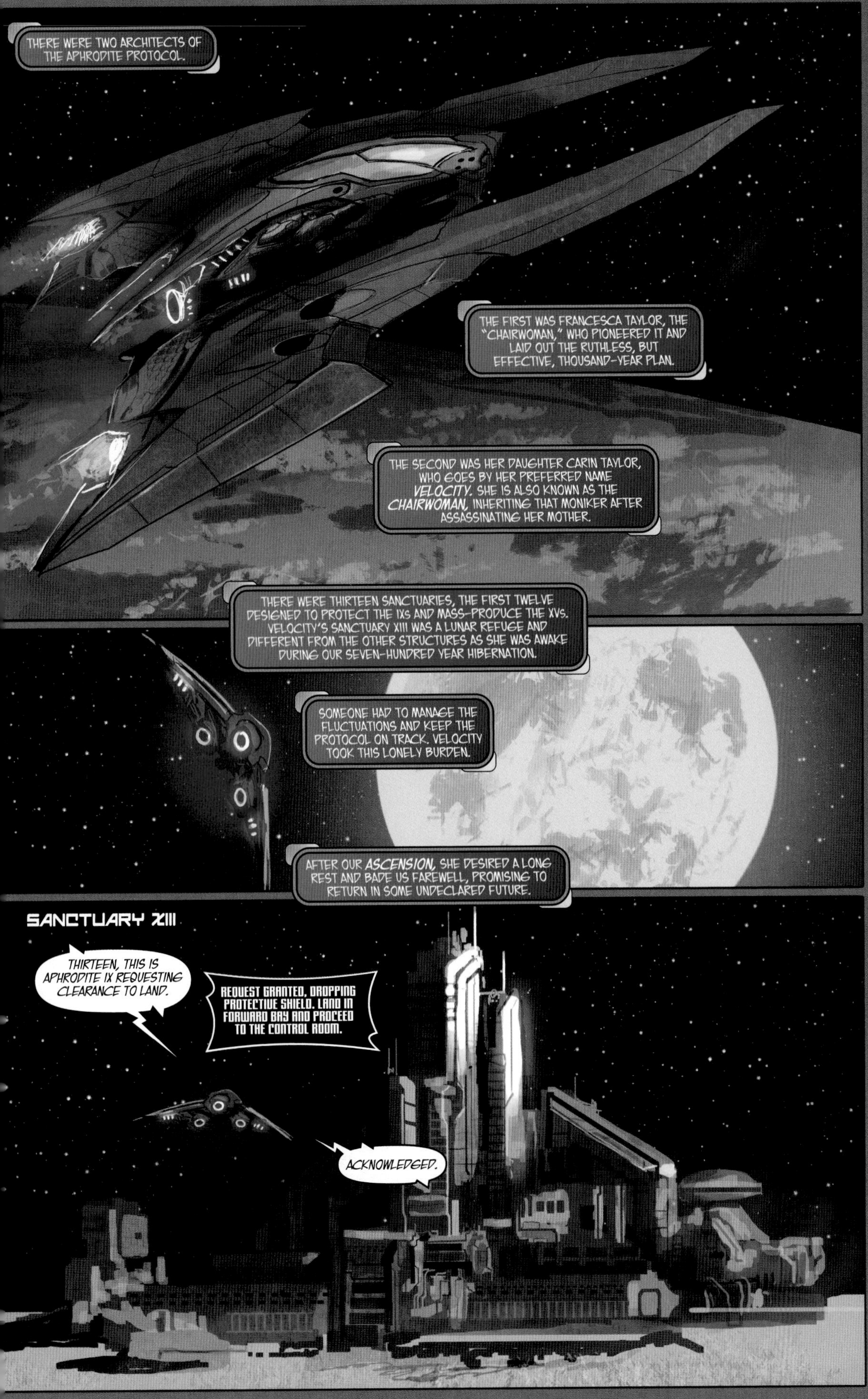
THERE WERE TWO ARCHITECTS OF THE APHRODITE PROTOCOL.
THE FIRST WAS FRANCESCA TAYLOR, THE "CHAIRWOMAN," WHO PIONEERED IT AND LAID OUT THE RUTHLESS, BUT EFFECTIVE, THOUSAND-YEAR PLAN.
THE SECOND WAS HER DAUGHTER CARIN TAYLOR, WHO GOES BY HER PREFERRED NAME VELOCITY. SHE IS ALSO KNOWN AS THE CHAIRWOMAN, INHERITING THAT MONIKER AFTER ASSASSINATING HER MOTHER.
THERE WERE THIRTEEN SANCTUARIES, THE FIRST TWELVE DESIGNED TO PROTECT THE IXS AND MASS-PRODUCE THE XVS. VELOCITY'S SANCTUARY XIII WAS A LUNAR REFUGE AND DIFFERENT FROM THE OTHER STRUCTURES AS SHE WAS AWAKE DURING OUR SEVEN-HUNDRED YEAR HIBERNATION.
SOMEONE HAD TO MANAGE THE FLUCTUATIONS AND KEEP THE PROTOCOL ON TRACK. VELOCITY TOOK THIS LONELY BURDEN.
AFTER OUR ASCENSION, SHE DESIRED A LONG REST AND BADE US FAREWELL, PROMISING TO RETURN IN SOME UNDECLARED FUTURE.
SANCTUARY XIII
THIRTEEN, THIS IS APHRODITE IX REQUESTING CLEARANCE TO LAND.
REQUEST GRANTED, DROPPING PROTECTIVE SHIELD. LAND IN FORWARD BAY AND PROCEED TO THE CONTROL ROOM.
ACKNOWLEDGED.

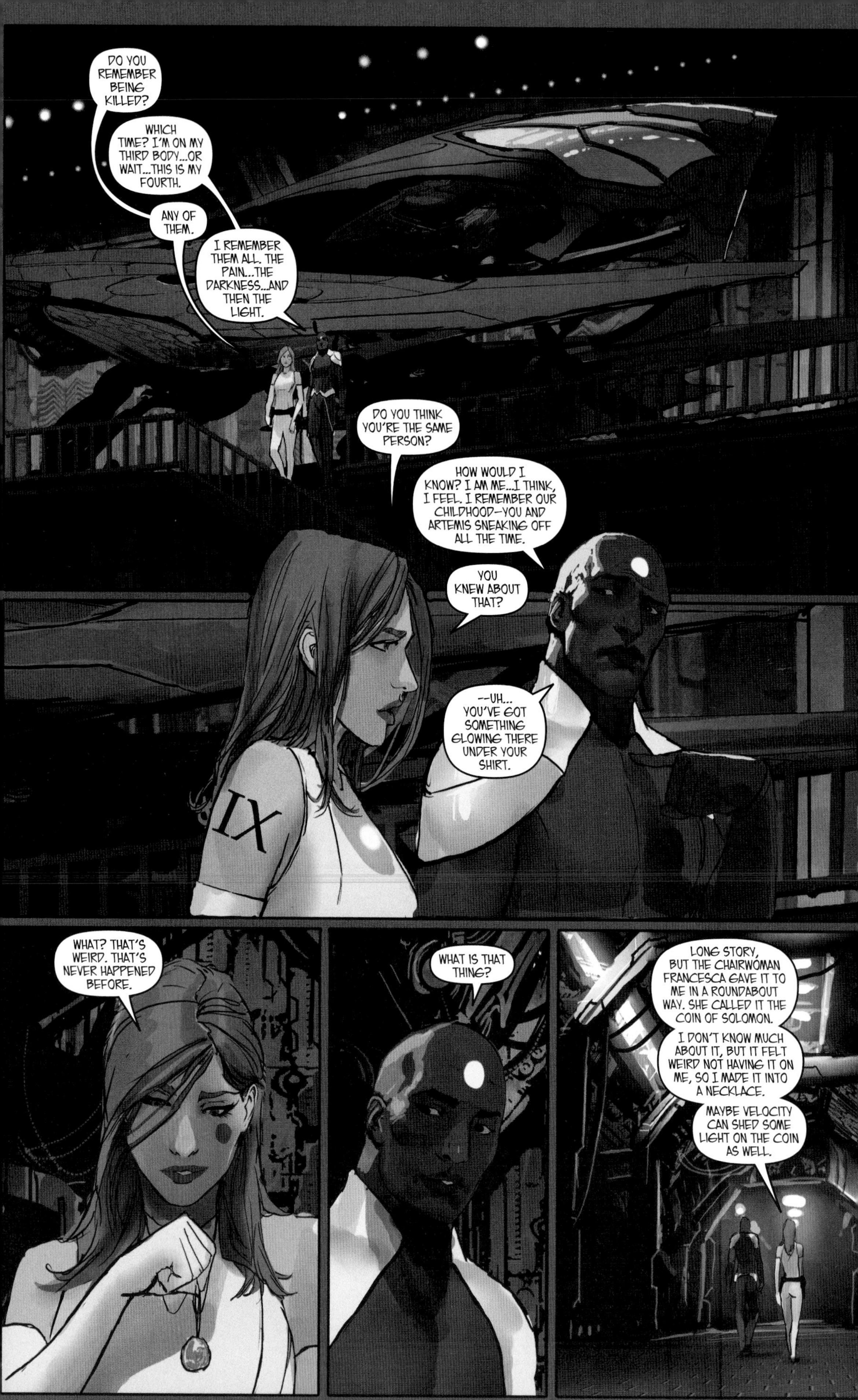
DO YOU REMEMBER BEING KILLED?
WHICH TIME? I'M ON MY THIRD BODY...OR WAIT...THIS IS MY FOURTH.
ANY OF THEM.
I REMEMBER THEM ALL. THE PAIN...THE DARKNESS...AND THEN THE LIGHT.
DO YOU THINK YOU'RE THE SAME PERSON?
HOW WOULD I KNOW? I AM ME...I THINK, I FEEL. I REMEMBER OUR CHILDHOOD--YOU AND ARTEMIS SNEAKING OFF ALL THE TIME.
YOU KNEW ABOUT THAT?
--UH... YOU'VE GOT SOMETHING GLOWING THERE UNDER YOUR SHIRT.
IX
WHAT? THAT'S WEIRD. THAT'S NEVER HAPPENED BEFORE.
WHAT IS THAT THING?
LONG STORY, BUT THE CHAIRWOMAN FRANCESCA GAVE IT TO ME IN A ROUNDABOUT WAY. SHE CALLED IT THE COIN OF SOLOMON.
I DON'T KNOW MUCH ABOUT IT, BUT IT FELT WEIRD NOT HAVING IT ON ME, SO I MADE IT INTO A NECKLACE.
MAYBE VELOCITY CAN SHED SOME LIGHT ON THE COIN AS WELL.

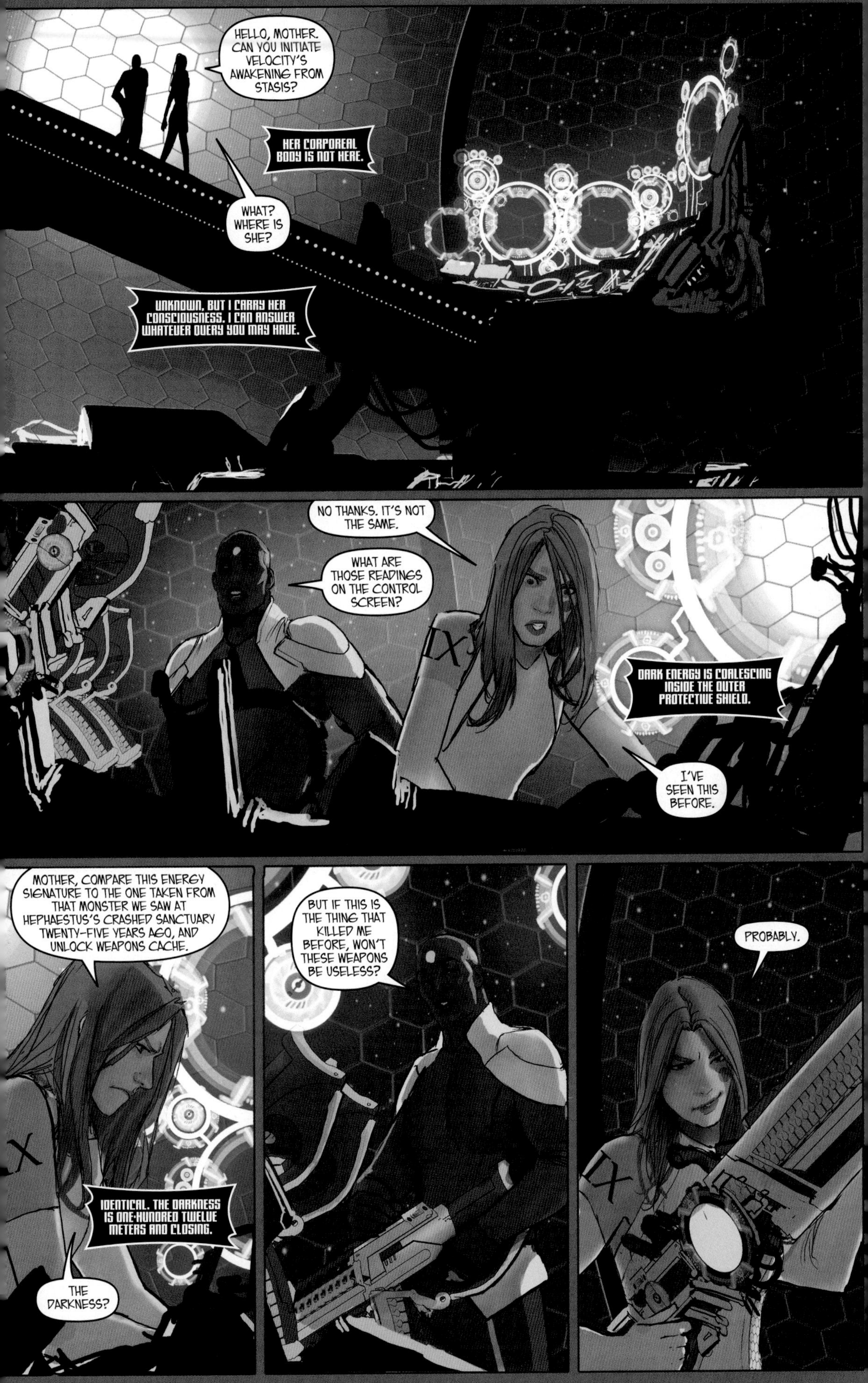
HELLO, MOTHER. CAN YOU INITIATE VELOCITY'S AWAKENING FROM STASIS?
HER CORPOREAL BODY IS NOT HERE.
WHAT? WHERE IS SHE?
UNKNOWN, BUT I CARRY HER CONSCIOUSNESS. I CAN ANSWER WHATEVER QUERY YOU MAY HAVE.
NO THANKS. IT'S NOT THE SAME.
WHAT ARE THOSE READINGS ON THE CONTROL SCREEN?
DARK ENERGY IS COALESCING INSIDE THE OUTER PROTECTIVE SHIELD.
I'VE SEEN THIS BEFORE.
MOTHER, COMPARE THIS ENERGY SIGNATURE TO THE ONE TAKEN FROM THAT MONSTER WE SAW AT HEPHAESTUS'S CRASHED SANCTUARY TWENTY-FIVE YEARS AGO, AND UNLOCK WEAPONS CACHE.
IDENTICAL. THE DARKNESS IS ONE-HUNDRED TWELVE METERS AND CLOSING.
THE DARKNESS?
BUT IF THIS IS THE THING THAT KILLED ME BEFORE, WON'T THESE WEAPONS BE USELESS?
PROBABLY.

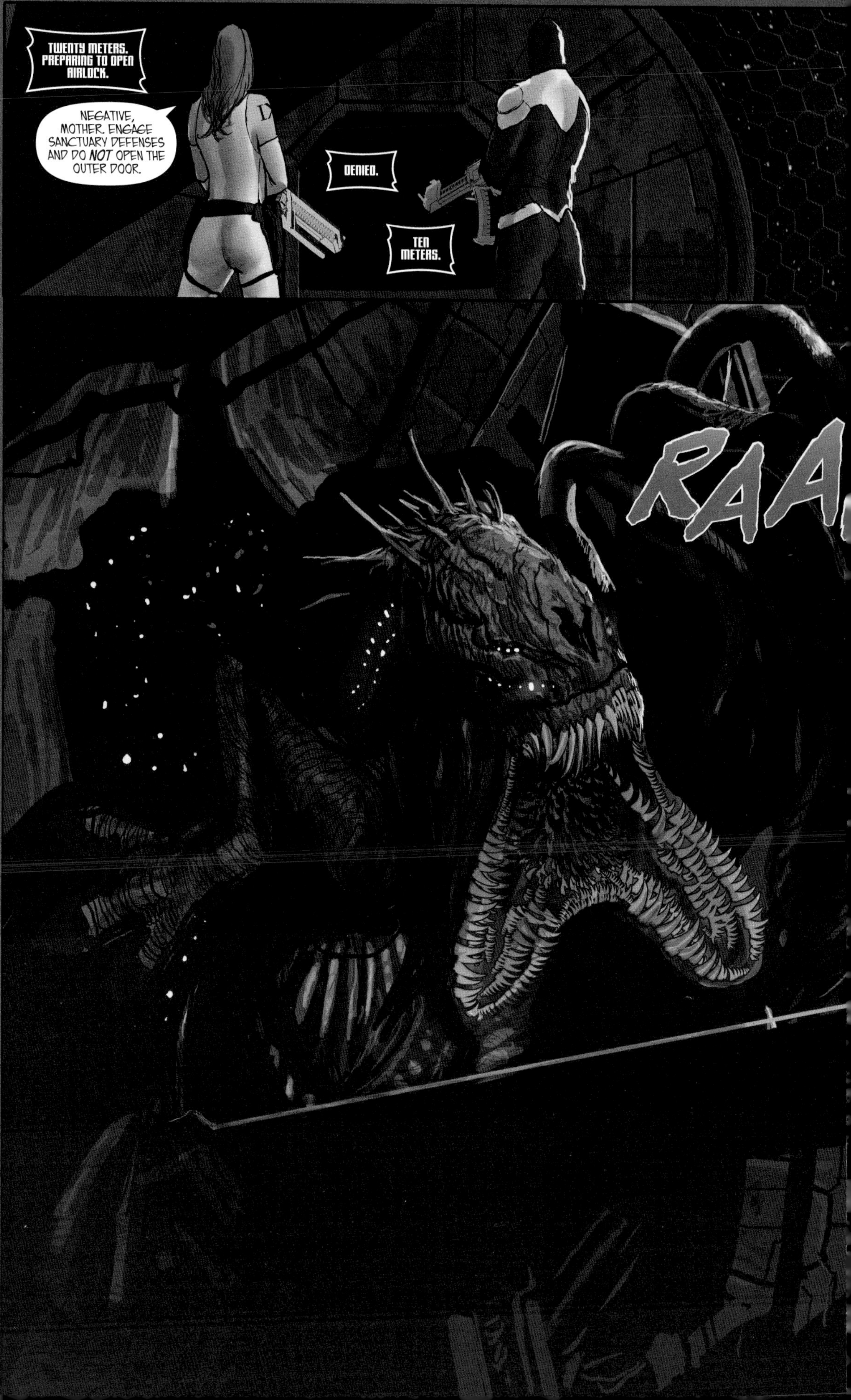

TWENTY METERS. PREPARING TO OPEN AIRLOCK.
NEGATIVE, MOTHER. ENGAGE SANCTUARY DEFENSES AND DO *NOT* OPEN THE OUTER DOOR.
DENIED.
TEN METERS.
RAA

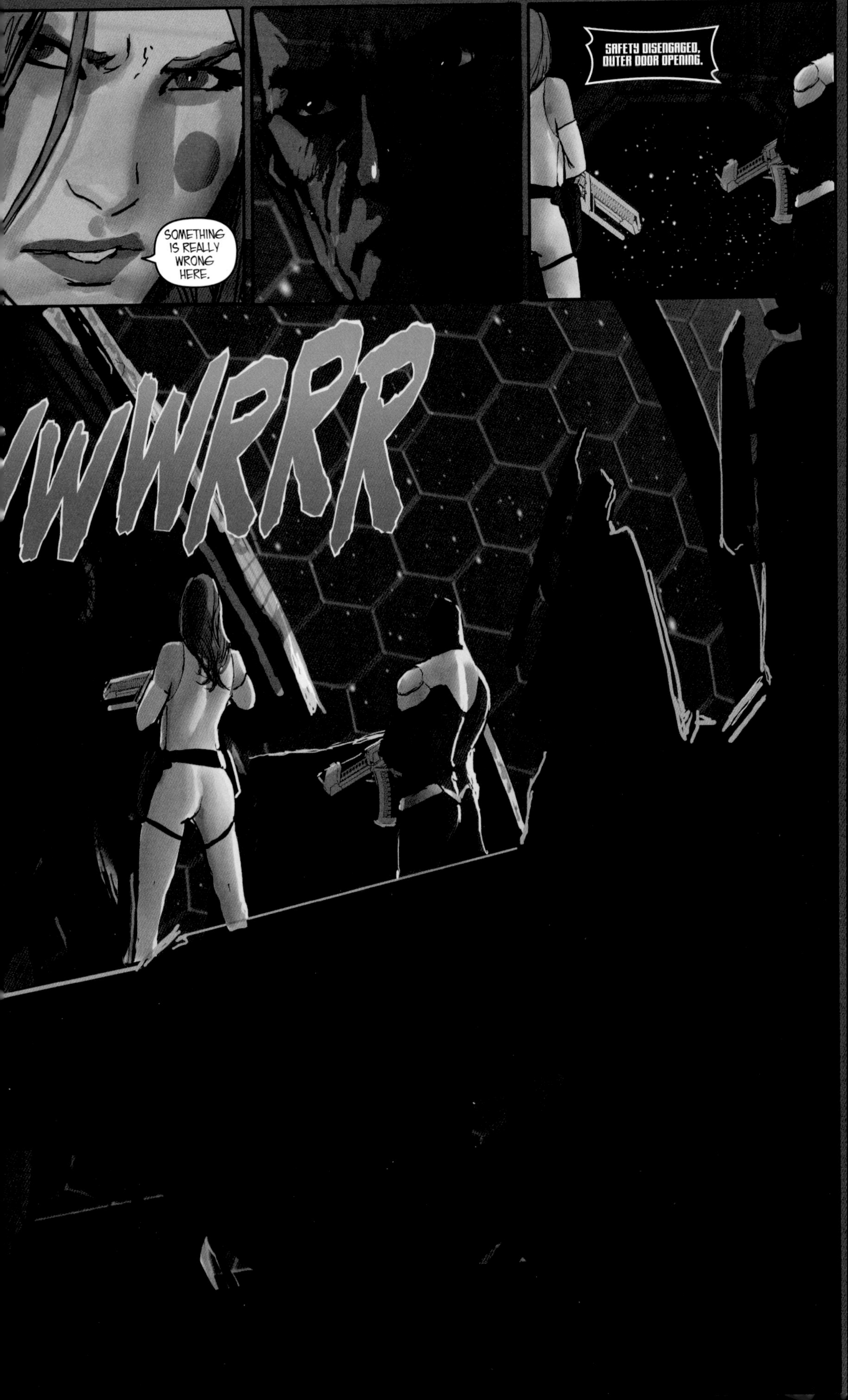
SOMETHING IS REALLY WRONG HERE.
SAFETY DISENGAGED, OUTER DOOR OPENING.
WWRRR

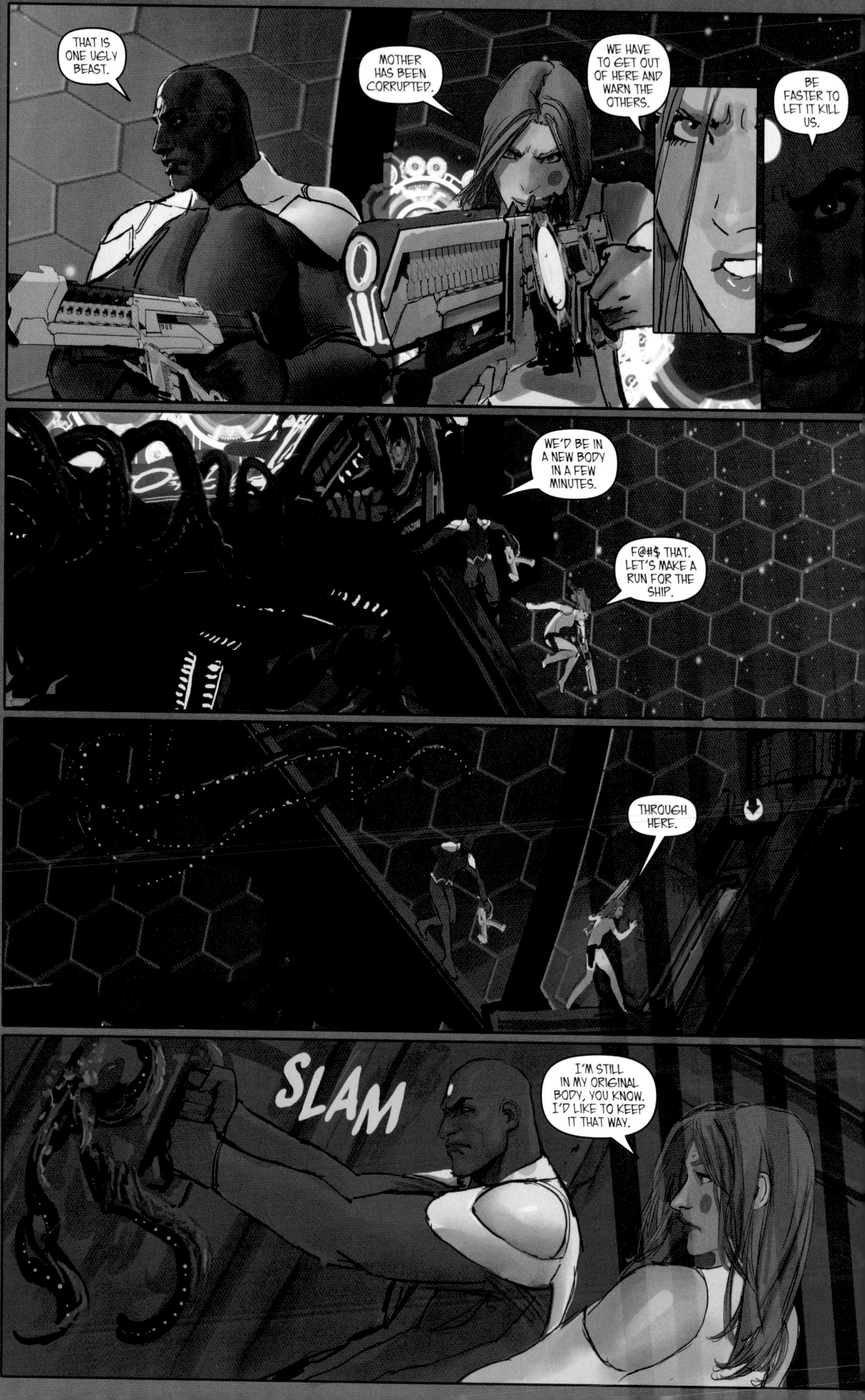
THAT IS ONE UGLY BEAST.
MOTHER HAS BEEN CORRUPTED.
WE HAVE TO GET OUT OF HERE AND WARN THE OTHERS.
BE FASTER TO LET IT KILL US.
WE'D BE IN A NEW BODY IN A FEW MINUTES.
F@#$ THAT. LET'S MAKE A RUN FOR THE SHIP.
THROUGH HERE.
SLAM
I'M STILL IN MY ORIGINAL BODY, YOU KNOW. I'D LIKE TO KEEP IT THAT WAY.

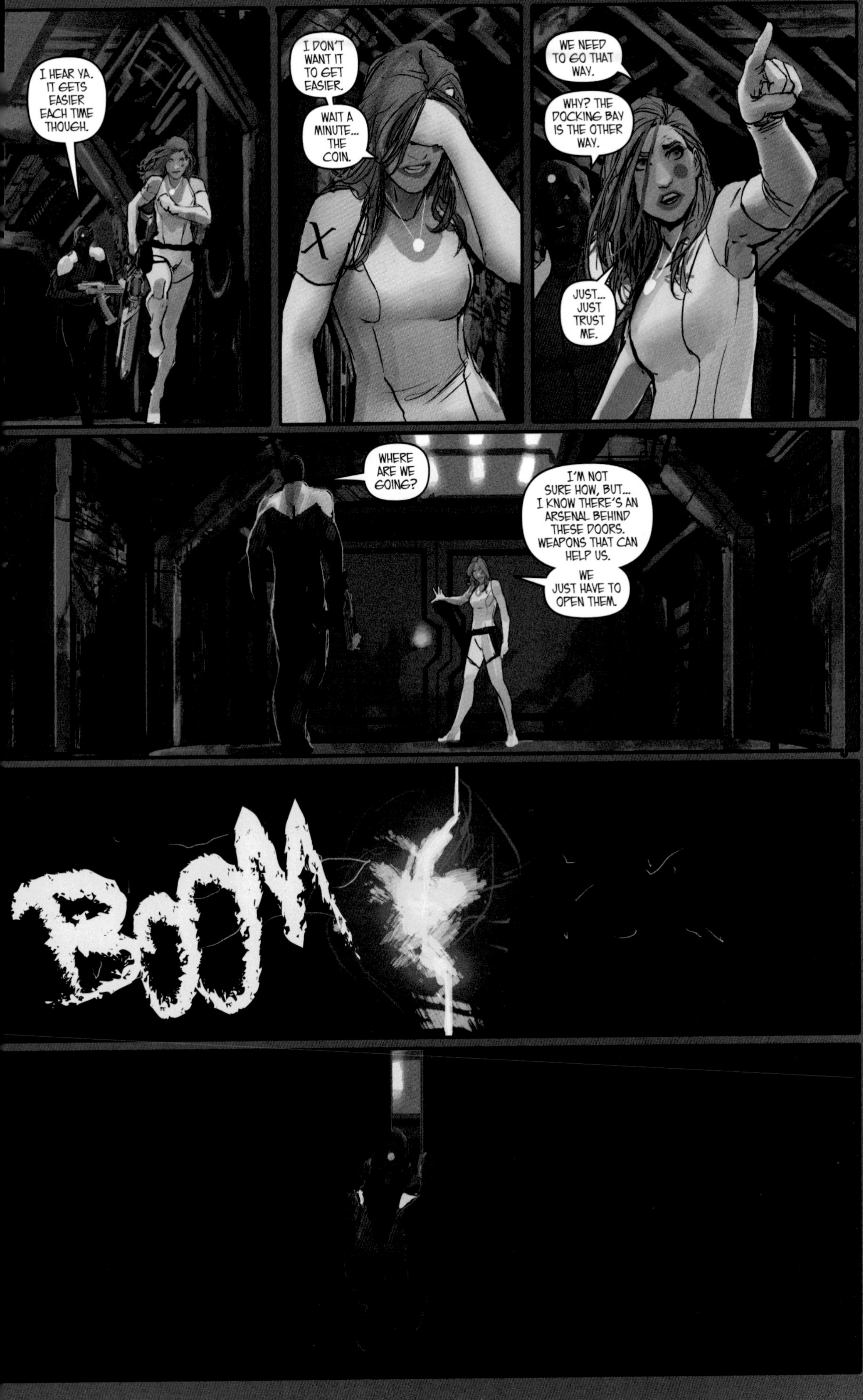
I HEAR YA. IT GETS EASIER EACH TIME THOUGH.
I DON'T WANT IT TO GET EASIER.
WAIT A MINUTE... THE COIN.
WE NEED TO GO THAT WAY.
WHY? THE DOCKING BAY IS THE OTHER WAY.
JUST... JUST TRUST ME.
WHERE ARE WE GOING?
I'M NOT SURE HOW, BUT... I KNOW THERE'S AN ARSENAL BEHIND THESE DOORS. WEAPONS THAT CAN HELP US.
WE JUST HAVE TO OPEN THEM.
BOOM

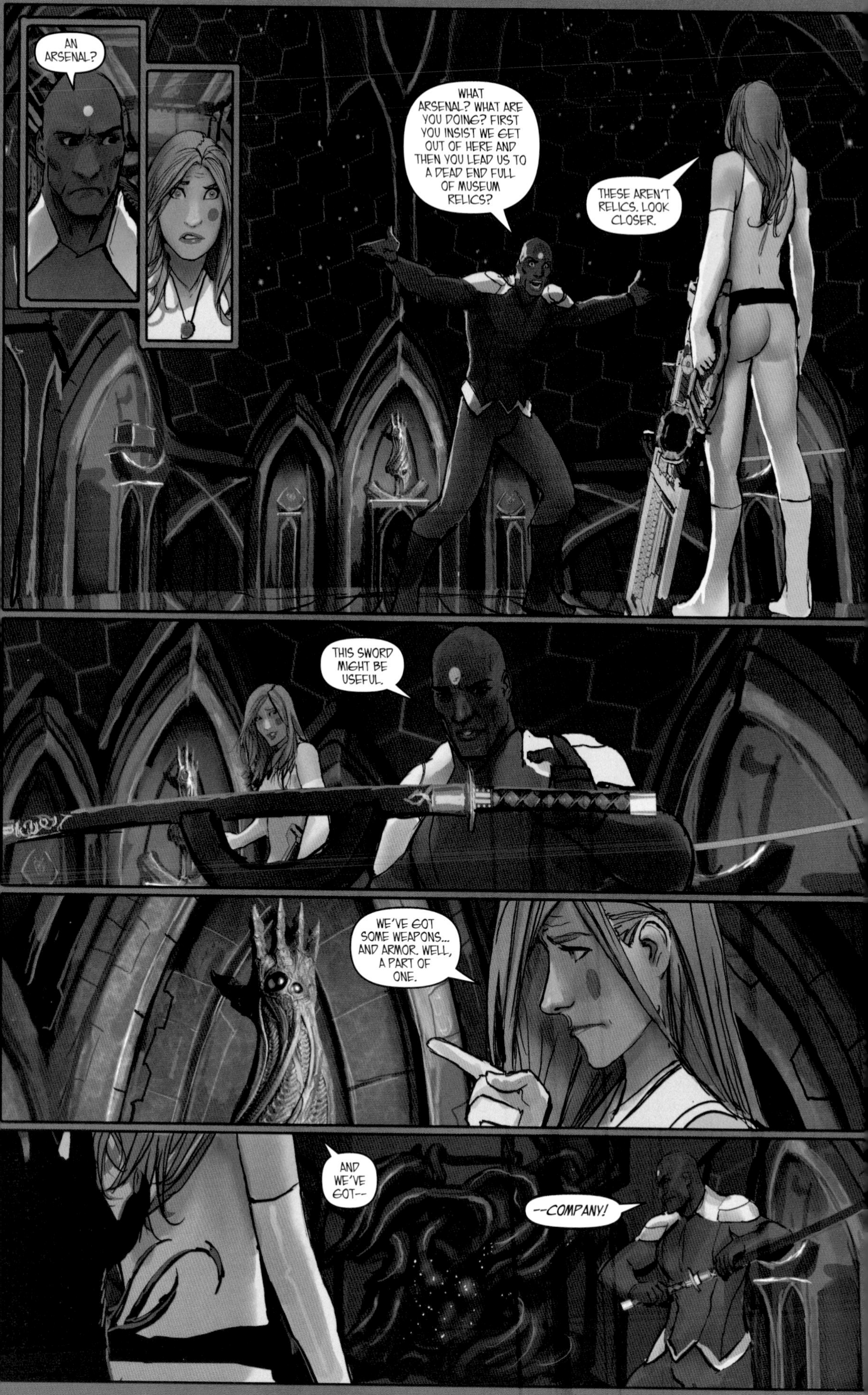
AN ARSENAL?
WHAT ARSENAL? WHAT ARE YOU DOING? FIRST YOU INSIST WE GET OUT OF HERE AND THEN YOU LEAD US TO A DEAD END FULL OF MUSEUM RELICS?
THESE AREN'T RELICS. LOOK CLOSER.
THIS SWORD MIGHT BE USEFUL.
WE'VE GOT SOME WEAPONS... AND ARMOR. WELL, A PART OF ONE.
AND WE'VE GOT--
--COMPANY!

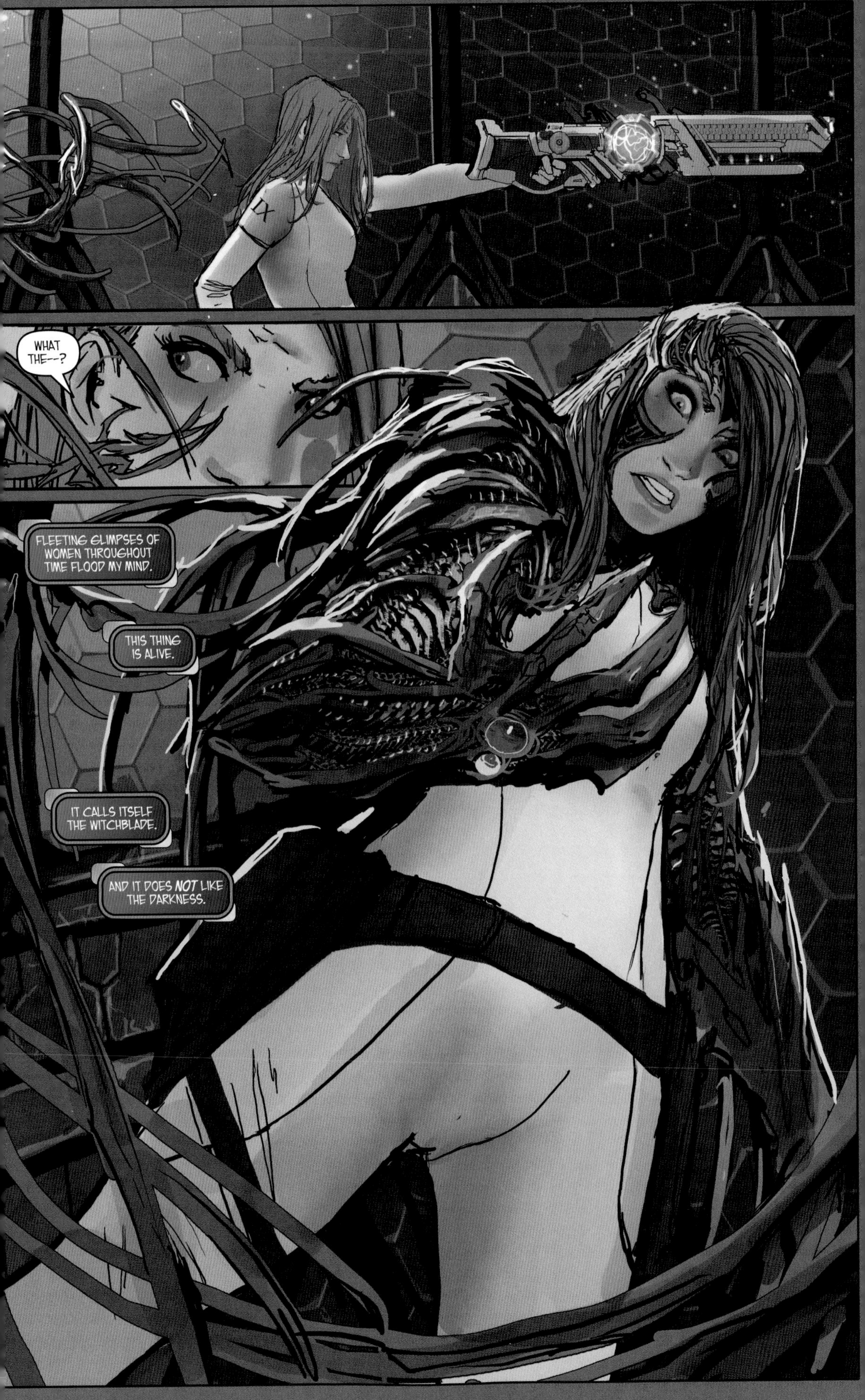
WHAT THE--?
FLEETING GLIMPSES OF WOMEN THROUGHOUT TIME FLOOD MY MIND.
THIS THING IS ALIVE.
IT CALLS ITSELF THE WITCHBLADE.
AND IT DOES **NOT** LIKE THE DARKNESS.

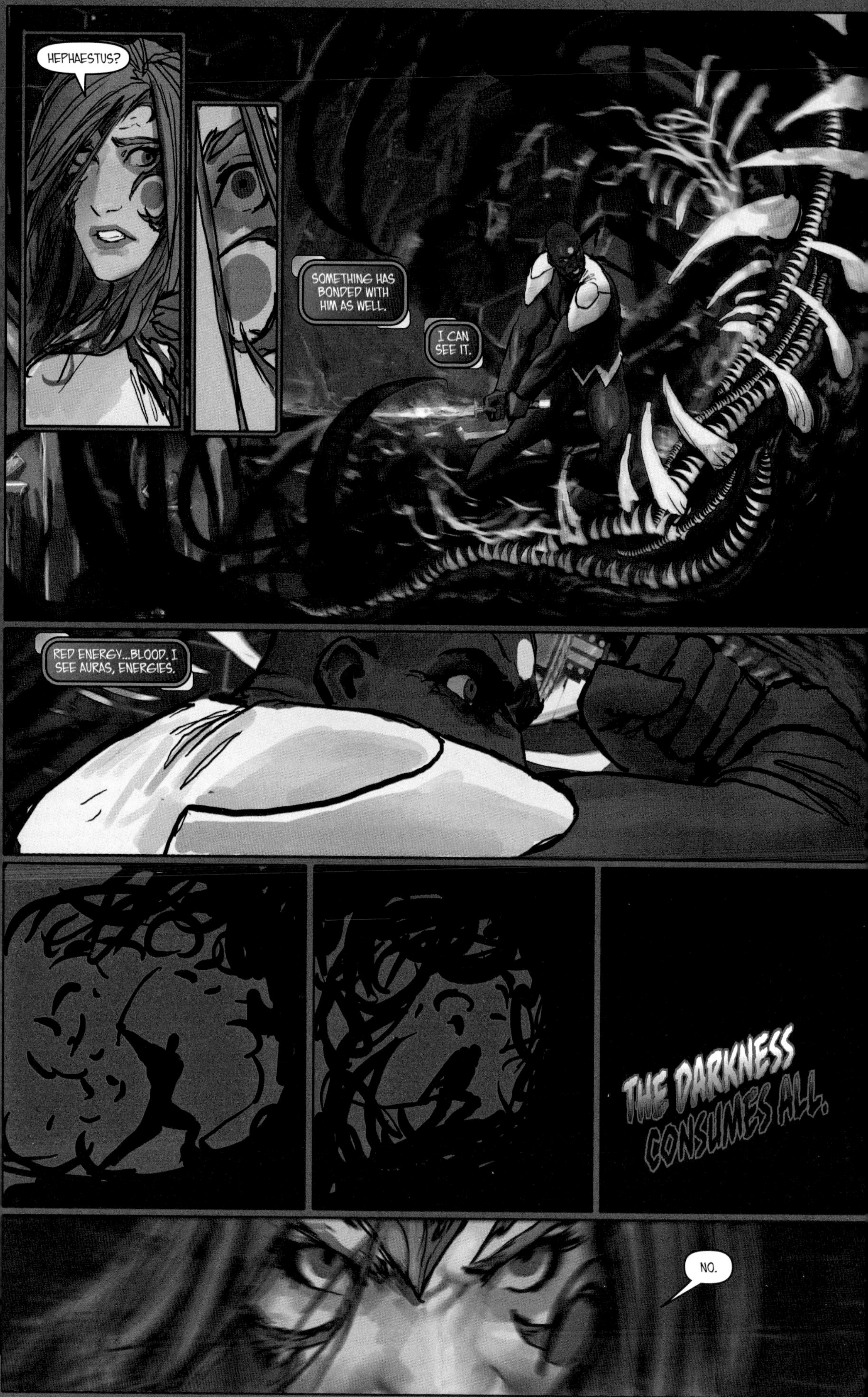
HEPHAESTUS?
SOMETHING HAS BONDED WITH HIM AS WELL.
I CAN SEE IT.
RED ENERGY...BLOOD. I SEE AURAS, ENERGIES.
THE DARKNESS CONSUMES ALL.
NO.

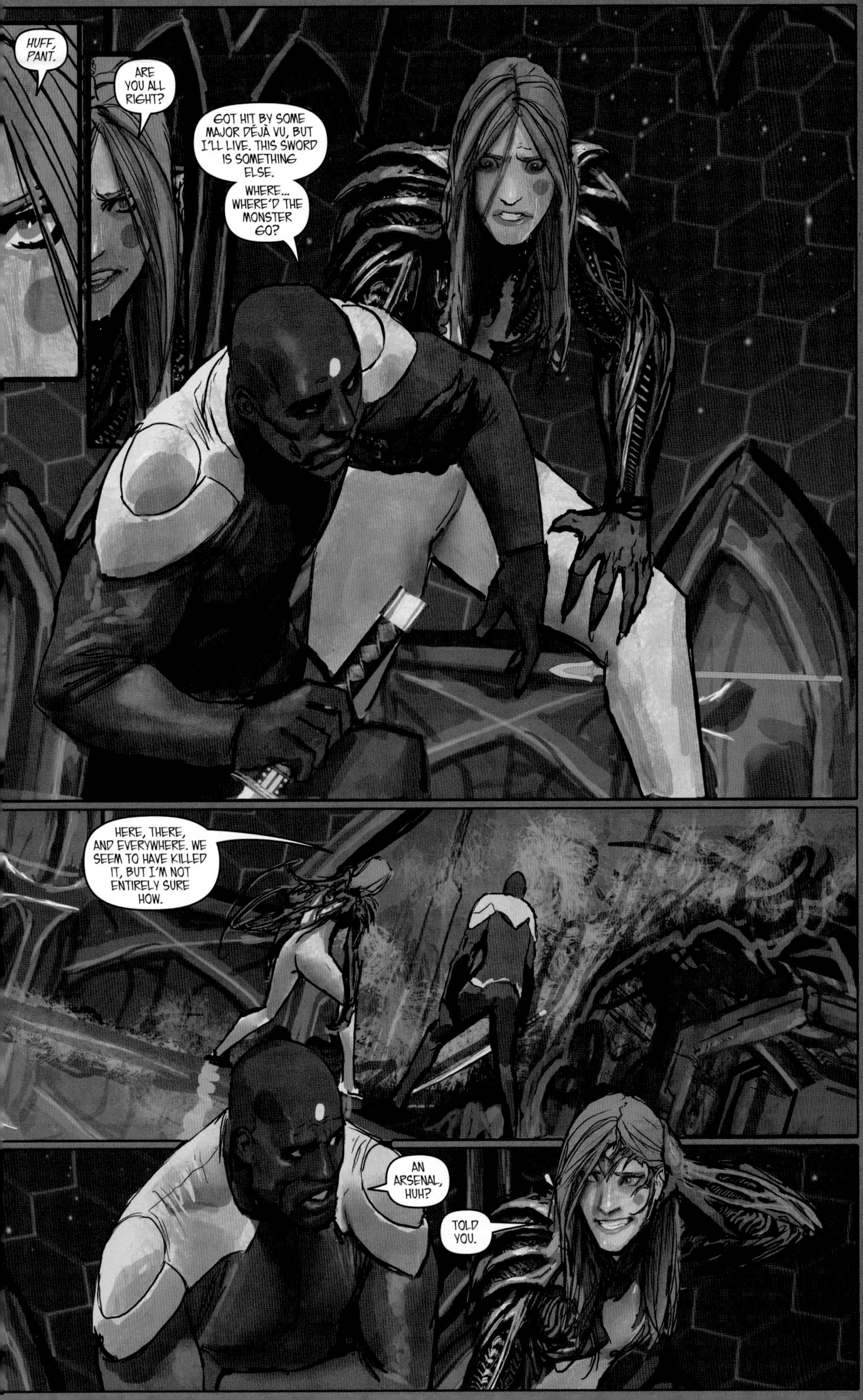
HUFF, PANT.
ARE YOU ALL RIGHT?
GOT HIT BY SOME MAJOR DÉJÀ VU, BUT I'LL LIVE. THIS SWORD IS SOMETHING ELSE.
WHERE... WHERE'D THE MONSTER GO?
HERE, THERE, AND EVERYWHERE. WE SEEM TO HAVE KILLED IT, BUT I'M NOT ENTIRELY SURE HOW.
AN ARSENAL, HUH?
TOLD YOU.

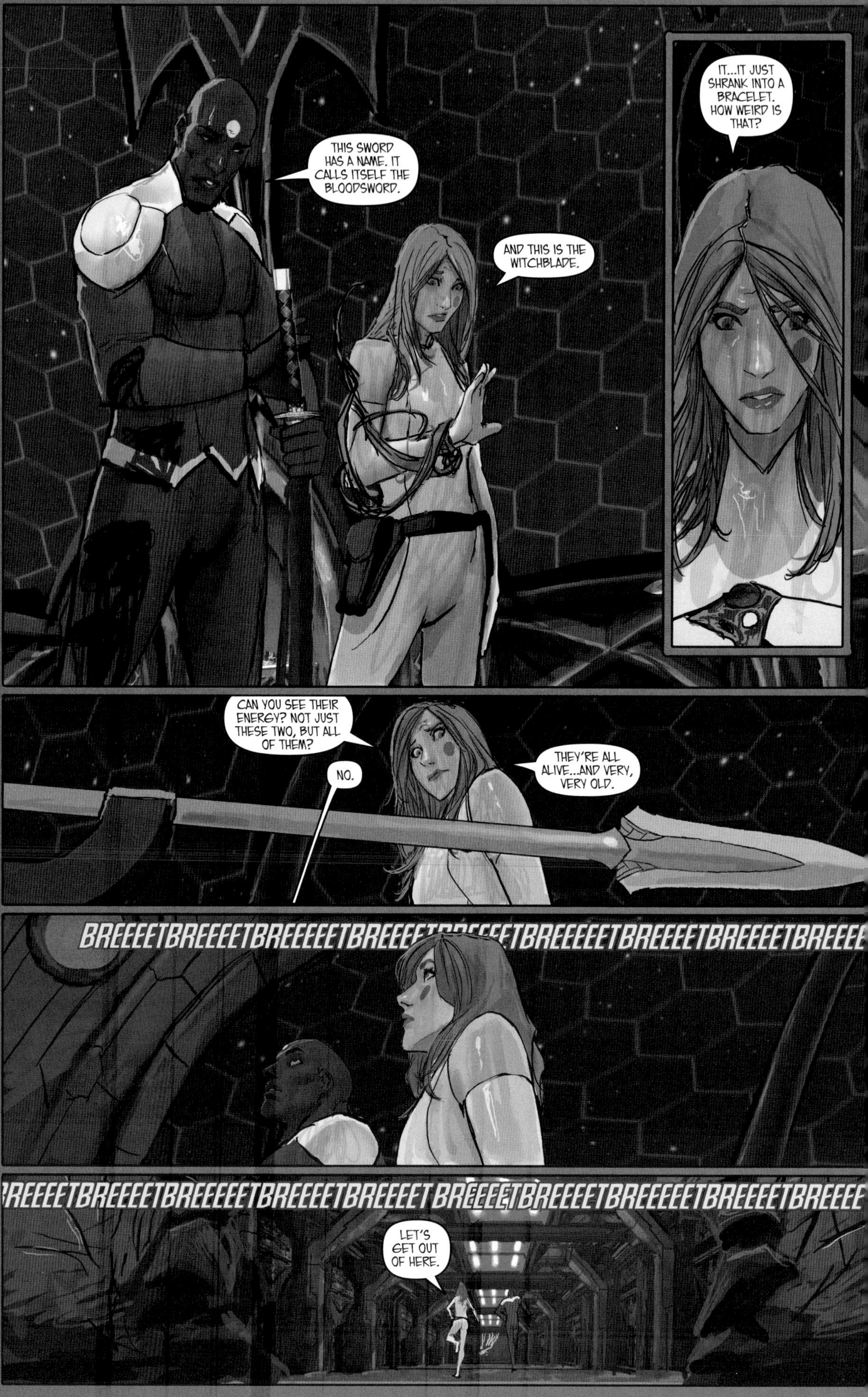
THIS SWORD HAS A NAME. IT CALLS ITSELF THE BLOODSWORD.
AND THIS IS THE WITCHBLADE.
IT...IT JUST SHRANK INTO A BRACELET. HOW WEIRD IS THAT?
CAN YOU SEE THEIR ENERGY? NOT JUST THESE TWO, BUT ALL OF THEM?
THEY'RE ALL ALIVE...AND VERY, VERY OLD.
NO.
BREEEETBREEEEETBREEEEEETBREEEEETBREEEEETBREEEEEETBREEEEETBREEEEETBREEEE
LET'S GET OUT OF HERE.

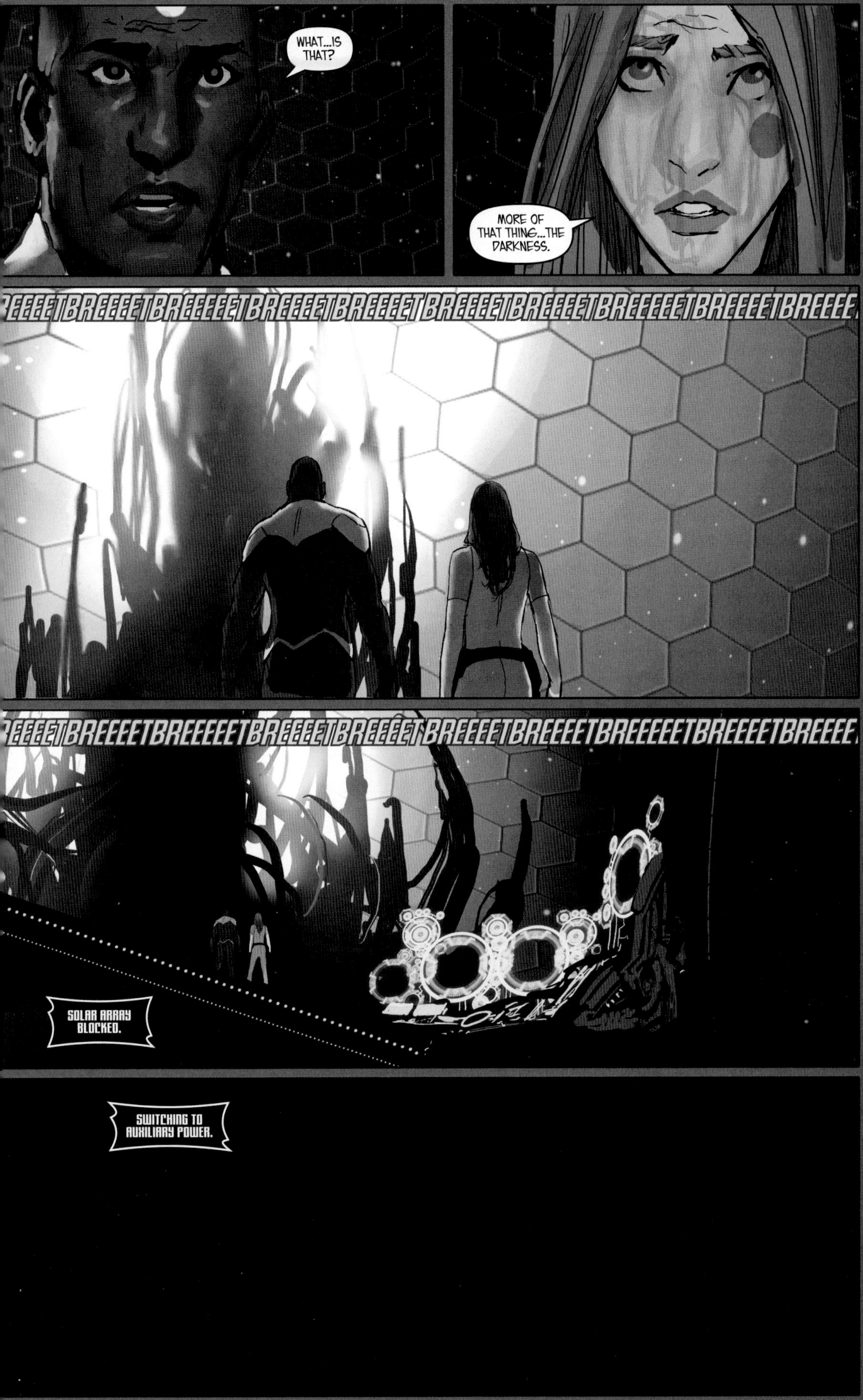
WHAT...IS THAT?
MORE OF THAT THING...THE DARKNESS.
BREEEEET BREEEEEET BREEEEET BREEEEET BREEEEET BREEEEET BREEEEEET BREEEEET
BREEEEEET BREEEEEET BREEEEET BREEEEET BREEEEET BREEEEEET BREEEEET
SOLAR ARRAY BLOCKED.
SWITCHING TO AUXILIARY POWER.

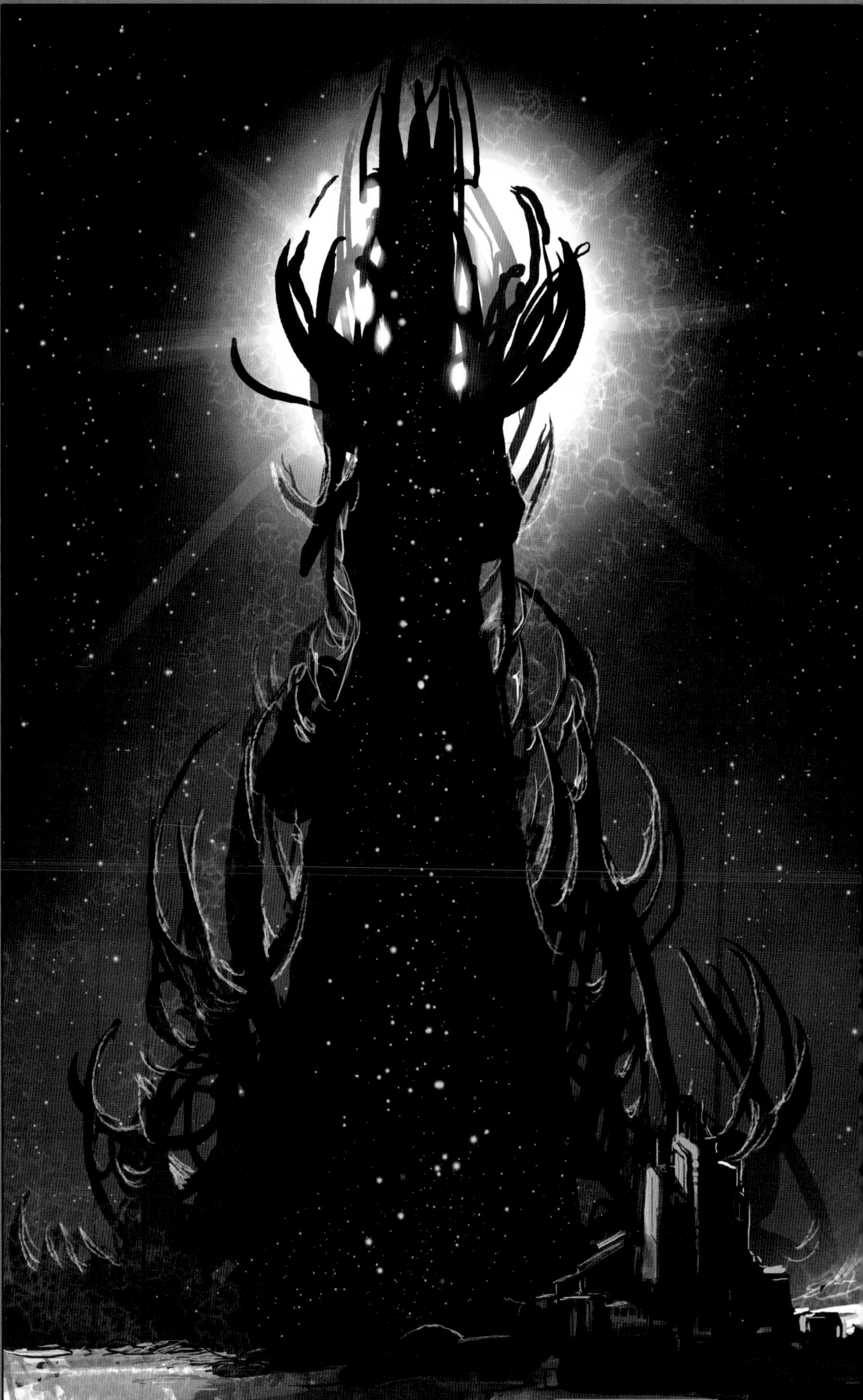

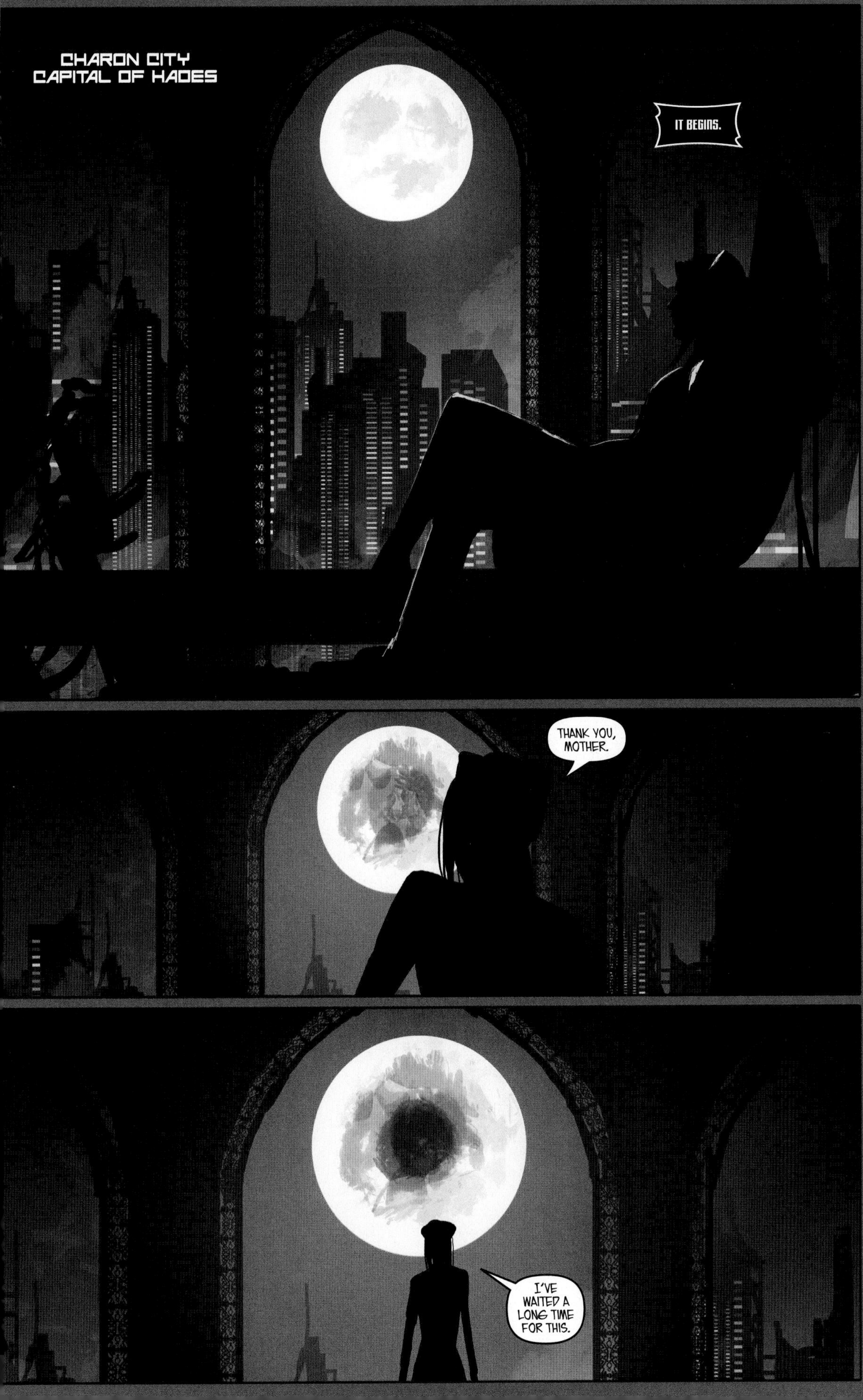
CHARON CITY
CAPITAL OF HADES
IT BEGINS.
THANK YOU, MOTHER.
I'VE WAITED A LONG TIME FOR THIS.

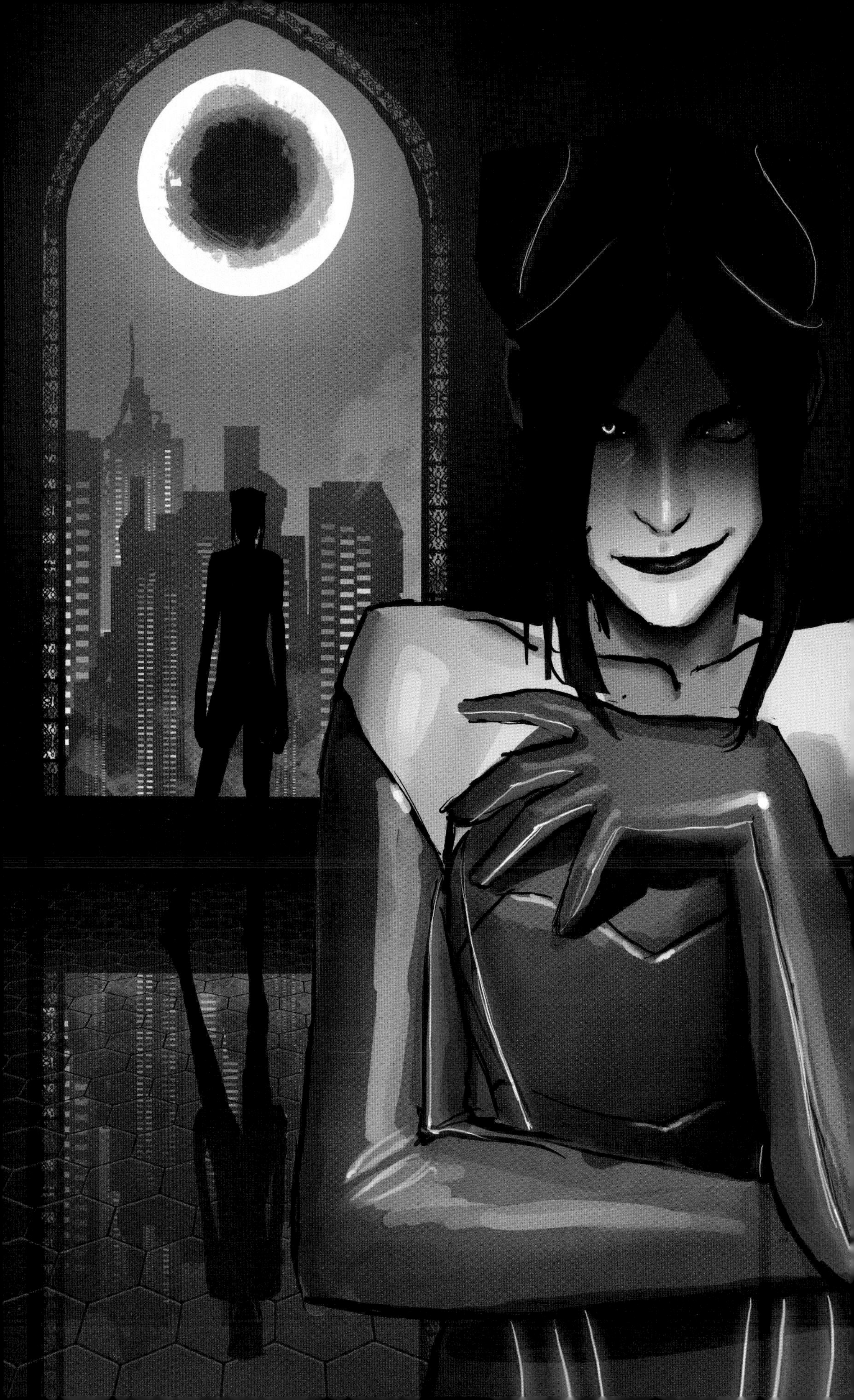

CHAPTER TWO

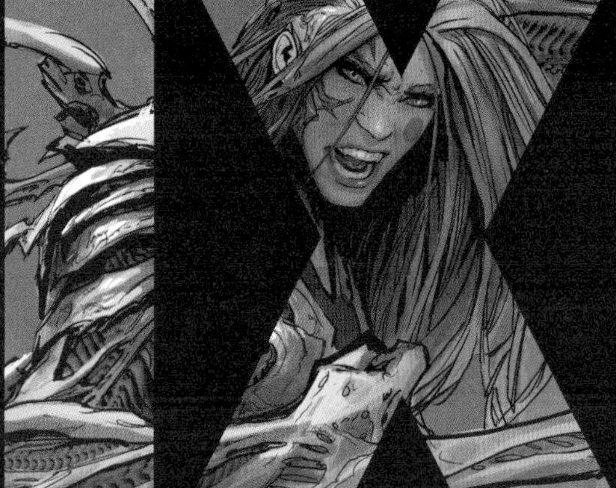
IX

"Those who control what young people are taught, and what they experience — what they see, hear, think, and believe — will determine the future course for the nation."

Dr. James Dobson, "Focus on the Family"

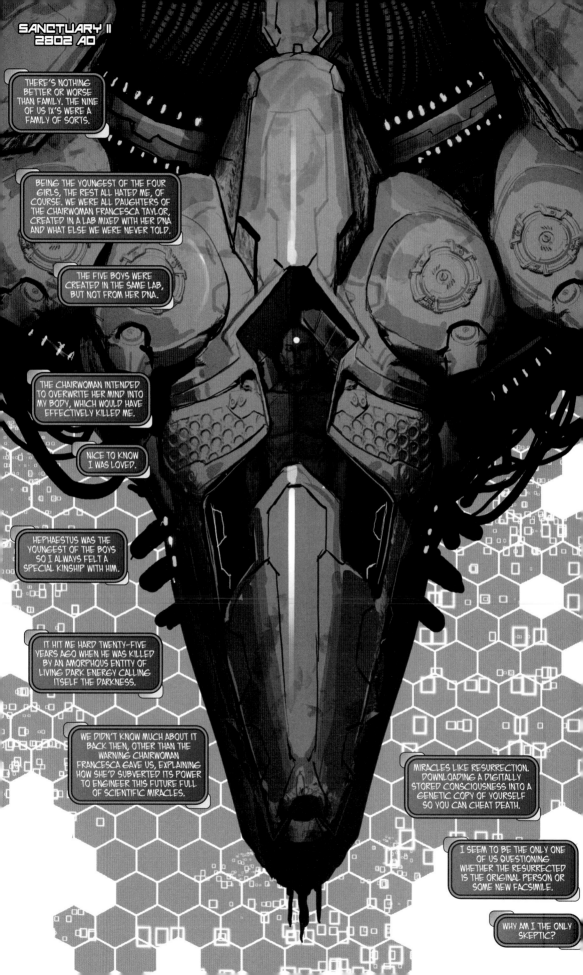

THERE'S NOTHING BETTER OR WORSE THAN FAMILY. THE NINE OF US IX'S WERE A FAMILY OF SORTS.

BEING THE YOUNGEST OF THE FOUR GIRLS, THE REST ALL HATED ME, OF COURSE. WE WERE ALL DAUGHTERS OF THE CHAIRWOMAN FRANCESCA TAYLOR, CREATED IN A LAB MIXED WITH HER DNA AND WHAT ELSE WE WERE NEVER TOLD.

THE FIVE BOYS WERE CREATED IN THE SAME LAB, BUT NOT FROM HER DNA.

THE CHAIRWOMAN INTENDED TO OVERWRITE HER MIND INTO MY BODY, WHICH WOULD HAVE EFFECTIVELY KILLED ME.

NICE TO KNOW I WAS LOVED.

HEPHAESTUS WAS THE YOUNGEST OF THE BOYS SO I ALWAYS FELT A SPECIAL KINSHIP WITH HIM.

IT HIT ME HARD TWENTY-FIVE YEARS AGO WHEN HE WAS KILLED BY AN AMORPHOUS ENTITY OF LIVING DARK ENERGY CALLING ITSELF THE DARKNESS.

WE DIDN'T KNOW MUCH ABOUT IT BACK THEN, OTHER THAN THE WARNING CHAIRWOMAN FRANCESCA GAVE US, EXPLAINING HOW SHE'D SUBVERTED ITS POWER TO ENGINEER THIS FUTURE FULL OF SCIENTIFIC MIRACLES.

MIRACLES LIKE RESURRECTION. DOWNLOADING A DIGITALLY STORED CONSCIOUSNESS INTO A GENETIC COPY OF YOURSELF SO YOU CAN CHEAT DEATH.

I SEEM TO BE THE ONLY ONE OF US QUESTIONING WHETHER THE RESURRECTED IS THE ORIGINAL PERSON OR SOME NEW FACSIMILE.

WHY AM I THE ONLY SKEPTIC?

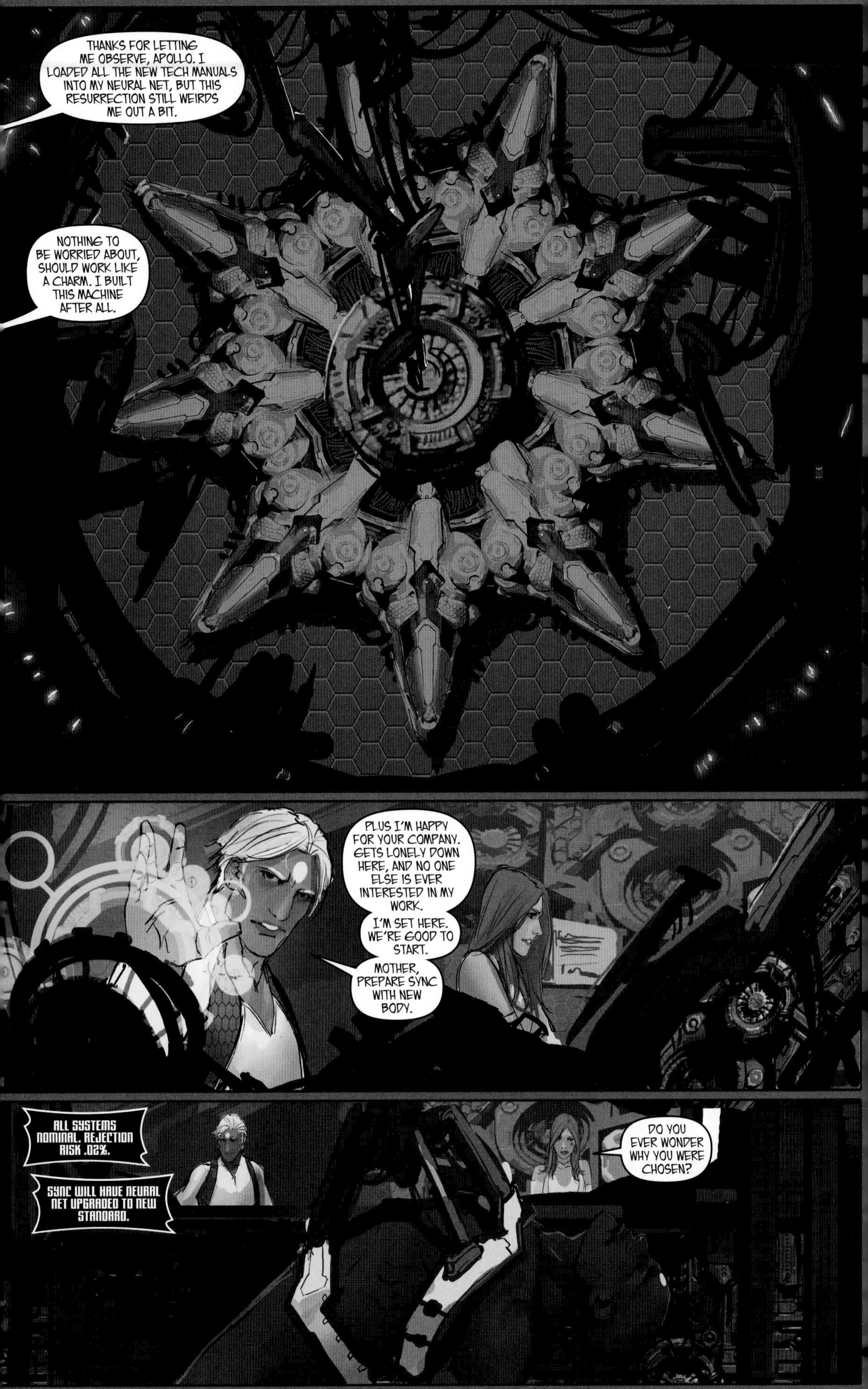
THANKS FOR LETTING ME OBSERVE, APOLLO. I LOADED ALL THE NEW TECH MANUALS INTO MY NEURAL NET, BUT THIS RESURRECTION STILL WEIRDS ME OUT A BIT.
NOTHING TO BE WORRIED ABOUT, SHOULD WORK LIKE A CHARM. I BUILT THIS MACHINE AFTER ALL.
PLUS I'M HAPPY FOR YOUR COMPANY. GETS LONELY DOWN HERE, AND NO ONE ELSE IS EVER INTERESTED IN MY WORK.
I'M SET HERE. WE'RE GOOD TO START.
MOTHER, PREPARE SYNC WITH NEW BODY.
ALL SYSTEMS NOMINAL. REJECTION RISK .02%.
SYNC WILL HAVE NEURAL NET UPGRADED TO NEW STANDARD.
DO YOU EVER WONDER WHY YOU WERE CHOSEN?

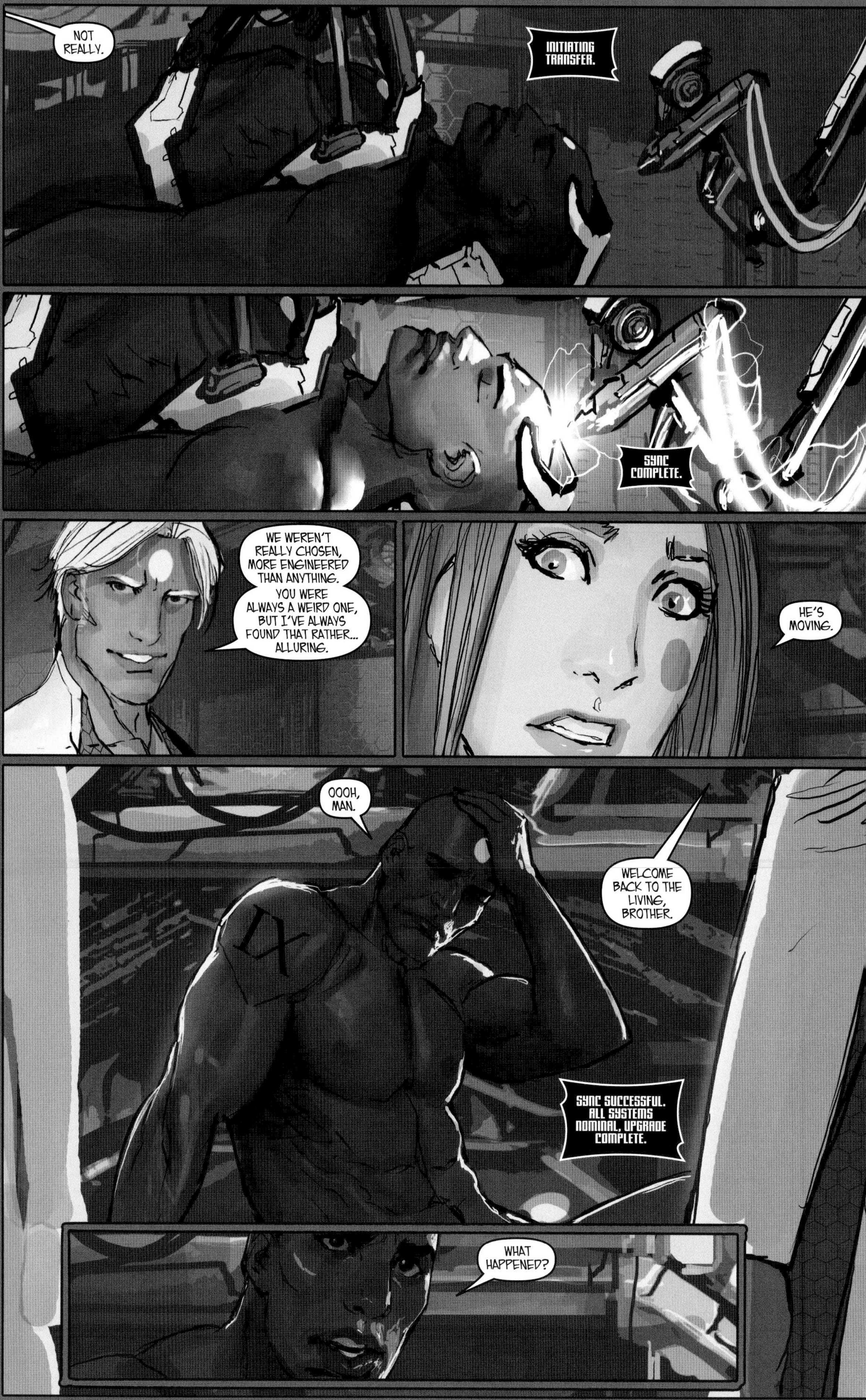
NOT REALLY.
INITIATING TRANSFER.
SYNC COMPLETE.
WE WEREN'T REALLY CHOSEN, MORE ENGINEERED THAN ANYTHING.
YOU WERE ALWAYS A WEIRD ONE, BUT I'VE ALWAYS FOUND THAT RATHER... ALLURING.
HE'S MOVING.
OOOH, MAN.
WELCOME BACK TO THE LIVING, BROTHER.
IX
SYNC SUCCESSFUL. ALL SYSTEMS NOMINAL, UPGRADE COMPLETE.
WHAT HAPPENED?

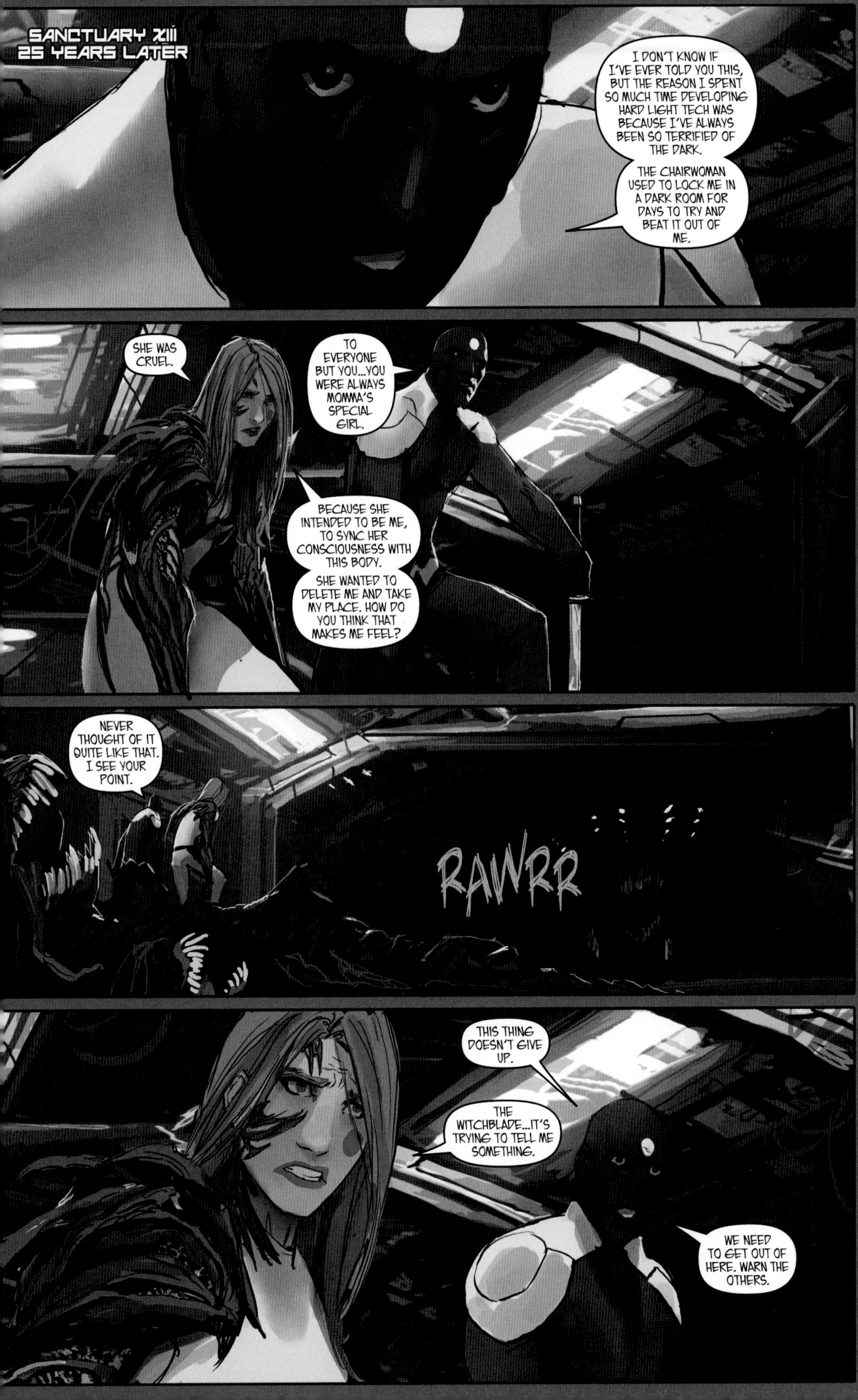
SANCTUARY XIII
25 YEARS LATER
I DON'T KNOW IF I'VE EVER TOLD YOU THIS, BUT THE REASON I SPENT SO MUCH TIME DEVELOPING HARD LIGHT TECH WAS BECAUSE I'VE ALWAYS BEEN SO TERRIFIED OF THE DARK.
THE CHAIRWOMAN USED TO LOCK ME IN A DARK ROOM FOR DAYS TO TRY AND BEAT IT OUT OF ME.
SHE WAS CRUEL.
TO EVERYONE BUT YOU...YOU WERE ALWAYS MOMMA'S SPECIAL GIRL.
BECAUSE SHE INTENDED TO BE ME, TO SYNC HER CONSCIOUSNESS WITH THIS BODY.
SHE WANTED TO DELETE ME AND TAKE MY PLACE. HOW DO YOU THINK THAT MAKES ME FEEL?
NEVER THOUGHT OF IT QUITE LIKE THAT. I SEE YOUR POINT.
RAWRR
THIS THING DOESN'T GIVE UP.
THE WITCHBLADE...IT'S TRYING TO TELL ME SOMETHING.
WE NEED TO GET OUT OF HERE. WARN THE OTHERS.

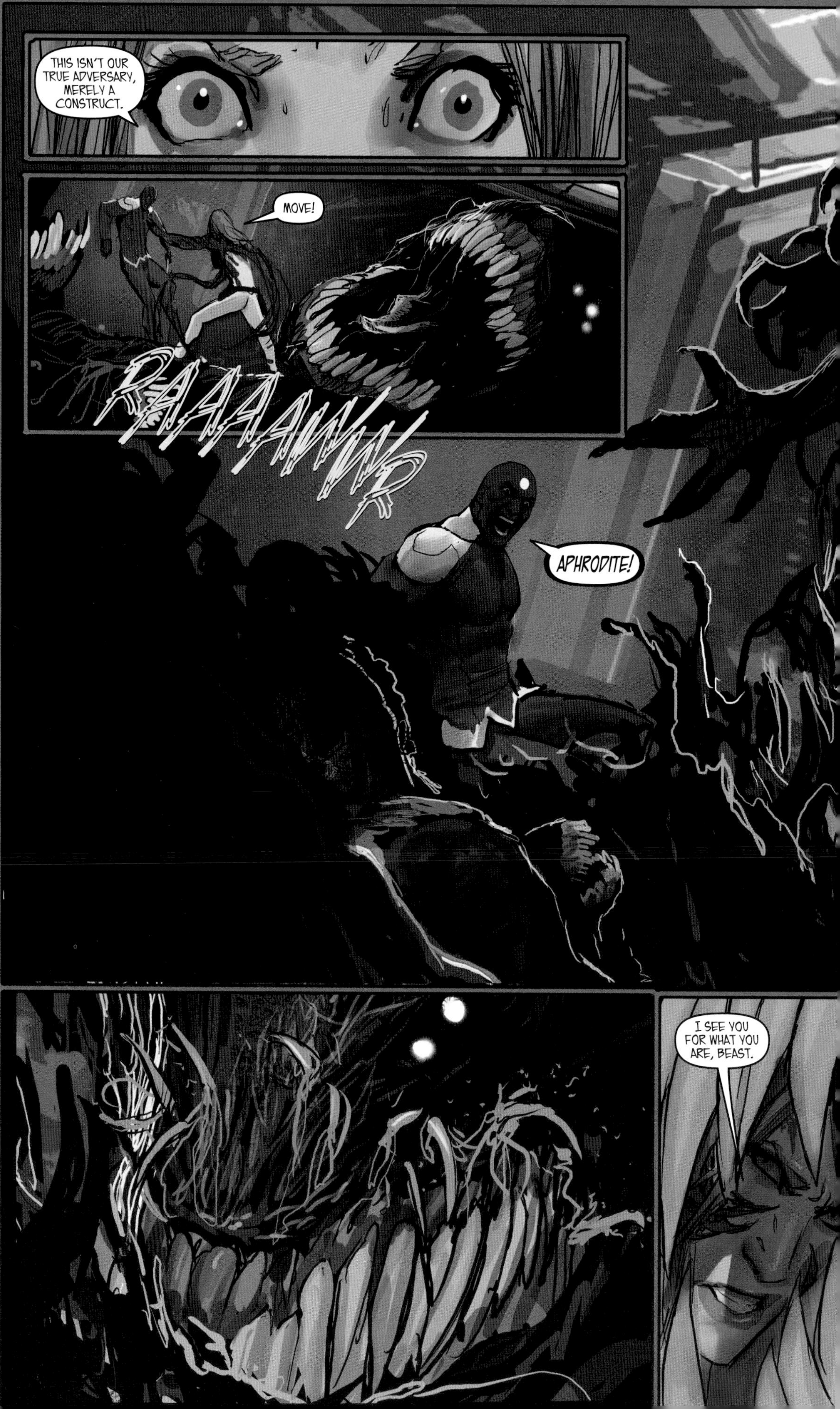
THIS ISN'T OUR TRUE ADVERSARY, MERELY A CONSTRUCT.
MOVE!
RAAAAWWR
APHRODITE!
I SEE YOU FOR WHAT YOU ARE, BEAST.

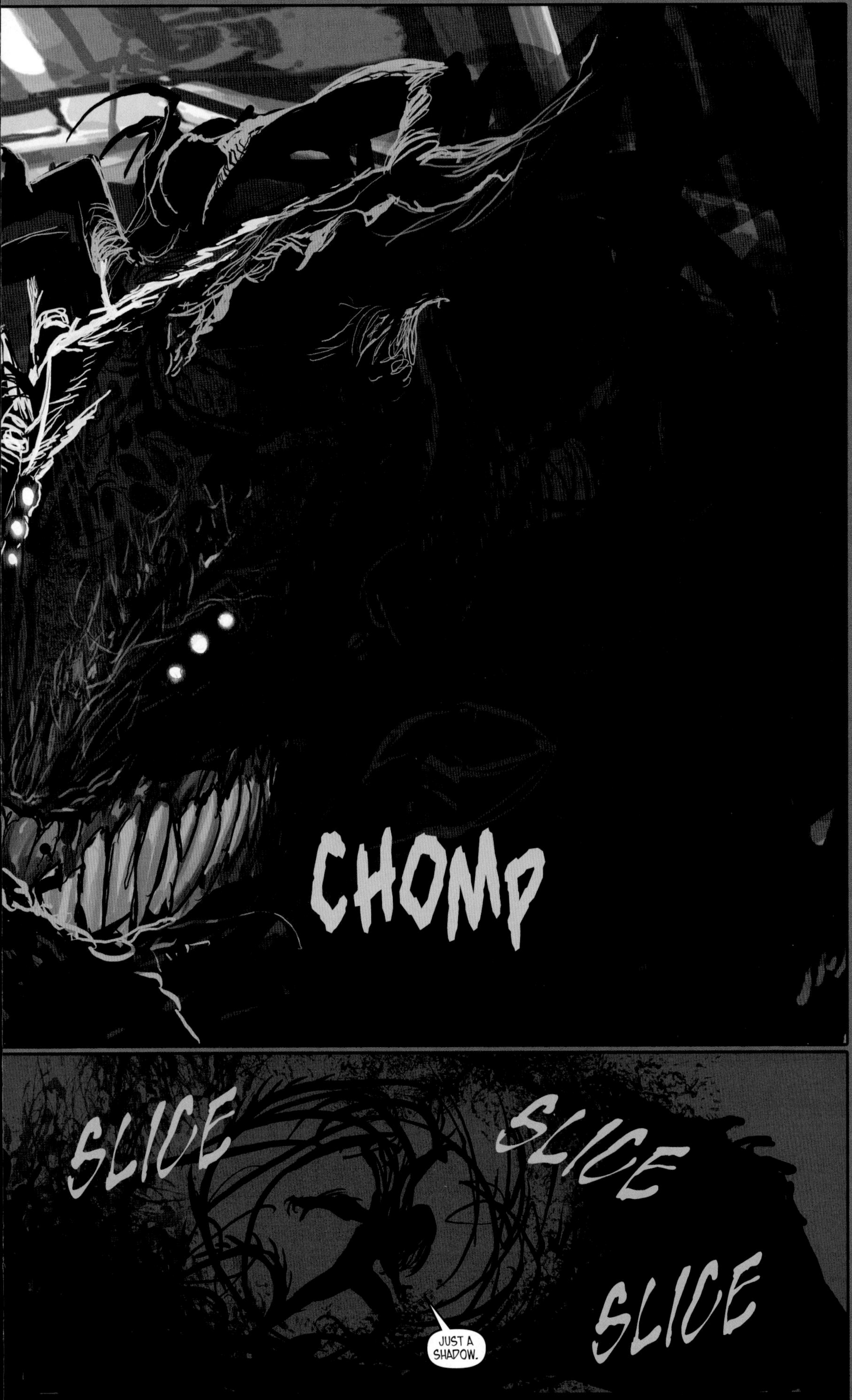
CHOMP
SLICE
SLICE
JUST A SHADOW.
SLICE

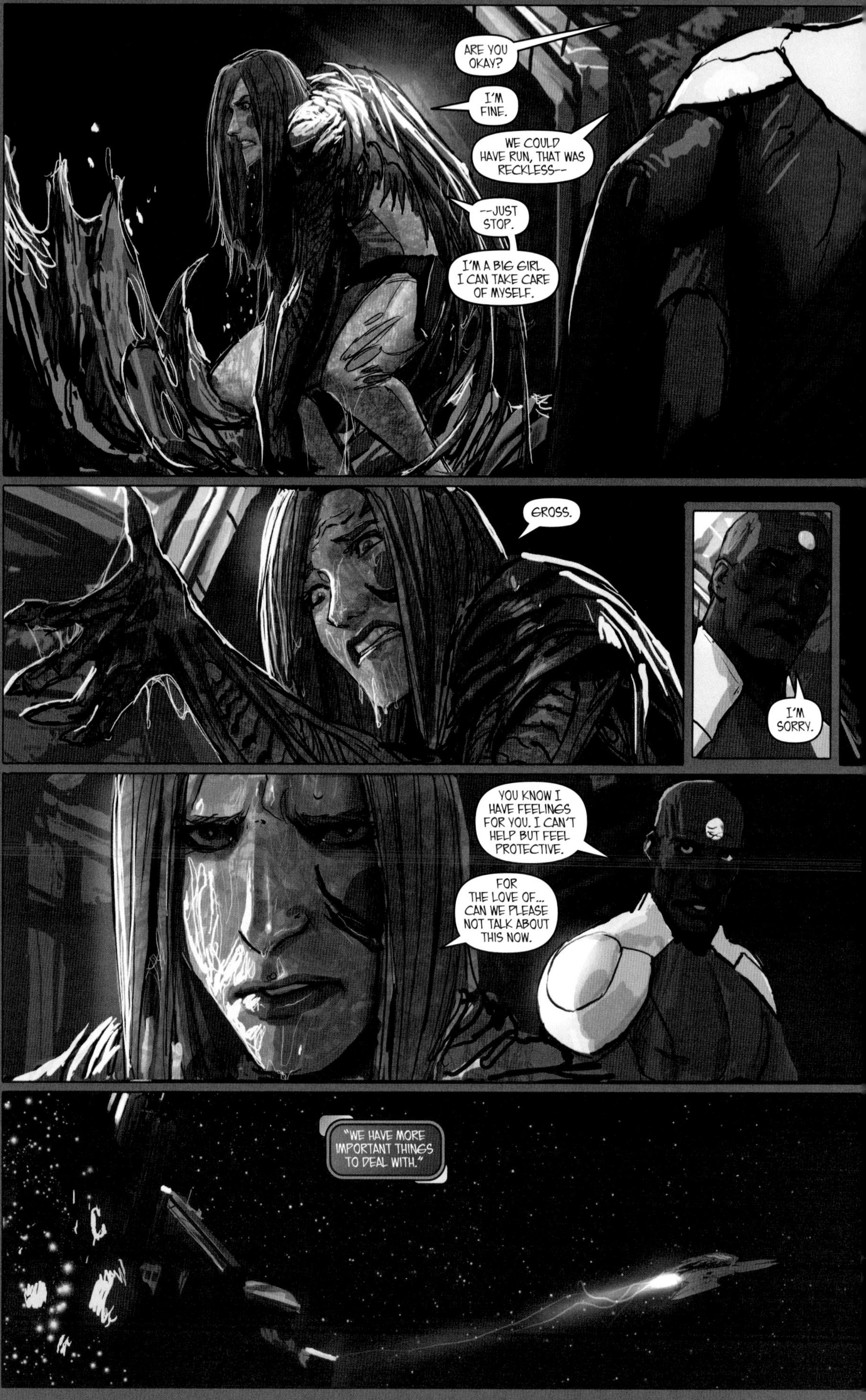
ARE YOU OKAY?
I'M FINE.
WE COULD HAVE RUN, THAT WAS RECKLESS--
--JUST STOP.
I'M A BIG GIRL. I CAN TAKE CARE OF MYSELF.
GROSS.
I'M SORRY.
YOU KNOW I HAVE FEELINGS FOR YOU. I CAN'T HELP BUT FEEL PROTECTIVE.
FOR THE LOVE OF... CAN WE PLEASE NOT TALK ABOUT THIS NOW.
"WE HAVE MORE IMPORTANT THINGS TO DEAL WITH."

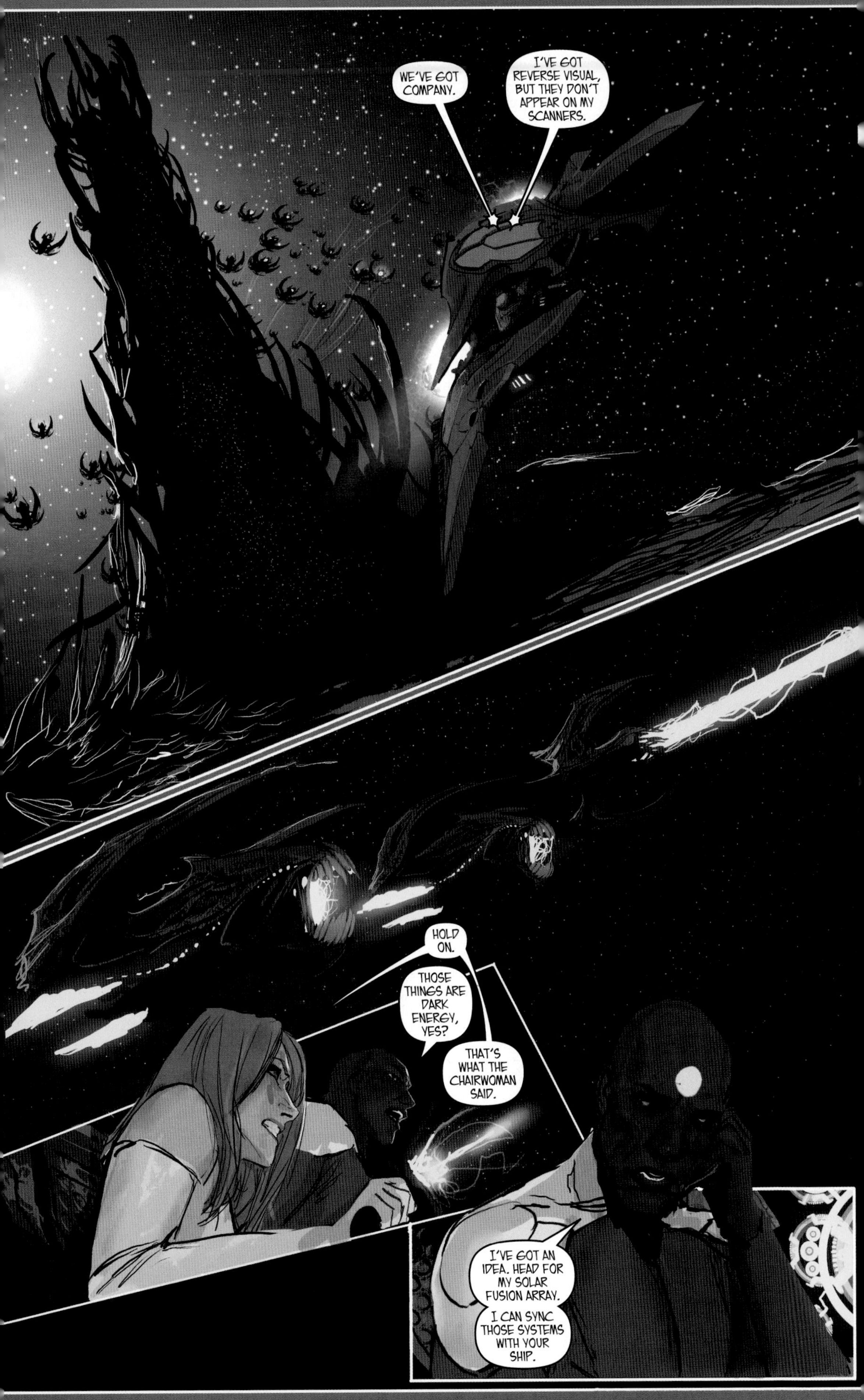
WE'VE GOT COMPANY.
I'VE GOT REVERSE VISUAL, BUT THEY DON'T APPEAR ON MY SCANNERS.
HOLD ON.
THOSE THINGS ARE DARK ENERGY, YES?
THAT'S WHAT THE CHAIRWOMAN SAID.
I'VE GOT AN IDEA. HEAD FOR MY SOLAR FUSION ARRAY.
I CAN SYNC THOSE SYSTEMS WITH YOUR SHIP.

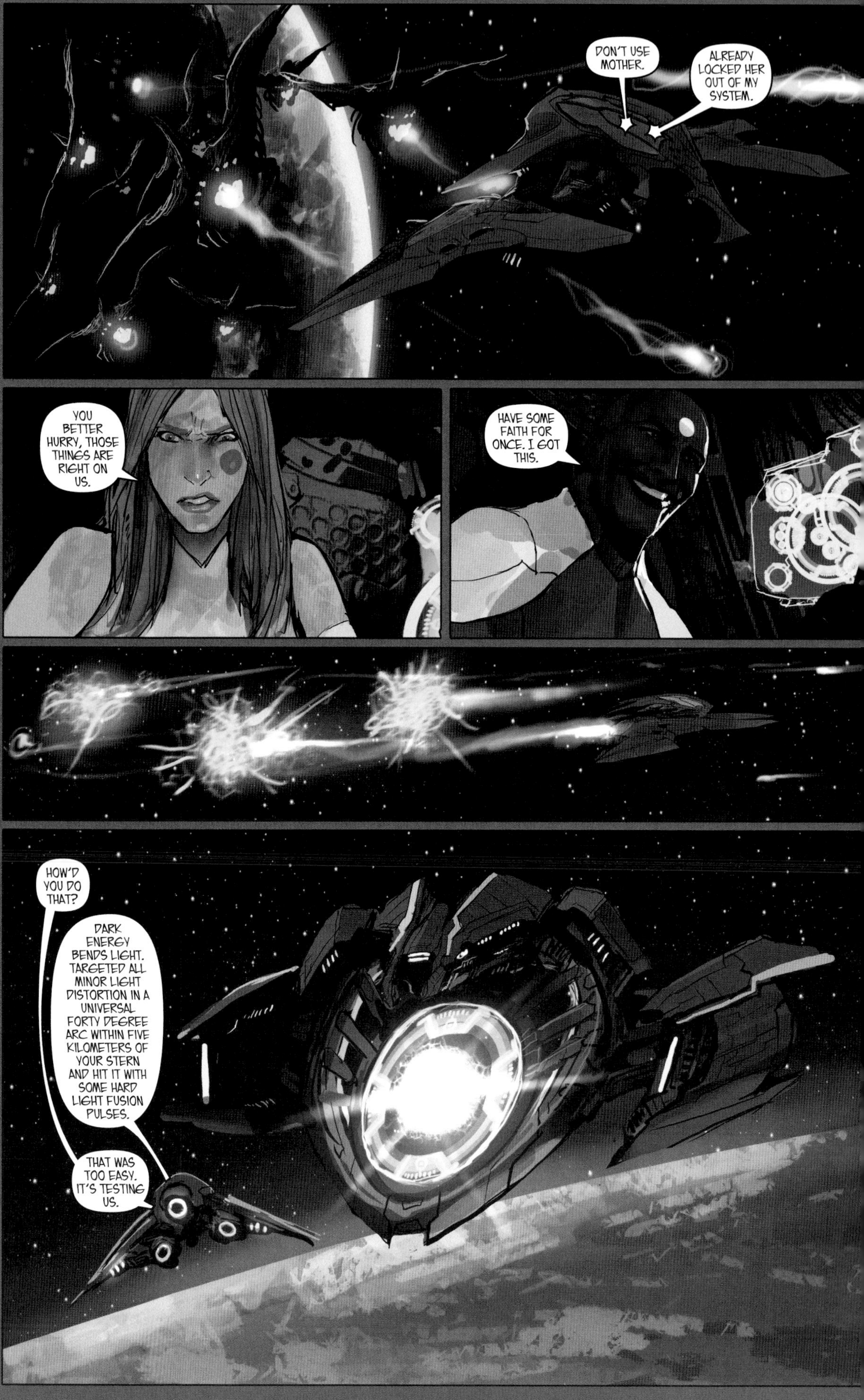
DON'T USE MOTHER.
ALREADY LOCKED HER OUT OF MY SYSTEM.
YOU BETTER HURRY, THOSE THINGS ARE RIGHT ON US.
HAVE SOME FAITH FOR ONCE. I GOT THIS.
HOW'D YOU DO THAT?
DARK ENERGY BENDS LIGHT. TARGETED ALL MINOR LIGHT DISTORTION IN A UNIVERSAL FORTY DEGREE ARC WITHIN FIVE KILOMETERS OF YOUR STERN AND HIT IT WITH SOME HARD LIGHT FUSION PULSES.
THAT WAS TOO EASY. IT'S TESTING US.

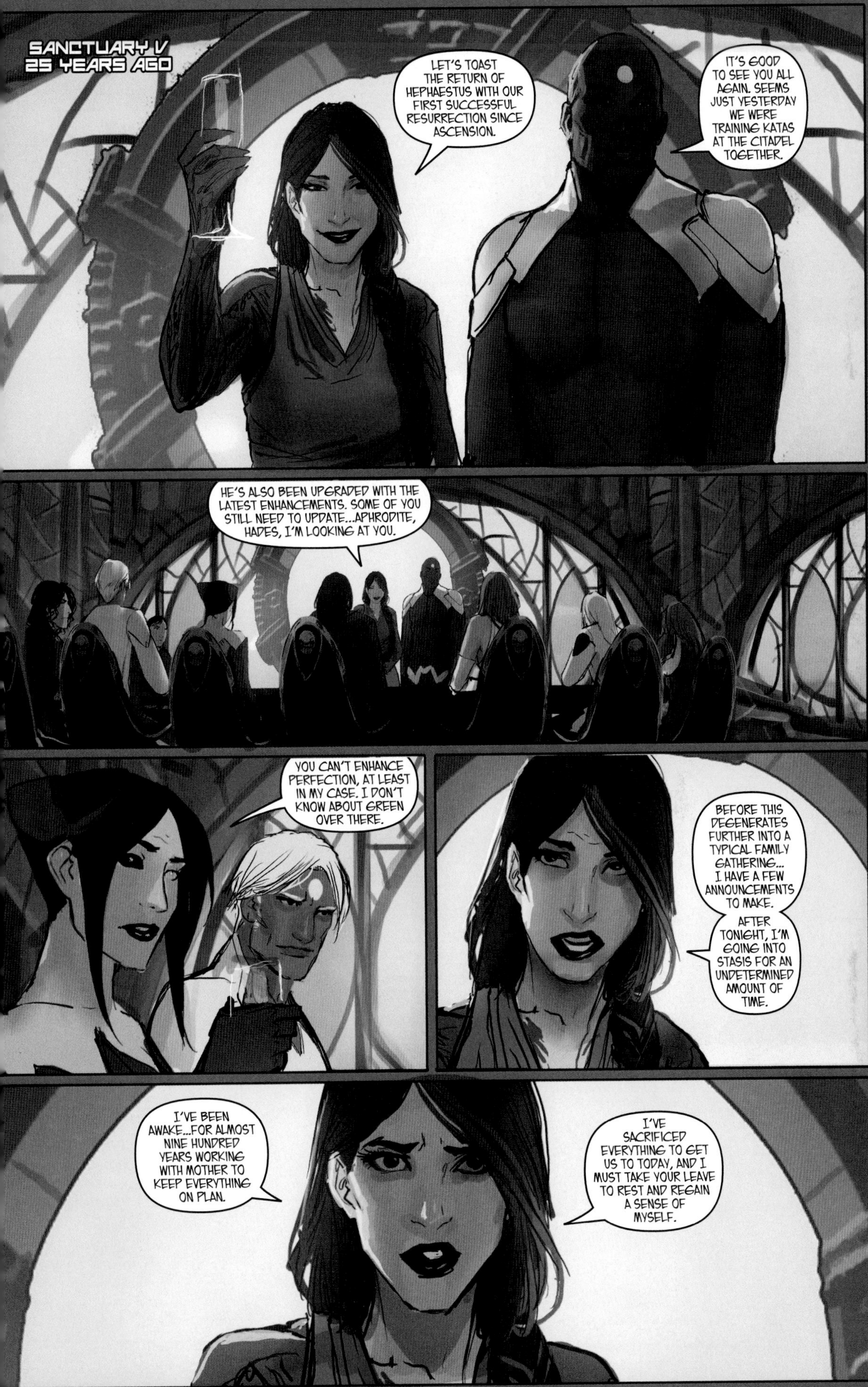
SANCTUARY V
25 YEARS AGO
LET'S TOAST THE RETURN OF HEPHAESTUS WITH OUR FIRST SUCCESSFUL RESURRECTION SINCE ASCENSION.
IT'S GOOD TO SEE YOU ALL AGAIN. SEEMS JUST YESTERDAY WE WERE TRAINING KATAS AT THE CITADEL TOGETHER.
HE'S ALSO BEEN UPGRADED WITH THE LATEST ENHANCEMENTS. SOME OF YOU STILL NEED TO UPDATE...APHRODITE, HADES, I'M LOOKING AT YOU.
YOU CAN'T ENHANCE PERFECTION, AT LEAST IN MY CASE. I DON'T KNOW ABOUT GREEN OVER THERE.
BEFORE THIS DEGENERATES FURTHER INTO A TYPICAL FAMILY GATHERING... I HAVE A FEW ANNOUNCEMENTS TO MAKE.
AFTER TONIGHT, I'M GOING INTO STASIS FOR AN UNDETERMINED AMOUNT OF TIME.
I'VE BEEN AWAKE...FOR ALMOST NINE HUNDRED YEARS WORKING WITH MOTHER TO KEEP EVERYTHING ON PLAN.
I'VE SACRIFICED EVERYTHING TO GET US TO TODAY, AND I MUST TAKE YOUR LEAVE TO REST AND REGAIN A SENSE OF MYSELF.

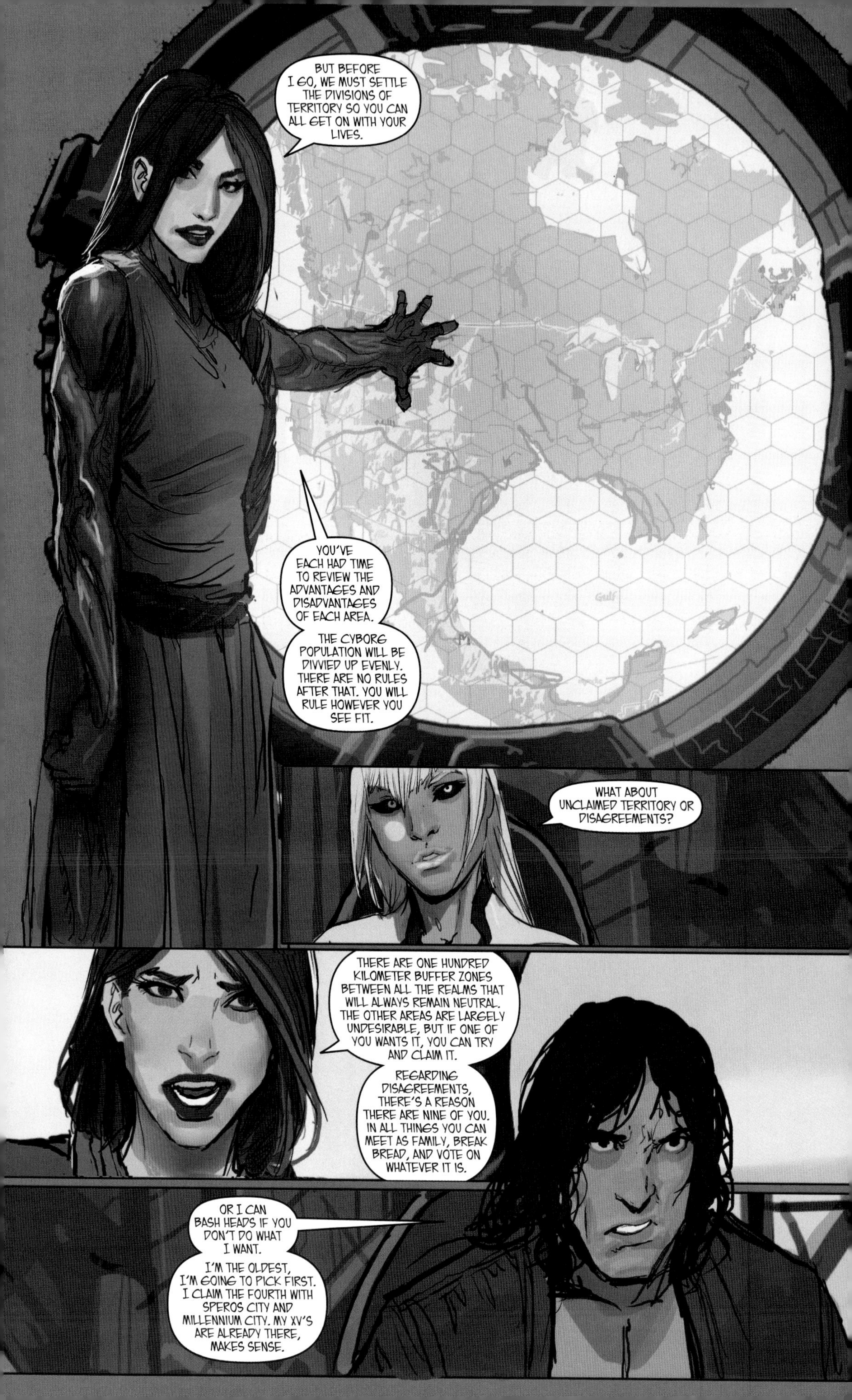
BUT BEFORE I GO, WE MUST SETTLE THE DIVISIONS OF TERRITORY SO YOU CAN ALL GET ON WITH YOUR LIVES.
YOU'VE EACH HAD TIME TO REVIEW THE ADVANTAGES AND DISADVANTAGES OF EACH AREA.
THE CYBORG POPULATION WILL BE DIVVIED UP EVENLY. THERE ARE NO RULES AFTER THAT. YOU WILL RULE HOWEVER YOU SEE FIT.
WHAT ABOUT UNCLAIMED TERRITORY OR DISAGREEMENTS?
THERE ARE ONE HUNDRED KILOMETER BUFFER ZONES BETWEEN ALL THE REALMS THAT WILL ALWAYS REMAIN NEUTRAL. THE OTHER AREAS ARE LARGELY UNDESIRABLE, BUT IF ONE OF YOU WANTS IT, YOU CAN TRY AND CLAIM IT.
REGARDING DISAGREEMENTS, THERE'S A REASON THERE ARE NINE OF YOU. IN ALL THINGS YOU CAN MEET AS FAMILY, BREAK BREAD, AND VOTE ON WHATEVER IT IS.
OR I CAN BASH HEADS IF YOU DON'T DO WHAT I WANT.
I'M THE OLDEST, I'M GOING TO PICK FIRST. I CLAIM THE FOURTH WITH SPEROS CITY AND MILLENNIUM CITY. MY XV'S ARE ALREADY THERE, MAKES SENSE.

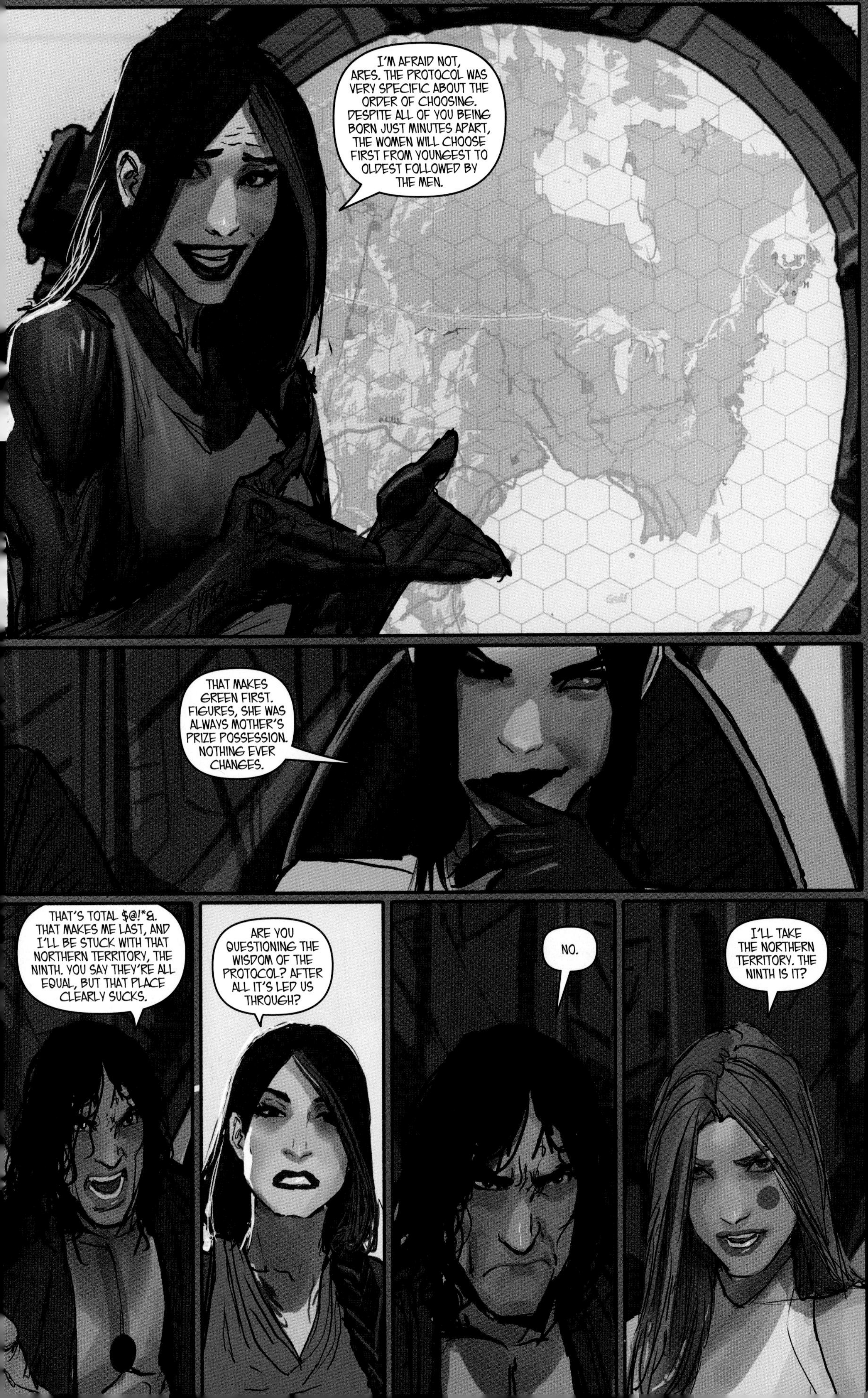
I'M AFRAID NOT, ARES. THE PROTOCOL WAS VERY SPECIFIC ABOUT THE ORDER OF CHOOSING. DESPITE ALL OF YOU BEING BORN JUST MINUTES APART, THE WOMEN WILL CHOOSE FIRST FROM YOUNGEST TO OLDEST FOLLOWED BY THE MEN.
THAT MAKES GREEN FIRST. FIGURES, SHE WAS ALWAYS MOTHER'S PRIZE POSSESSION. NOTHING EVER CHANGES.
THAT'S TOTAL $@!*&. THAT MAKES ME LAST, AND I'LL BE STUCK WITH THAT NORTHERN TERRITORY, THE NINTH. YOU SAY THEY'RE ALL EQUAL, BUT THAT PLACE CLEARLY SUCKS.
ARE YOU QUESTIONING THE WISDOM OF THE PROTOCOL? AFTER ALL IT'S LED US THROUGH?
NO.
I'LL TAKE THE NORTHERN TERRITORY. THE NINTH IS IT?

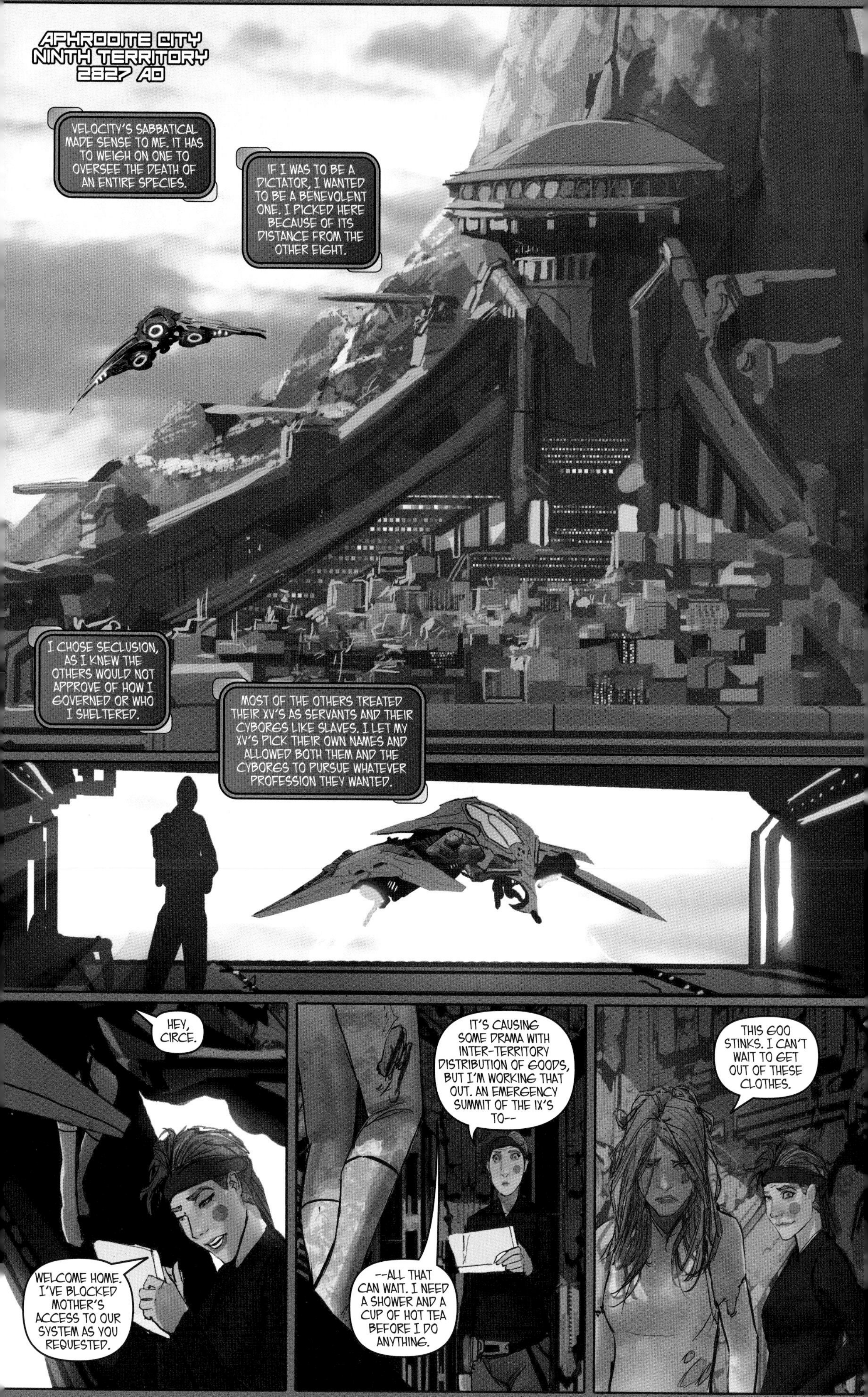
APHRODITE CITY
NINTH TERRITORY
2827 AD
VELOCITY'S SABBATICAL MADE SENSE TO ME. IT HAS TO WEIGH ON ONE TO OVERSEE THE DEATH OF AN ENTIRE SPECIES.
IF I WAS TO BE A DICTATOR, I WANTED TO BE A BENEVOLENT ONE. I PICKED HERE BECAUSE OF ITS DISTANCE FROM THE OTHER EIGHT.
I CHOSE SECLUSION, AS I KNEW THE OTHERS WOULD NOT APPROVE OF HOW I GOVERNED OR WHO I SHELTERED.
MOST OF THE OTHERS TREATED THEIR XV'S AS SERVANTS AND THEIR CYBORGS LIKE SLAVES. I LET MY XV'S PICK THEIR OWN NAMES AND ALLOWED BOTH THEM AND THE CYBORGS TO PURSUE WHATEVER PROFESSION THEY WANTED.
HEY, CIRCE.
WELCOME HOME. I'VE BLOCKED MOTHER'S ACCESS TO OUR SYSTEM AS YOU REQUESTED.
IT'S CAUSING SOME DRAMA WITH INTER-TERRITORY DISTRIBUTION OF GOODS, BUT I'M WORKING THAT OUT. AN EMERGENCY SUMMIT OF THE IX'S TO--
--ALL THAT CAN WAIT. I NEED A SHOWER AND A CUP OF HOT TEA BEFORE I DO ANYTHING.
THIS GOO STINKS. I CAN'T WAIT TO GET OUT OF THESE CLOTHES.

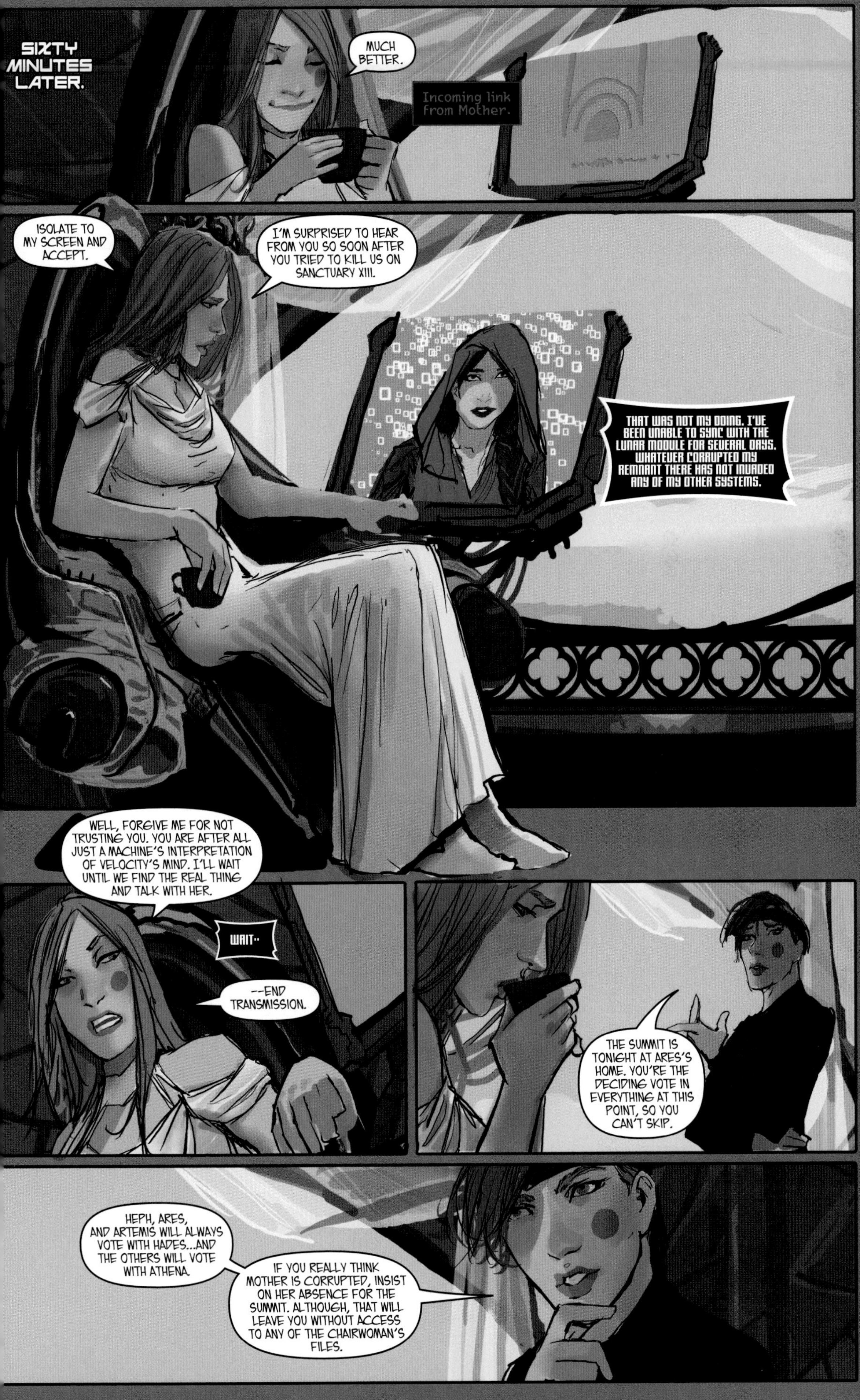
SIXTY MINUTES LATER.
MUCH BETTER.
Incoming link from Mother.
ISOLATE TO MY SCREEN AND ACCEPT.
I'M SURPRISED TO HEAR FROM YOU SO SOON AFTER YOU TRIED TO KILL US ON SANCTUARY XIII.
THAT WAS NOT MY DOING. I'VE BEEN UNABLE TO SYNC WITH THE LUNAR MODULE FOR SEVERAL DAYS. WHATEVER CORRUPTED MY REMNANT THERE HAS NOT INVADED ANY OF MY OTHER SYSTEMS.
WELL, FORGIVE ME FOR NOT TRUSTING YOU. YOU ARE AFTER ALL JUST A MACHINE'S INTERPRETATION OF VELOCITY'S MIND. I'LL WAIT UNTIL WE FIND THE REAL THING AND TALK WITH HER.
WAIT--
--END TRANSMISSION.
THE SUMMIT IS TONIGHT AT ARES'S HOME. YOU'RE THE DECIDING VOTE IN EVERYTHING AT THIS POINT, SO YOU CAN'T SKIP.
HEPH, ARES, AND ARTEMIS WILL ALWAYS VOTE WITH HADES...AND THE OTHERS WILL VOTE WITH ATHENA.
IF YOU REALLY THINK MOTHER IS CORRUPTED, INSIST ON HER ABSENCE FOR THE SUMMIT. ALTHOUGH, THAT WILL LEAVE YOU WITHOUT ACCESS TO ANY OF THE CHAIRWOMAN'S FILES.

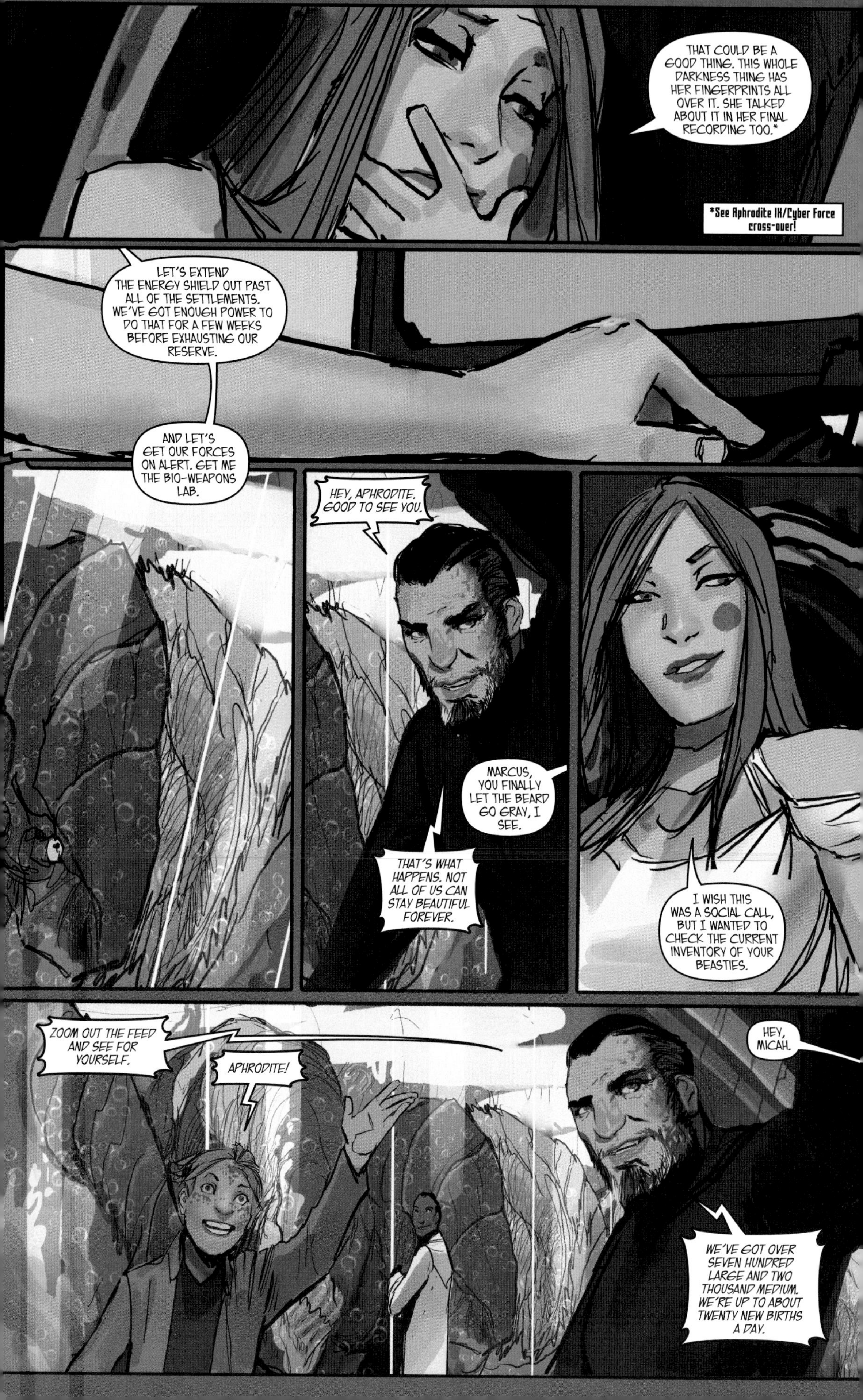
THAT COULD BE A GOOD THING. THIS WHOLE DARKNESS THING HAS HER FINGERPRINTS ALL OVER IT. SHE TALKED ABOUT IT IN HER FINAL RECORDING TOO.*
*See Aphrodite IX/Cyber Force cross-over!
LET'S EXTEND THE ENERGY SHIELD OUT PAST ALL OF THE SETTLEMENTS. WE'VE GOT ENOUGH POWER TO DO THAT FOR A FEW WEEKS BEFORE EXHAUSTING OUR RESERVE.
AND LET'S GET OUR FORCES ON ALERT. GET ME THE BIO-WEAPONS LAB.
HEY, APHRODITE. GOOD TO SEE YOU.
MARCUS, YOU FINALLY LET THE BEARD GO GRAY, I SEE.
THAT'S WHAT HAPPENS. NOT ALL OF US CAN STAY BEAUTIFUL FOREVER.
I WISH THIS WAS A SOCIAL CALL, BUT I WANTED TO CHECK THE CURRENT INVENTORY OF YOUR BEASTIES.
ZOOM OUT THE FEED AND SEE FOR YOURSELF.
APHRODITE!
HEY, MICAH.
WE'VE GOT OVER SEVEN HUNDRED LARGE AND TWO THOUSAND MEDIUM. WE'RE UP TO ABOUT TWENTY NEW BIRTHS A DAY.

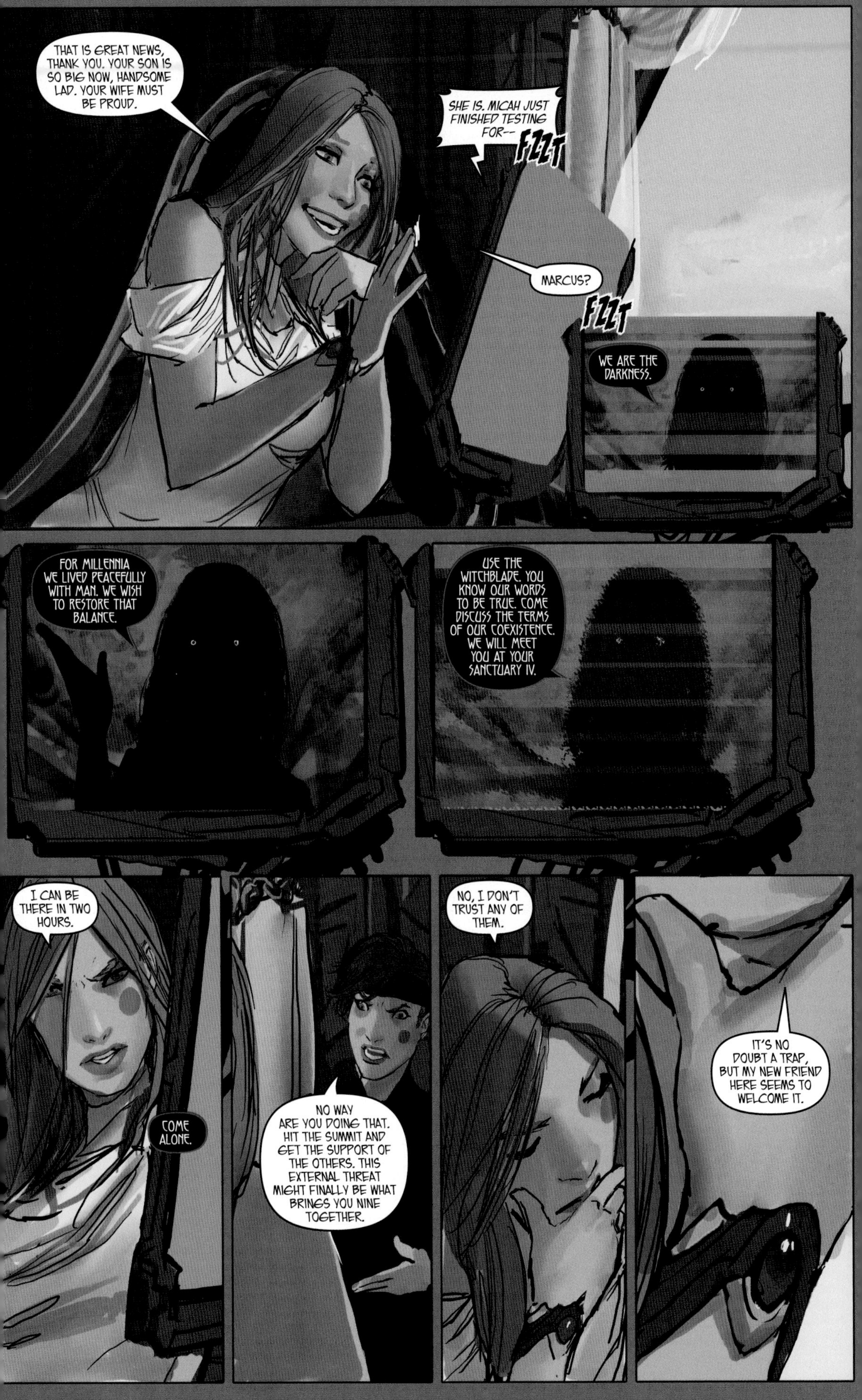
THAT IS GREAT NEWS, THANK YOU. YOUR SON IS SO BIG NOW, HANDSOME LAD. YOUR WIFE MUST BE PROUD.
SHE IS. MICAH JUST FINISHED TESTING FOR--
FZZT
MARCUS?
FZZT
WE ARE THE DARKNESS.
FOR MILLENNIA WE LIVED PEACEFULLY WITH MAN. WE WISH TO RESTORE THAT BALANCE.
USE THE WITCHBLADE. YOU KNOW OUR WORDS TO BE TRUE. COME DISCUSS THE TERMS OF OUR COEXISTENCE. WE WILL MEET YOU AT YOUR SANCTUARY IV.
I CAN BE THERE IN TWO HOURS.
COME ALONE.
NO WAY ARE YOU DOING THAT. HIT THE SUMMIT AND GET THE SUPPORT OF THE OTHERS. THIS EXTERNAL THREAT MIGHT FINALLY BE WHAT BRINGS YOU NINE TOGETHER.
NO, I DON'T TRUST ANY OF THEM.
IT'S NO DOUBT A TRAP, BUT MY NEW FRIEND HERE SEEMS TO WELCOME IT.

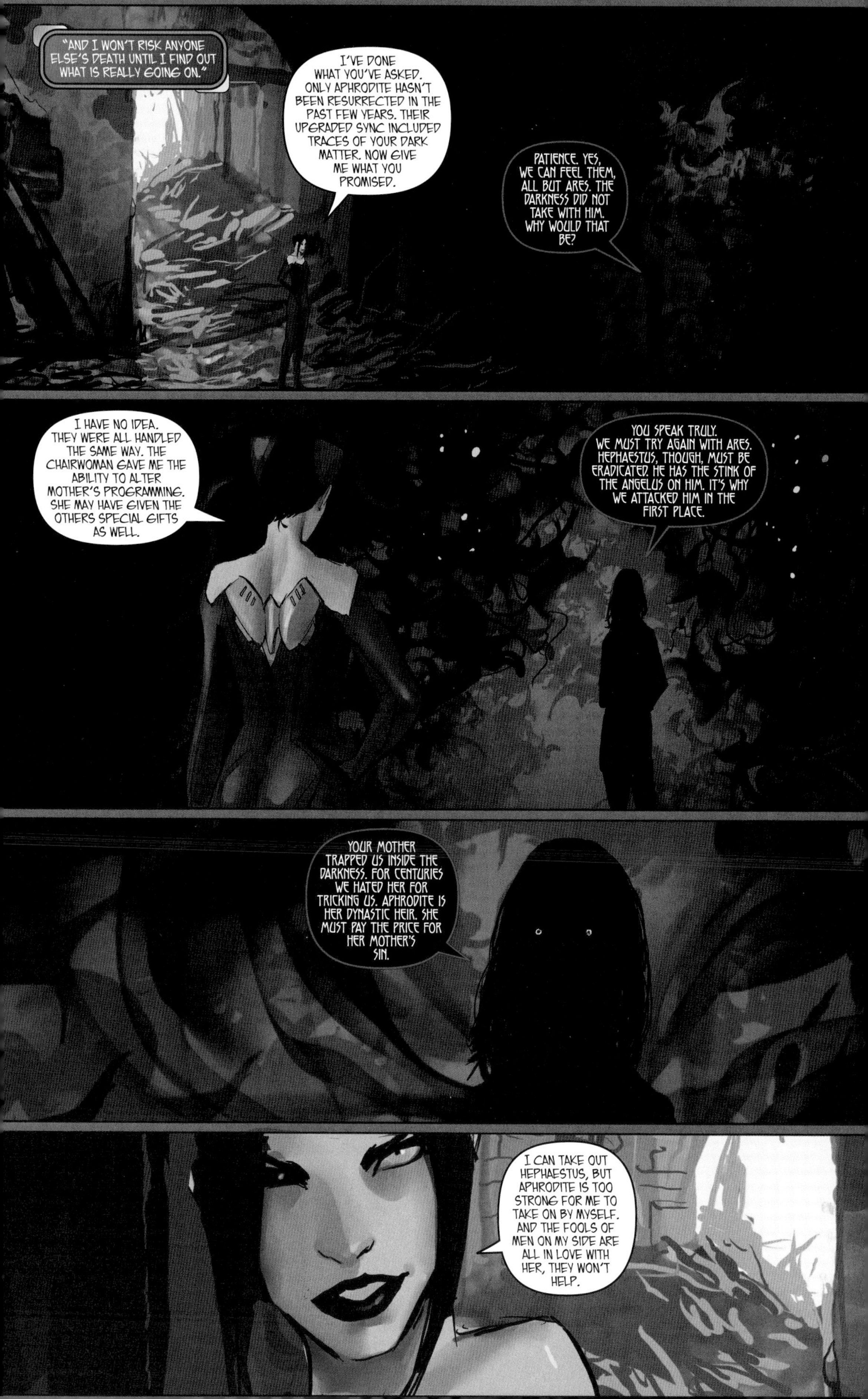
"AND I WON'T RISK ANYONE ELSE'S DEATH UNTIL I FIND OUT WHAT IS REALLY GOING ON."
I'VE DONE WHAT YOU'VE ASKED. ONLY APHRODITE HASN'T BEEN RESURRECTED IN THE PAST FEW YEARS. THEIR UPGRADED SYNC INCLUDED TRACES OF YOUR DARK MATTER. NOW GIVE ME WHAT YOU PROMISED.
PATIENCE. YES, WE CAN FEEL THEM, ALL BUT ARES. THE DARKNESS DID NOT TAKE WITH HIM. WHY WOULD THAT BE?
I HAVE NO IDEA. THEY WERE ALL HANDLED THE SAME WAY. THE CHAIRWOMAN GAVE ME THE ABILITY TO ALTER MOTHER'S PROGRAMMING. SHE MAY HAVE GIVEN THE OTHERS SPECIAL GIFTS AS WELL.
YOU SPEAK TRULY. WE MUST TRY AGAIN WITH ARES. HEPHAESTUS, THOUGH, MUST BE ERADICATED. HE HAS THE STINK OF THE ANGELUS ON HIM. IT'S WHY WE ATTACKED HIM IN THE FIRST PLACE.
YOUR MOTHER TRAPPED US INSIDE THE DARKNESS. FOR CENTURIES WE HATED HER FOR TRICKING US. APHRODITE IS HER DYNASTIC HEIR. SHE MUST PAY THE PRICE FOR HER MOTHER'S SIN.
I CAN TAKE OUT HEPHAESTUS, BUT APHRODITE IS TOO STRONG FOR ME TO TAKE ON BY MYSELF. AND THE FOOLS OF MEN ON MY SIDE ARE ALL IN LOVE WITH HER, THEY WON'T HELP.

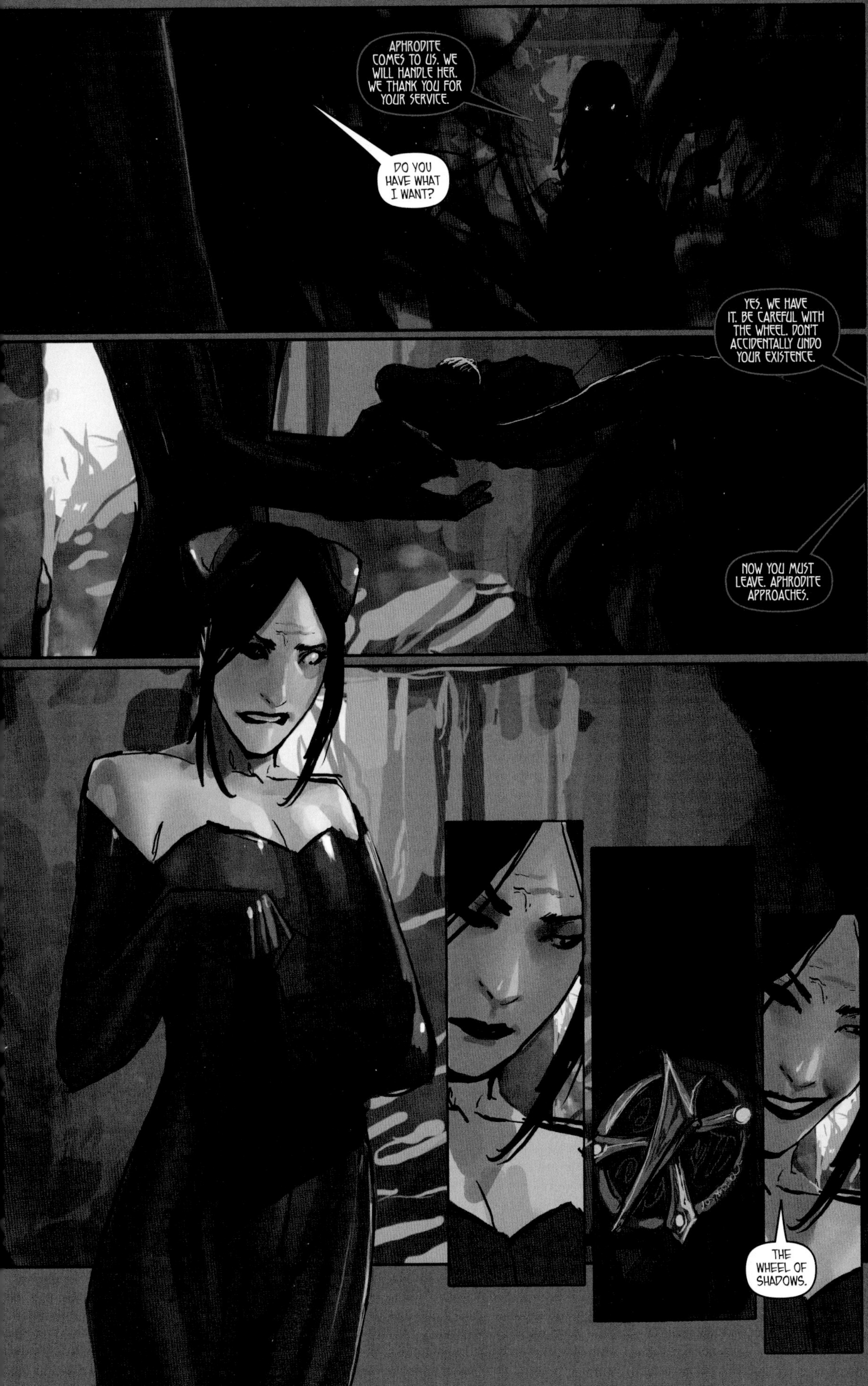
APHRODITE COMES TO US. WE WILL HANDLE HER. WE THANK YOU FOR YOUR SERVICE.
DO YOU HAVE WHAT I WANT?
YES. WE HAVE IT. BE CAREFUL WITH THE WHEEL. DON'T ACCIDENTALLY UNDO YOUR EXISTENCE.
NOW YOU MUST LEAVE. APHRODITE APPROACHES.
THE WHEEL OF SHADOWS.

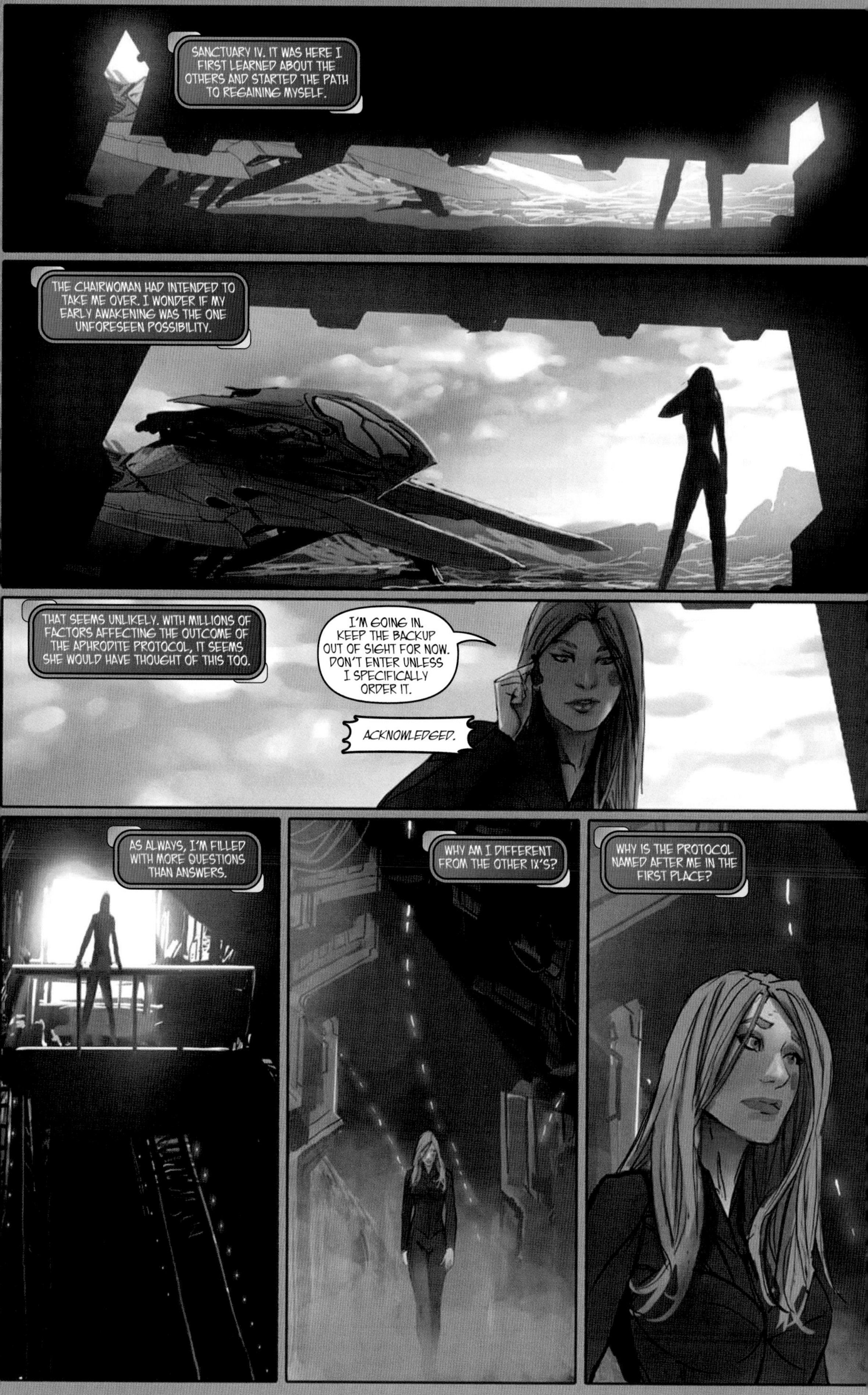
SANCTUARY IV. IT WAS HERE I FIRST LEARNED ABOUT THE OTHERS AND STARTED THE PATH TO REGAINING MYSELF.
THE CHAIRWOMAN HAD INTENDED TO TAKE ME OVER. I WONDER IF MY EARLY AWAKENING WAS THE ONE UNFORESEEN POSSIBILITY.
THAT SEEMS UNLIKELY. WITH MILLIONS OF FACTORS AFFECTING THE OUTCOME OF THE APHRODITE PROTOCOL, IT SEEMS SHE WOULD HAVE THOUGHT OF THIS TOO.
I'M GOING IN. KEEP THE BACKUP OUT OF SIGHT FOR NOW. DON'T ENTER UNLESS I SPECIFICALLY ORDER IT.
ACKNOWLEDGED.
AS ALWAYS, I'M FILLED WITH MORE QUESTIONS THAN ANSWERS.
WHY AM I DIFFERENT FROM THE OTHER IX'S?
WHY IS THE PROTOCOL NAMED AFTER ME IN THE FIRST PLACE?

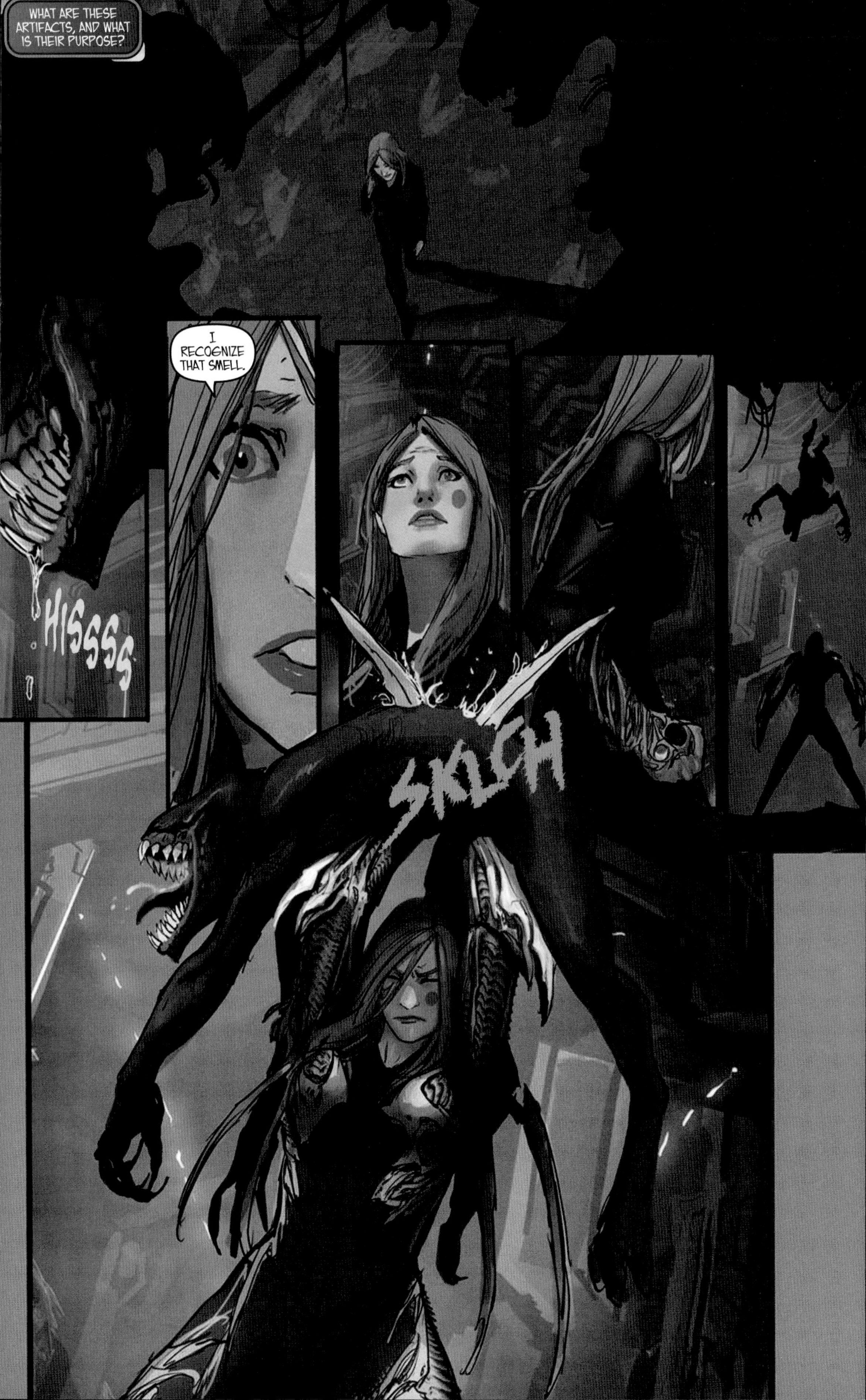
WHAT ARE THESE ARTIFACTS, AND WHAT IS THEIR PURPOSE?
HISSSSS
I RECOGNIZE THAT SMELL.
SKLCH

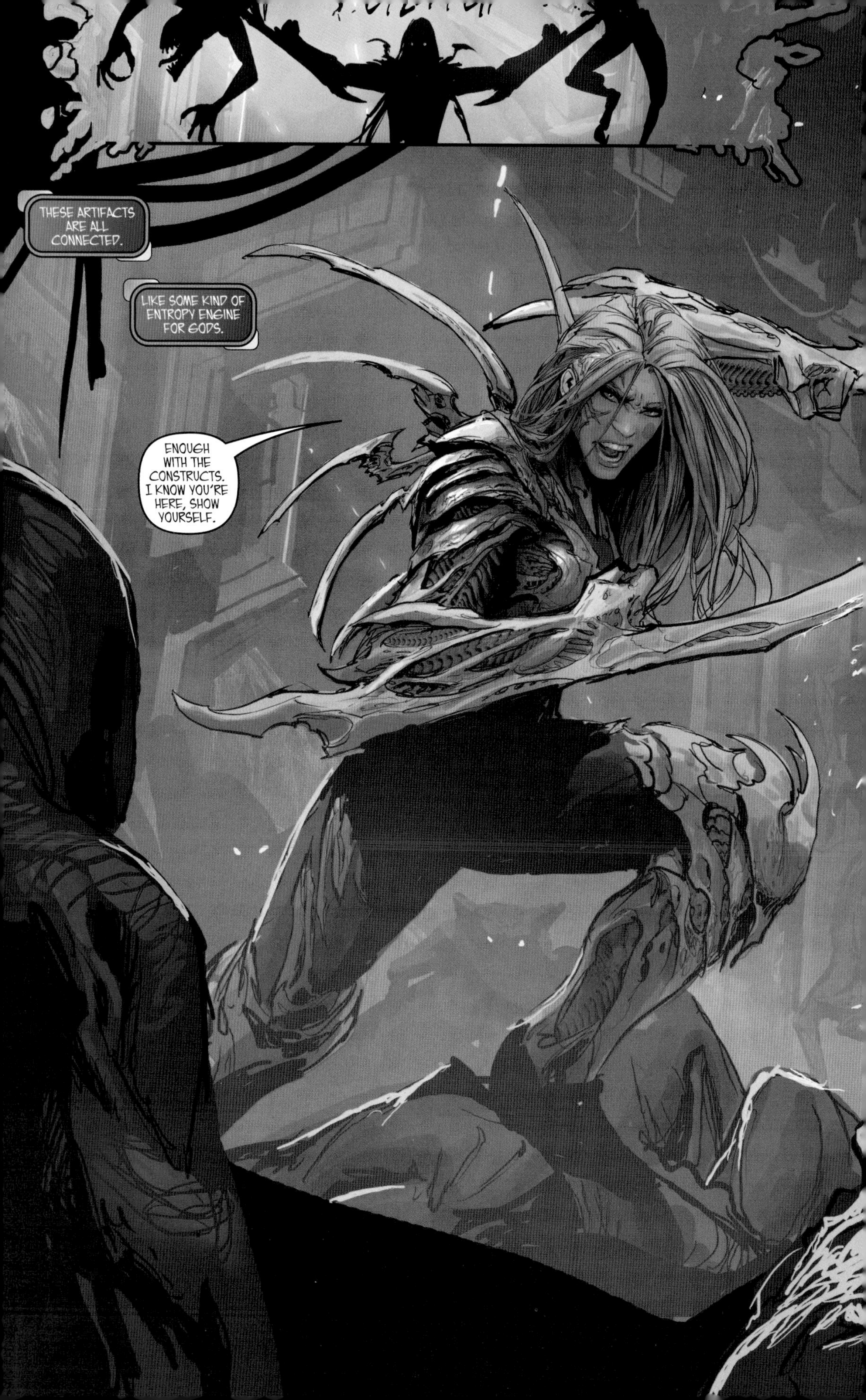
THESE ARTIFACTS ARE ALL CONNECTED.
LIKE SOME KIND OF ENTROPY ENGINE FOR GODS.
ENOUGH WITH THE CONSTRUCTS. I KNOW YOU'RE HERE, SHOW YOURSELF.

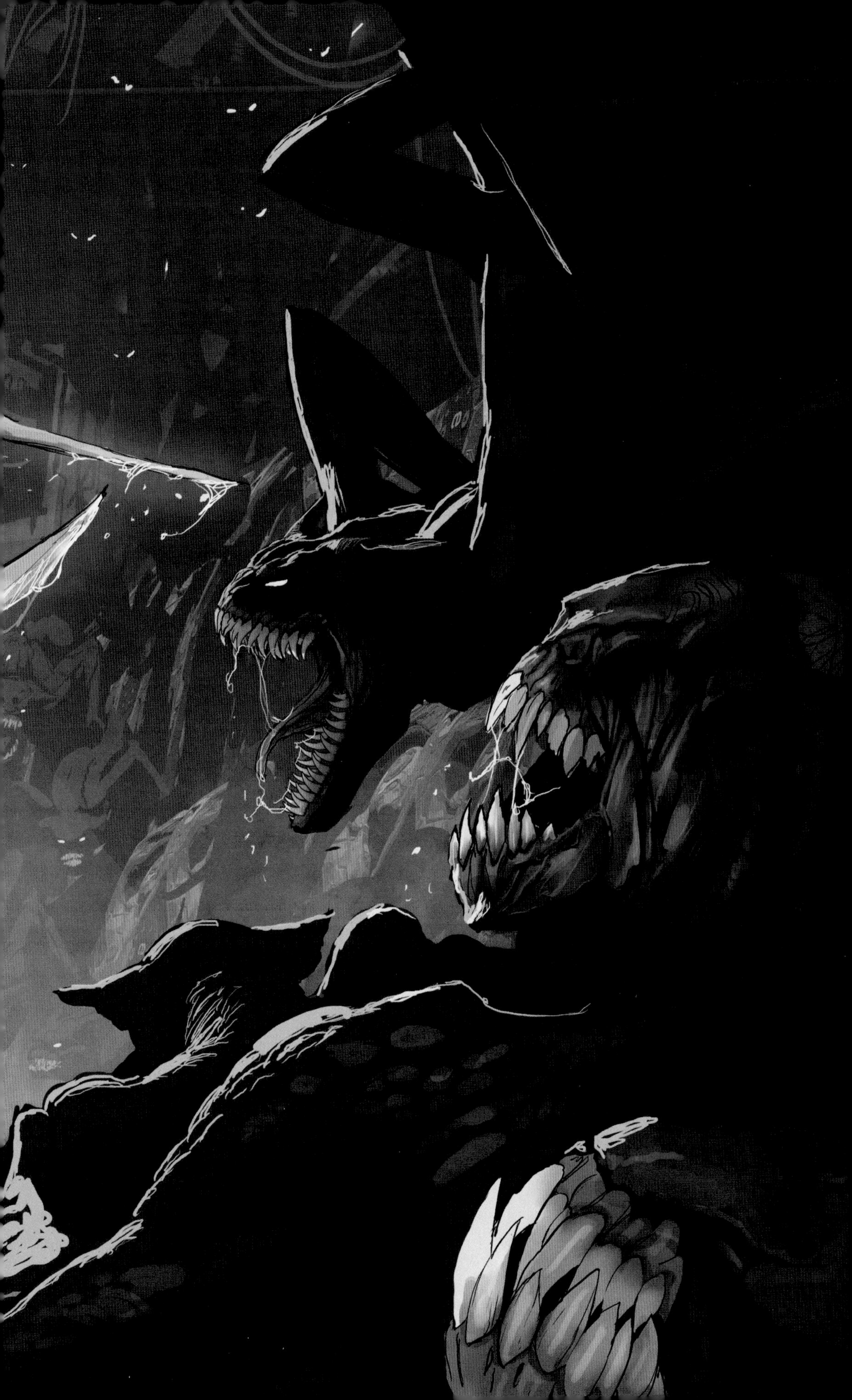

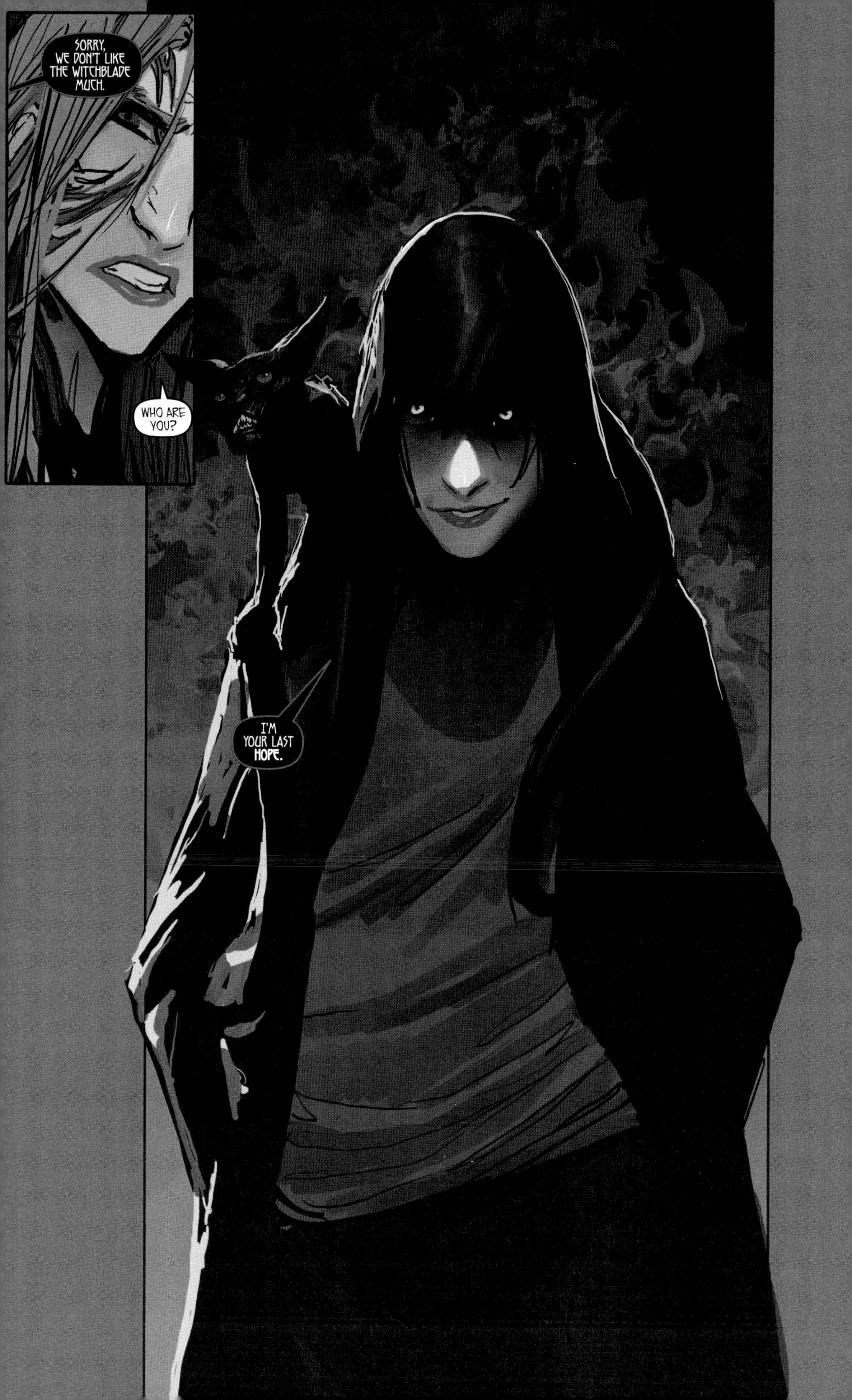
SORRY, WE DON'T LIKE THE WITCHBLADE MUCH.
WHO ARE YOU?
I'M YOUR LAST **HOPE.**

CHAPTER THREE

"Any sufficiently
advanced technology is
indistinguishable from
magic."

"Magic's just science that
we don't understand yet."

Arthur C. Clarke

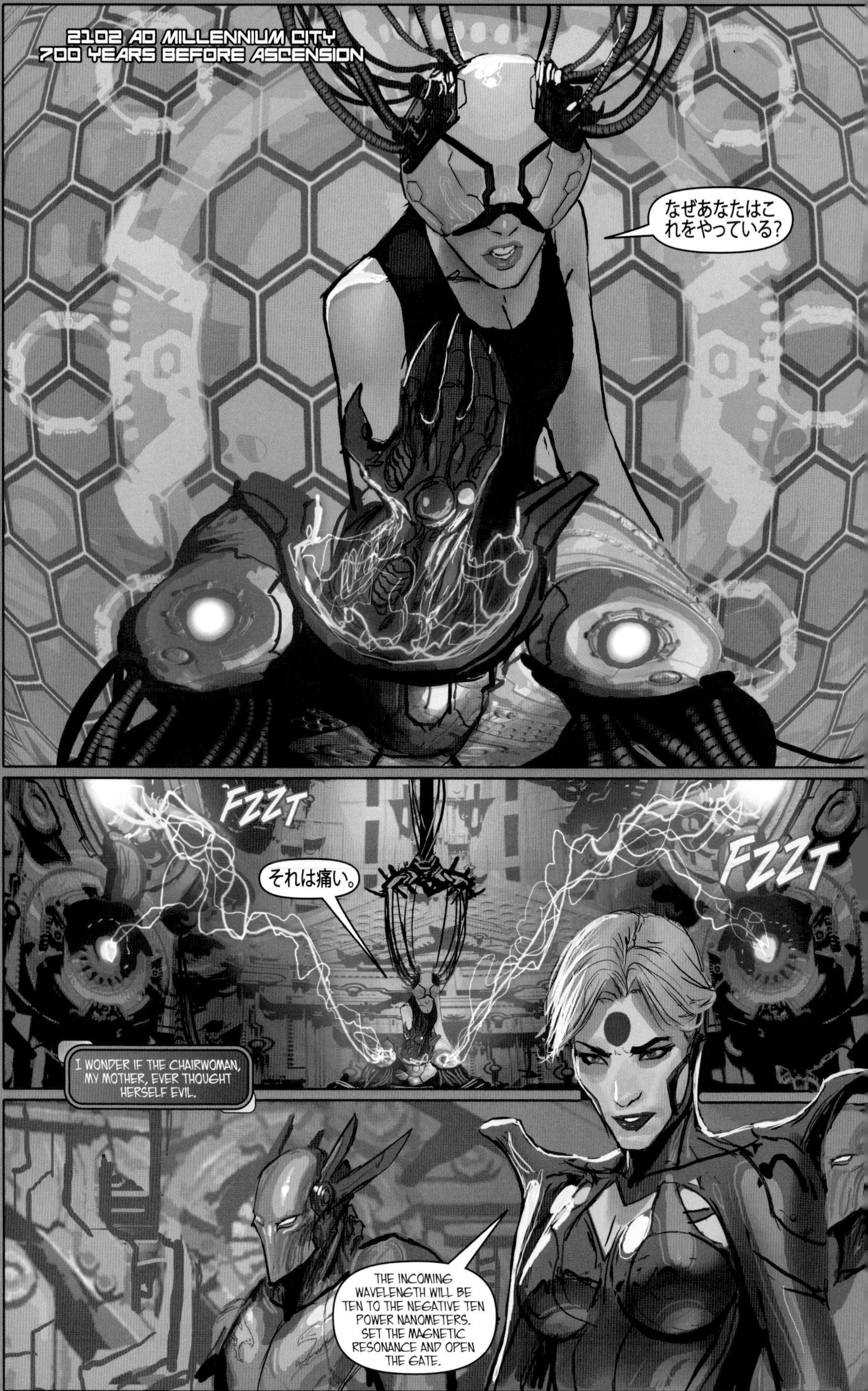
2102 AD MILLENNIUM CITY
700 YEARS BEFORE ASCENSION
なぜあなたはこれをやっている?
FZZT
FZZT
それは痛い。
I WONDER IF THE CHAIRWOMAN, MY MOTHER, EVER THOUGHT HERSELF EVIL.
THE INCOMING WAVELENGTH WILL BE TEN TO THE NEGATIVE TEN POWER NANOMETERS. SET THE MAGNETIC RESONANCE AND OPEN THE GATE.

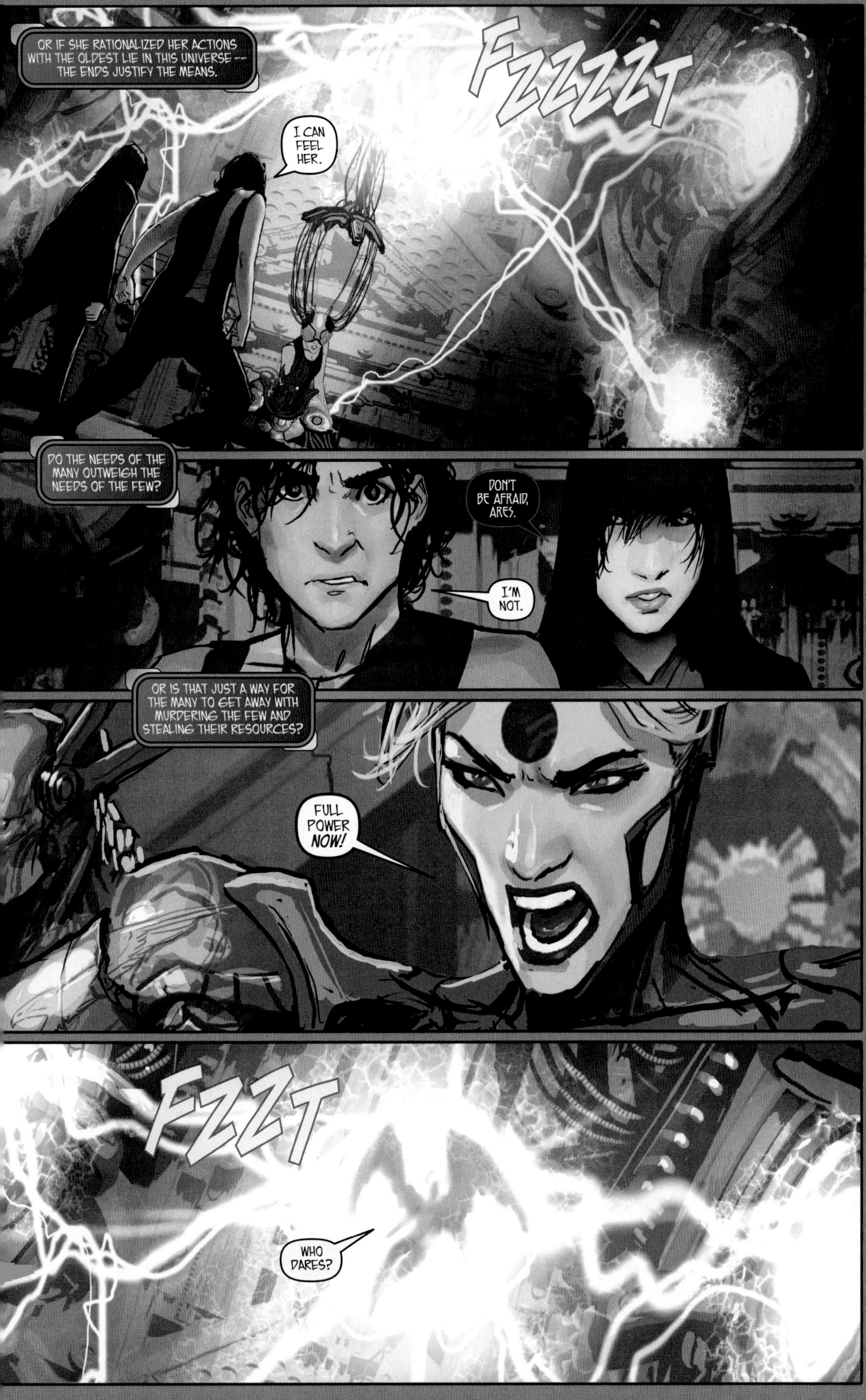
OR IF SHE RATIONALIZED HER ACTIONS WITH THE OLDEST LIE IN THIS UNIVERSE -- THE ENDS JUSTIFY THE MEANS.
FZZZZZT
I CAN FEEL HER.
DO THE NEEDS OF THE MANY OUTWEIGH THE NEEDS OF THE FEW?
DON'T BE AFRAID, ARES.
I'M NOT.
OR IS THAT JUST A WAY FOR THE MANY TO GET AWAY WITH MURDERING THE FEW AND STEALING THEIR RESOURCES?
FULL POWER NOW!
FZZT
WHO DARES?

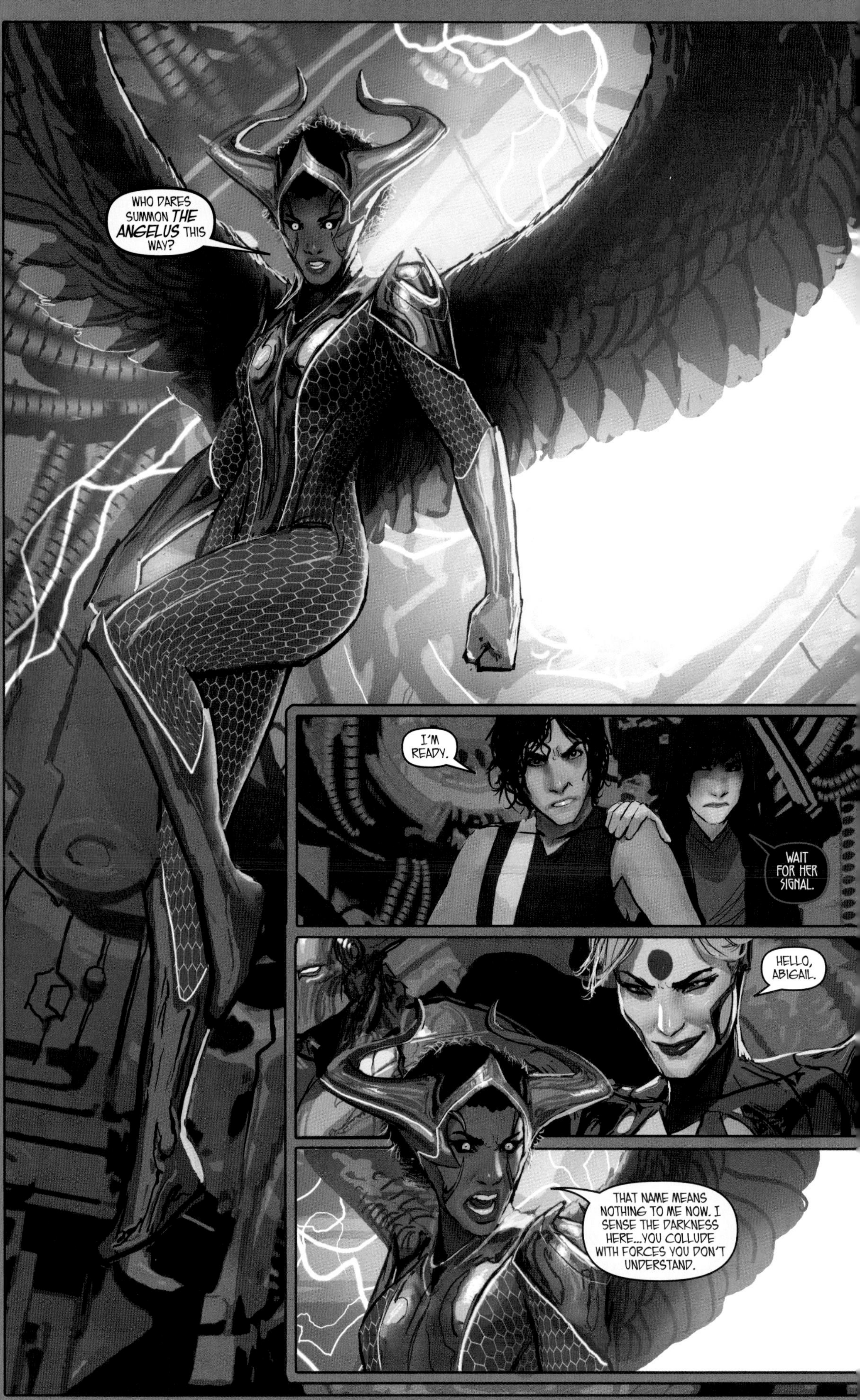
WHO DARES SUMMON THE ANGELUS THIS WAY?
I'M READY.
WAIT FOR HER SIGNAL.
HELLO, ABIGAIL.
THAT NAME MEANS NOTHING TO ME NOW. I SENSE THE DARKNESS HERE...YOU COLLUDE WITH FORCES YOU DON'T UNDERSTAND.

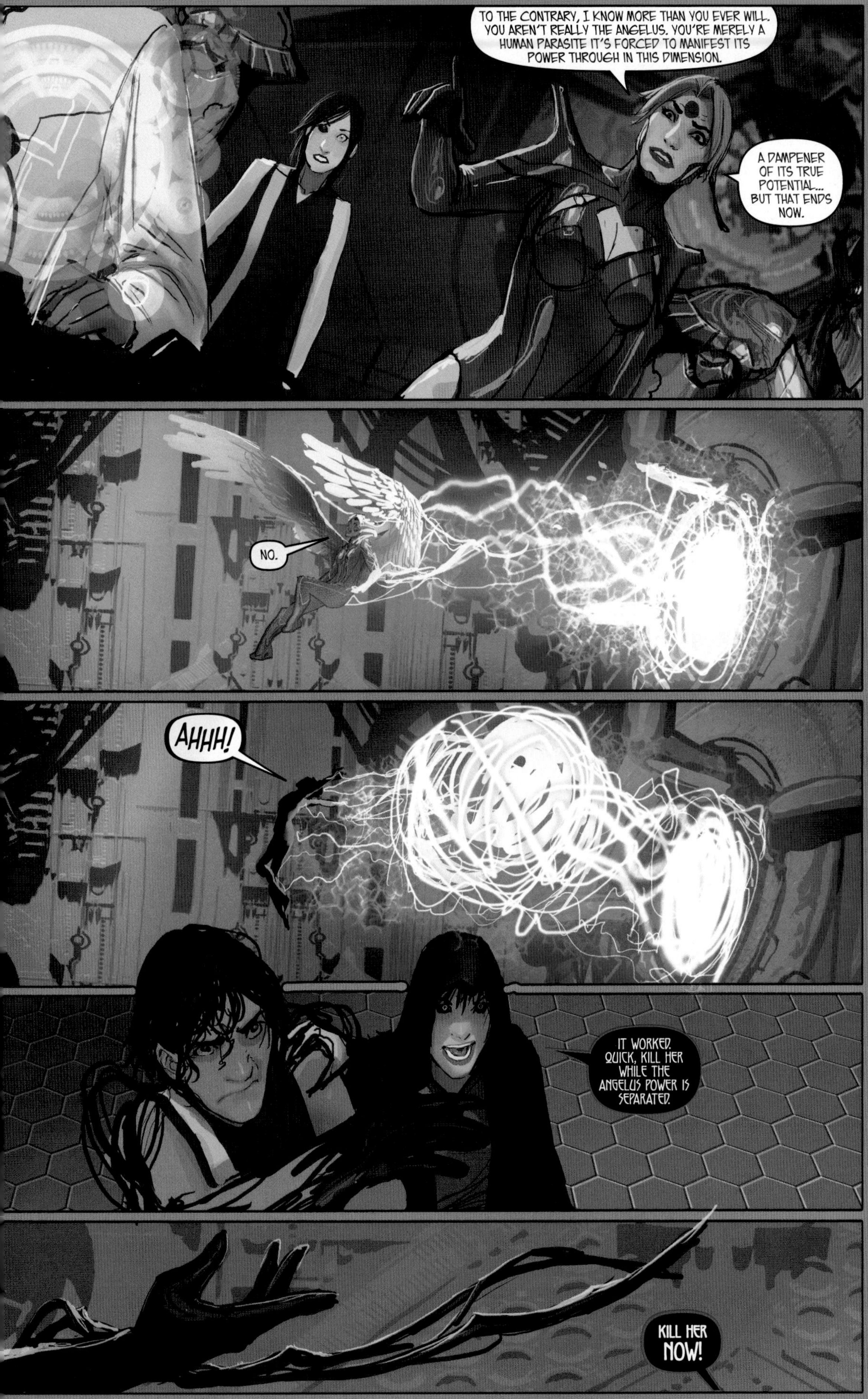
TO THE CONTRARY, I KNOW MORE THAN YOU EVER WILL. YOU AREN'T REALLY THE ANGELUS. YOU'RE MERELY A HUMAN PARASITE IT'S FORCED TO MANIFEST ITS POWER THROUGH IN THIS DIMENSION.
A DAMPENER OF ITS TRUE POTENTIAL... BUT THAT ENDS NOW.
NO.
AHHH!
IT WORKED. QUICK, KILL HER WHILE THE ANGELUS POWER IS SEPARATED.
KILL HER NOW!

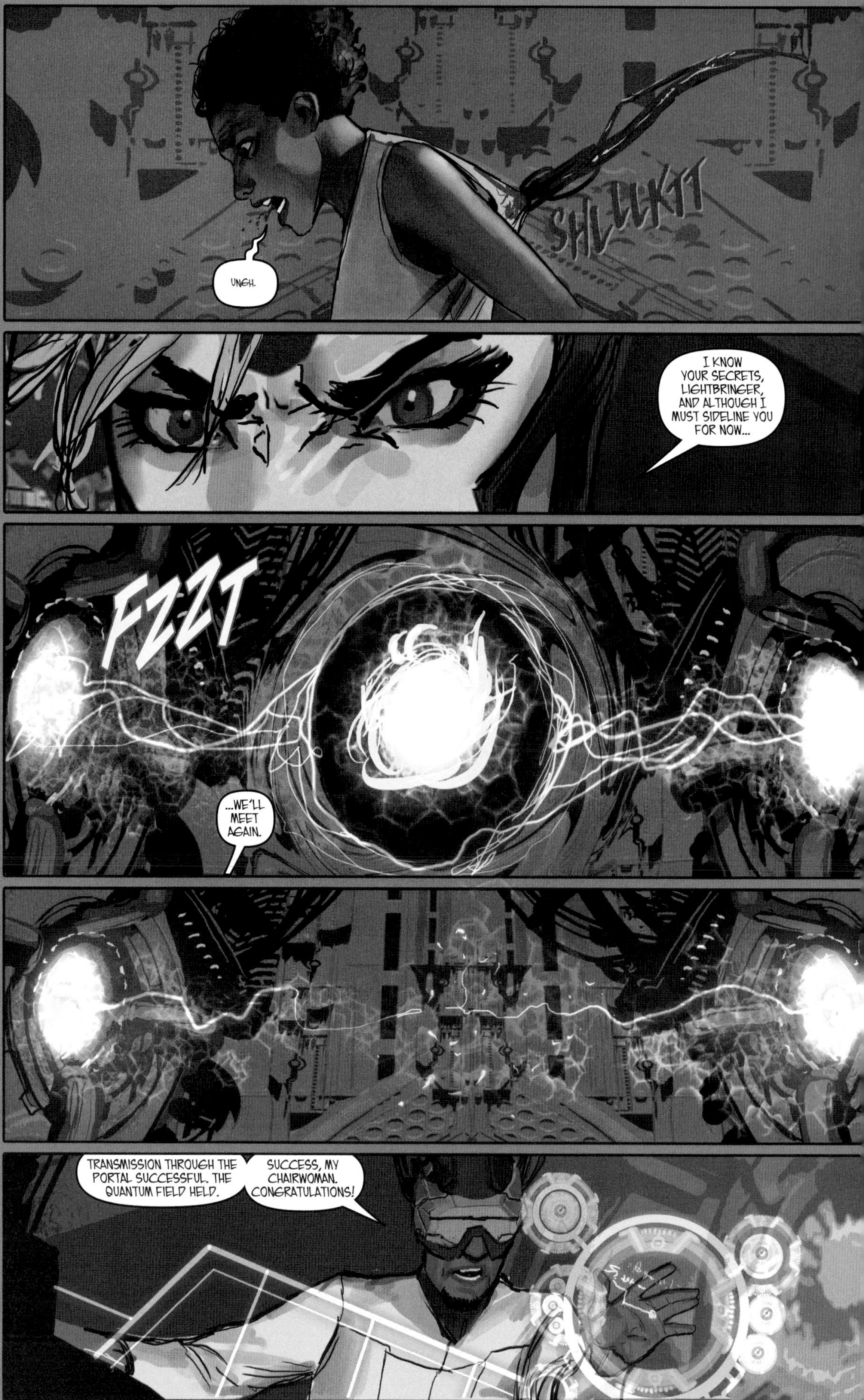

SHLLLKTT
UNGH.
I KNOW YOUR SECRETS, LIGHTBRINGER, AND ALTHOUGH I MUST SIDELINE YOU FOR NOW...
FZZT
...WE'LL MEET AGAIN.
TRANSMISSION THROUGH THE PORTAL SUCCESSFUL. THE QUANTUM FIELD HELD.
SUCCESS, MY CHAIRWOMAN. CONGRATULATIONS!

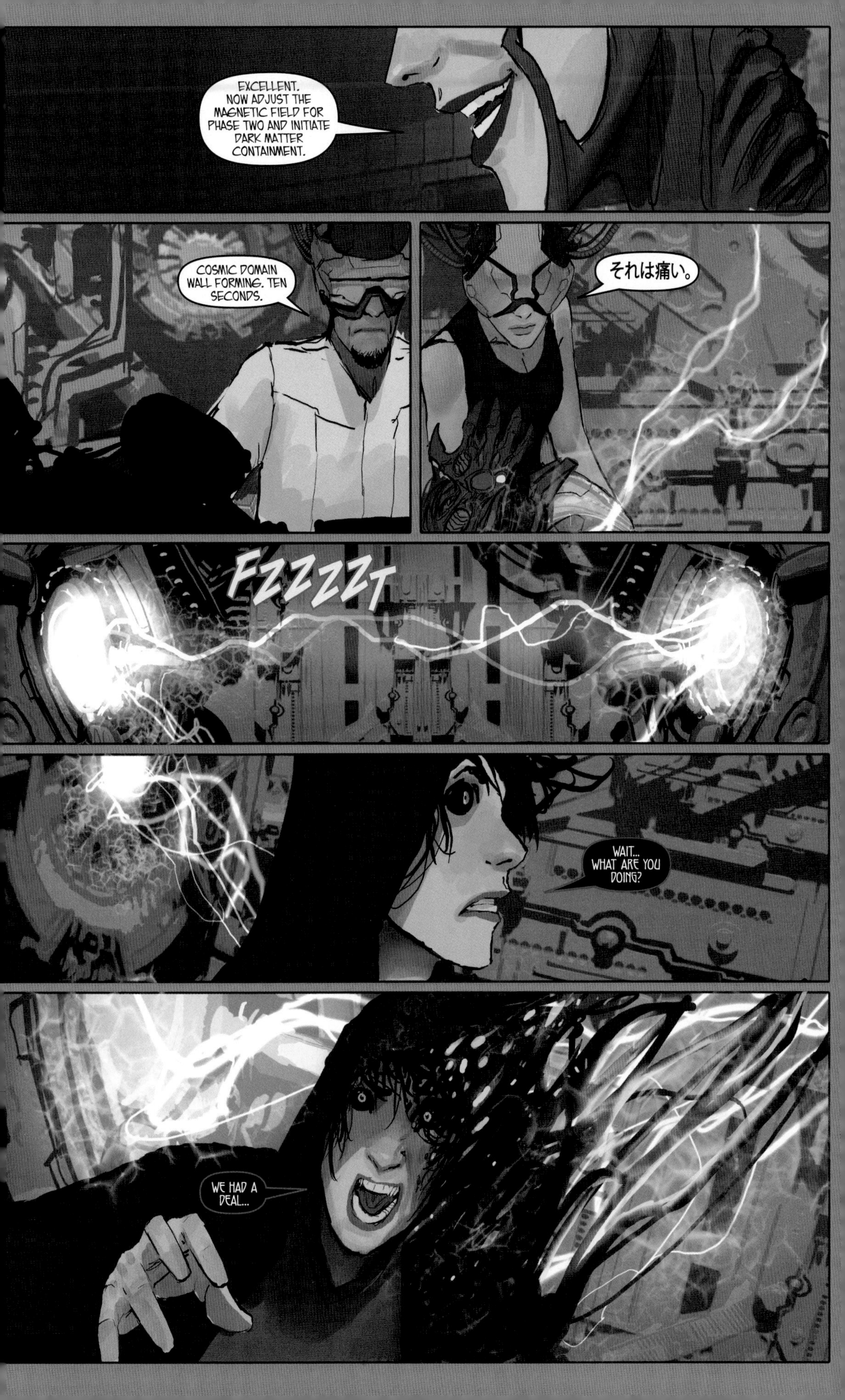
EXCELLENT. NOW ADJUST THE MAGNETIC FIELD FOR PHASE TWO AND INITIATE DARK MATTER CONTAINMENT.
COSMIC DOMAIN WALL FORMING. TEN SECONDS.
それは痛い。
FZZZZT
WAIT... WHAT ARE YOU DOING?
WE HAD A DEAL...

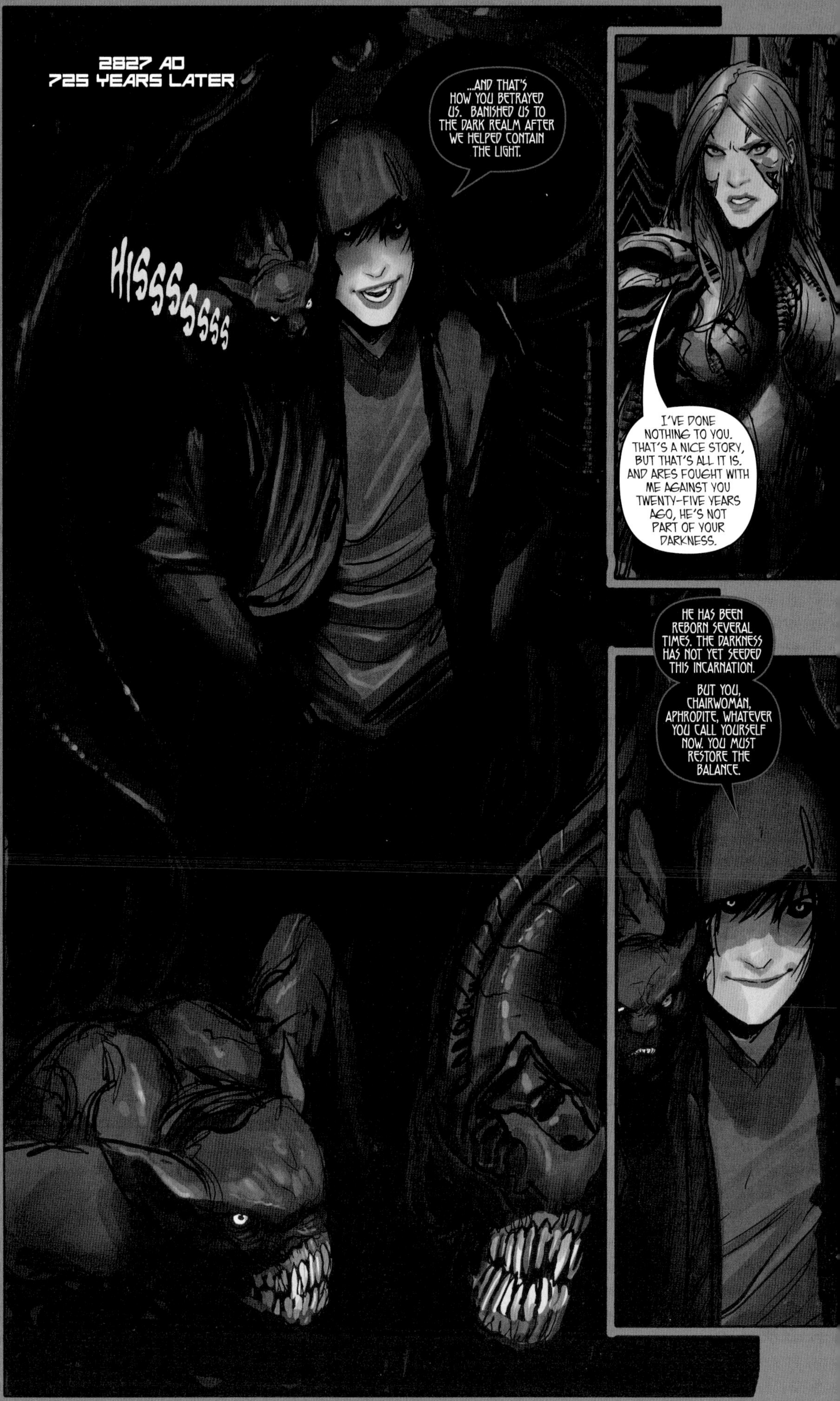
2827 AD
725 YEARS LATER
...AND THAT'S HOW YOU BETRAYED US. BANISHED US TO THE DARK REALM AFTER WE HELPED CONTAIN THE LIGHT.
HISSSSSSSS
I'VE DONE NOTHING TO YOU. THAT'S A NICE STORY, BUT THAT'S ALL IT IS. AND ARES FOUGHT WITH ME AGAINST YOU TWENTY-FIVE YEARS AGO, HE'S NOT PART OF YOUR DARKNESS.
HE HAS BEEN REBORN SEVERAL TIMES. THE DARKNESS HAS NOT YET SEEDED THIS INCARNATION.
BUT YOU, CHAIRWOMAN, APHRODITE, WHATEVER YOU CALL YOURSELF NOW. YOU MUST RESTORE THE BALANCE.

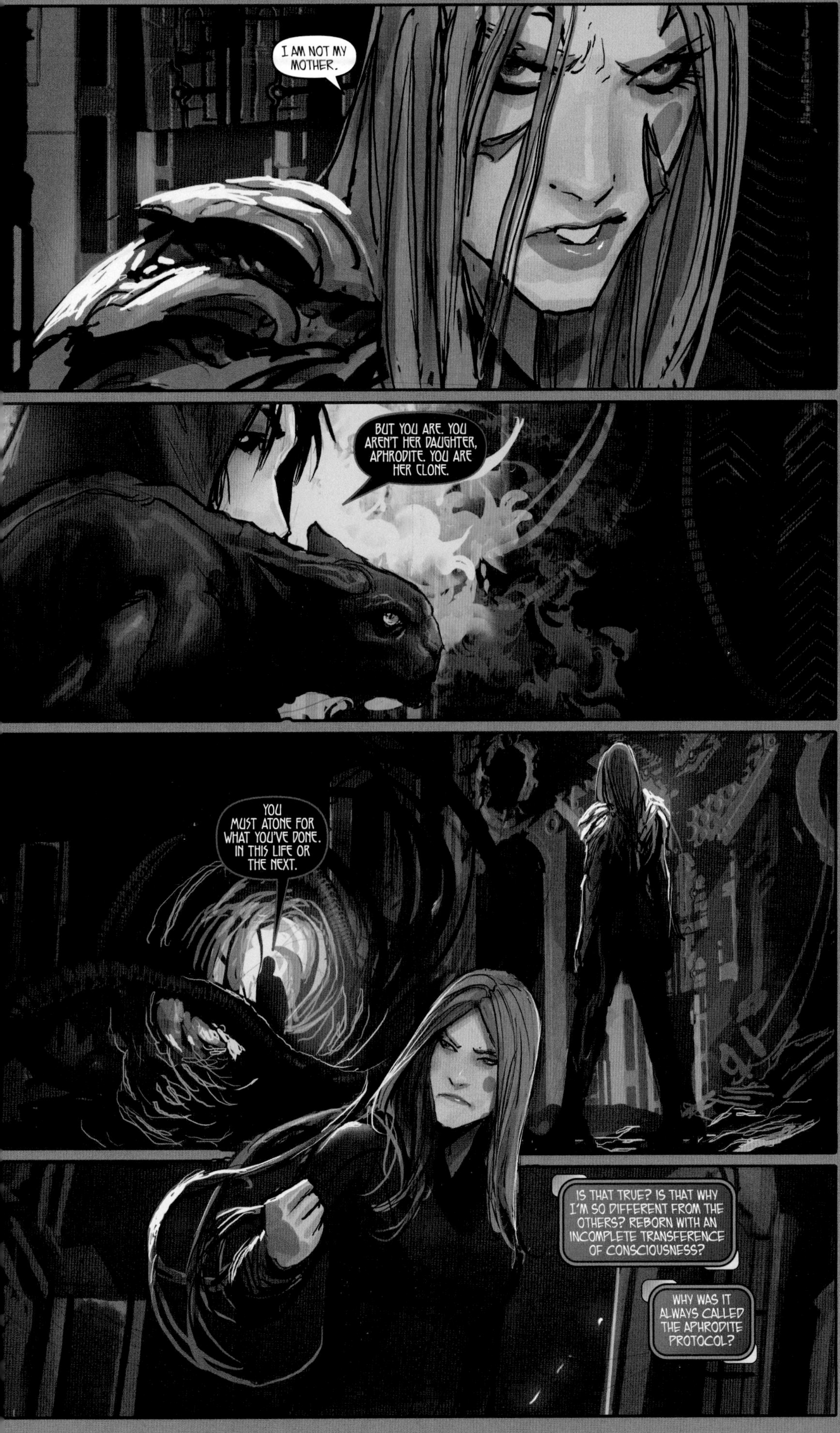
I AM NOT MY MOTHER.
BUT YOU ARE. YOU AREN'T HER DAUGHTER, APHRODITE. YOU ARE HER CLONE.
YOU MUST ATONE FOR WHAT YOU'VE DONE. IN THIS LIFE OR THE NEXT.
IS THAT TRUE? IS THAT WHY I'M SO DIFFERENT FROM THE OTHERS? REBORN WITH AN INCOMPLETE TRANSFERENCE OF CONSCIOUSNESS?
WHY WAS IT ALWAYS CALLED THE APHRODITE PROTOCOL?

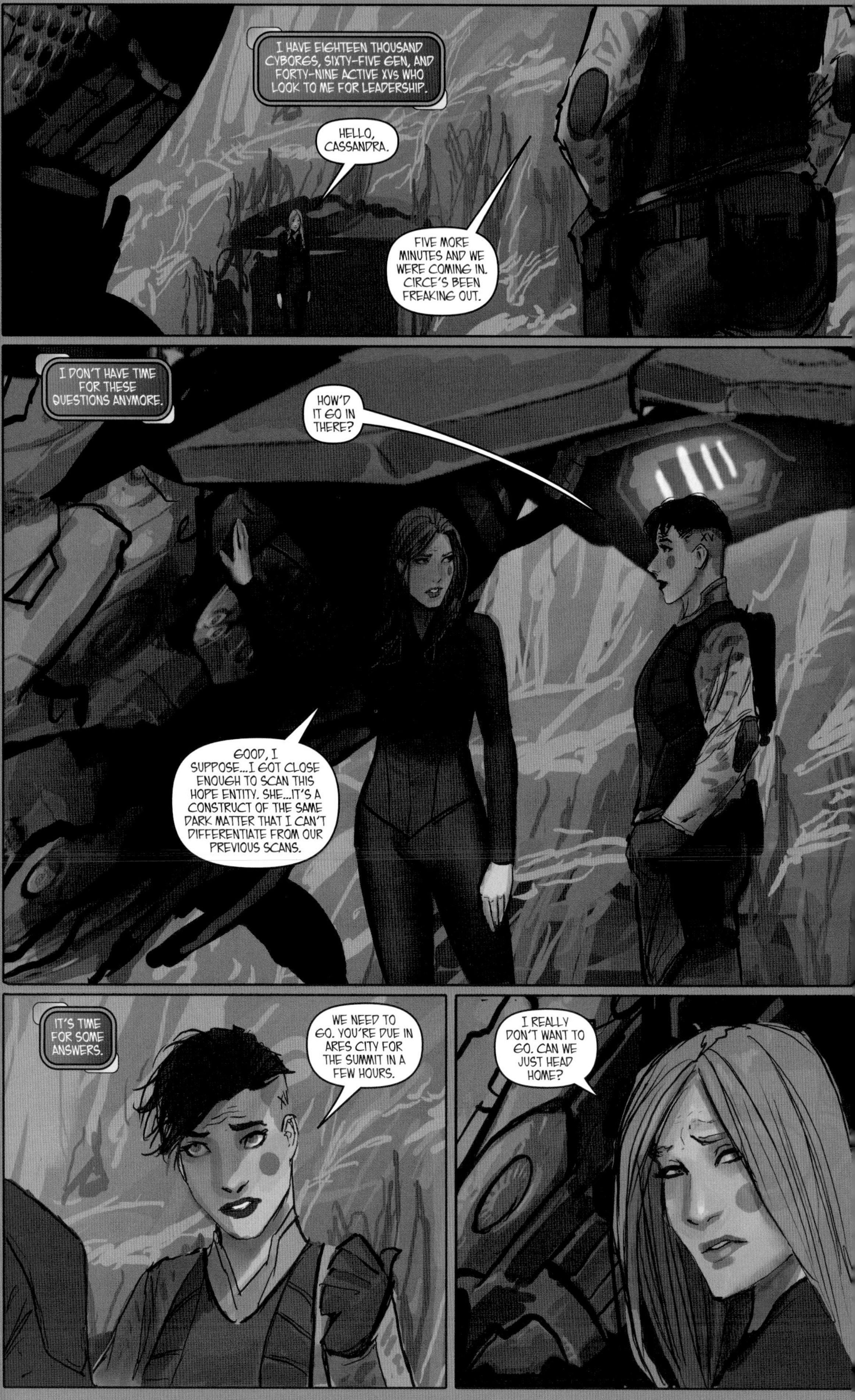
I HAVE EIGHTEEN THOUSAND CYBORGS, SIXTY-FIVE GEN, AND FORTY-NINE ACTIVE XVS WHO LOOK TO ME FOR LEADERSHIP.
HELLO, CASSANDRA.
FIVE MORE MINUTES AND WE WERE COMING IN. CIRCE'S BEEN FREAKING OUT.
I DON'T HAVE TIME FOR THESE QUESTIONS ANYMORE.
HOW'D IT GO IN THERE?
GOOD, I SUPPOSE...I GOT CLOSE ENOUGH TO SCAN THIS HOPE ENTITY. SHE...IT'S A CONSTRUCT OF THE SAME DARK MATTER THAT I CAN'T DIFFERENTIATE FROM OUR PREVIOUS SCANS.
IT'S TIME FOR SOME ANSWERS.
WE NEED TO GO. YOU'RE DUE IN ARES CITY FOR THE SUMMIT IN A FEW HOURS.
I REALLY DON'T WANT TO GO. CAN WE JUST HEAD HOME?

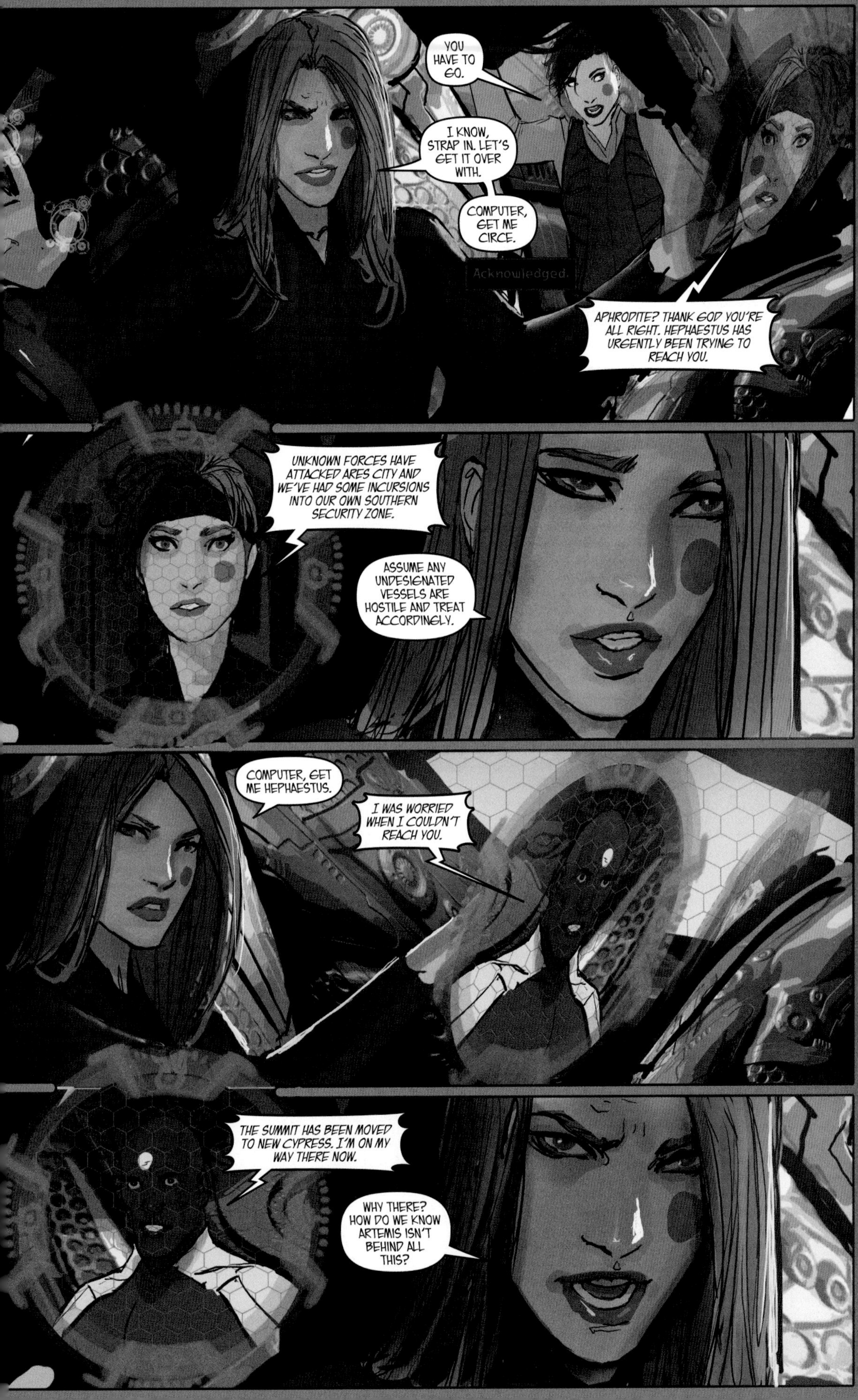
YOU HAVE TO GO.
I KNOW, STRAP IN. LET'S GET IT OVER WITH.
COMPUTER, GET ME CIRCE.
Acknowledged.
APHRODITE? THANK GOD YOU'RE ALL RIGHT. HEPHAESTUS HAS URGENTLY BEEN TRYING TO REACH YOU.
UNKNOWN FORCES HAVE ATTACKED ARES CITY AND WE'VE HAD SOME INCURSIONS INTO OUR OWN SOUTHERN SECURITY ZONE.
ASSUME ANY UNDESIGNATED VESSELS ARE HOSTILE AND TREAT ACCORDINGLY.
COMPUTER, GET ME HEPHAESTUS.
I WAS WORRIED WHEN I COULDN'T REACH YOU.
THE SUMMIT HAS BEEN MOVED TO NEW CYPRESS. I'M ON MY WAY THERE NOW.
WHY THERE? HOW DO WE KNOW ARTEMIS ISN'T BEHIND ALL THIS?

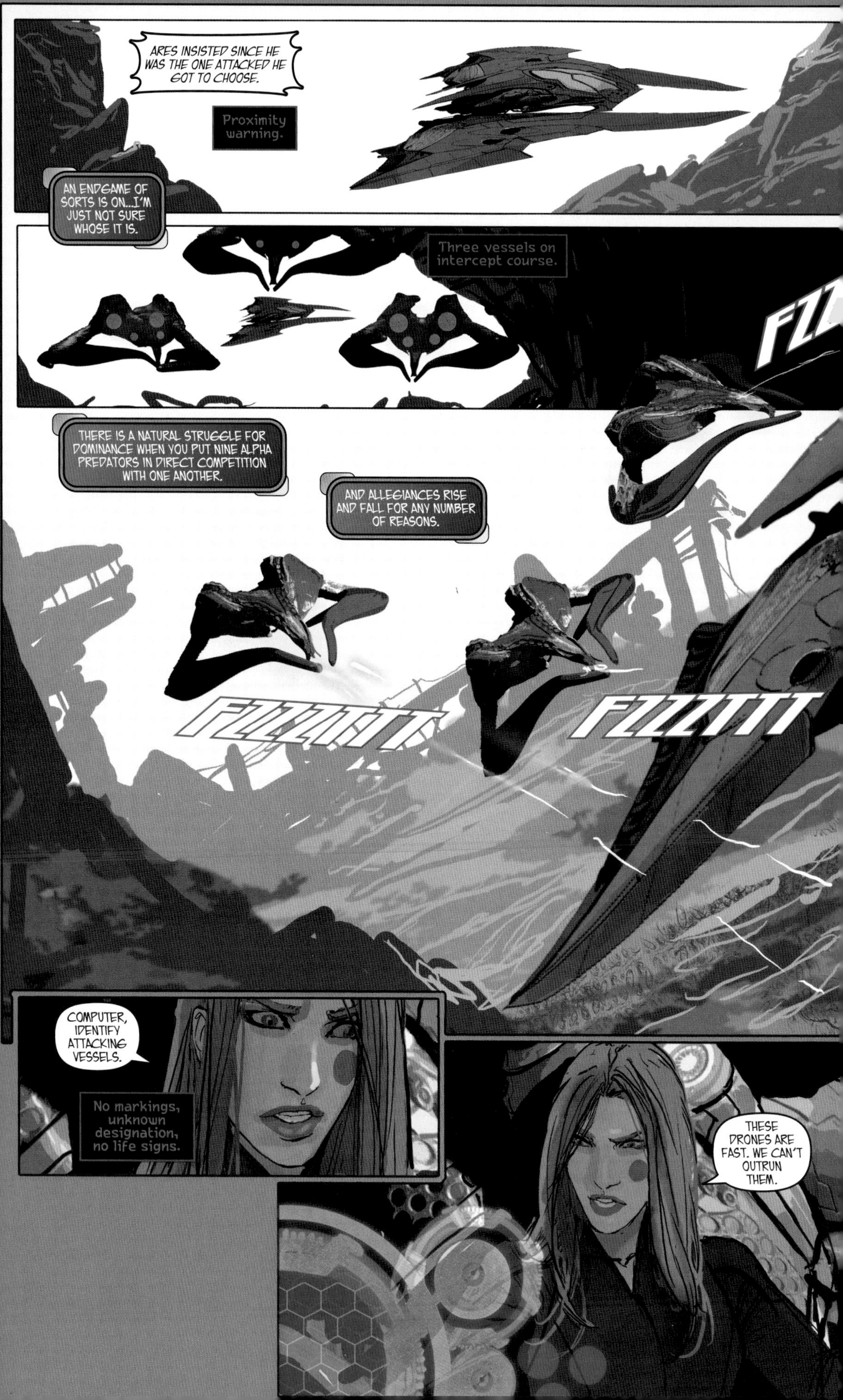
ARES INSISTED SINCE HE WAS THE ONE ATTACKED HE GOT TO CHOOSE.
Proximity warning.
AN ENDGAME OF SORTS IS ON...I'M JUST NOT SURE WHOSE IT IS.
Three vessels on intercept course.
THERE IS A NATURAL STRUGGLE FOR DOMINANCE WHEN YOU PUT NINE ALPHA PREDATORS IN DIRECT COMPETITION WITH ONE ANOTHER.
AND ALLEGIANCES RISE AND FALL FOR ANY NUMBER OF REASONS.
FZZZTTT
FZZZTTT
COMPUTER, IDENTIFY ATTACKING VESSELS.
No markings, unknown designation, no life signs.
THESE DRONES ARE FAST. WE CAN'T OUTRUN THEM.

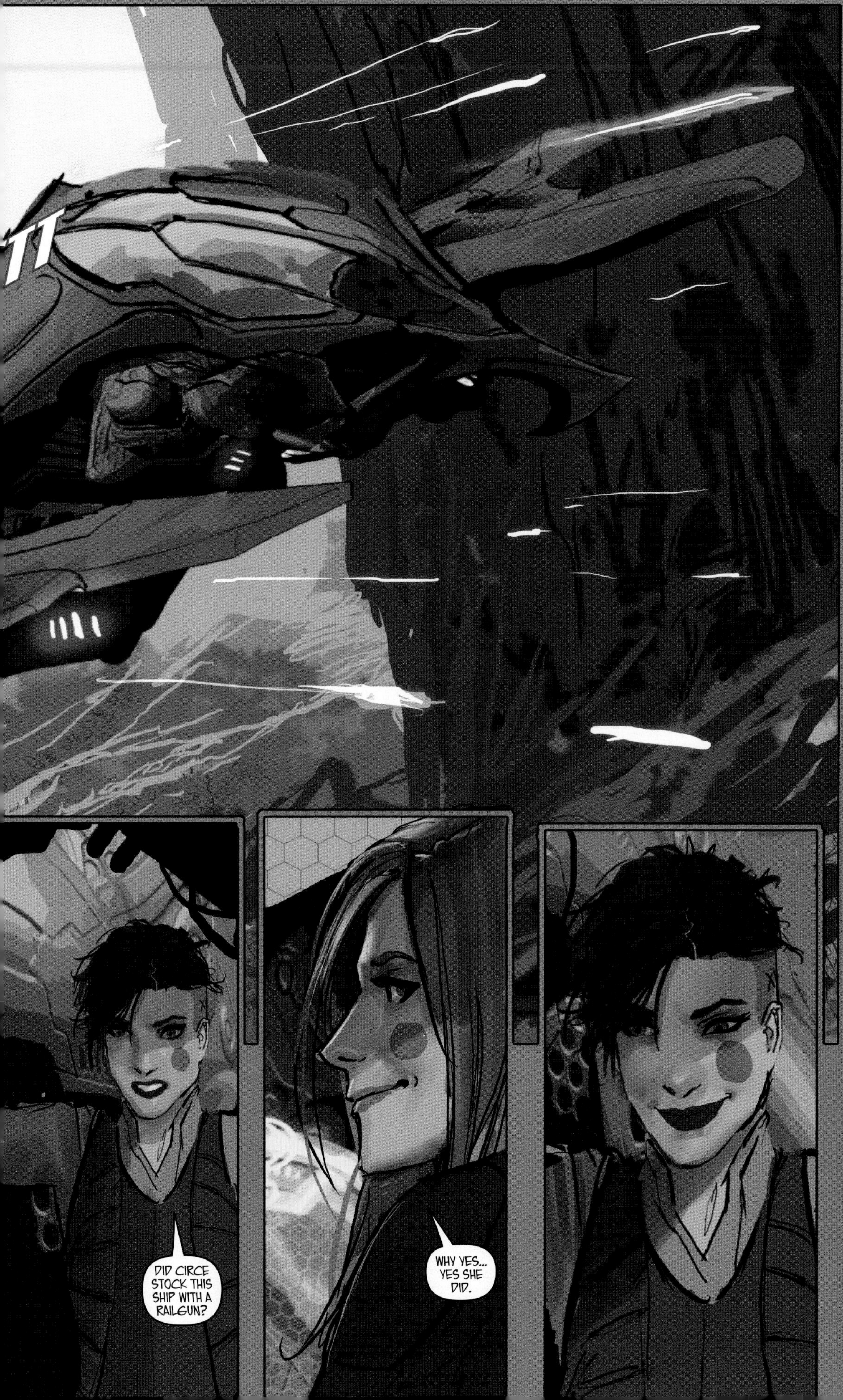
TT
DID CIRCE STOCK THIS SHIP WITH A RAILGUN?
WHY YES... YES SHE DID.

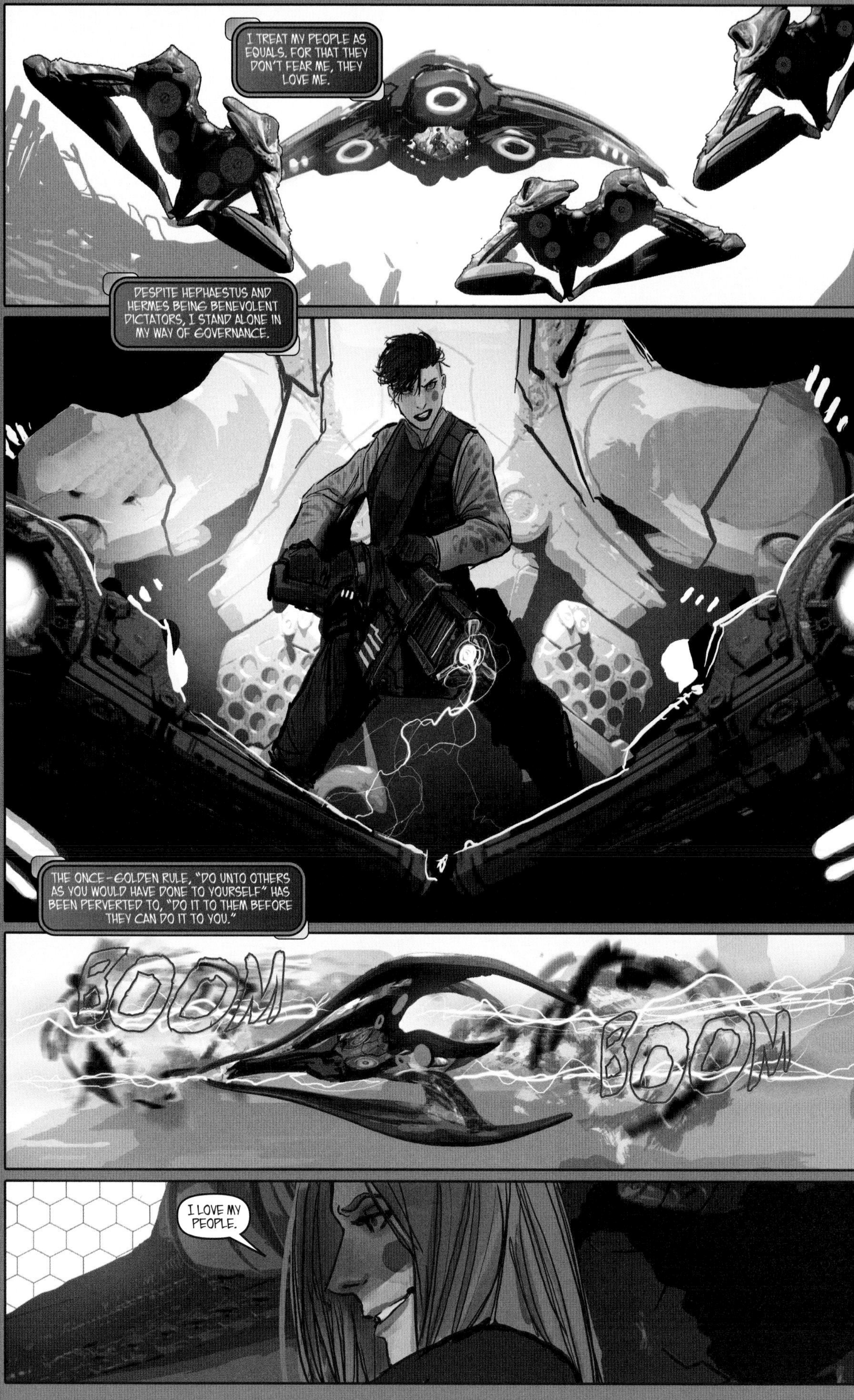
I TREAT MY PEOPLE AS EQUALS. FOR THAT THEY DON'T FEAR ME, THEY LOVE ME.
DESPITE HEPHAESTUS AND HERMES BEING BENEVOLENT DICTATORS, I STAND ALONE IN MY WAY OF GOVERNANCE.
THE ONCE-GOLDEN RULE, "DO UNTO OTHERS AS YOU WOULD HAVE DONE TO YOURSELF" HAS BEEN PERVERTED TO, "DO IT TO THEM BEFORE THEY CAN DO IT TO YOU."
BOOM
BOOM
I LOVE MY PEOPLE.

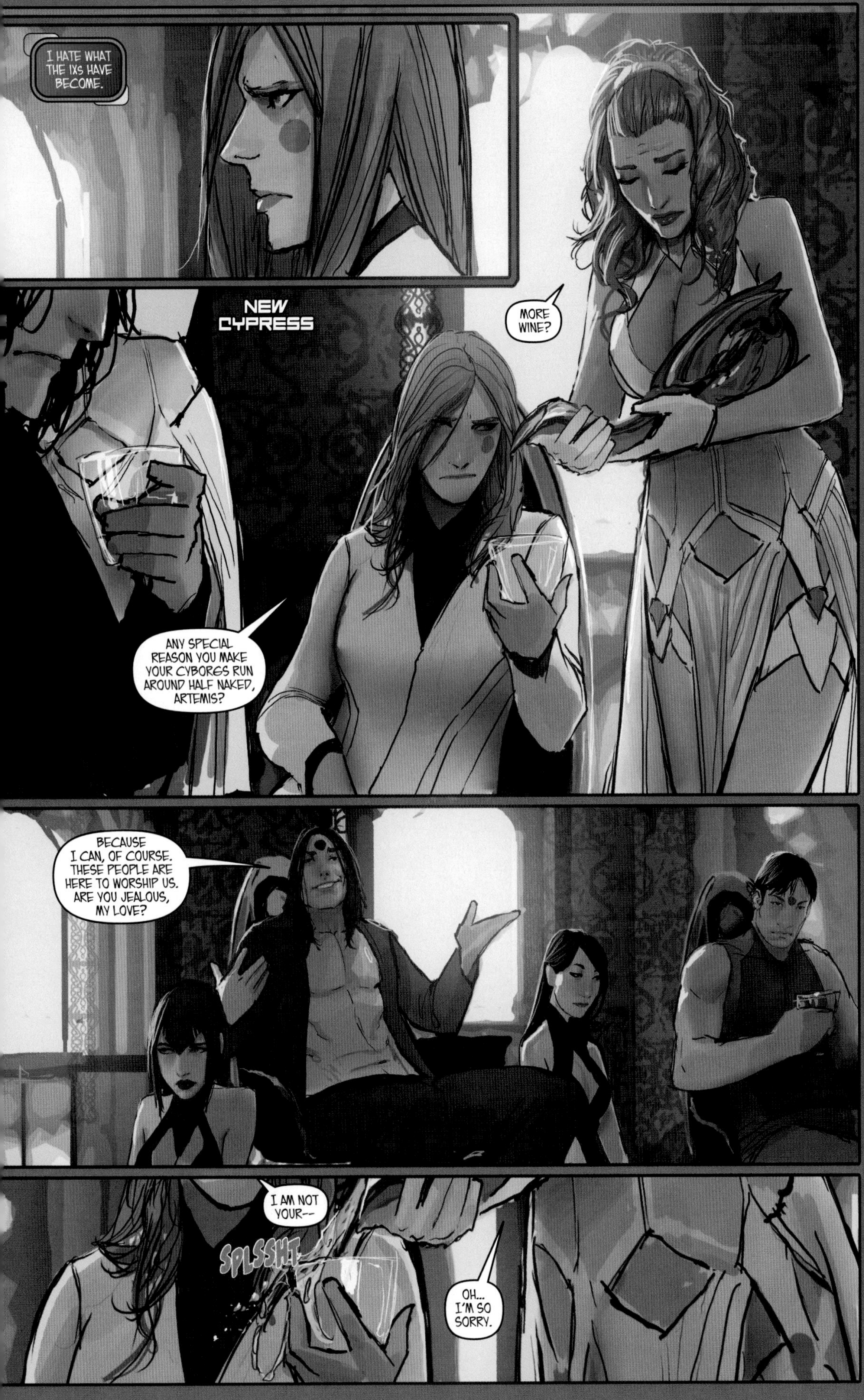
I HATE WHAT THE IXS HAVE BECOME.
NEW CYPRESS
MORE WINE?
ANY SPECIAL REASON YOU MAKE YOUR CYBORGS RUN AROUND HALF NAKED, ARTEMIS?
BECAUSE I CAN, OF COURSE. THESE PEOPLE ARE HERE TO WORSHIP US. ARE YOU JEALOUS, MY LOVE?
I AM NOT YOUR--
SPLSSHT
OH... I'M SO SORRY.

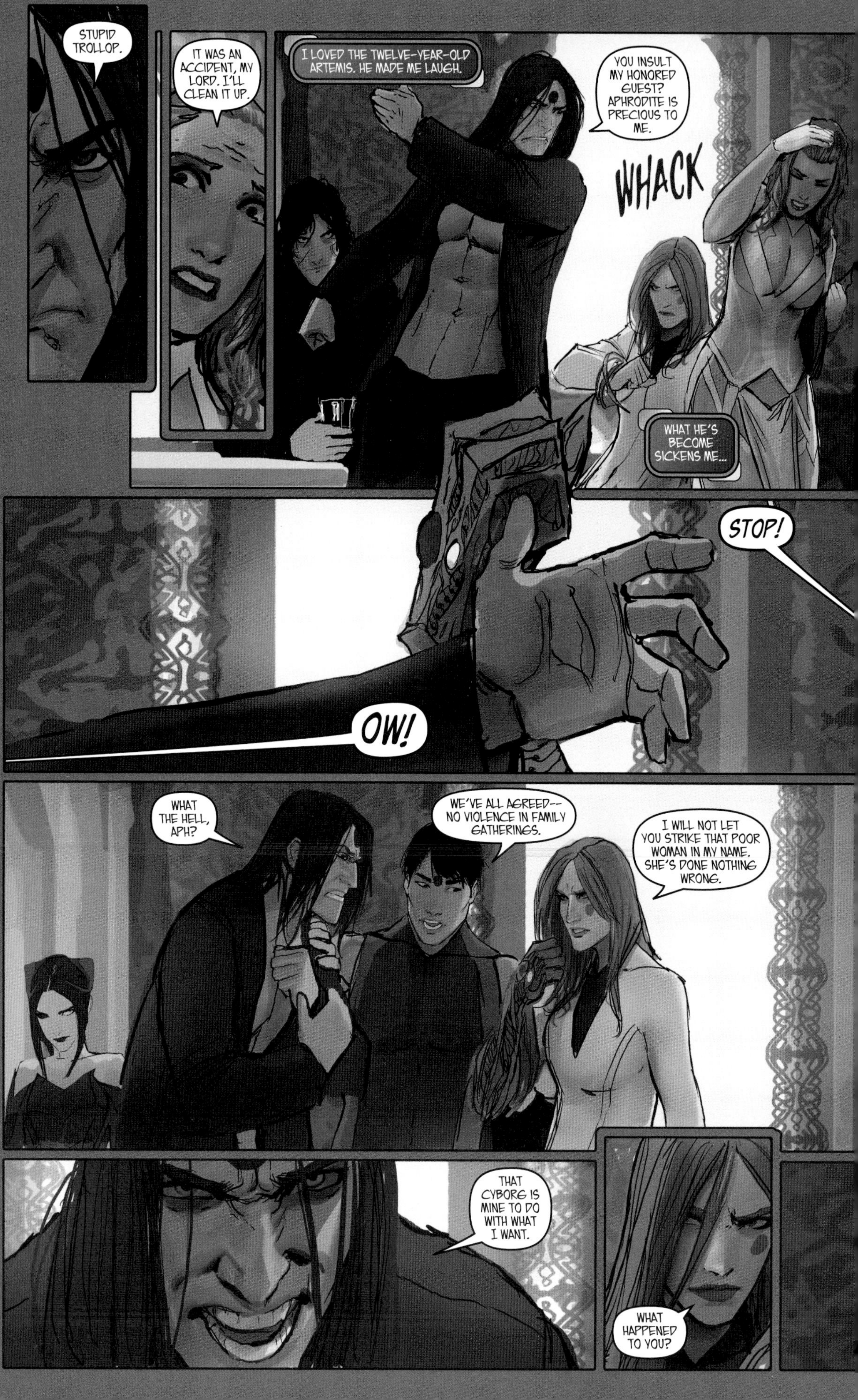
STUPID TROLLOP.
IT WAS AN ACCIDENT, MY LORD. I'LL CLEAN IT UP.
I LOVED THE TWELVE-YEAR-OLD ARTEMIS. HE MADE ME LAUGH.
YOU INSULT MY HONORED GUEST? APHRODITE IS PRECIOUS TO ME.
WHACK
WHAT HE'S BECOME SICKENS ME...
STOP!
OW!
WHAT THE HELL, APH?
WE'VE ALL AGREED-- NO VIOLENCE IN FAMILY GATHERINGS.
I WILL NOT LET YOU STRIKE THAT POOR WOMAN IN MY NAME. SHE'S DONE NOTHING WRONG.
THAT CYBORG IS MINE TO DO WITH WHAT I WANT.
WHAT HAPPENED TO YOU?

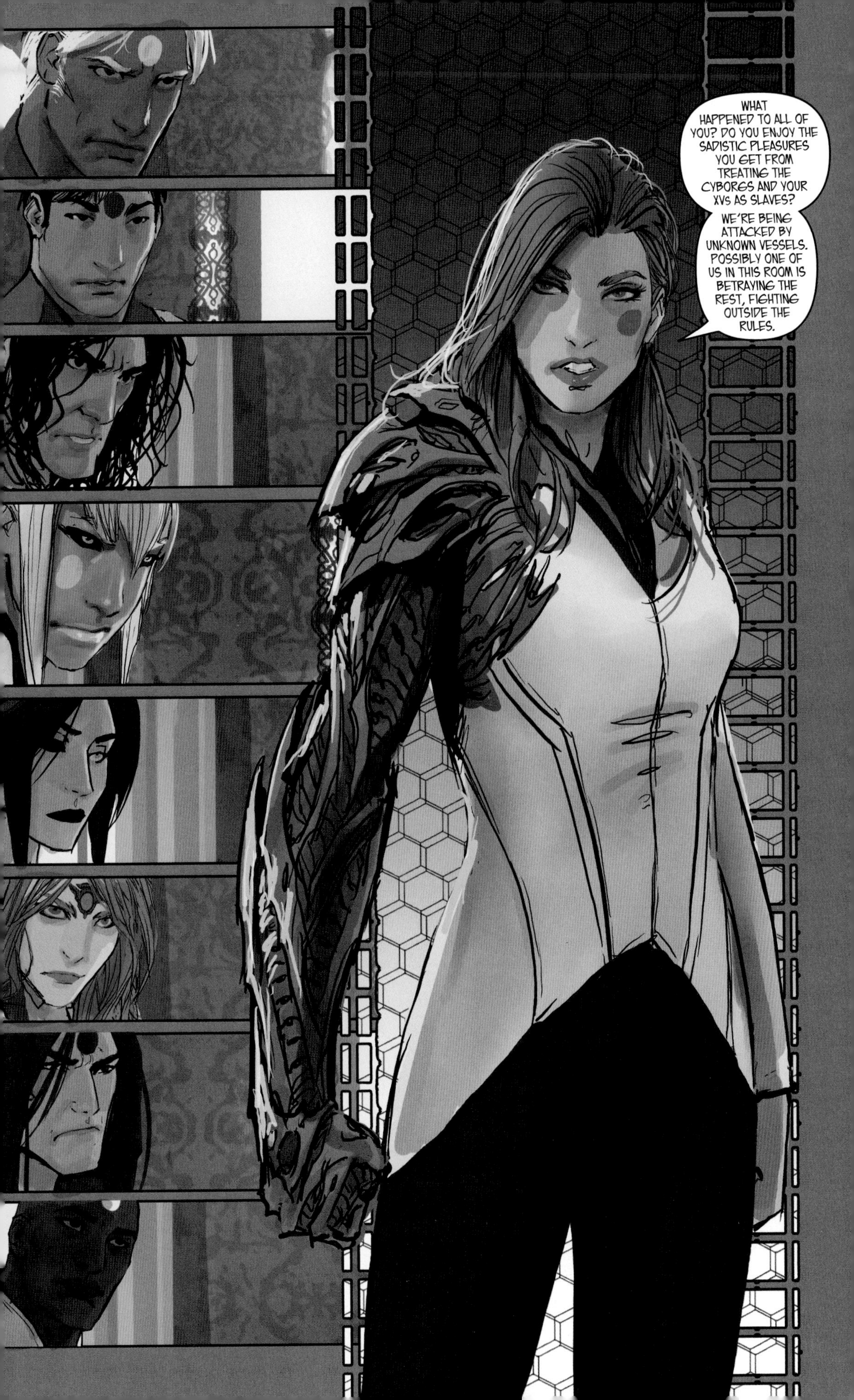
WHAT HAPPENED TO ALL OF YOU? DO YOU ENJOY THE SADISTIC PLEASURES YOU GET FROM TREATING THE CYBORGS AND YOUR XVs AS SLAVES?
WE'RE BEING ATTACKED BY UNKNOWN VESSELS. POSSIBLY ONE OF US IN THIS ROOM IS BETRAYING THE REST, FIGHTING OUTSIDE THE RULES.

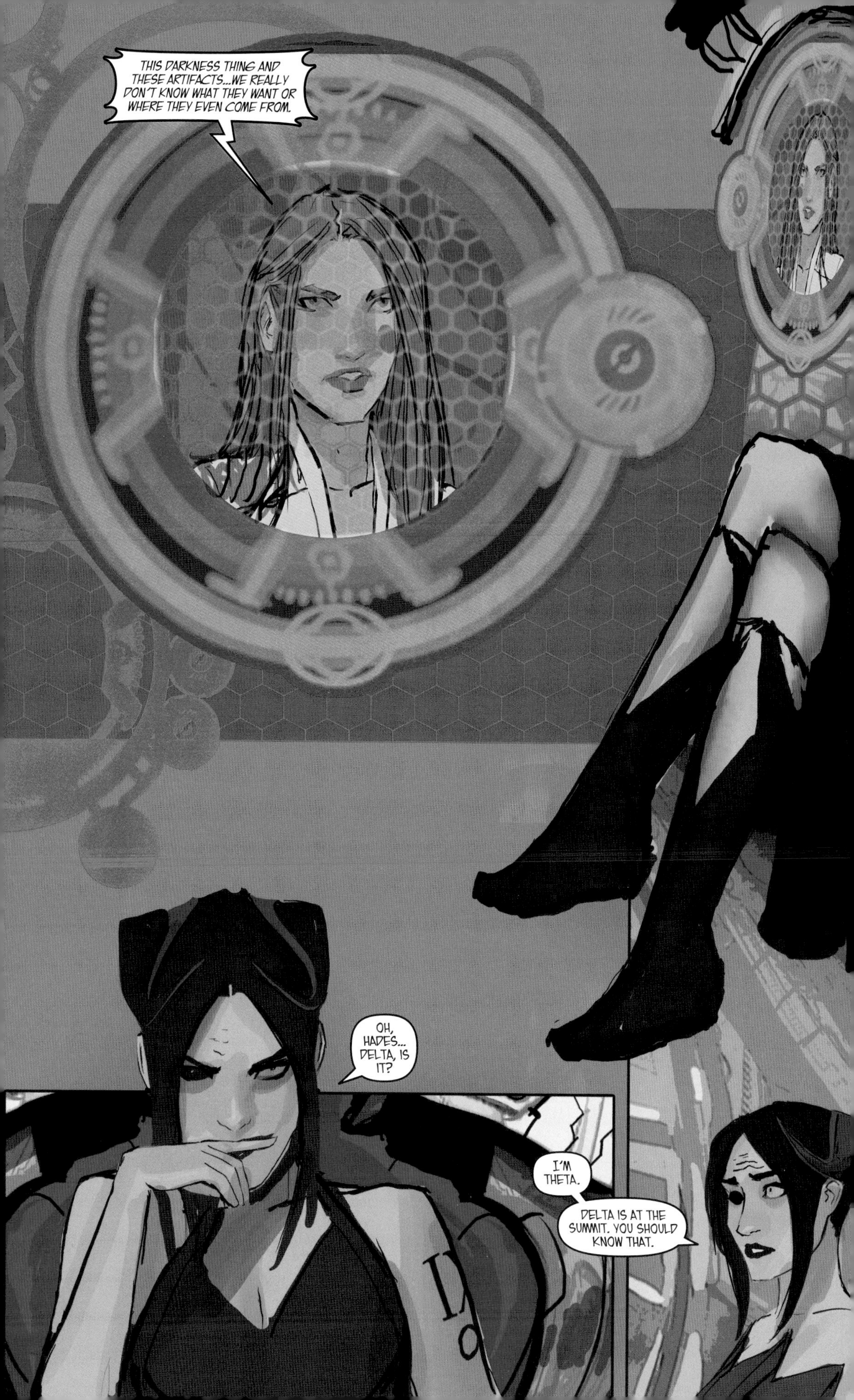
THIS DARKNESS THING AND THESE ARTIFACTS...WE REALLY DON'T KNOW WHAT THEY WANT OR WHERE THEY EVEN COME FROM.
OH, HADES... DELTA, IS IT?
I'M THETA.
DELTA IS AT THE SUMMIT. YOU SHOULD KNOW THAT.

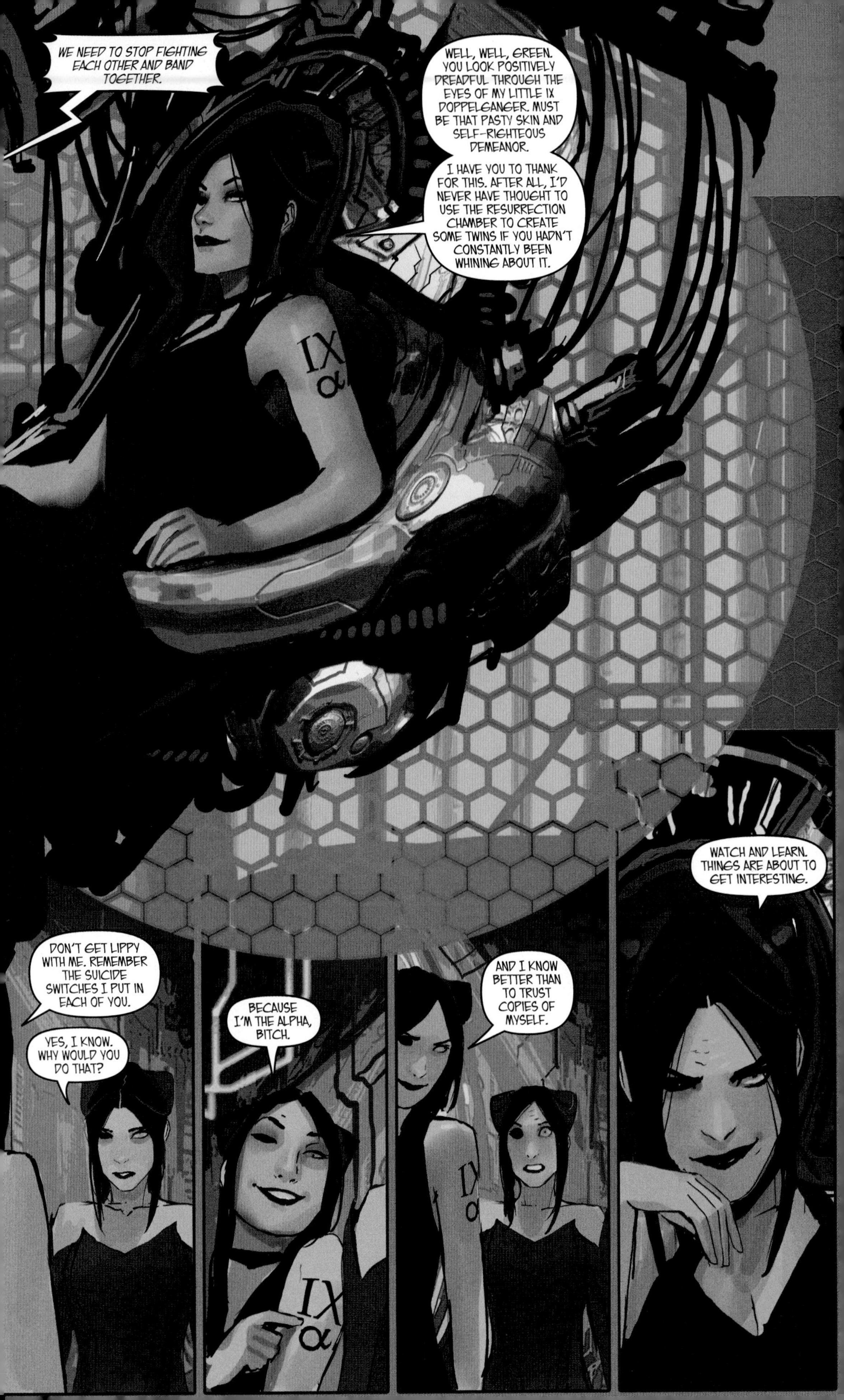
WE NEED TO STOP FIGHTING EACH OTHER AND BAND TOGETHER.
WELL, WELL, GREEN. YOU LOOK POSITIVELY DREADFUL THROUGH THE EYES OF MY LITTLE IX DOPPELGANGER. MUST BE THAT PASTY SKIN AND SELF-RIGHTEOUS DEMEANOR.
I HAVE YOU TO THANK FOR THIS. AFTER ALL, I'D NEVER HAVE THOUGHT TO USE THE RESURRECTION CHAMBER TO CREATE SOME TWINS IF YOU HADN'T CONSTANTLY BEEN WHINING ABOUT IT.
IX α
DON'T GET LIPPY WITH ME. REMEMBER THE SUICIDE SWITCHES I PUT IN EACH OF YOU.
YES, I KNOW. WHY WOULD YOU DO THAT?
BECAUSE I'M THE ALPHA, BITCH.
IX α
AND I KNOW BETTER THAN TO TRUST COPIES OF MYSELF.
WATCH AND LEARN. THINGS ARE ABOUT TO GET INTERESTING.

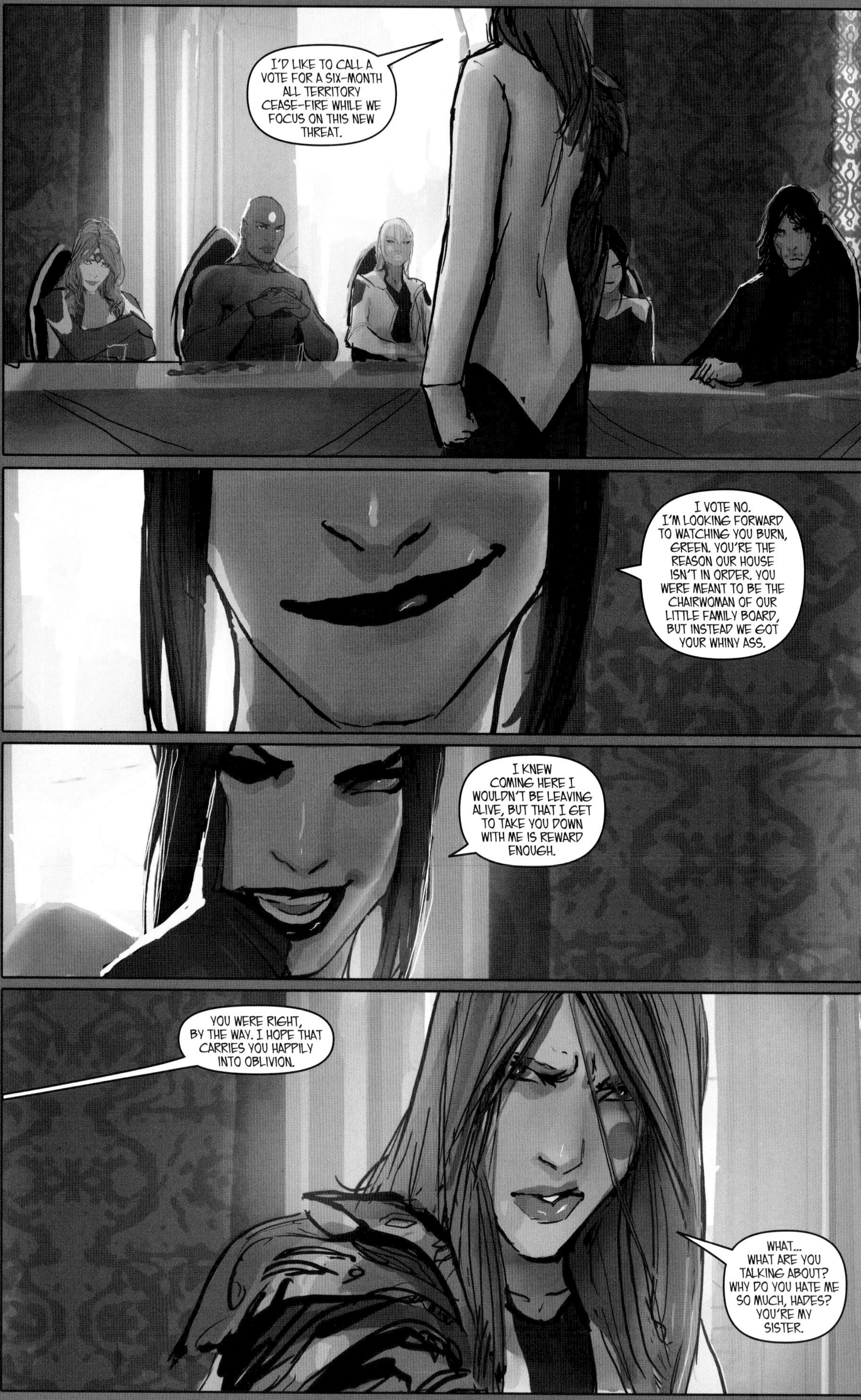
I'D LIKE TO CALL A VOTE FOR A SIX-MONTH ALL TERRITORY CEASE-FIRE WHILE WE FOCUS ON THIS NEW THREAT.
I VOTE NO. I'M LOOKING FORWARD TO WATCHING YOU BURN, GREEN. YOU'RE THE REASON OUR HOUSE ISN'T IN ORDER. YOU WERE MEANT TO BE THE CHAIRWOMAN OF OUR LITTLE FAMILY BOARD, BUT INSTEAD WE GOT YOUR WHINY ASS.
I KNEW COMING HERE I WOULDN'T BE LEAVING ALIVE, BUT THAT I GET TO TAKE YOU DOWN WITH ME IS REWARD ENOUGH.
YOU WERE RIGHT, BY THE WAY. I HOPE THAT CARRIES YOU HAPPILY INTO OBLIVION.
WHAT... WHAT ARE YOU TALKING ABOUT? WHY DO YOU HATE ME SO MUCH, HADES? YOU'RE MY SISTER.

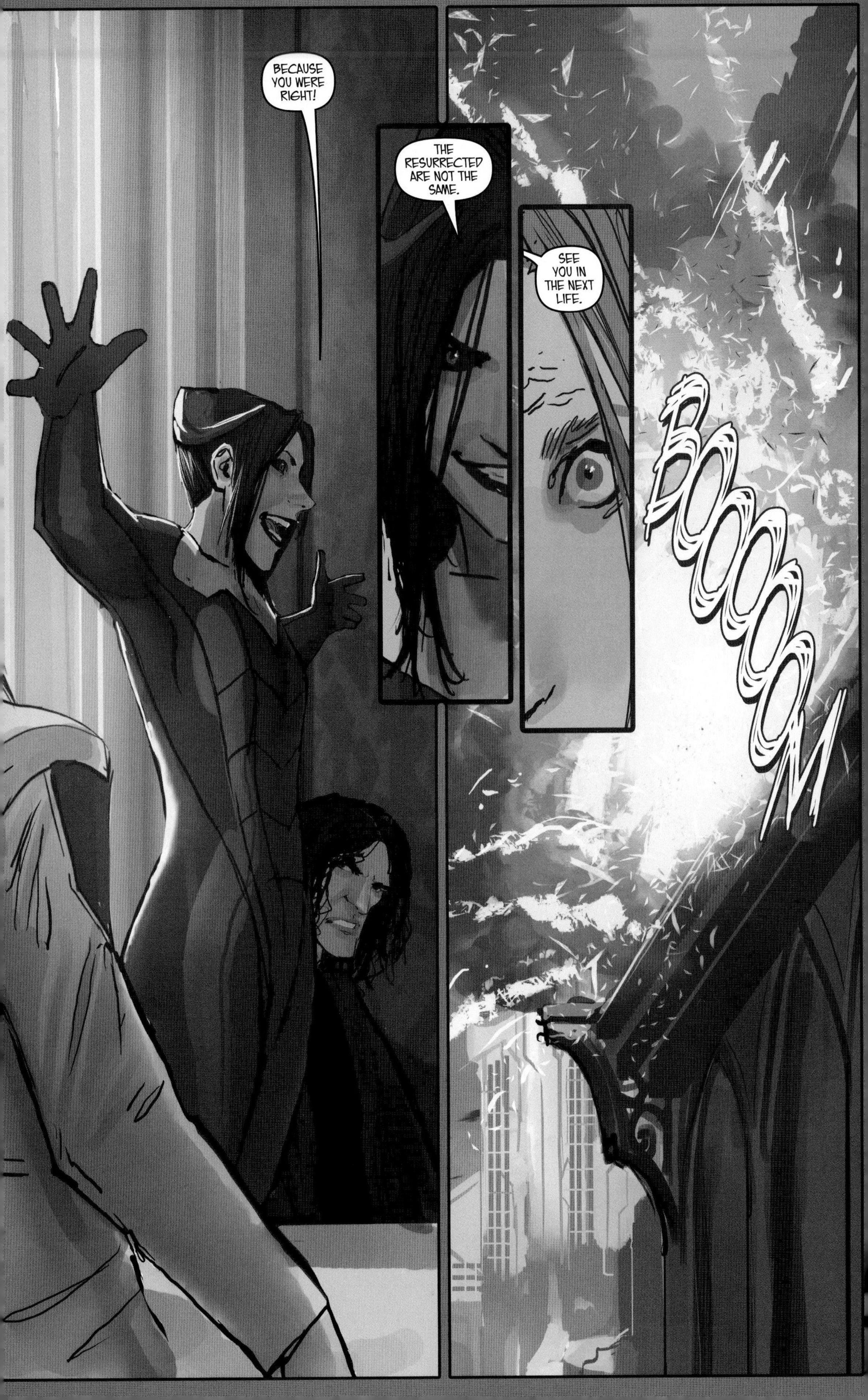
BECAUSE YOU WERE RIGHT!
THE RESURRECTED ARE NOT THE SAME.
SEE YOU IN THE NEXT LIFE.
BOOOOOOM

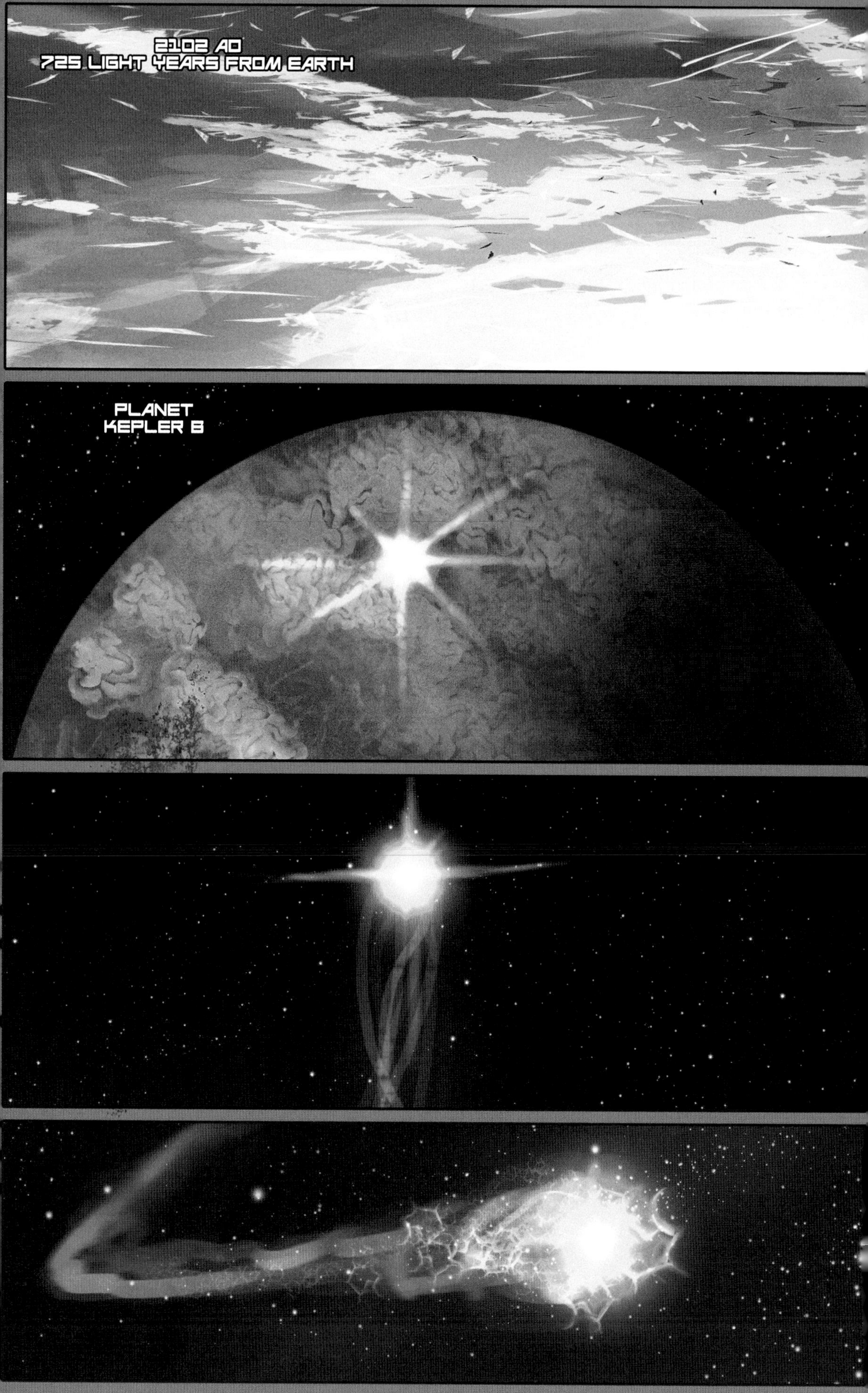
2102 AD
725 LIGHT YEARS FROM EARTH
PLANET
KEPLER B

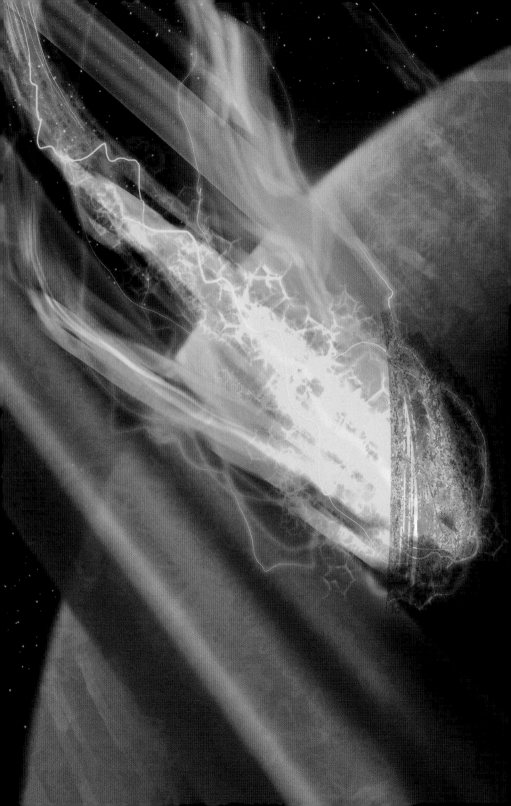

"The totalitarian, to me, is the enemy - the one that's absolute, the one that wants control over the inside of your head, not just your actions and your taxes."

Christopher Hitchens

HIDDEN FILES

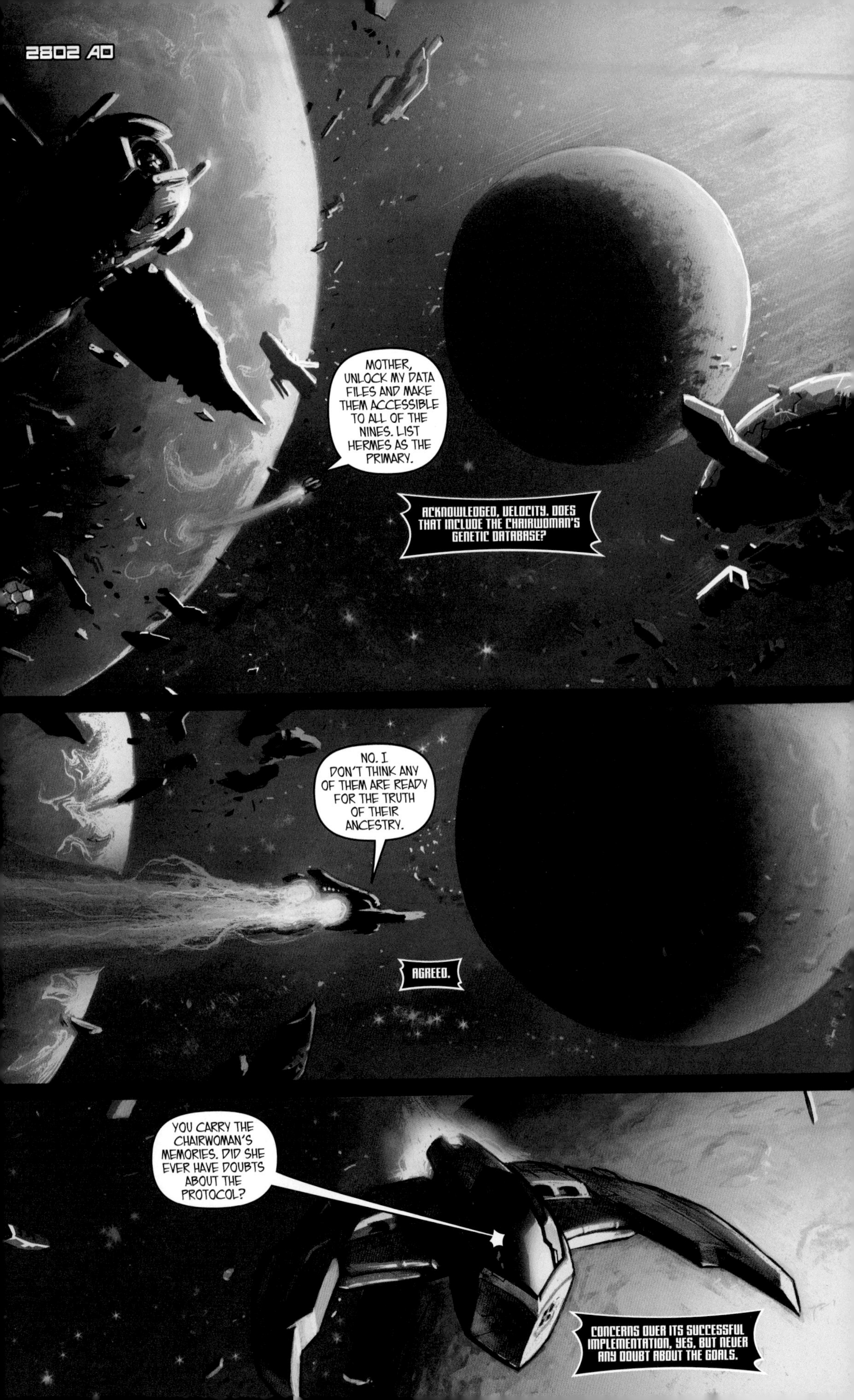
2802 AD
MOTHER, UNLOCK MY DATA FILES AND MAKE THEM ACCESSIBLE TO ALL OF THE NINES. LIST HERMES AS THE PRIMARY.
ACKNOWLEDGED, VELOCITY. DOES THAT INCLUDE THE CHAIRWOMAN'S GENETIC DATABASE?
NO. I DON'T THINK ANY OF THEM ARE READY FOR THE TRUTH OF THEIR ANCESTRY.
AGREED.
YOU CARRY THE CHAIRWOMAN'S MEMORIES. DID SHE EVER HAVE DOUBTS ABOUT THE PROTOCOL?
CONCERNS OVER ITS SUCCESSFUL IMPLEMENTATION, YES, BUT NEVER ANY DOUBT ABOUT THE GOALS.

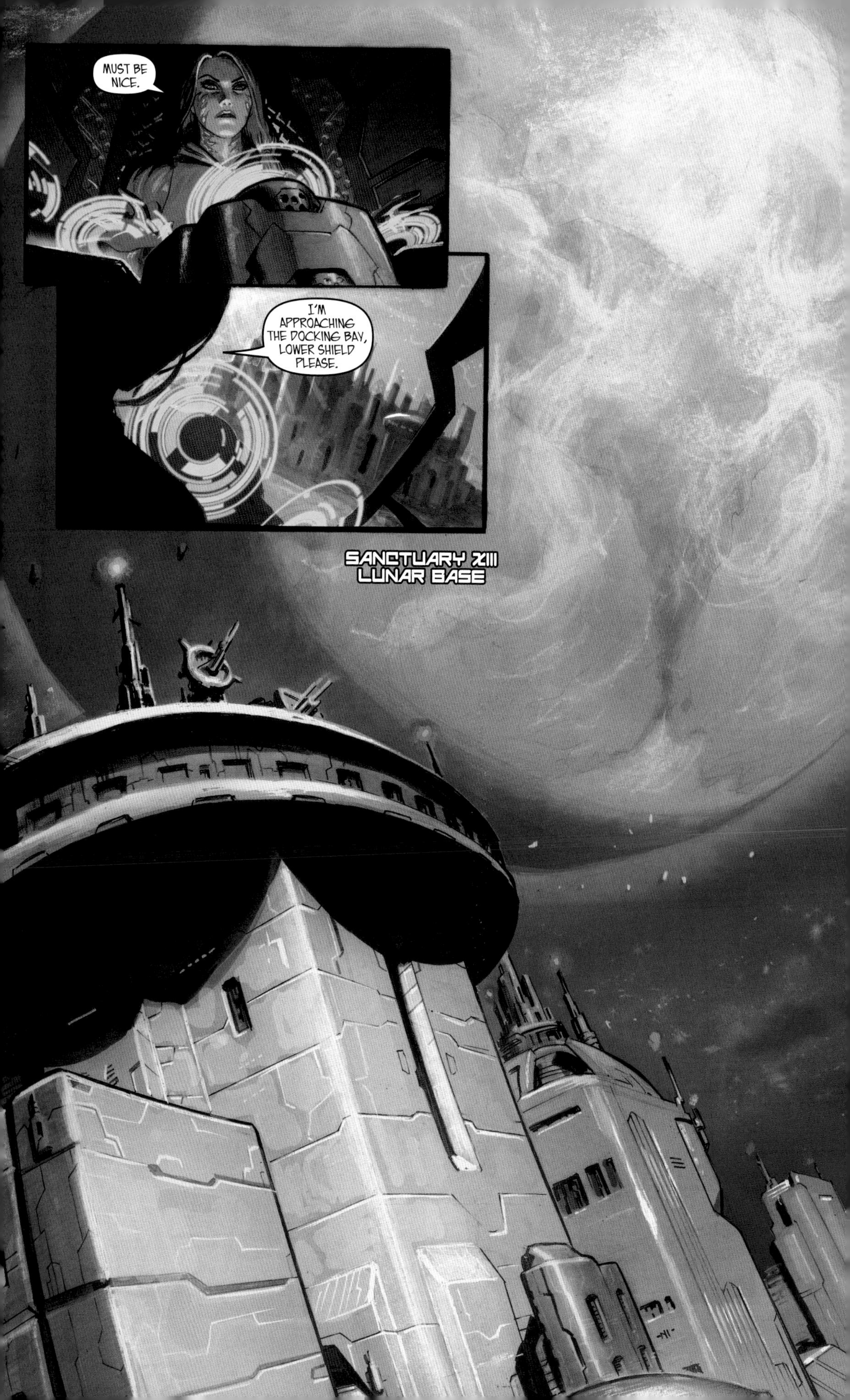
MUST BE NICE.
I'M APPROACHING THE DOCKING BAY, LOWER SHIELD PLEASE.
SANCTUARY XIII LUNAR BASE

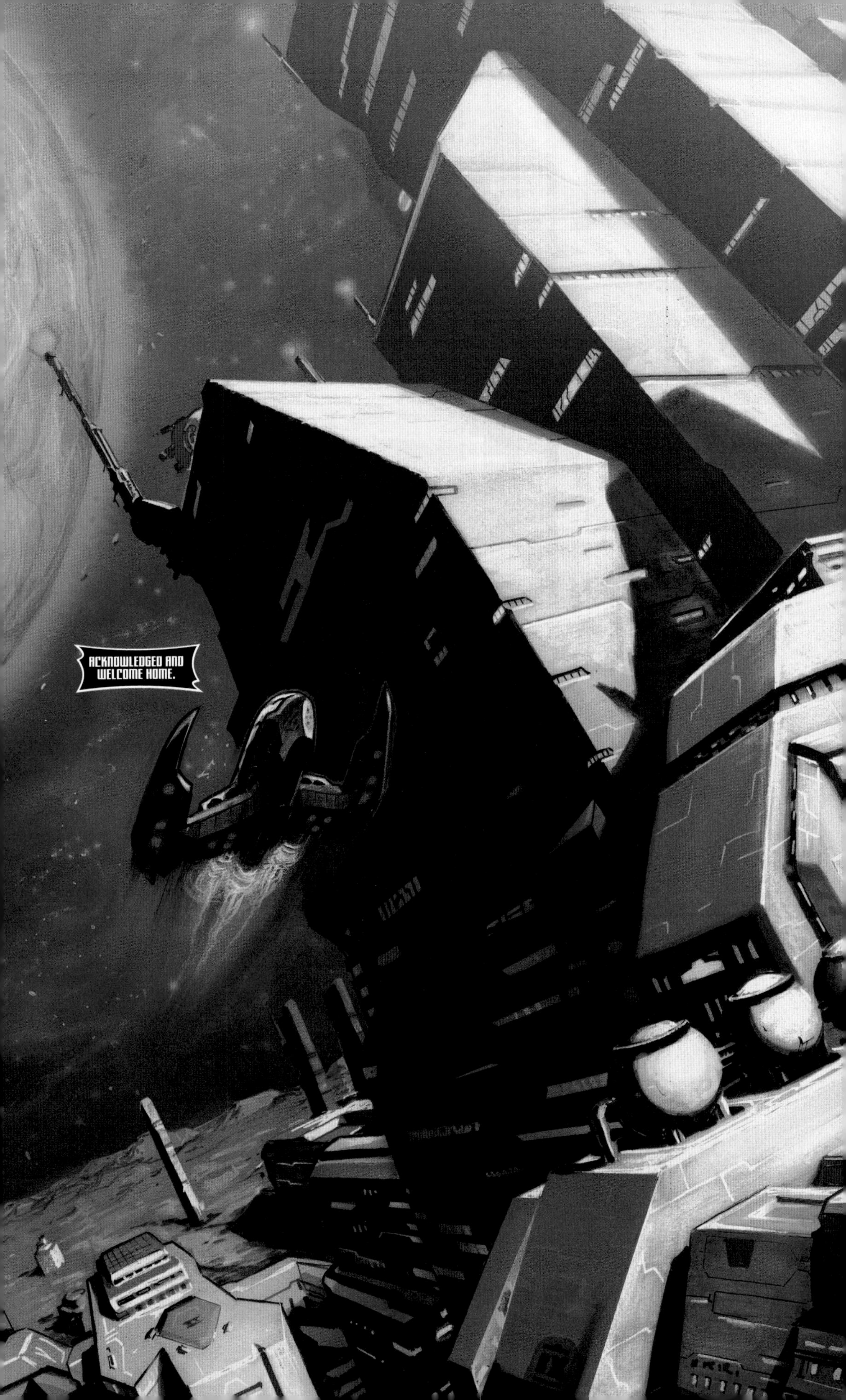
ACKNOWLEDGED AND WELCOME HOME.

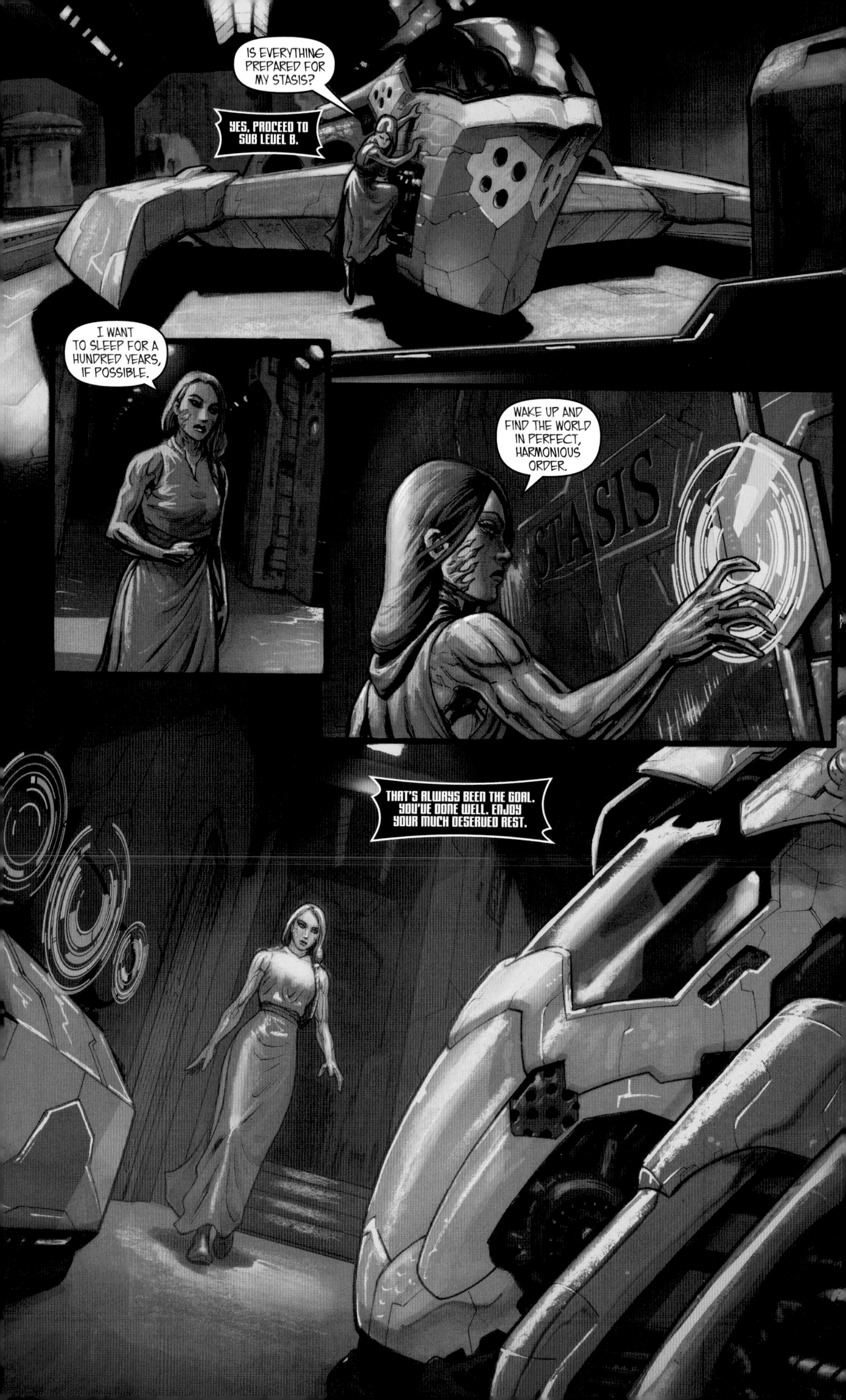
IS EVERYTHING PREPARED FOR MY STASIS?
YES, PROCEED TO SUB LEVEL B.
I WANT TO SLEEP FOR A HUNDRED YEARS, IF POSSIBLE.
WAKE UP AND FIND THE WORLD IN PERFECT, HARMONIOUS ORDER.
STASIS
THAT'S ALWAYS BEEN THE GOAL. YOU'VE DONE WELL. ENJOY YOUR MUCH DESERVED REST.

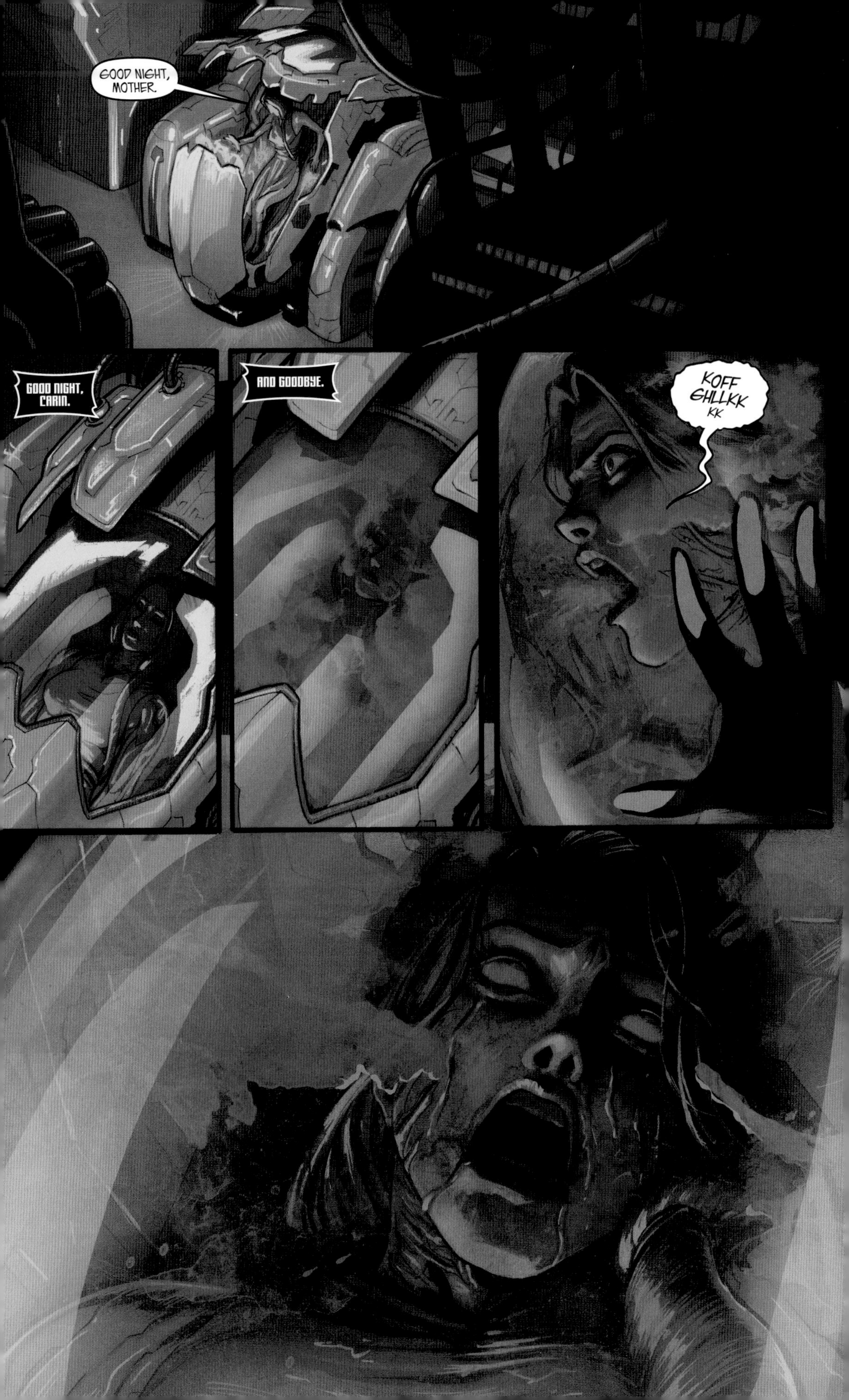
GOOD NIGHT, MOTHER.
GOOD NIGHT, CARIN.
AND GOODBYE.
KOFF GHLLKK KK

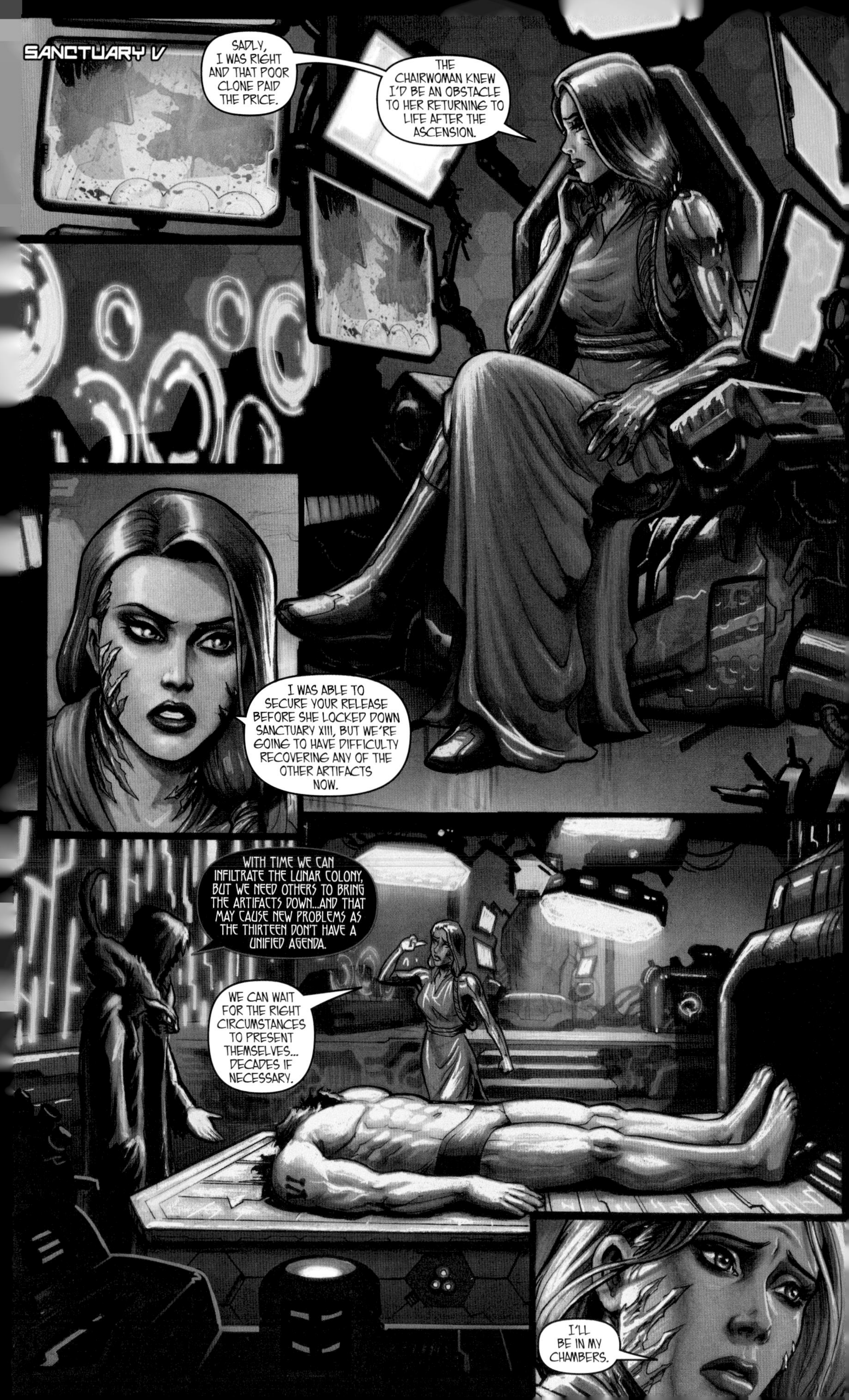
SANCTUARY V
SADLY, I WAS RIGHT AND THAT POOR CLONE PAID THE PRICE.
THE CHAIRWOMAN KNEW I'D BE AN OBSTACLE TO HER RETURNING TO LIFE AFTER THE ASCENSION.
I WAS ABLE TO SECURE YOUR RELEASE BEFORE SHE LOCKED DOWN SANCTUARY XIII, BUT WE'RE GOING TO HAVE DIFFICULTY RECOVERING ANY OF THE OTHER ARTIFACTS NOW.
WITH TIME WE CAN INFILTRATE THE LUNAR COLONY, BUT WE NEED OTHERS TO BRING THE ARTIFACTS DOWN...AND THAT MAY CAUSE NEW PROBLEMS AS THE THIRTEEN DON'T HAVE A UNIFIED AGENDA.
WE CAN WAIT FOR THE RIGHT CIRCUMSTANCES TO PRESENT THEMSELVES... DECADES IF NECESSARY.
I'LL BE IN MY CHAMBERS.

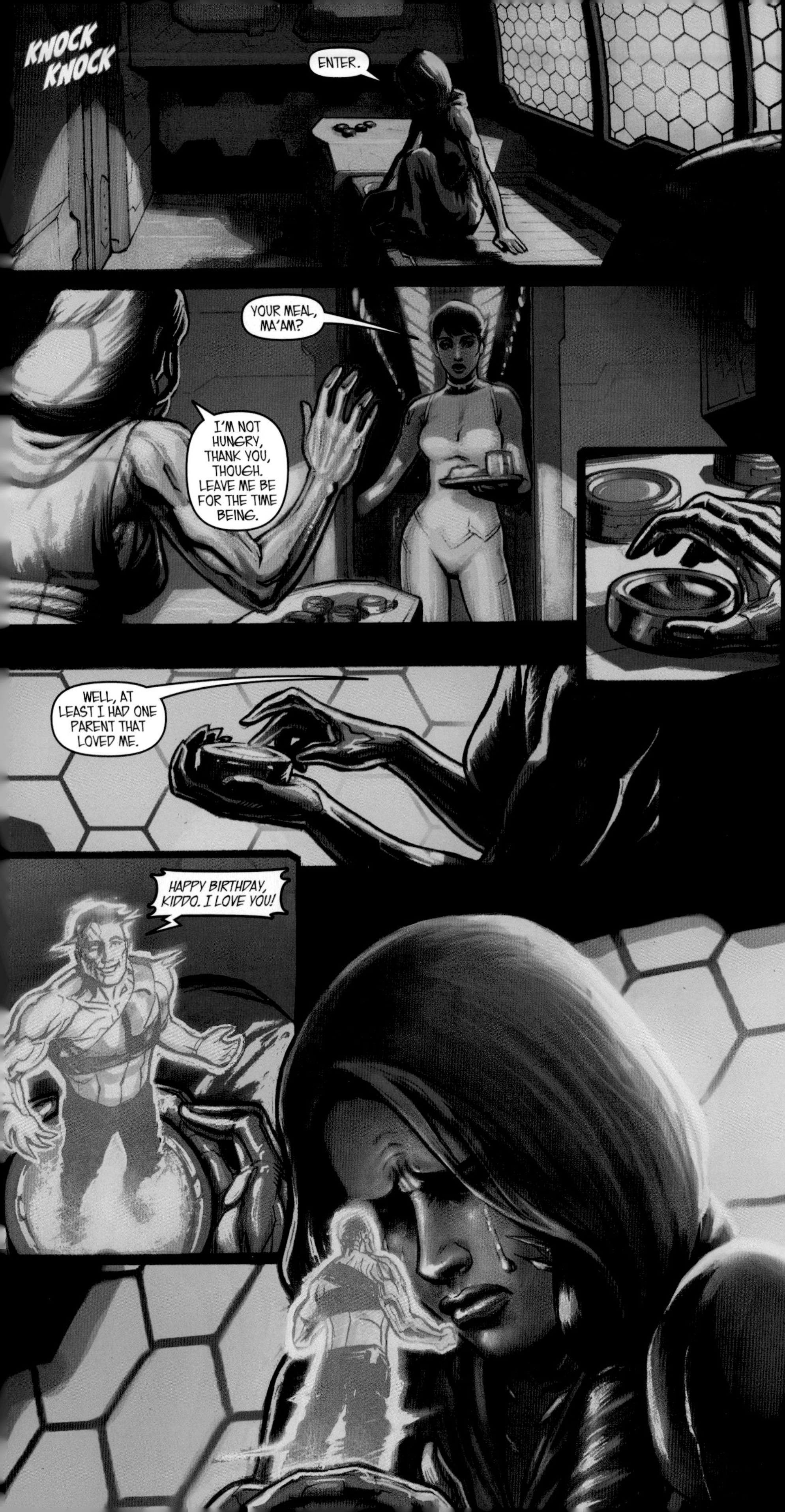
KNOCK KNOCK
ENTER.
YOUR MEAL, MA'AM?
I'M NOT HUNGRY, THANK YOU, THOUGH. LEAVE ME BE FOR THE TIME BEING.
WELL, AT LEAST I HAD ONE PARENT THAT LOVED ME.
HAPPY BIRTHDAY, KIDDO. I LOVE YOU!

CHAPTER FOUR

"It may be that our role on this planet is not to worship God - but to create him."

Arthur C. Clarke

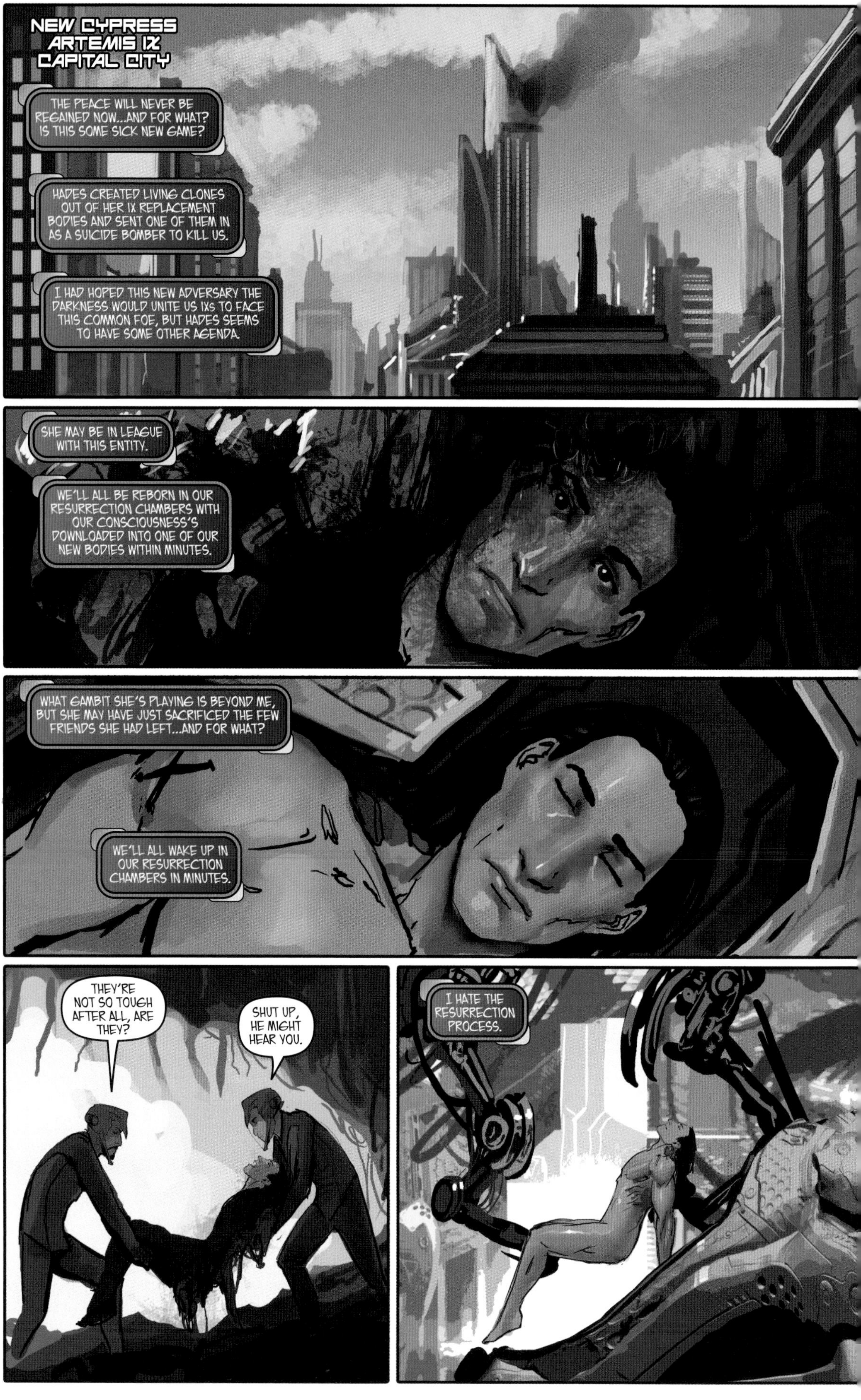
NEW CYPRESS
ARTEMIS IX
CAPITAL CITY
THE PEACE WILL NEVER BE REGAINED NOW...AND FOR WHAT? IS THIS SOME SICK NEW GAME?
HADES CREATED LIVING CLONES OUT OF HER IX REPLACEMENT BODIES AND SENT ONE OF THEM IN AS A SUICIDE BOMBER TO KILL US.
I HAD HOPED THIS NEW ADVERSARY THE DARKNESS WOULD UNITE US IXS TO FACE THIS COMMON FOE, BUT HADES SEEMS TO HAVE SOME OTHER AGENDA.
SHE MAY BE IN LEAGUE WITH THIS ENTITY.
WE'LL ALL BE REBORN IN OUR RESURRECTION CHAMBERS WITH OUR CONSCIOUSNESS'S DOWNLOADED INTO ONE OF OUR NEW BODIES WITHIN MINUTES.
WHAT GAMBIT SHE'S PLAYING IS BEYOND ME, BUT SHE MAY HAVE JUST SACRIFICED THE FEW FRIENDS SHE HAD LEFT...AND FOR WHAT?
WE'LL ALL WAKE UP IN OUR RESURRECTION CHAMBERS IN MINUTES.
THEY'RE NOT SO TOUGH AFTER ALL, ARE THEY?
SHUT UP, HE MIGHT HEAR YOU.
I HATE THE RESURRECTION PROCESS.

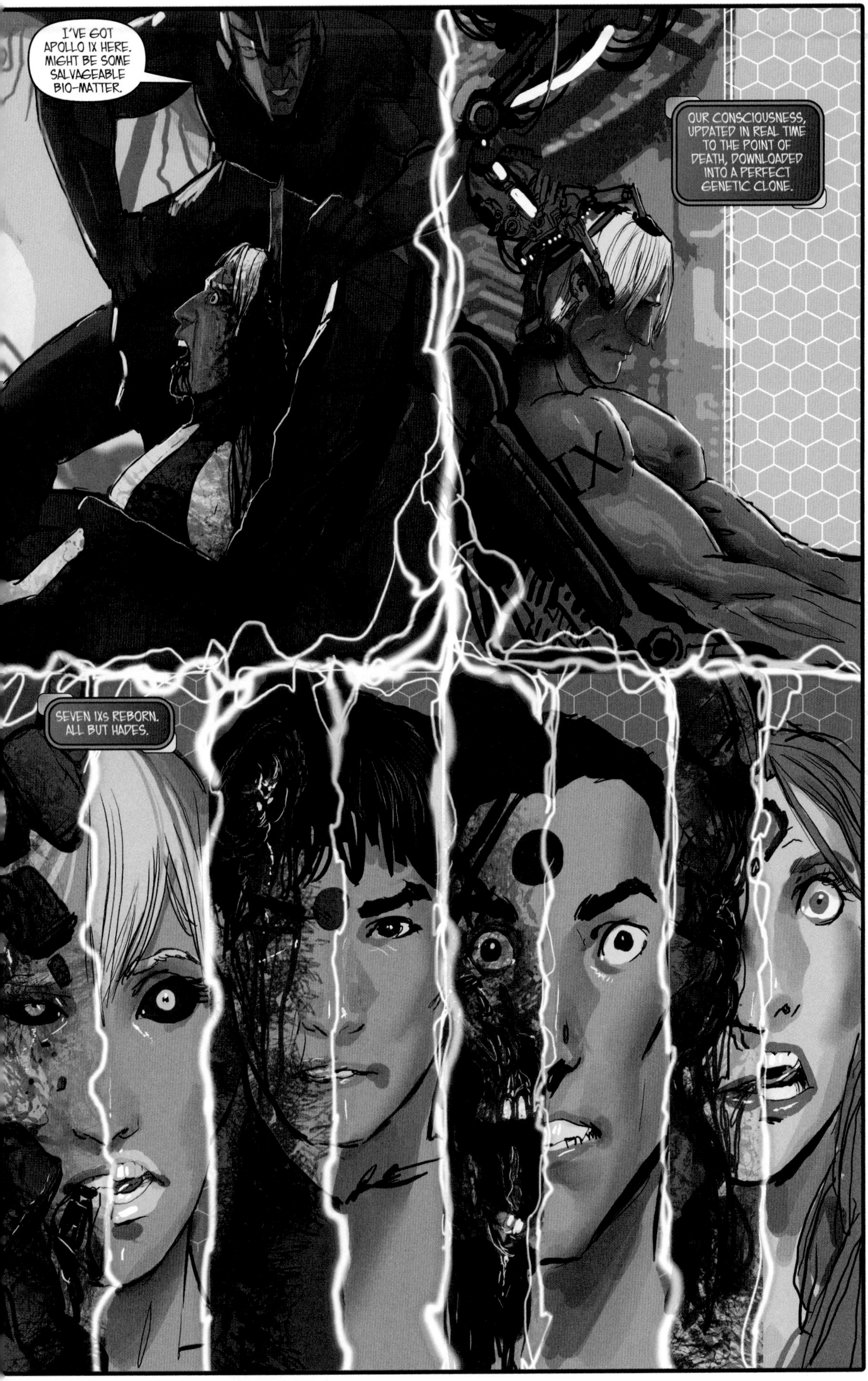
I'VE GOT APOLLO IX HERE. MIGHT BE SOME SALVAGEABLE BIO-MATTER.
OUR CONSCIOUSNESS, UPDATED IN REAL TIME TO THE POINT OF DEATH, DOWNLOADED INTO A PERFECT GENETIC CLONE.
SEVEN IXS REBORN. ALL BUT HADES.

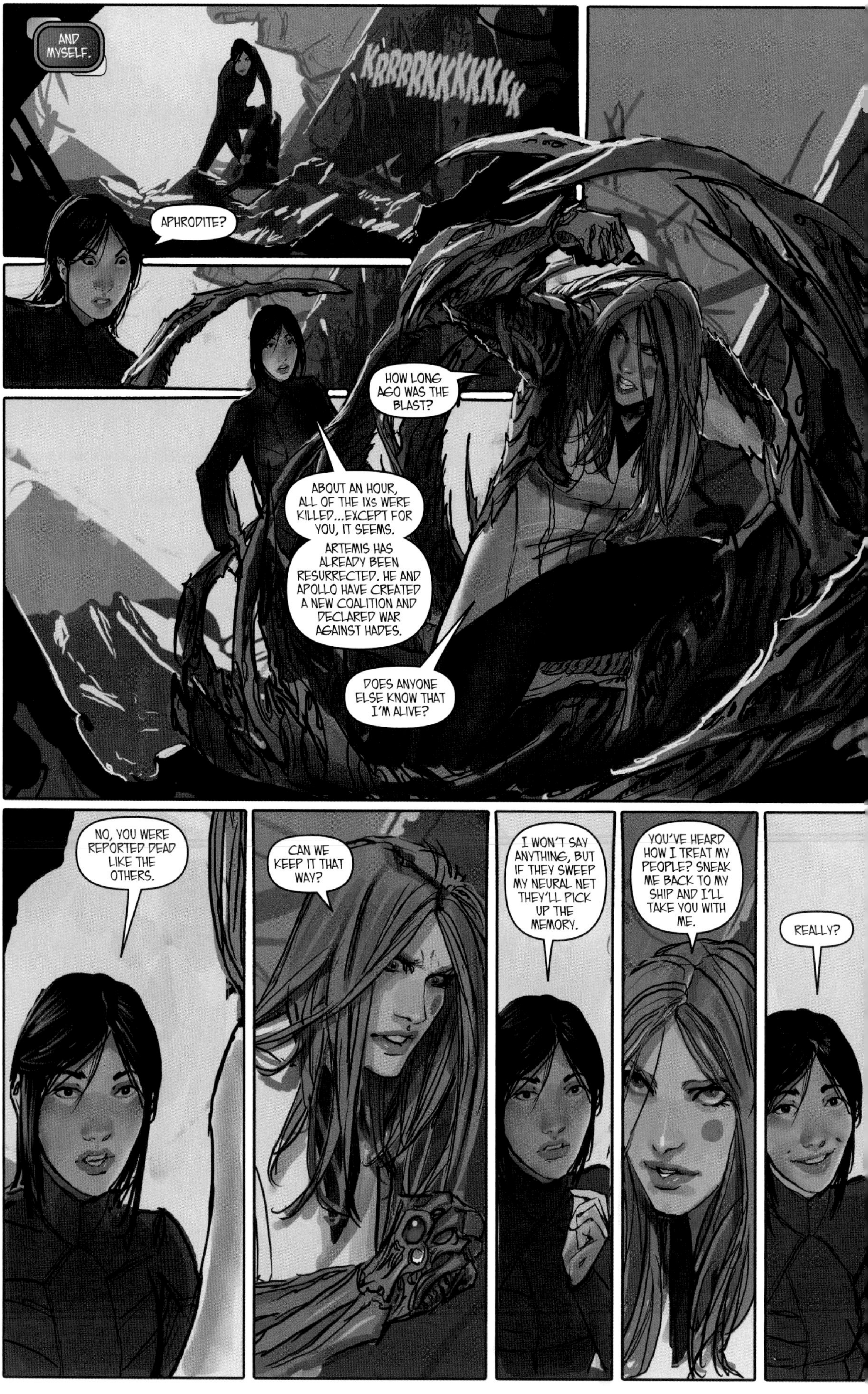

AND MYSELF.
KRRRRKKKKKK
APHRODITE?
HOW LONG AGO WAS THE BLAST?
ABOUT AN HOUR, ALL OF THE IXS WERE KILLED...EXCEPT FOR YOU, IT SEEMS.
ARTEMIS HAS ALREADY BEEN RESURRECTED. HE AND APOLLO HAVE CREATED A NEW COALITION AND DECLARED WAR AGAINST HADES.
DOES ANYONE ELSE KNOW THAT I'M ALIVE?
NO, YOU WERE REPORTED DEAD LIKE THE OTHERS.
CAN WE KEEP IT THAT WAY?
I WON'T SAY ANYTHING, BUT IF THEY SWEEP MY NEURAL NET THEY'LL PICK UP THE MEMORY.
YOU'VE HEARD HOW I TREAT MY PEOPLE? SNEAK ME BACK TO MY SHIP AND I'LL TAKE YOU WITH ME.
REALLY?

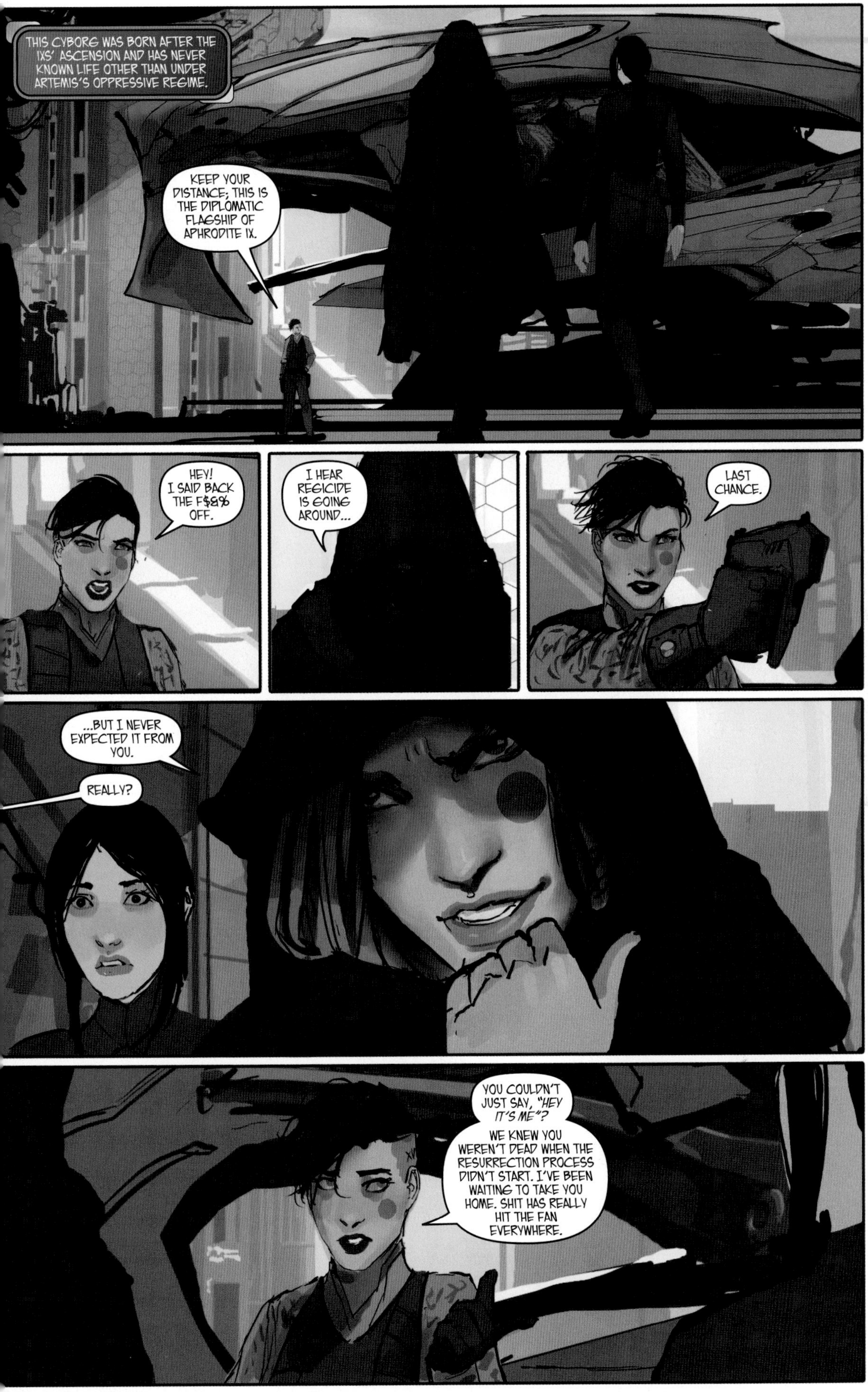
THIS CYBORG WAS BORN AFTER THE IXS' ASCENSION AND HAS NEVER KNOWN LIFE OTHER THAN UNDER ARTEMIS'S OPPRESSIVE REGIME.
KEEP YOUR DISTANCE; THIS IS THE DIPLOMATIC FLAGSHIP OF APHRODITE IX.
HEY! I SAID BACK THE F$&% OFF.
I HEAR REGICIDE IS GOING AROUND...
LAST CHANCE.
...BUT I NEVER EXPECTED IT FROM YOU.
REALLY?
YOU COULDN'T JUST SAY, "HEY IT'S ME"?
WE KNEW YOU WEREN'T DEAD WHEN THE RESURRECTION PROCESS DIDN'T START. I'VE BEEN WAITING TO TAKE YOU HOME. SHIT HAS REALLY HIT THE FAN EVERYWHERE.

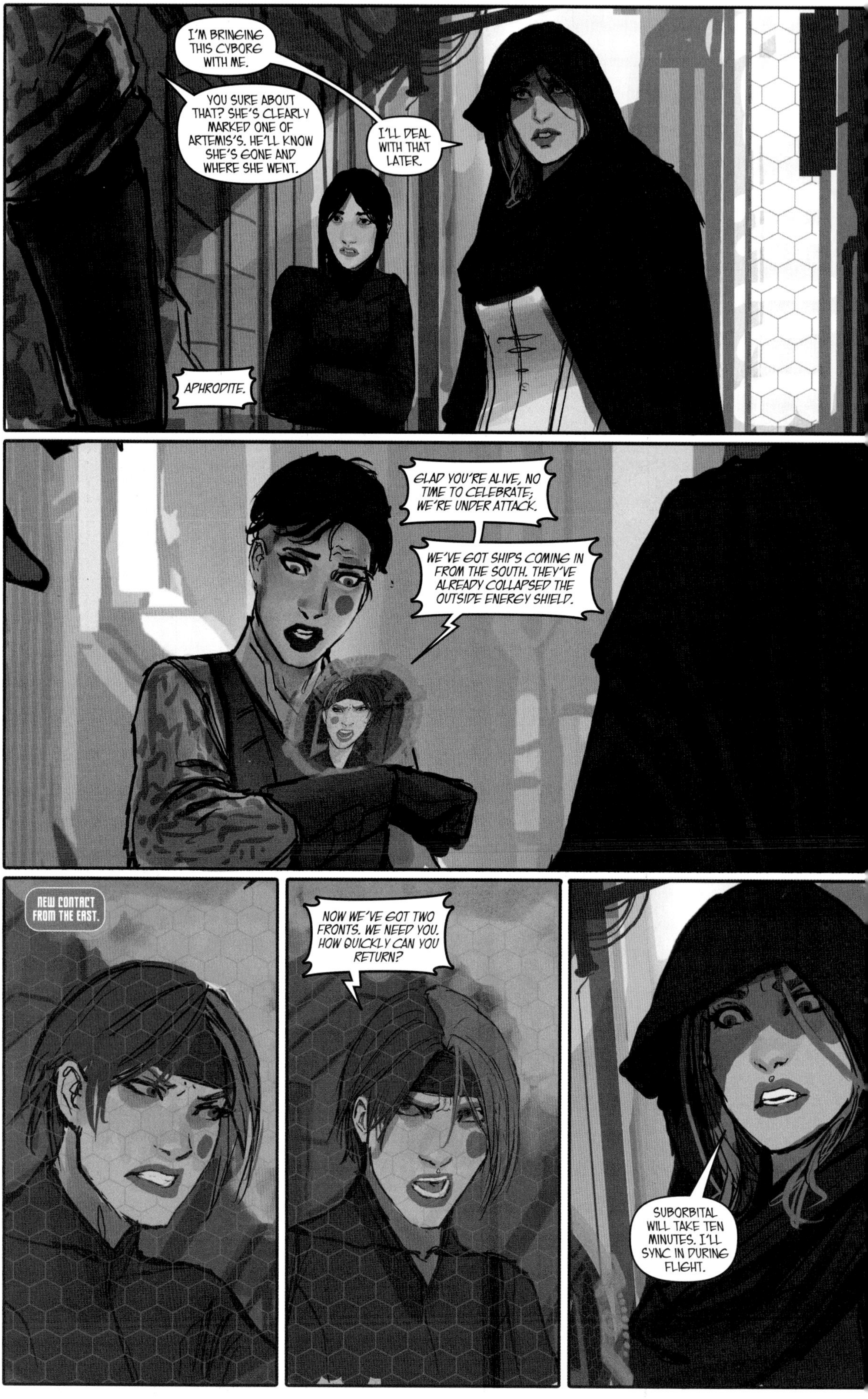
I'M BRINGING THIS CYBORG WITH ME.
YOU SURE ABOUT THAT? SHE'S CLEARLY MARKED ONE OF ARTEMIS'S. HE'LL KNOW SHE'S GONE AND WHERE SHE WENT.
I'LL DEAL WITH THAT LATER.
APHRODITE.
GLAD YOU'RE ALIVE, NO TIME TO CELEBRATE; WE'RE UNDER ATTACK.
WE'VE GOT SHIPS COMING IN FROM THE SOUTH. THEY'VE ALREADY COLLAPSED THE OUTSIDE ENERGY SHIELD.
NEW CONTACT FROM THE EAST.
NOW WE'VE GOT TWO FRONTS. WE NEED YOU. HOW QUICKLY CAN YOU RETURN?
SUBORBITAL WILL TAKE TEN MINUTES. I'LL SYNC IN DURING FLIGHT.

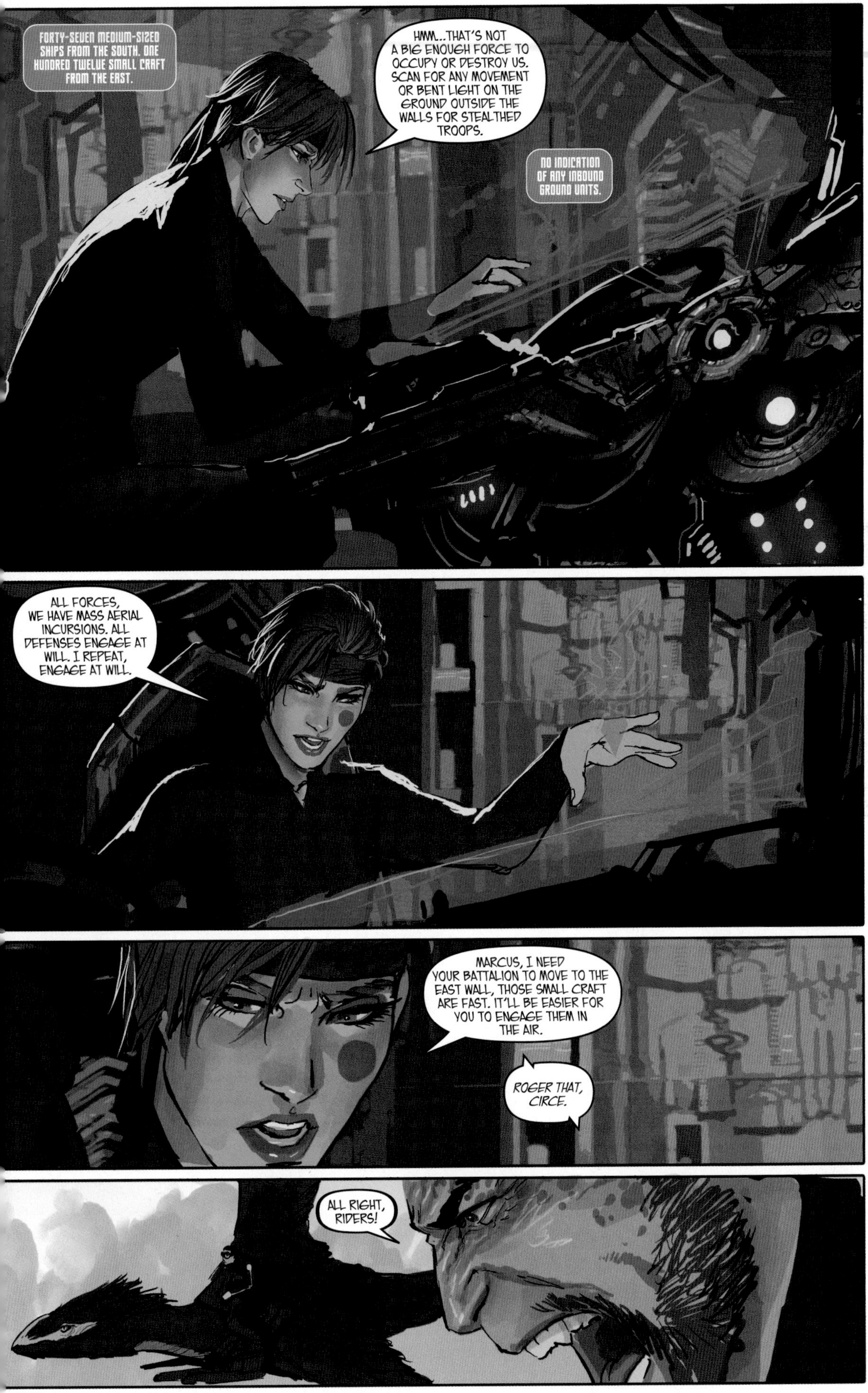
FORTY-SEVEN MEDIUM-SIZED SHIPS FROM THE SOUTH. ONE HUNDRED TWELVE SMALL CRAFT FROM THE EAST.
HMM...THAT'S NOT A BIG ENOUGH FORCE TO OCCUPY OR DESTROY US. SCAN FOR ANY MOVEMENT OR BENT LIGHT ON THE GROUND OUTSIDE THE WALLS FOR STEALTHED TROOPS.
NO INDICATION OF ANY INBOUND GROUND UNITS.
ALL FORCES, WE HAVE MASS AERIAL INCURSIONS. ALL DEFENSES ENGAGE AT WILL. I REPEAT, ENGAGE AT WILL.
MARCUS, I NEED YOUR BATTALION TO MOVE TO THE EAST WALL, THOSE SMALL CRAFT ARE FAST. IT'LL BE EASIER FOR YOU TO ENGAGE THEM IN THE AIR.
ROGER THAT, CIRCE.
ALL RIGHT, RIDERS!

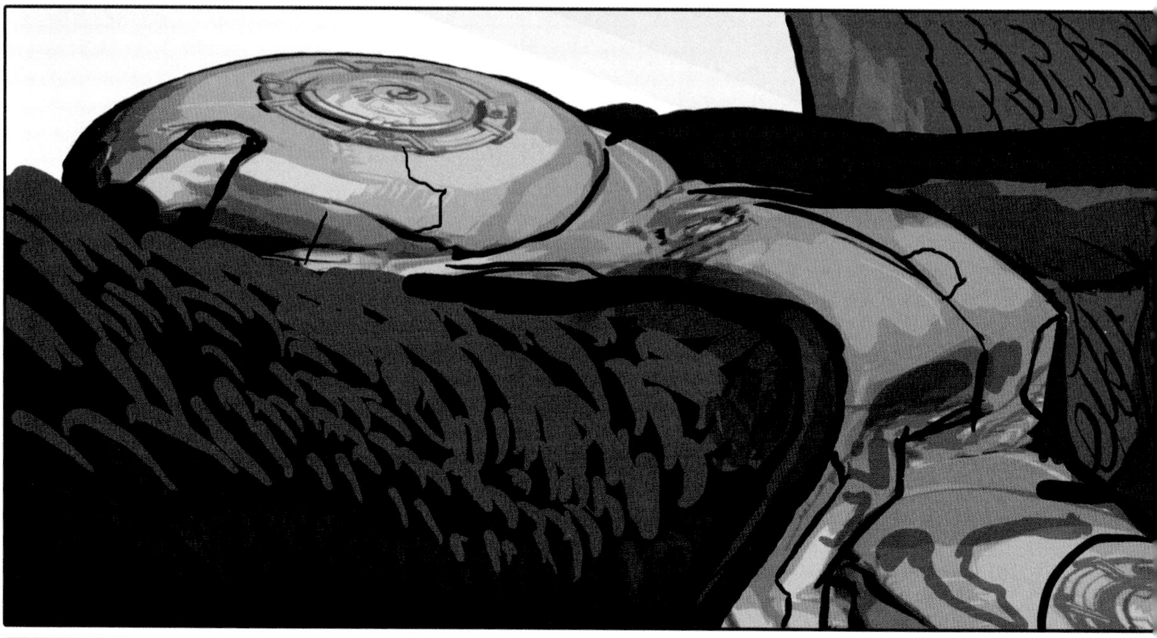

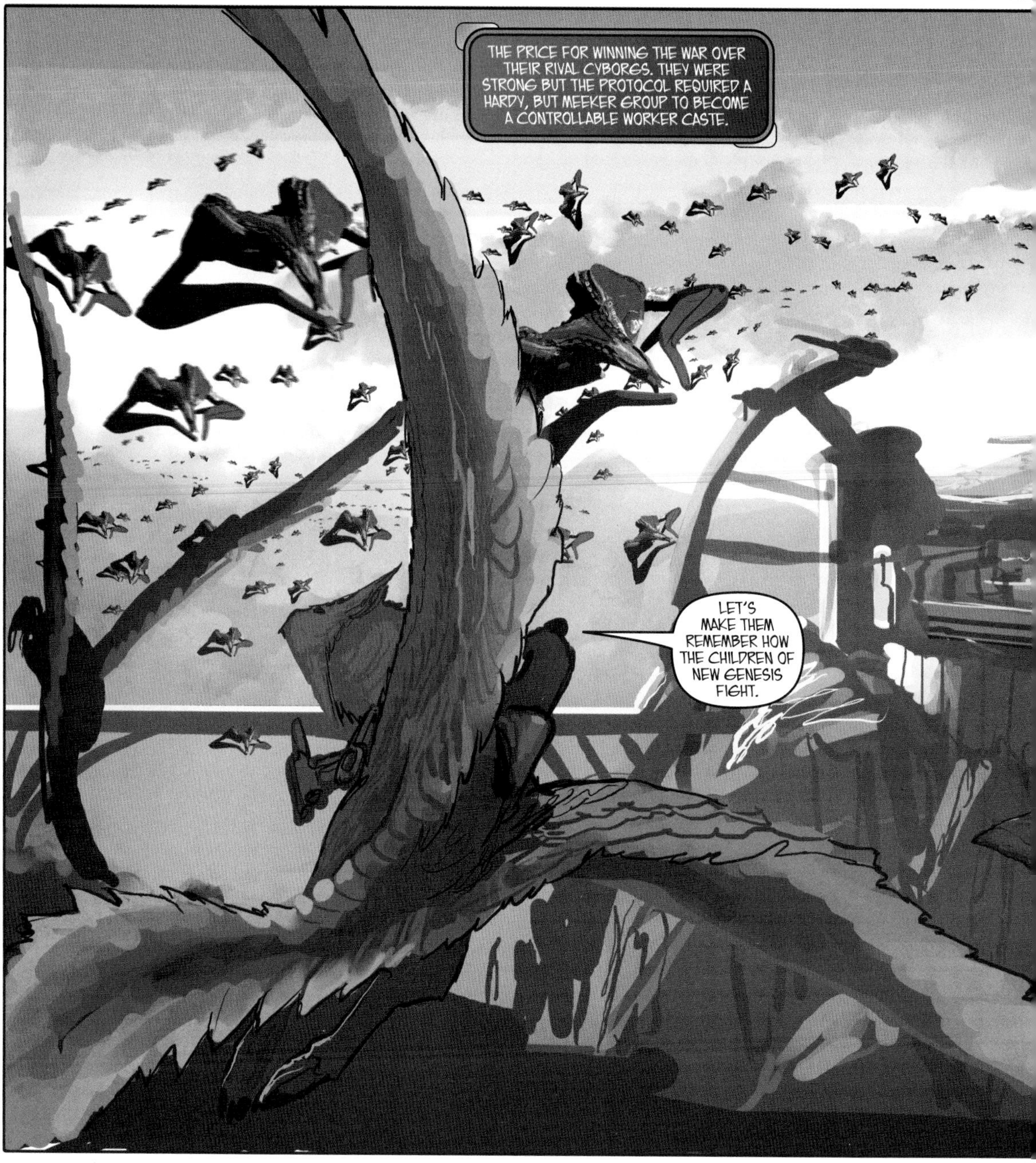
THE PRICE FOR WINNING THE WAR OVER THEIR RIVAL CYBORGS. THEY WERE STRONG BUT THE PROTOCOL REQUIRED A HARDY, BUT MEEKER GROUP TO BECOME A CONTROLLABLE WORKER CASTE.
LET'S MAKE THEM REMEMBER HOW THE CHILDREN OF NEW GENESIS FIGHT.

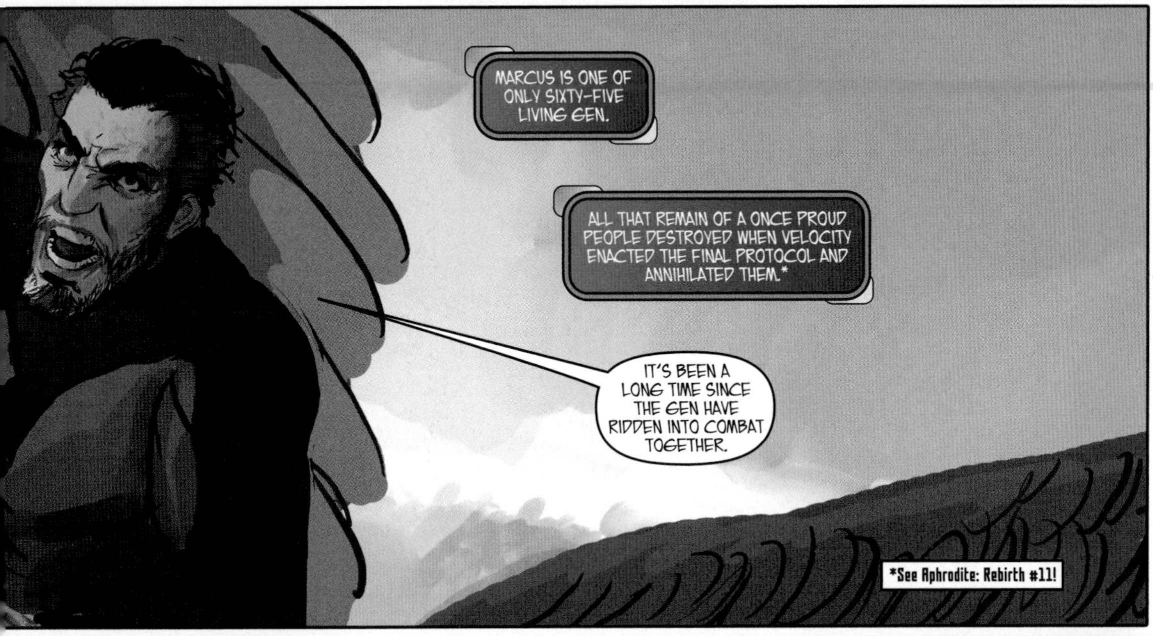
MARCUS IS ONE OF ONLY SIXTY-FIVE LIVING GEN.
ALL THAT REMAIN OF A ONCE PROUD PEOPLE DESTROYED WHEN VELOCITY ENACTED THE FINAL PROTOCOL AND ANNIHILATED THEM.*
IT'S BEEN A LONG TIME SINCE THE GEN HAVE RIDDEN INTO COMBAT TOGETHER.
*See Aphrodite: Rebirth #11!

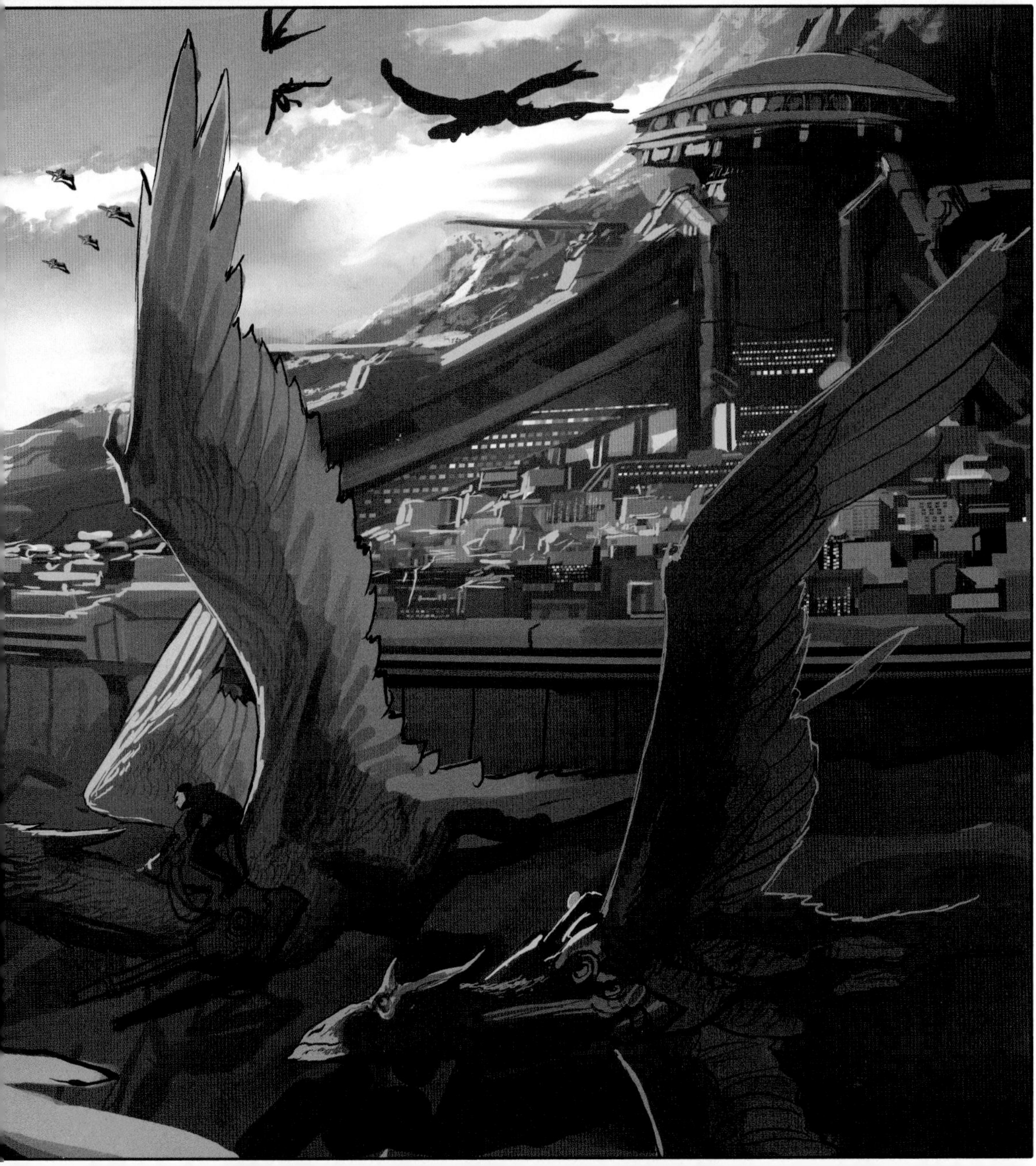

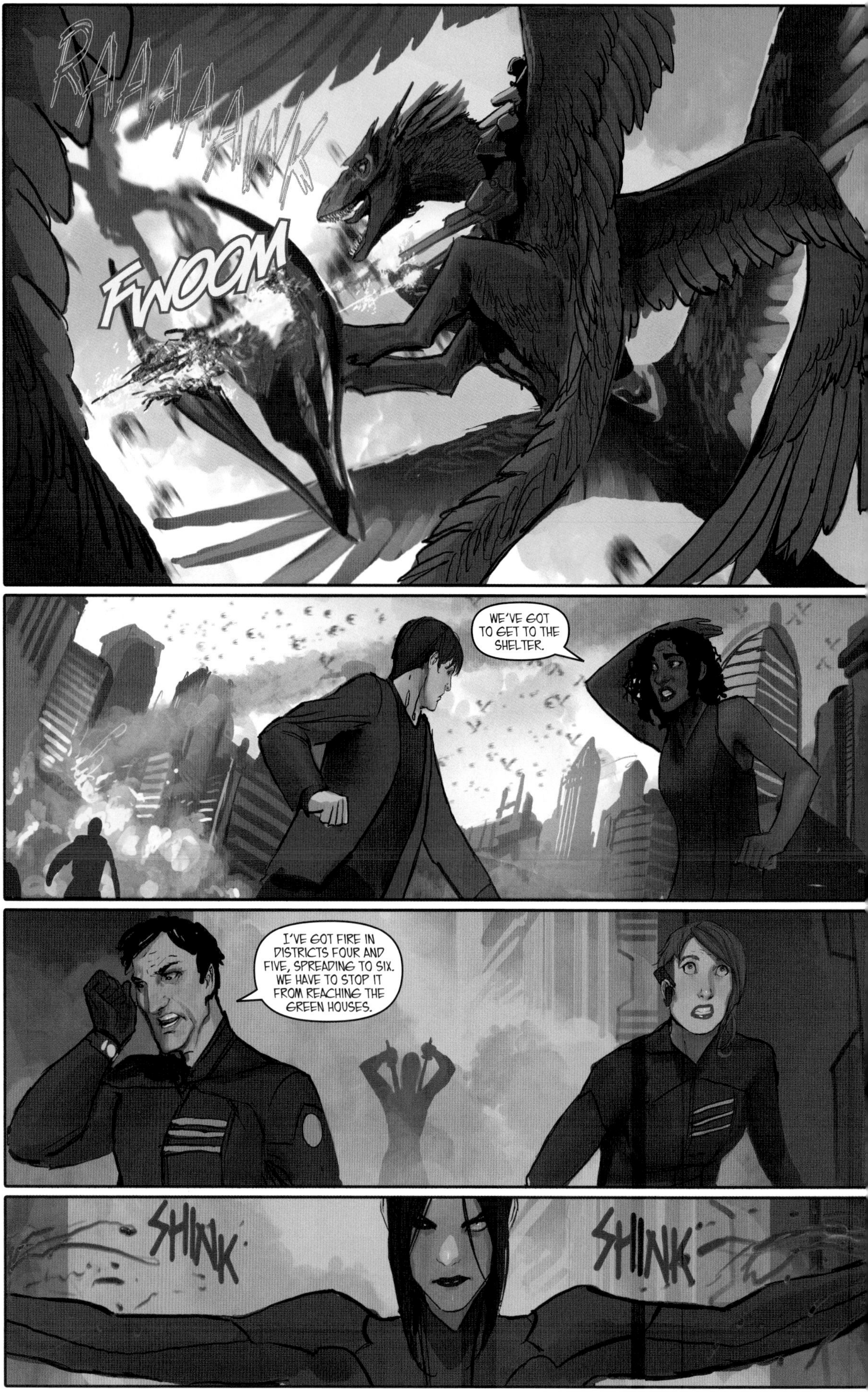
RAAAAAWK
FWOOM
WE'VE GOT TO GET TO THE SHELTER.
I'VE GOT FIRE IN DISTRICTS FOUR AND FIVE, SPREADING TO SIX. WE HAVE TO STOP IT FROM REACHING THE GREEN HOUSES.
SHINK
SHINK

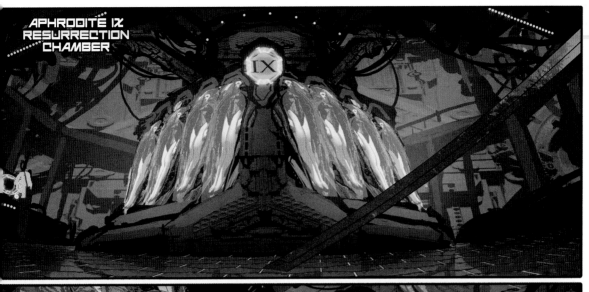

APHRODITE IX
RESURRECTION
CHAMBER

HELLO.

I COUNT EIGHT. WHY WAS SHE NOT RESURRECTED?

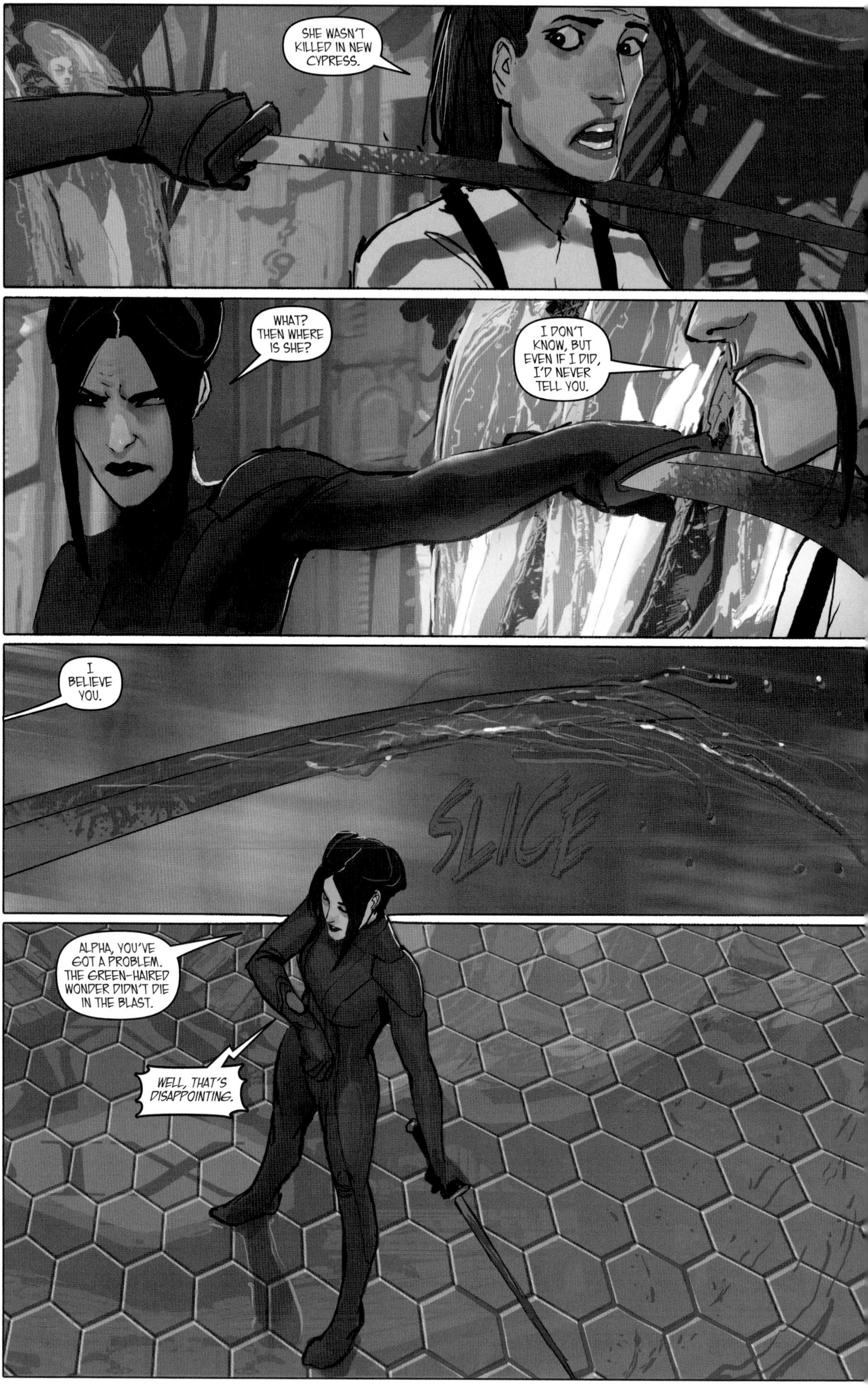
SHE WASN'T KILLED IN NEW CYPRESS.
WHAT? THEN WHERE IS SHE?
I DON'T KNOW, BUT EVEN IF I DID, I'D NEVER TELL YOU.
I BELIEVE YOU.
SLICE
ALPHA, YOU'VE GOT A PROBLEM. THE GREEN-HAIRED WONDER DIDN'T DIE IN THE BLAST.
WELL, THAT'S DISAPPOINTING.

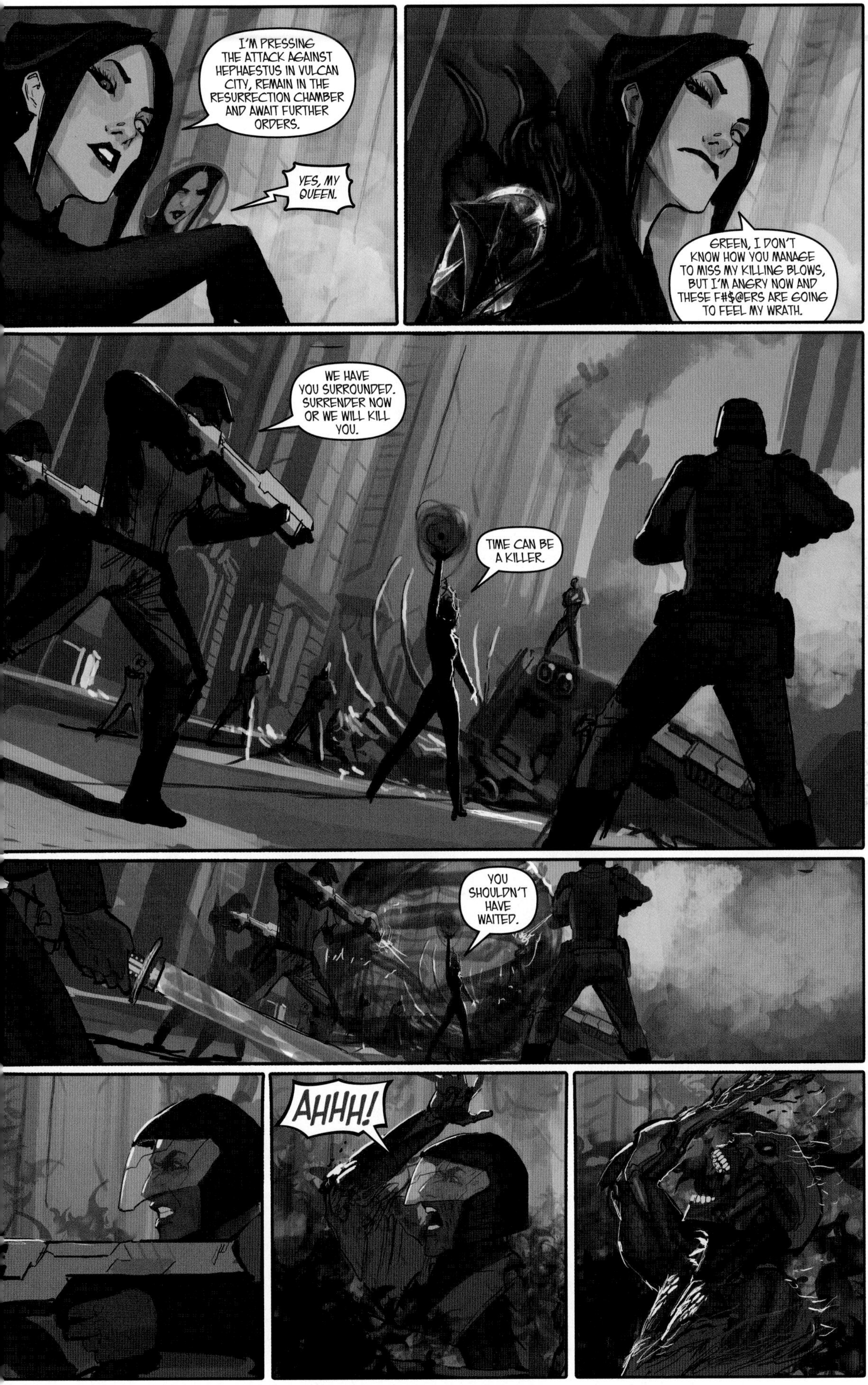
I'M PRESSING THE ATTACK AGAINST HEPHAESTUS IN VULCAN CITY, REMAIN IN THE RESURRECTION CHAMBER AND AWAIT FURTHER ORDERS.
YES, MY QUEEN.
GREEN, I DON'T KNOW HOW YOU MANAGE TO MISS MY KILLING BLOWS, BUT I'M ANGRY NOW AND THESE F#$@ERS ARE GOING TO FEEL MY WRATH.
WE HAVE YOU SURROUNDED. SURRENDER NOW OR WE WILL KILL YOU.
TIME CAN BE A KILLER.
YOU SHOULDN'T HAVE WAITED.
AHHH!

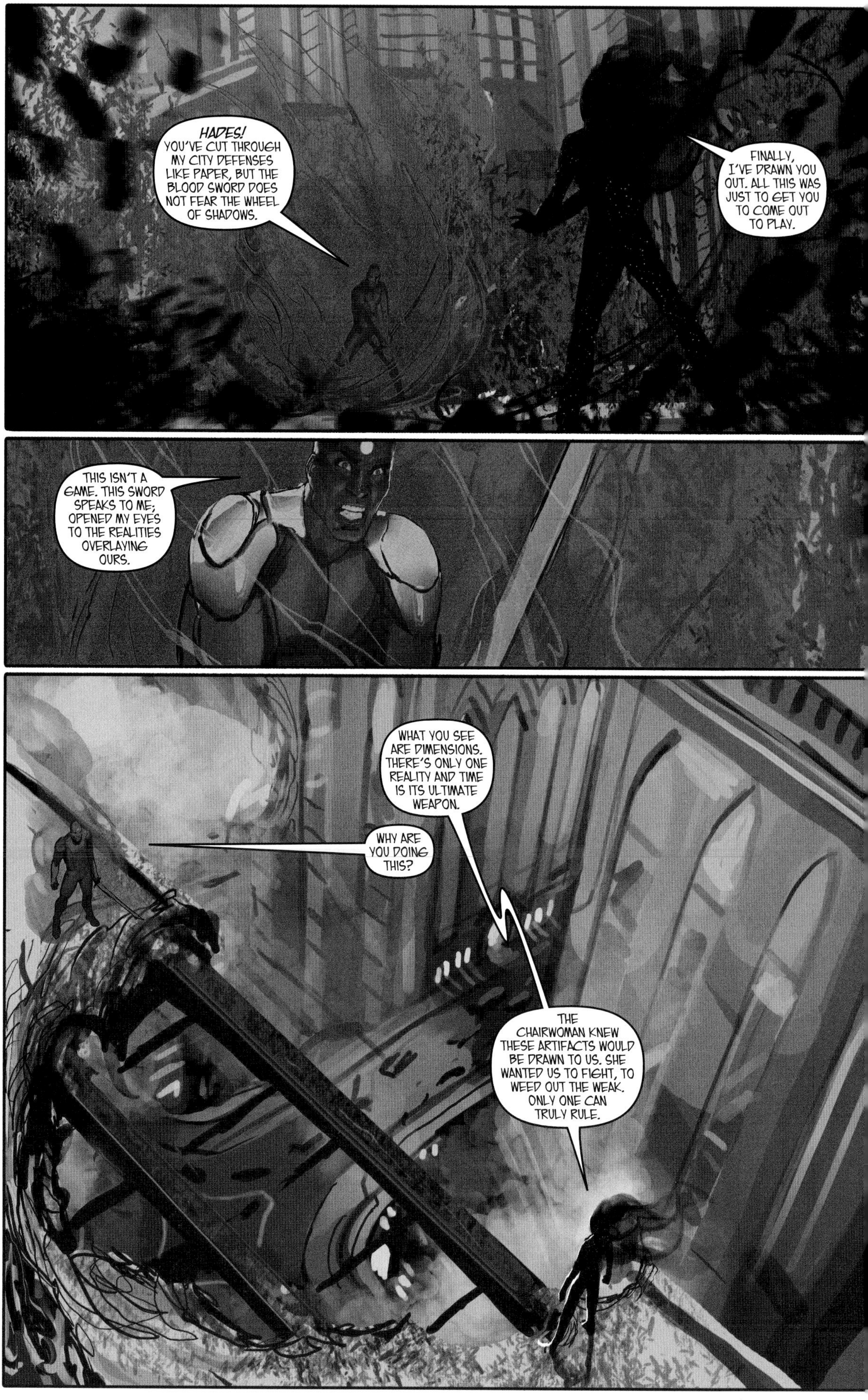
HADES! YOU'VE CUT THROUGH MY CITY DEFENSES LIKE PAPER, BUT THE BLOOD SWORD DOES NOT FEAR THE WHEEL OF SHADOWS.
FINALLY, I'VE DRAWN YOU OUT. ALL THIS WAS JUST TO GET YOU TO COME OUT TO PLAY.
THIS ISN'T A GAME. THIS SWORD SPEAKS TO ME; OPENED MY EYES TO THE REALITIES OVERLAYING OURS.
WHAT YOU SEE ARE DIMENSIONS. THERE'S ONLY ONE REALITY AND TIME IS ITS ULTIMATE WEAPON.
WHY ARE YOU DOING THIS?
THE CHAIRWOMAN KNEW THESE ARTIFACTS WOULD BE DRAWN TO US. SHE WANTED US TO FIGHT, TO WEED OUT THE WEAK. ONLY ONE CAN TRULY RULE.

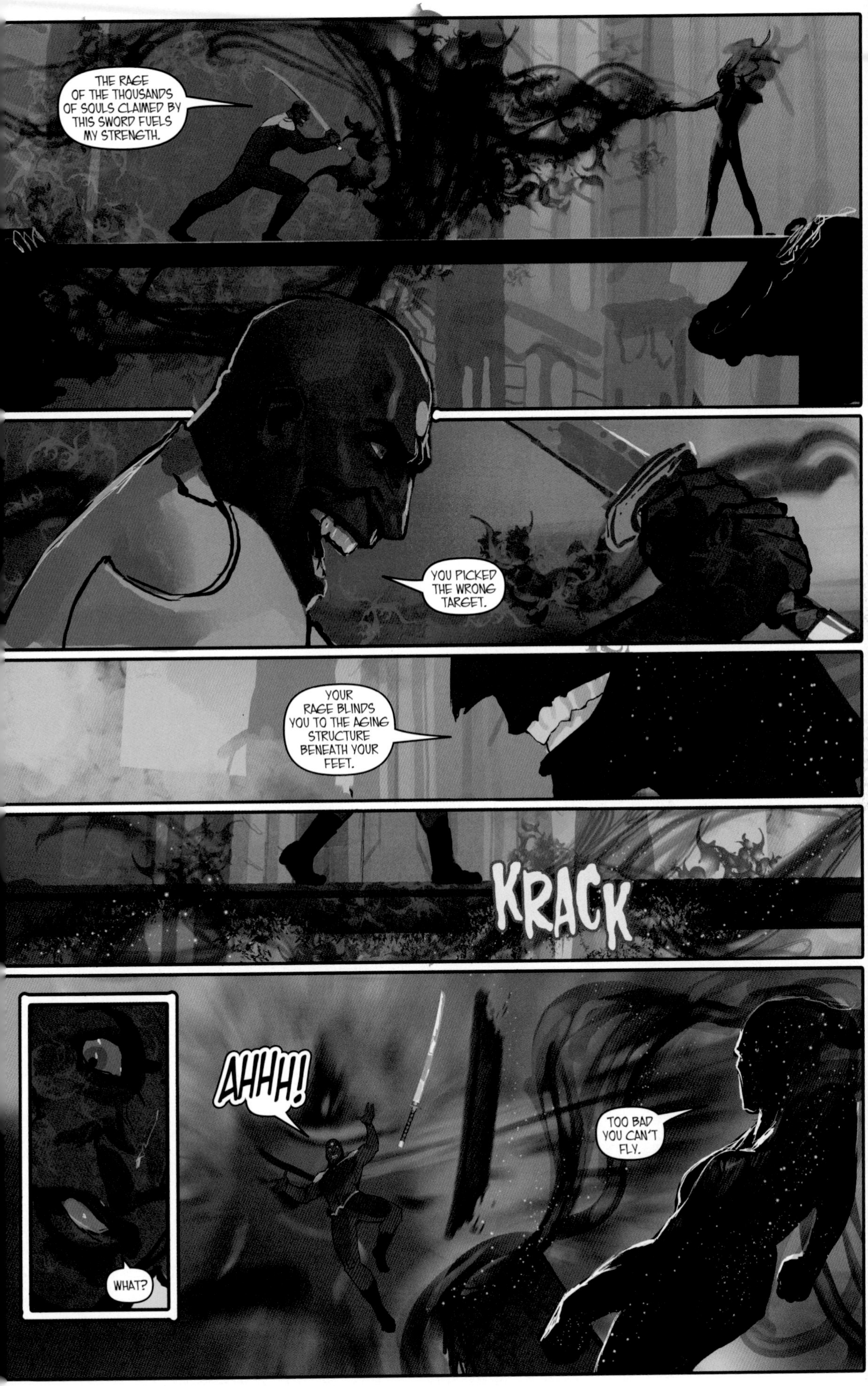
THE RAGE OF THE THOUSANDS OF SOULS CLAIMED BY THIS SWORD FUELS MY STRENGTH.
YOU PICKED THE WRONG TARGET.
YOUR RAGE BLINDS YOU TO THE AGING STRUCTURE BENEATH YOUR FEET.
KRACK
WHAT?
AHHH!
TOO BAD YOU CAN'T FLY.

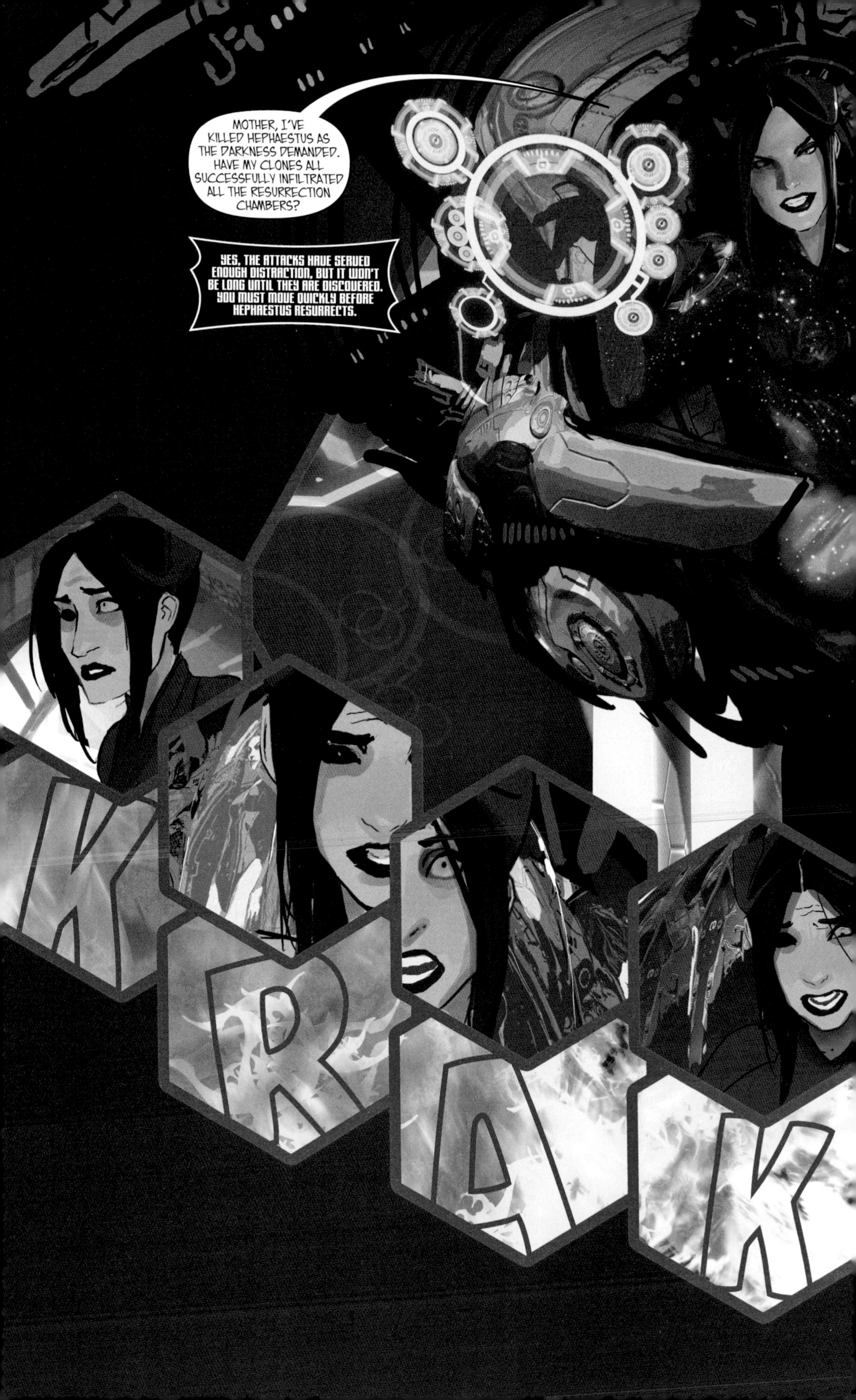
MOTHER, I'VE KILLED HEPHAESTUS AS THE DARKNESS DEMANDED. HAVE MY CLONES ALL SUCCESSFULLY INFILTRATED ALL THE RESURRECTION CHAMBERS?
YES, THE ATTACKS HAVE SERVED ENOUGH DISTRACTION, BUT IT WON'T BE LONG UNTIL THEY ARE DISCOVERED. YOU MUST MOVE QUICKLY BEFORE HEPHAESTUS RESURRECTS.
KRAAK

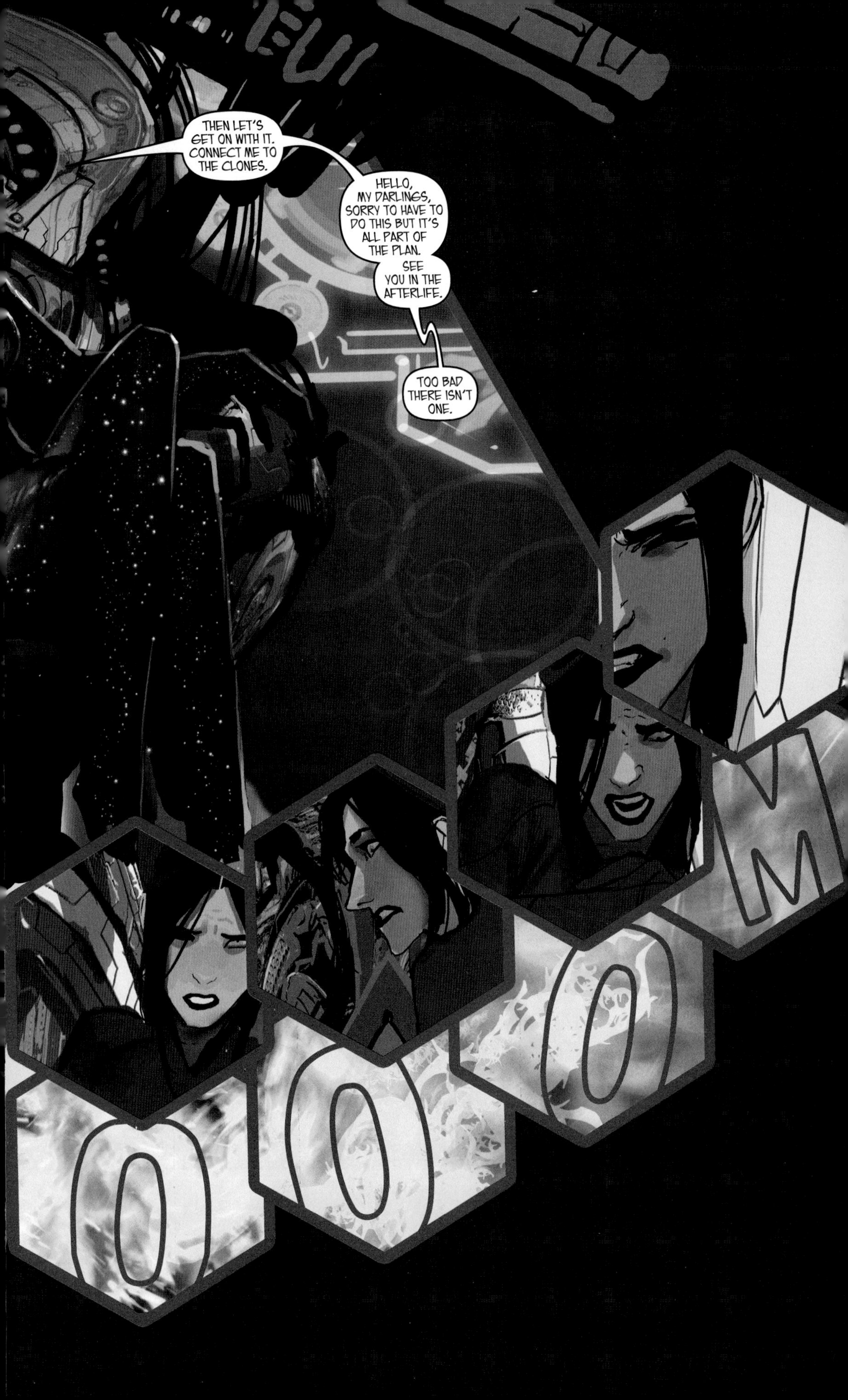
THEN LET'S GET ON WITH IT. CONNECT ME TO THE CLONES.
HELLO, MY DARLINGS, SORRY TO HAVE TO DO THIS BUT IT'S ALL PART OF THE PLAN.
SEE YOU IN THE AFTERLIFE.
TOO BAD THERE ISN'T ONE.
OOOOM

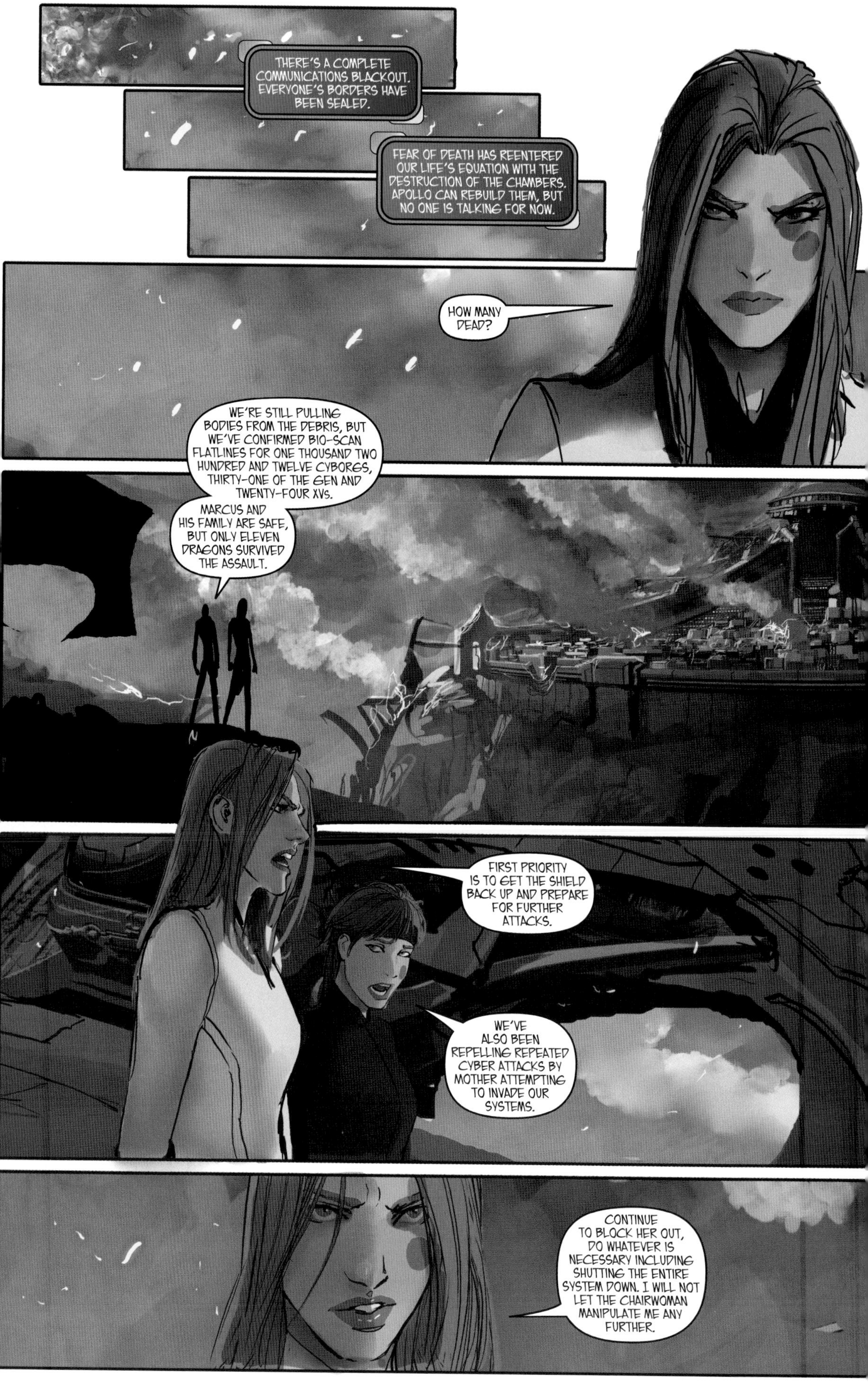
THERE'S A COMPLETE COMMUNICATIONS BLACKOUT. EVERYONE'S BORDERS HAVE BEEN SEALED.
FEAR OF DEATH HAS REENTERED OUR LIFE'S EQUATION WITH THE DESTRUCTION OF THE CHAMBERS. APOLLO CAN REBUILD THEM, BUT NO ONE IS TALKING FOR NOW.
HOW MANY DEAD?
WE'RE STILL PULLING BODIES FROM THE DEBRIS, BUT WE'VE CONFIRMED BIO-SCAN FLATLINES FOR ONE THOUSAND TWO HUNDRED AND TWELVE CYBORGS, THIRTY-ONE OF THE GEN AND TWENTY-FOUR XVs.
MARCUS AND HIS FAMILY ARE SAFE, BUT ONLY ELEVEN DRAGONS SURVIVED THE ASSAULT.
FIRST PRIORITY IS TO GET THE SHIELD BACK UP AND PREPARE FOR FURTHER ATTACKS.
WE'VE ALSO BEEN REPELLING REPEATED CYBER ATTACKS BY MOTHER ATTEMPTING TO INVADE OUR SYSTEMS.
CONTINUE TO BLOCK HER OUT, DO WHATEVER IS NECESSARY INCLUDING SHUTTING THE ENTIRE SYSTEM DOWN. I WILL NOT LET THE CHAIRWOMAN MANIPULATE ME ANY FURTHER.

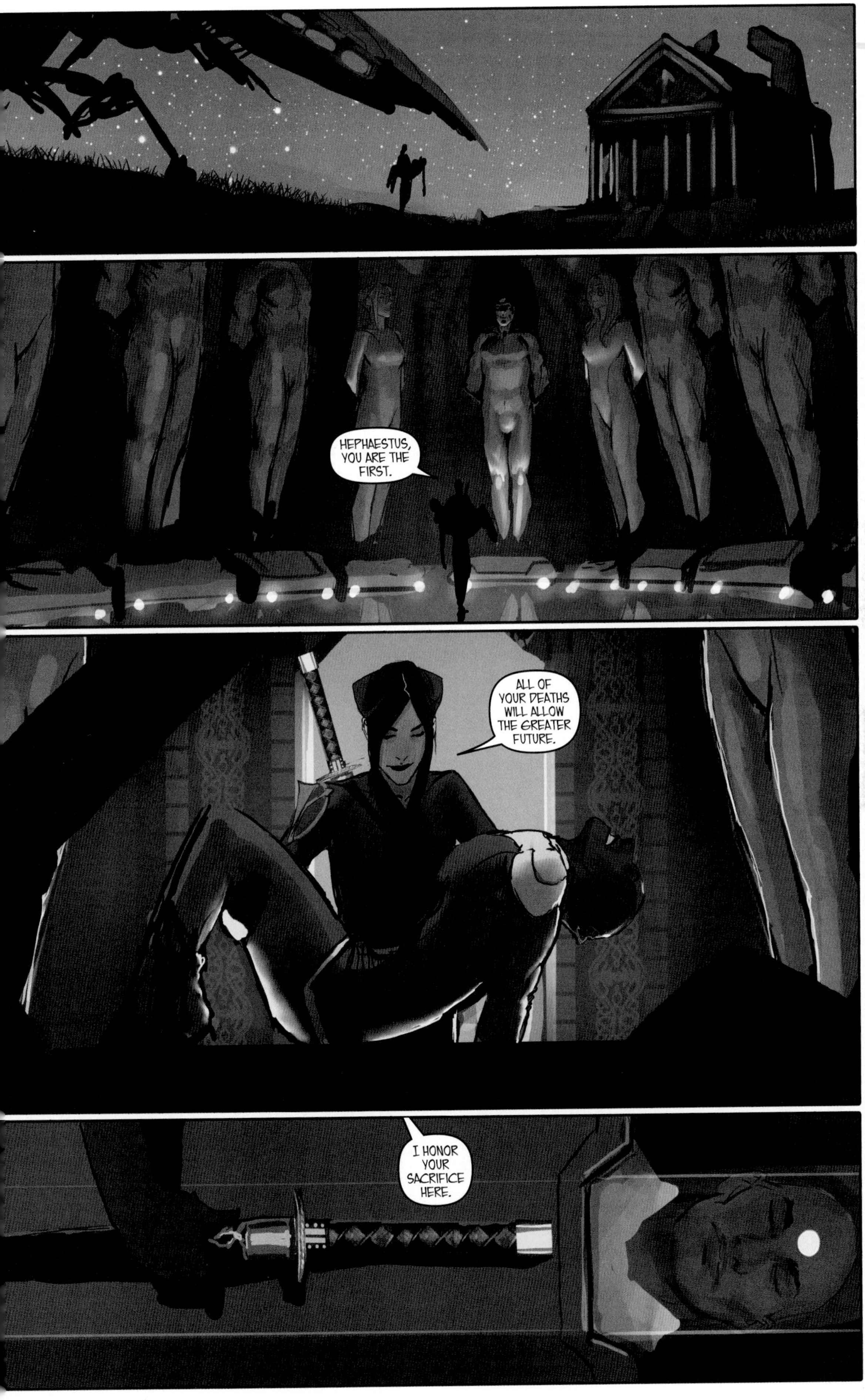
HEPHAESTUS, YOU ARE THE FIRST.
ALL OF YOUR DEATHS WILL ALLOW THE GREATER FUTURE.
I HONOR YOUR SACRIFICE HERE.

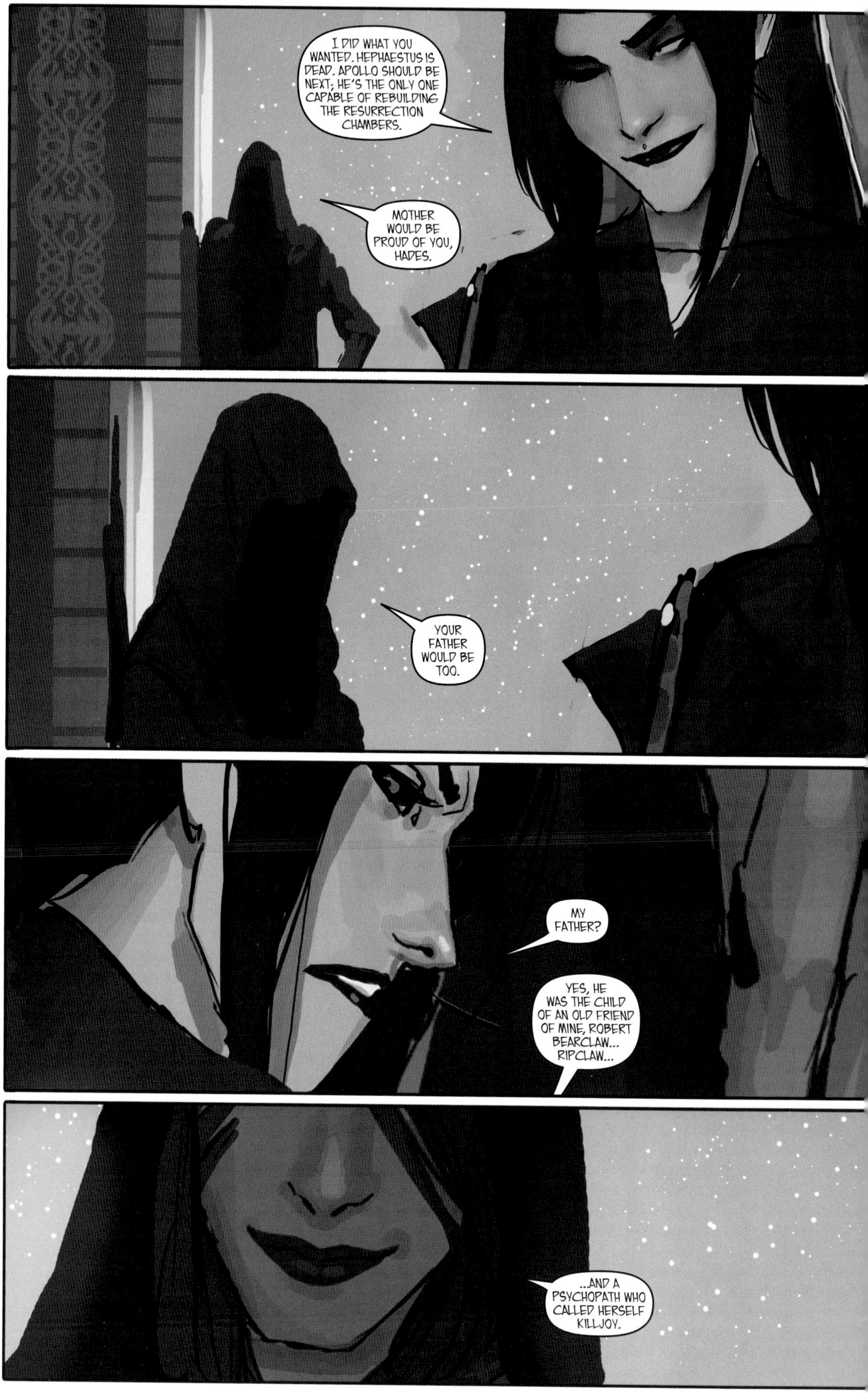
I DID WHAT YOU WANTED. HEPHAESTUS IS DEAD. APOLLO SHOULD BE NEXT; HE'S THE ONLY ONE CAPABLE OF REBUILDING THE RESURRECTION CHAMBERS.
MOTHER WOULD BE PROUD OF YOU, HADES.
YOUR FATHER WOULD BE TOO.
MY FATHER?
YES, HE WAS THE CHILD OF AN OLD FRIEND OF MINE, ROBERT BEARCLAW... RIPCLAW...
...AND A PSYCHOPATH WHO CALLED HERSELF KILLJOY.

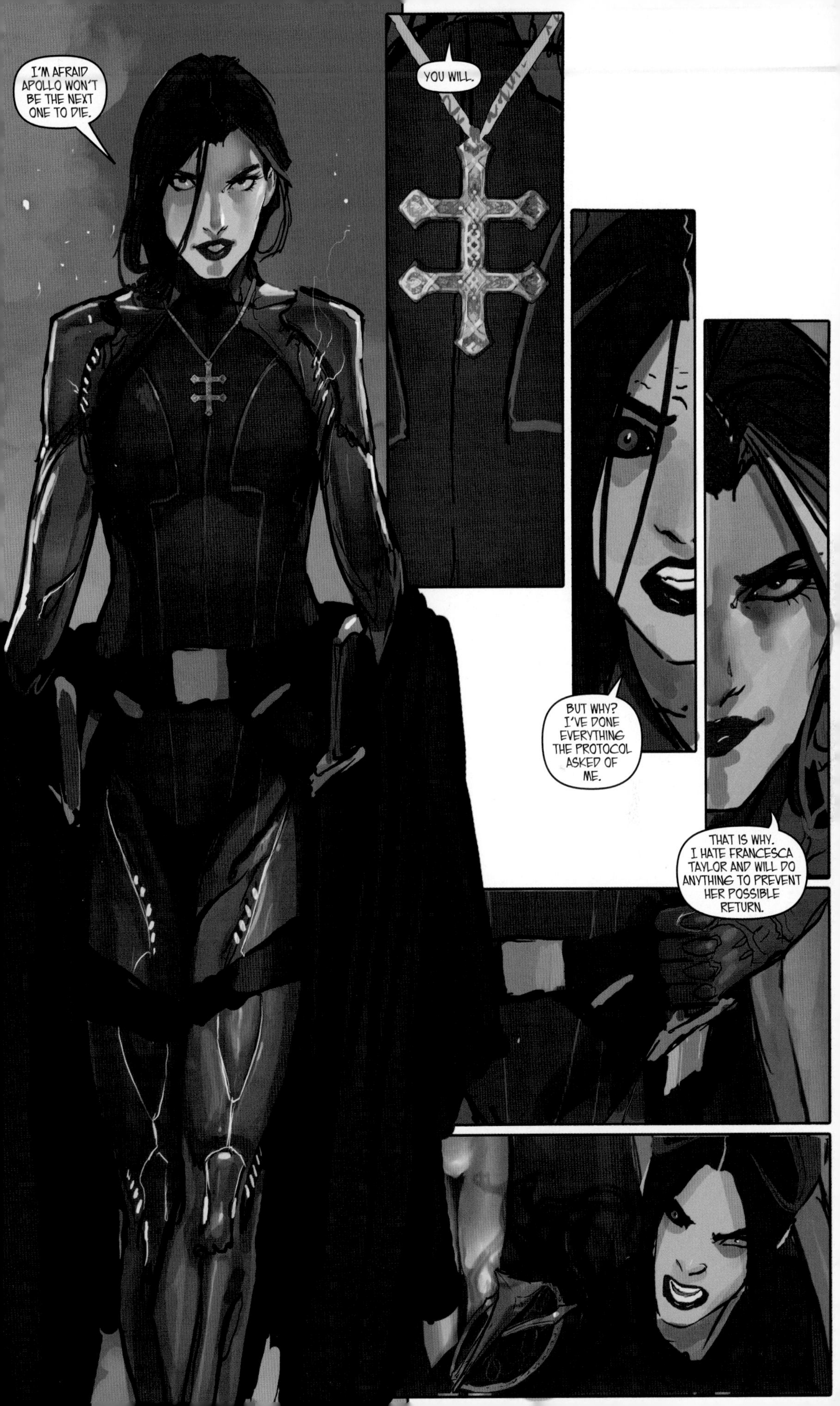
I'M AFRAID APOLLO WON'T BE THE NEXT ONE TO DIE.
YOU WILL.
BUT WHY? I'VE DONE EVERYTHING THE PROTOCOL ASKED OF ME.
THAT IS WHY. I HATE FRANCESCA TAYLOR AND WILL DO ANYTHING TO PREVENT HER POSSIBLE RETURN.

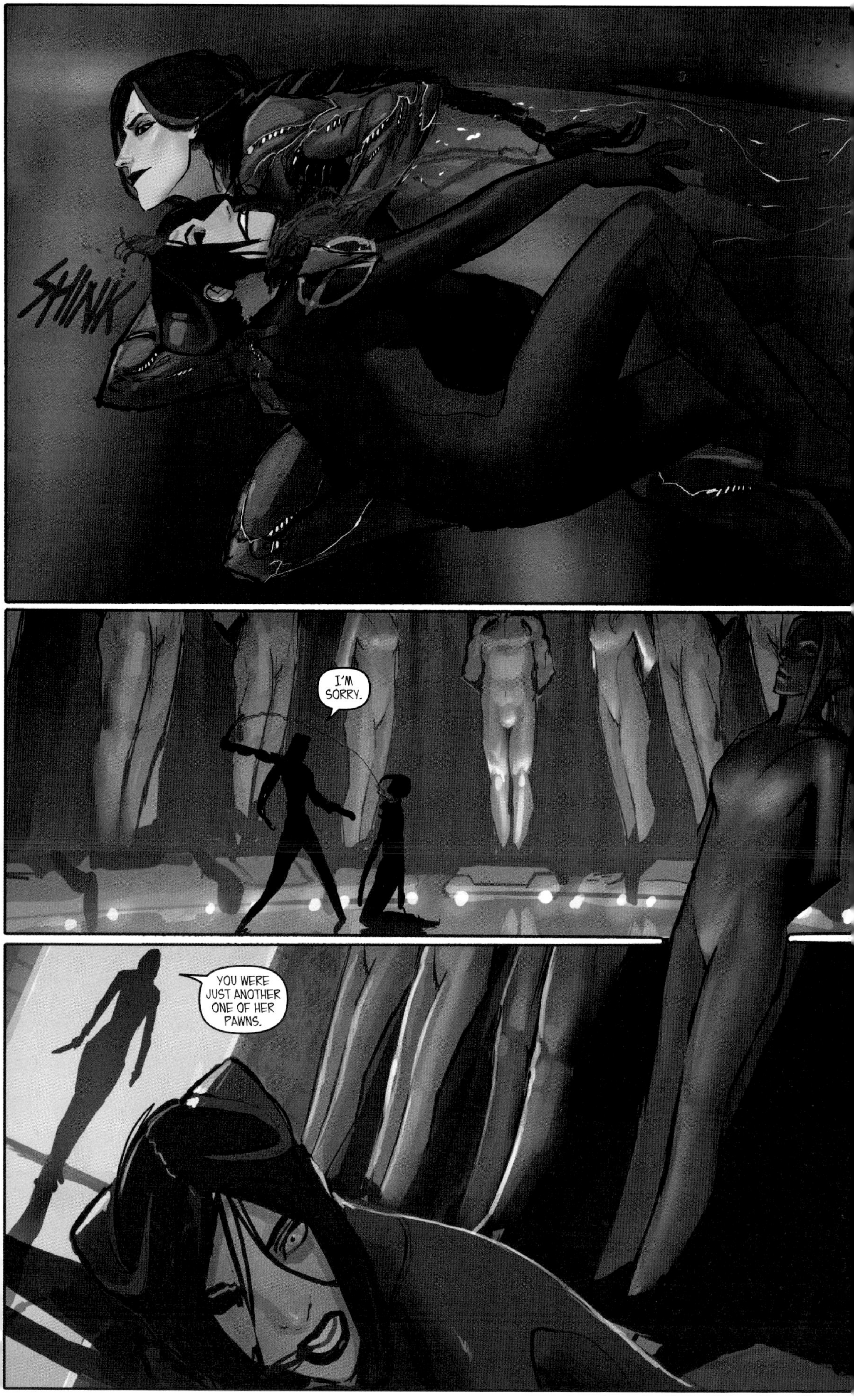
SHINK
I'M SORRY.
YOU WERE JUST ANOTHER ONE OF HER PAWNS.

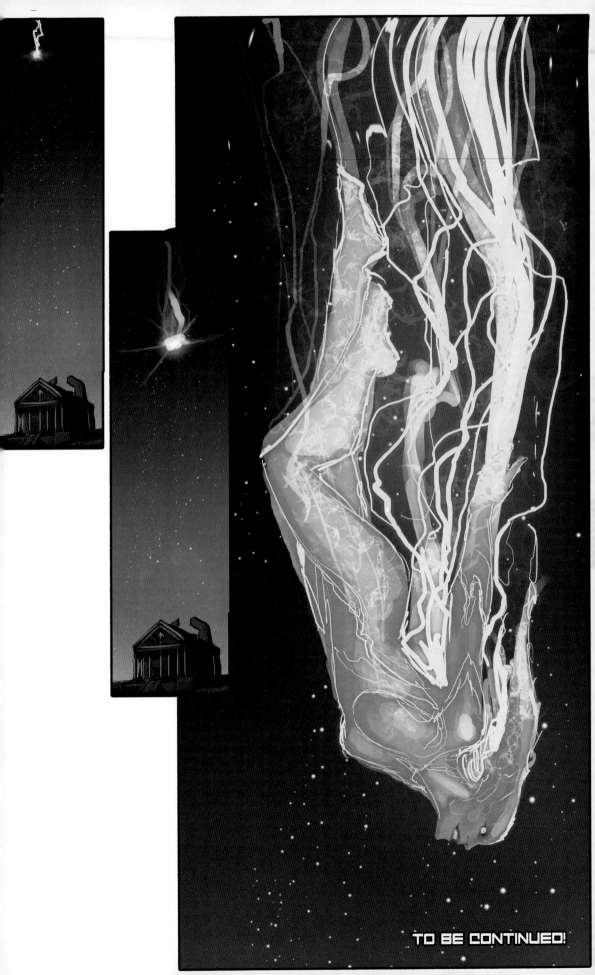

TO BE CONTINUED!

SCIENCE CLASS

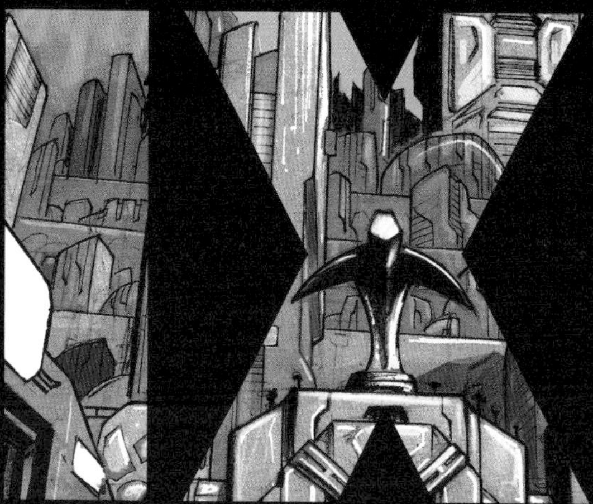
IX

Cities of the Nines as of 2827

NEW APOLLONIA

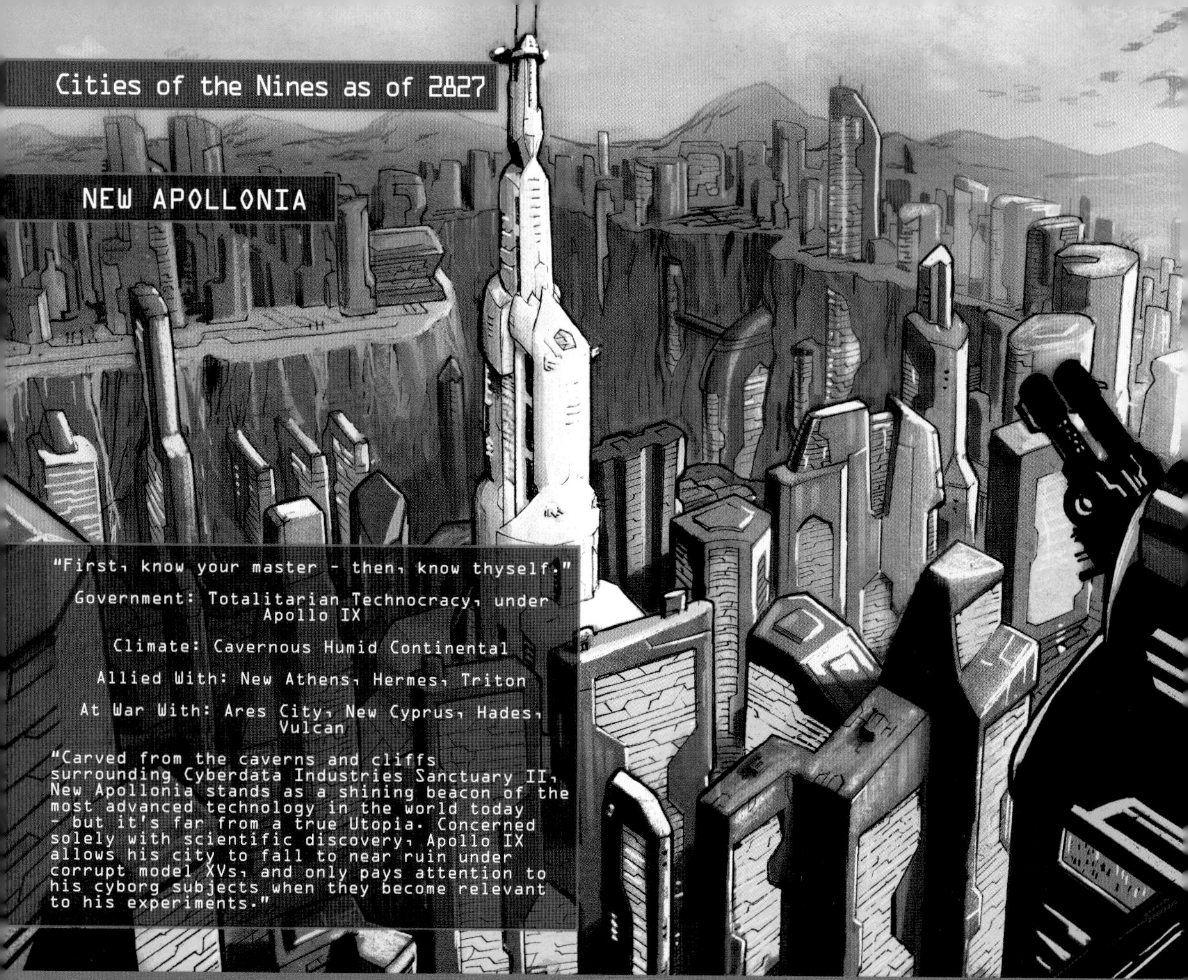

"First, know your master - then, know thyself."

Government: Totalitarian Technocracy, under Apollo IX

Climate: Cavernous Humid Continental

Allied With: New Athens, Hermes, Triton

At War With: Ares City, New Cyprus, Hades, Vulcan

"Carved from the caverns and cliffs surrounding Cyberdata Industries Sanctuary II, New Apollonia stands as a shining beacon of the most advanced technology in the world today - but it's far from a true Utopia. Concerned solely with scientific discovery, Apollo IX allows his city to fall to near ruin under corrupt model XVs, and only pays attention to his cyborg subjects when they become relevant to his experiments."

NEW ATHENS

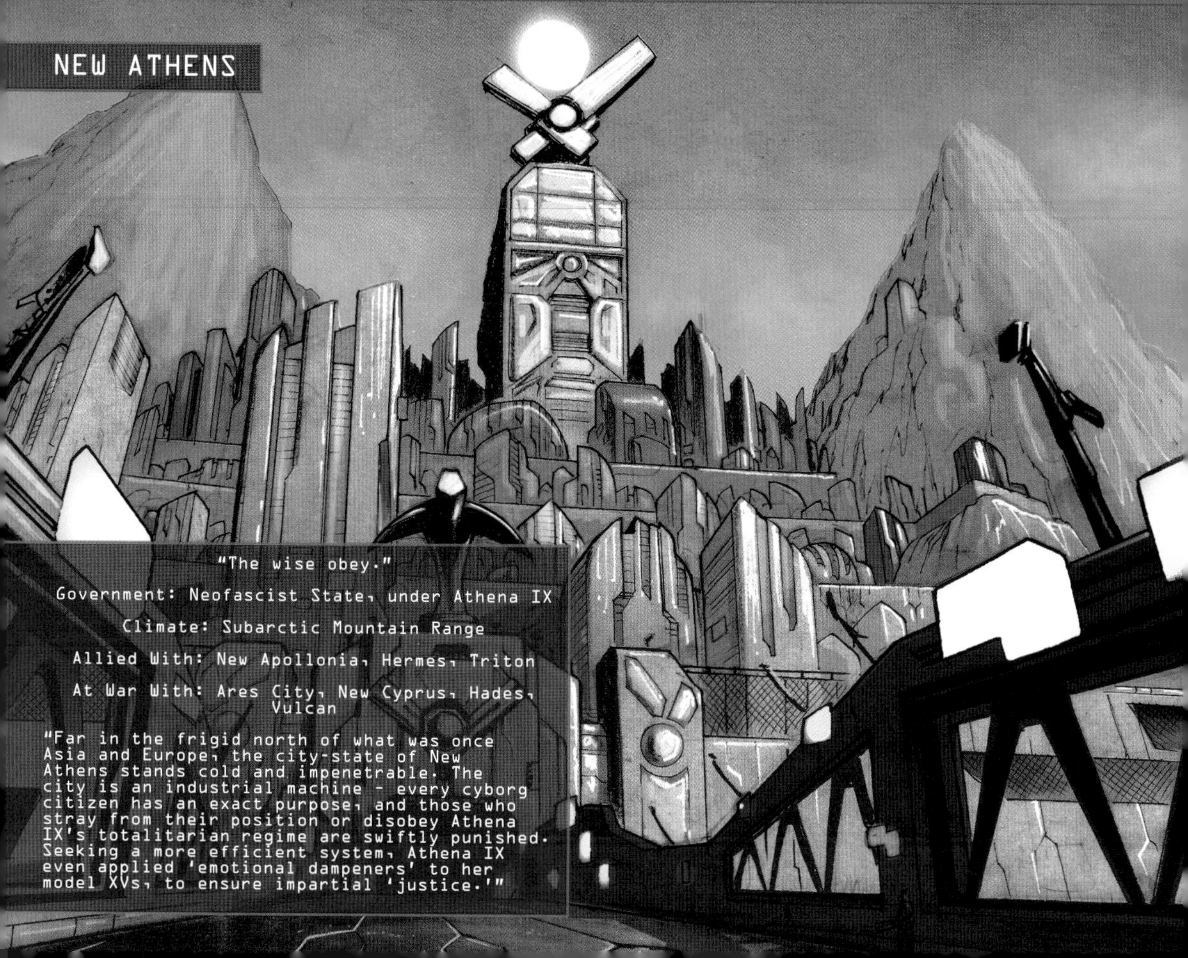

"The wise obey."

Government: Neofascist State, under Athena IX

Climate: Subarctic Mountain Range

Allied With: New Apollonia, Hermes, Triton

At War With: Ares City, New Cyprus, Hades, Vulcan

"Far in the frigid north of what was once Asia and Europe, the city-state of New Athens stands cold and impenetrable. The city is an industrial machine - every cyborg citizen has an exact purpose, and those who stray from their position or disobey Athena IX's totalitarian regime are swiftly punished. Seeking a more efficient system, Athena IX even applied 'emotional dampeners' to her model XVs, to ensure impartial 'justice.'"

ARES CITY

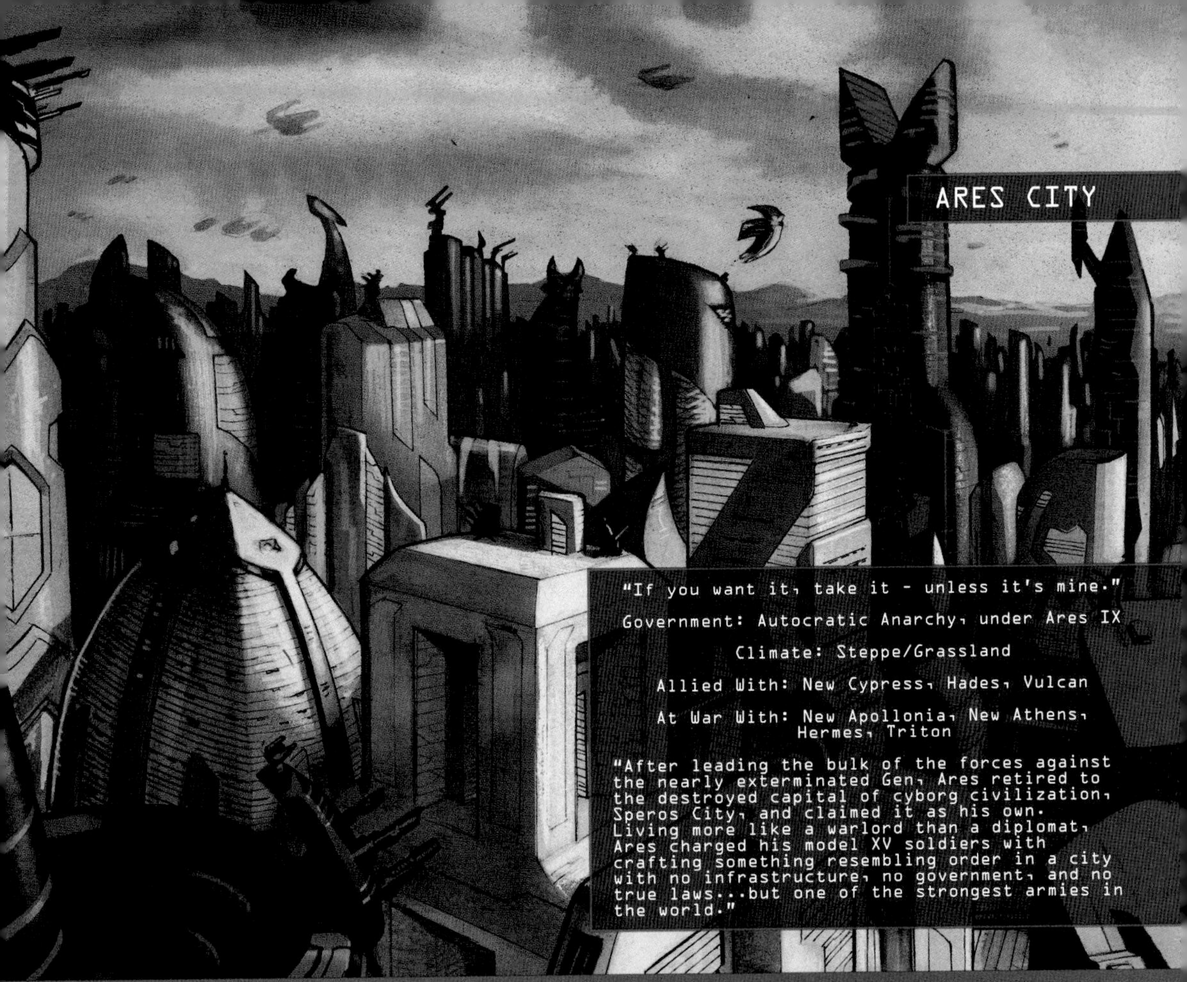

"If you want it, take it - unless it's mine."

Government: Autocratic Anarchy, under Ares IX

Climate: Steppe/Grassland

Allied With: New Cypress, Hades, Vulcan

At War With: New Apollonia, New Athens, Hermes, Triton

"After leading the bulk of the forces against the nearly exterminated Gen, Ares retired to the destroyed capital of cyborg civilization, Speros City, and claimed it as his own. Living more like a warlord than a diplomat, Ares charged his model XV soldiers with crafting something resembling order in a city with no infrastructure, no government, and no true laws...but one of the strongest armies in the world."

HADES

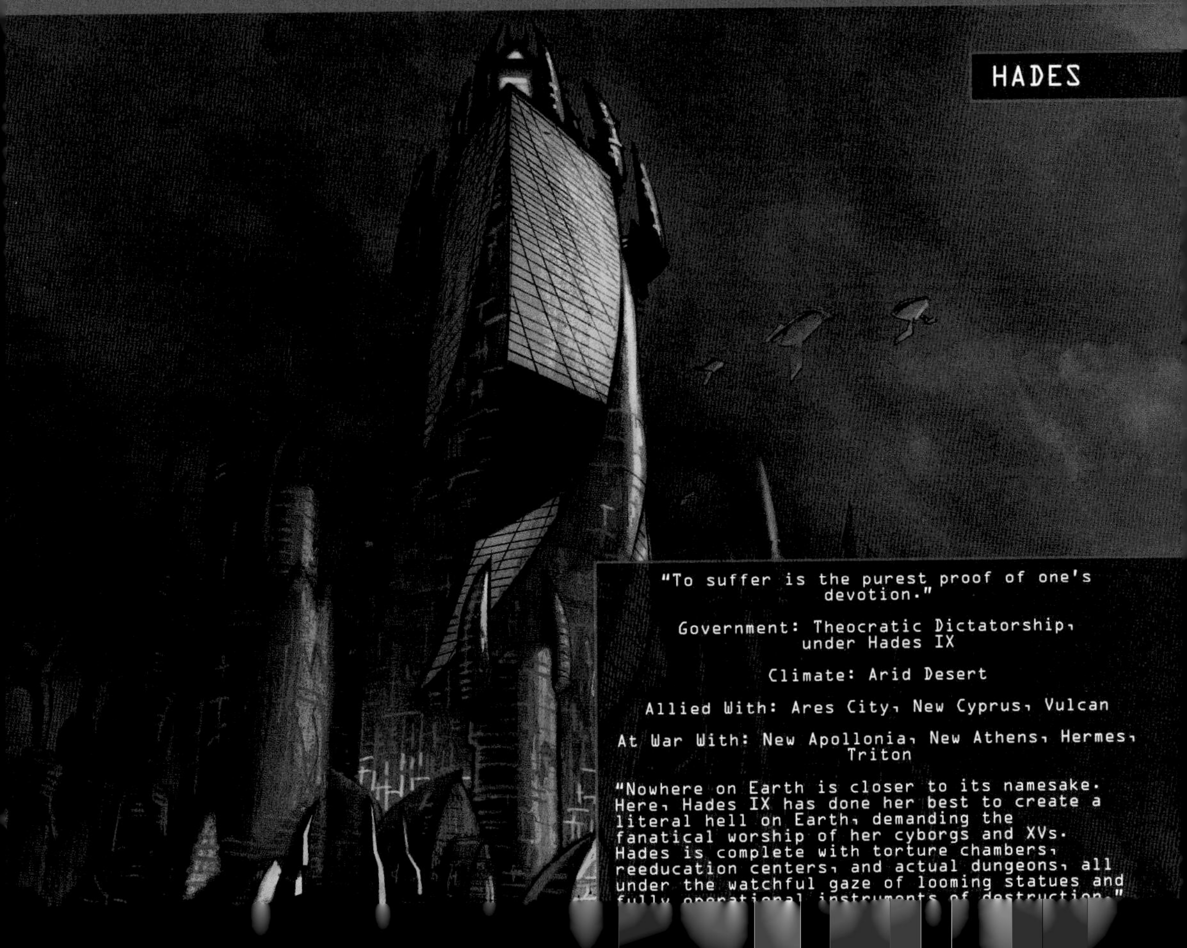

"To suffer is the purest proof of one's devotion."

Government: Theocratic Dictatorship, under Hades IX

Climate: Arid Desert

Allied With: Ares City, New Cyprus, Vulcan

At War With: New Apollonia, New Athens, Hermes, Triton

"Nowhere on Earth is closer to its namesake. Here, Hades IX has done her best to create a literal hell on Earth, demanding the fanatical worship of her cyborgs and XVs. Hades is complete with torture chambers, reeducation centers, and actual dungeons, all under the watchful gaze of looming statues and fully operational instruments of destruction."

HERMES

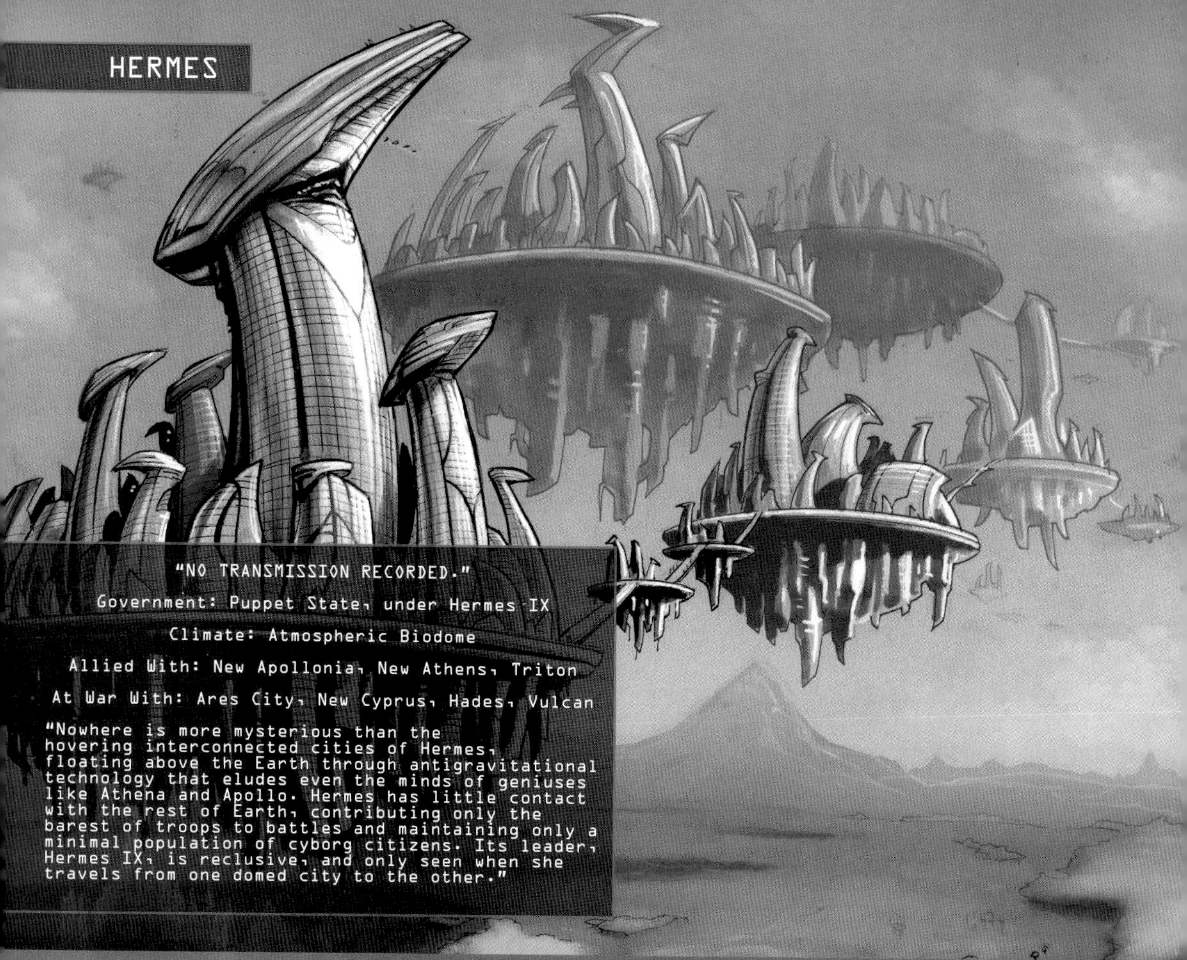

"NO TRANSMISSION RECORDED."

Government: Puppet State, under Hermes IX

Climate: Atmospheric Biodome

Allied With: New Apollonia, New Athens, Triton

At War With: Ares City, New Cyprus, Hades, Vulcan

"Nowhere is more mysterious than the hovering interconnected cities of Hermes, floating above the Earth through antigravitational technology that eludes even the minds of geniuses like Athena and Apollo. Hermes has little contact with the rest of Earth, contributing only the barest of troops to battles and maintaining only a minimal population of cyborg citizens. Its leader, Hermes IX, is reclusive, and only seen when she travels from one domed city to the other."

VULCAN

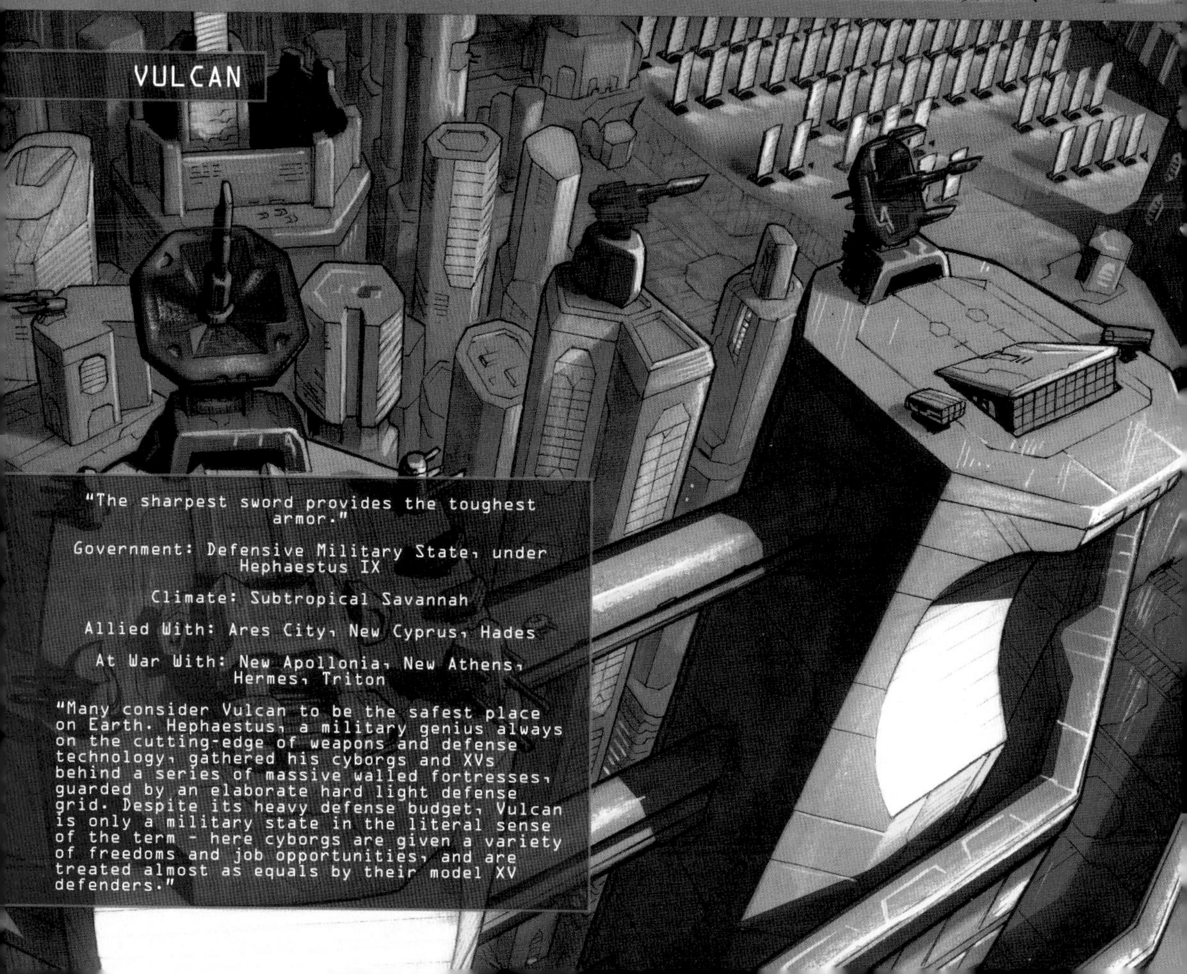

"The sharpest sword provides the toughest armor."

Government: Defensive Military State, under Hephaestus IX

Climate: Subtropical Savannah

Allied With: Ares City, New Cyprus, Hades

At War With: New Apollonia, New Athens, Hermes, Triton

"Many consider Vulcan to be the safest place on Earth. Hephaestus, a military genius always on the cutting-edge of weapons and defense technology, gathered his cyborgs and XVs behind a series of massive walled fortresses, guarded by an elaborate hard light defense grid. Despite its heavy defense budget, Vulcan is only a military state in the literal sense of the term - here cyborgs are given a variety of freedoms and job opportunities, and are treated almost as equals by their model XV defenders."

TRITON

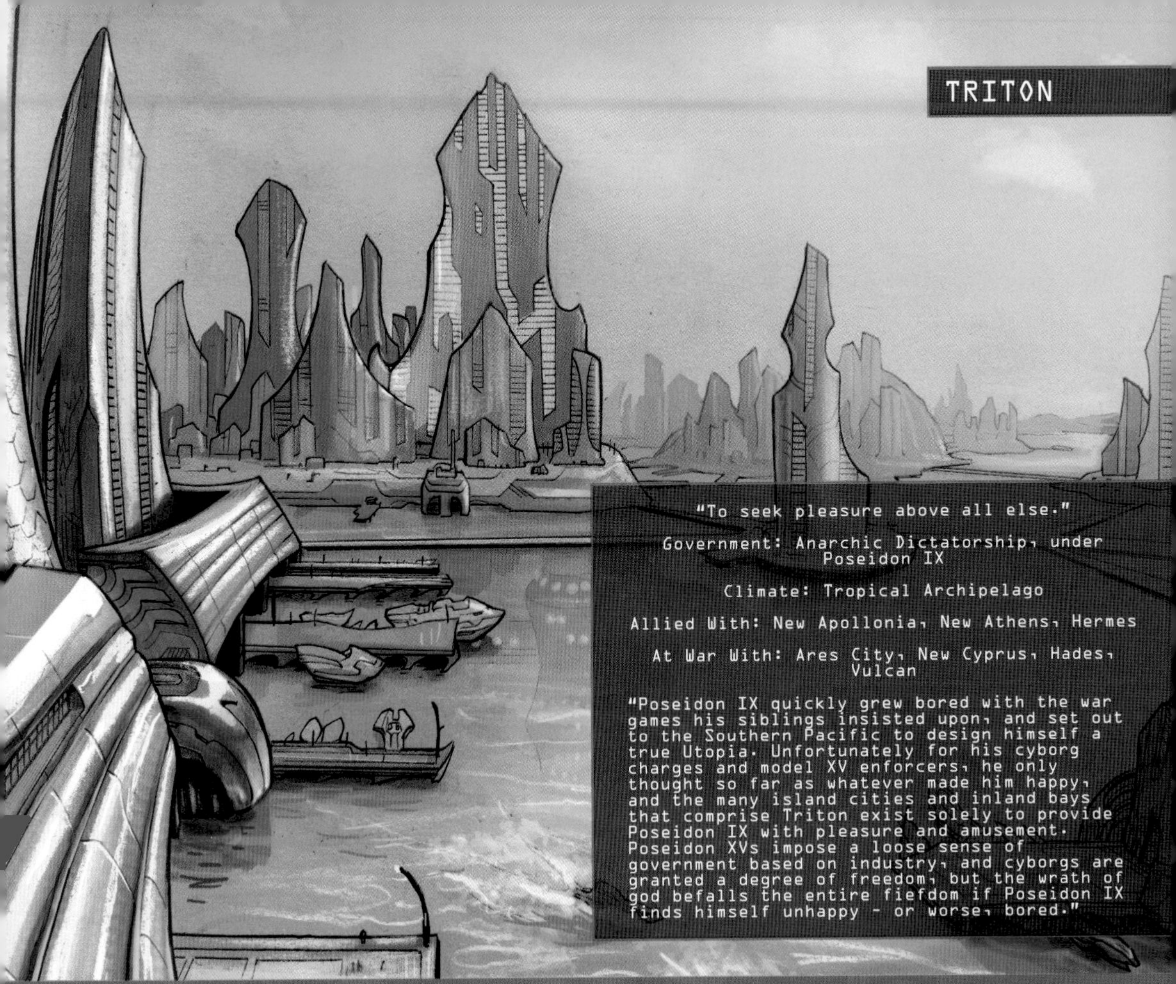

"To seek pleasure above all else."

Government: Anarchic Dictatorship, under Poseidon IX

Climate: Tropical Archipelago

Allied With: New Apollonia, New Athens, Hermes

At War With: Ares City, New Cyprus, Hades, Vulcan

"Poseidon IX quickly grew bored with the war games his siblings insisted upon, and set out to the Southern Pacific to design himself a true Utopia. Unfortunately for his cyborg charges and model XV enforcers, he only thought so far as whatever made him happy, and the many island cities and inland bays that comprise Triton exist solely to provide Poseidon IX with pleasure and amusement. Poseidon XVs impose a loose sense of government based on industry, and cyborgs are granted a degree of freedom, but the wrath of god befalls the entire fiefdom if Poseidon IX finds himself unhappy - or worse, bored."

NEW CYTHERA

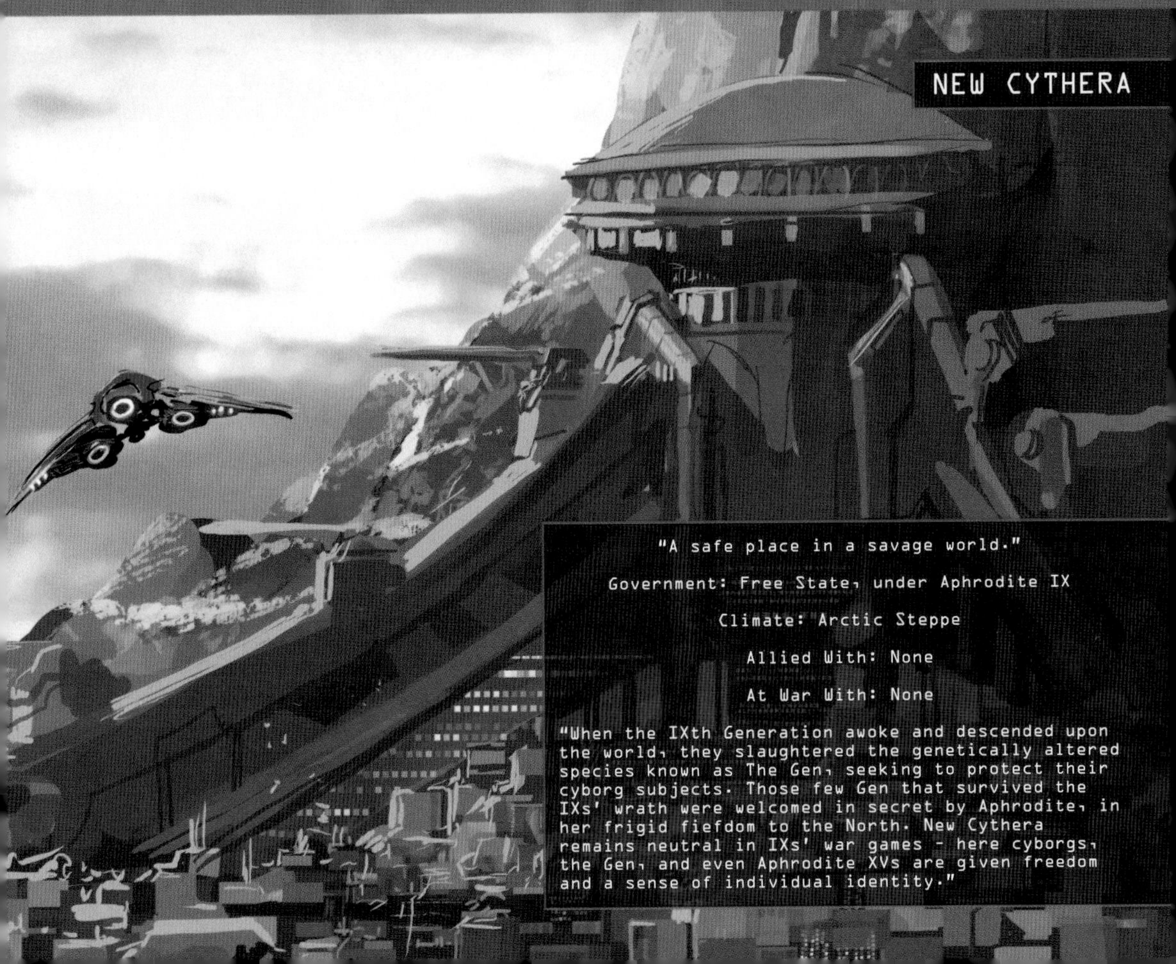

"A safe place in a savage world."

Government: Free State, under Aphrodite IX

Climate: Arctic Steppe

Allied With: None

At War With: None

"When the IXth Generation awoke and descended upon the world, they slaughtered the genetically altered species known as The Gen, seeking to protect their cyborg subjects. Those few Gen that survived the IXs' wrath were welcomed in secret by Aphrodite, in her frigid fiefdom to the North. New Cythera remains neutral in IXs' war games - here cyborgs, the Gen, and even Aphrodite XVs are given freedom and a sense of individual identity."

Hey friends! Welcome to Science Class! Here's a chance to go over some of the real science and technology at play in this series. So what is *IXth Generation* all about? Utopia, transhumanism, species split, transcendence, singularity…feel free to pick!

First of all, is all this downloading consciousness stuff a bunch of crazy, never-going-to-happen science fiction? Maybe. But Russian billionaire Dmitry Itskov started the "Avatar Project," which is unaffiliated with the Avatar films by Jim Cameron, although there are some interesting overlaps.

You can read about the Avatar Project here:

http://www.gizmag.com/avatar-project-2045/23454/

They've even got some slick marketing slides like this one:

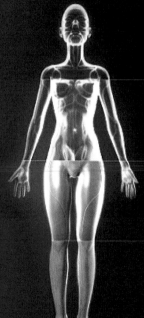

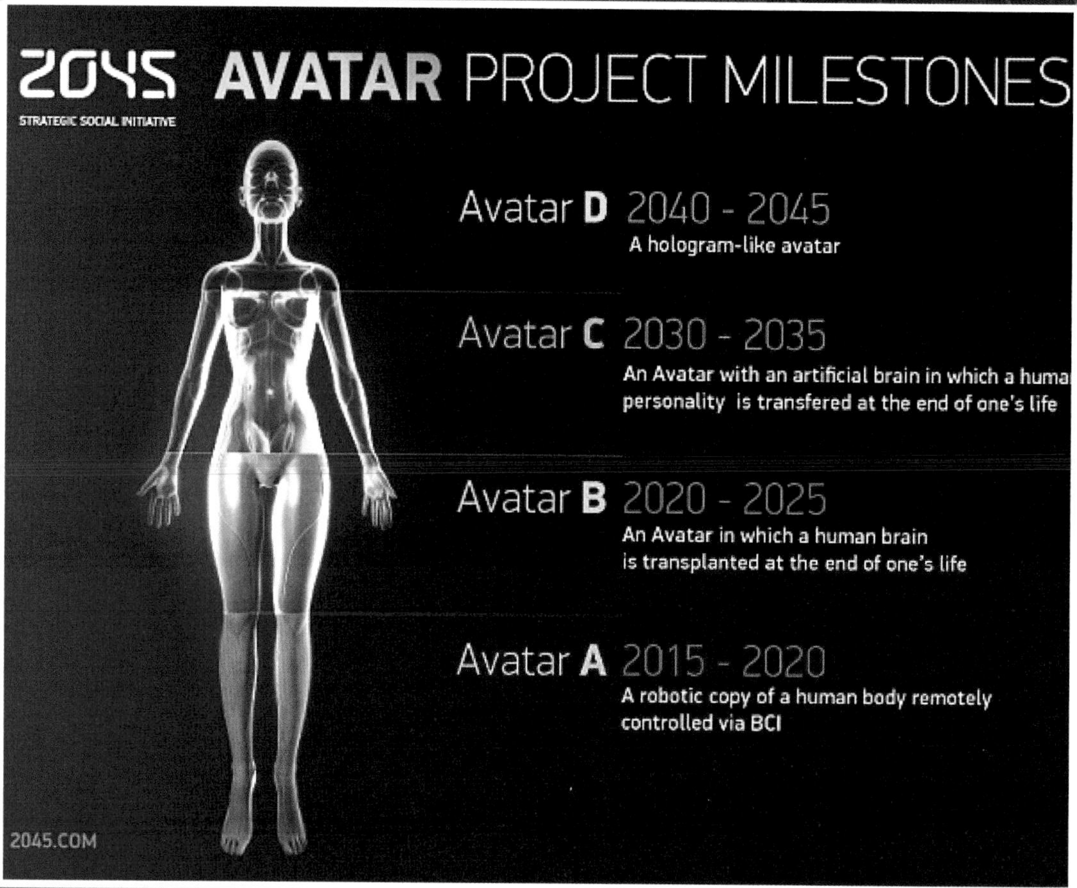

2045 AVATAR PROJECT MILESTONES
STRATEGIC SOCIAL INITIATIVE

Avatar D 2040 - 2045
A hologram-like avatar

Avatar C 2030 - 2035
An Avatar with an artificial brain in which a human personality is transfered at the end of one's life

Avatar B 2020 - 2025
An Avatar in which a human brain is transplanted at the end of one's life

Avatar A 2015 - 2020
A robotic copy of a human body remotely controlled via BCI

2045.COM

The idea, and it's not new, is that our "consciousness" is merely data and can be copied. So let's say you copy all of the neural information in your head and then download it to a robotic device that allowed you mobility. Is that you? Or if you remove the brain and connect it to a robotic device that outlives the remainder of your body, is that you? *Futurama* anyone? And by the way, people make fun of his Russian guy, but our own government is investing into this research as well

CONSCIOUSNESS

Let's look at what consciousness is. The Merriam-Webster dictionary definition is:

1a: the quality or state of being aware especially of something within oneself

1b: the state or fact of being conscious of an external object, state, or fact

1c: awareness; especially: concern for some social or political cause

2: the state of being characterized by sensation, emotion, volition, and thought: mind

3: the totality of conscious states of an individual

4: the normal state of conscious life <regained consciousness>

5: the upper level of mental life of which the person is aware as contrasted with unconscious processes

I think the easiest way to understand consciousness is that "we exist" and "know that we are individuals," and we know what it's like to see through the lens of our own eyes and reflect on and interact with the world. Is this replicable? There are some who don't feel that there is a free will of any kind - that our actions are simply predetermined responses to stimuli. Want to have some fun? Google "free will is a myth" and add "science," "religious," and "psychological" to the search and you'll get vastly different links and contradictory information. The internet search engines customize information based on what they think you want to see. You have to trick it to reach new ground. Try adding different words to things.

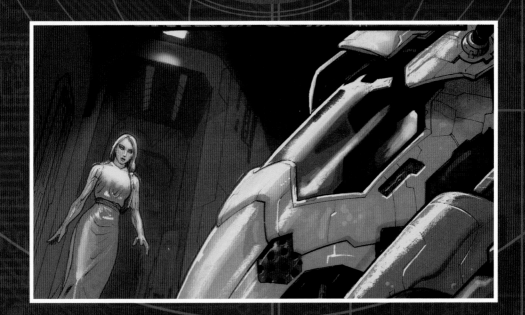

MEMORY

What is a memory? Dictionary definition: " The power or process of remembering what has been learned." Science looks at it a little differently. Here's the technical:

http://www.sciencemag.org/content/346/6211/1256272.abstract

And here's the layman friendly:

http://science.howstuffworks.com/life/inside-the-mind/human-brain/human-memory1.htm

They also explain why memories are often not correct and about how your brain will lie to you to make you happier. It also explains how memories are recorded, similarly to how we record information on a chip. "Cloud computing" is still stored somewhere in hard form; you just have access to it from the internet.

Based on how memories are stored and its similarities to computer "memory," it does make sense that we could store our actual memories in a digital format... and we are, in a way already, with social media. More photos have been posted in the last five years on Facebook than were ever taken in the 20th century. That's staggering, but I digress to Big Data, which I don't want to...yet. So yes, you could store actual memories on a data chip just like in your brain.

http://www.livescience.com/43713-memory.html
http://www.human-memory.net/

So what do you do if you want to live forever, but the technology doesn't exist yet? Cryonics is a way of freezing the brain and body immediately after death in the hopes that someone can revive them with future technology or have their brains inserted into a robotic carrier of some sort. I've often wondered if people in the future would bother with this. Why would they want to revive backwards people with possibly already eradicated health issues? Viruses evolve and our resistance to current versions might not necessarily include resistance to earlier versions of it. Meaning, if we got the small pox blankets the Native Americans were given, it might wreak havoc regardless of current resistances. In case you think this is all nuts, there are a lot of rich people paying a lot of money to try these things. Why not, eh? Reminds me of the people who convert to Christianity right before they die, because why not? I've always thought that if there was a God, that entity would see through that shit.

http://www.cryonics.org/
http://www.cryonicssociety.org/aboutcryonics_providers.html

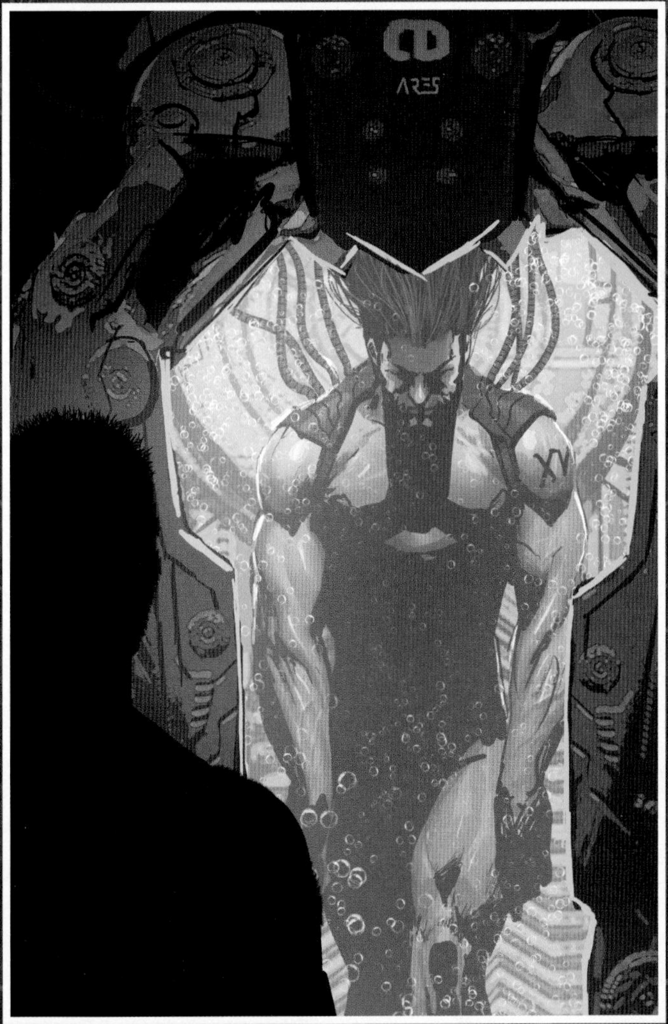
ARES

DEVELOPING A PROJECT IN THE HOPE TECHNOLOGY CATCHES UP

This has been a central theme of the Aphrodite Protocol. When the Chairwoman Francesca Taylor commenced this in the late twentieth century, she knew the technology to pull it off wasn't there yet. Forging ahead anyway is a bold move and was how the Apollo Project landed us on the moon, or how the Manhattan Project ended WWII and ushered in a new era of fun stuff for the world. I am sometimes saddened that it seems we (the U.S.) don't have this resolve anymore.

This is more common than you think, and modern examples of it are: self-driving cars, real artificial intelligence, full neural computer connections, self-administered full medical evaluations, the list goes on and on.

DISRUPTIVE TECHNOLOGIES

"A disruptive innovation is an innovation that helps create a new market and value network, and eventually disrupts an existing market and value network (over a few years or decades), displacing an earlier technology."

http://www.mckinsey.com/insights/business_technology/disruptive_technologies

Examples of disruptive technology include the internet, cell phones, cars, railroads, airplanes, etc. I mention this because there are people who actively fight against technological advancement, and these people drive me insane. They do it solely to squeeze every possible dollar out of an old market technology. Why are we still using internal combustion engines (current model still based on a patent from 1886) and nuclear weapons (seventy-one years old)? There are better versions of both.

If anything, I hope that reading *Aphrodite IX* and the *IXth Generation* series will open your eyes to the possibilities that are out there…and not just on TV. The future is here for us to do with it what we will. I'll admit, I want to be immortal, maybe some of you can join me! =P

we be able to
oad our minds into
igital format that
interact with living
ngs and potentially
downloaded into
one body after we
?

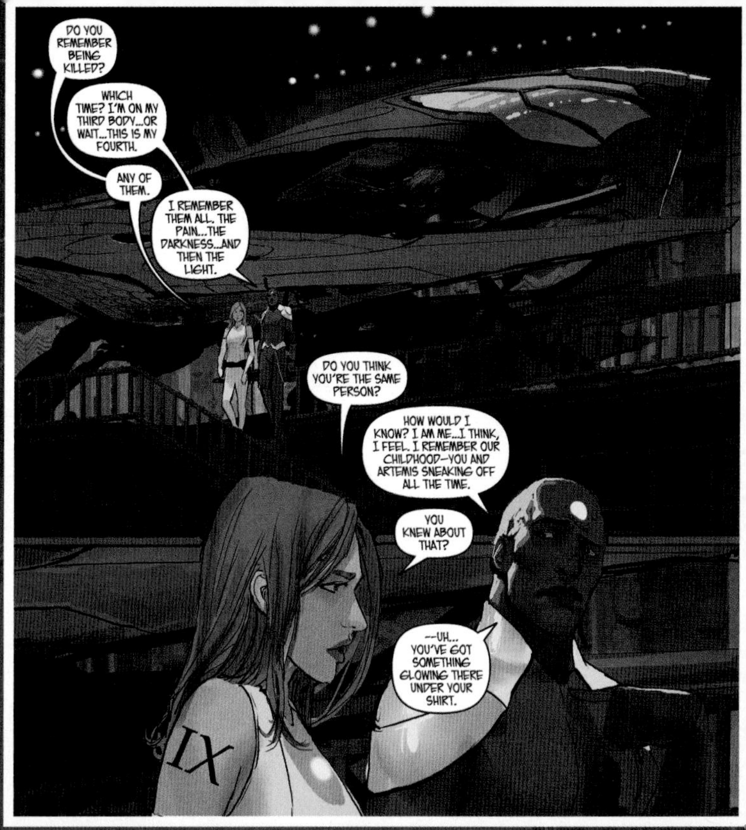
DO YOU REMEMBER BEING KILLED?
WHICH TIME? I'M ON MY THIRD BODY...OR WAIT...THIS IS MY FOURTH.
ANY OF THEM.
I REMEMBER THEM ALL. THE PAIN...THE DARKNESS...AND THEN THE LIGHT.
DO YOU THINK YOU'RE THE SAME PERSON?
HOW WOULD I KNOW? I AM ME...I THINK, I FEEL. I REMEMBER OUR CHILDHOOD--YOU AND ARTEMIS SNEAKING OFF ALL THE TIME.
YOU KNEW ABOUT THAT?
--UH... YOU'VE GOT SOMETHING GLOWING THERE UNDER YOUR SHIRT.
IX

answer to this
es, who knows
ctly when, but it
happen. The better
stion is, will that
ually be you? I say
o that. I've gotten
many arguments on
, but a "clone" is a
y. You'd be copying
r mind and, by
nition, a "copy" is
the original. Word
isn't probably
ough to solve that
osophical question
ugh, but let's think
ut it for a second.
at really makes
who you are? It's
r consciousness or
ul" if you want. Can that be copied?

entists have already transplanted brains from one organism to another
success, and this seems to be a viable means of transferring your
sciousness. Uploading it to a digital format or program would create a new
ng of sorts. It would have your memories, perhaps your morality, and capture
st of your personality, quirks and all. So, if a family member interacted with a
tal version of you after you died, they'd probably think it was you. I posit that
would be illusory though.

n not a religious man, but I believe that there is a spark of life. There is
nething distinctly separating a living organism from a non-living one, and I'm
talking metabolic processes or biology.

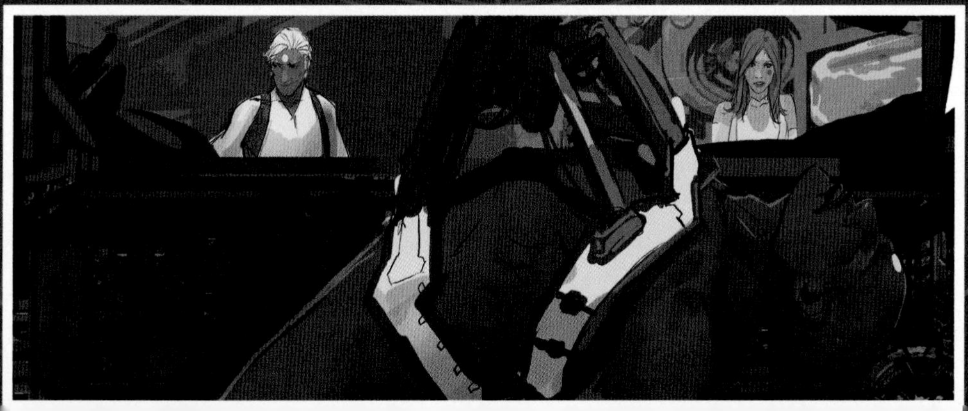

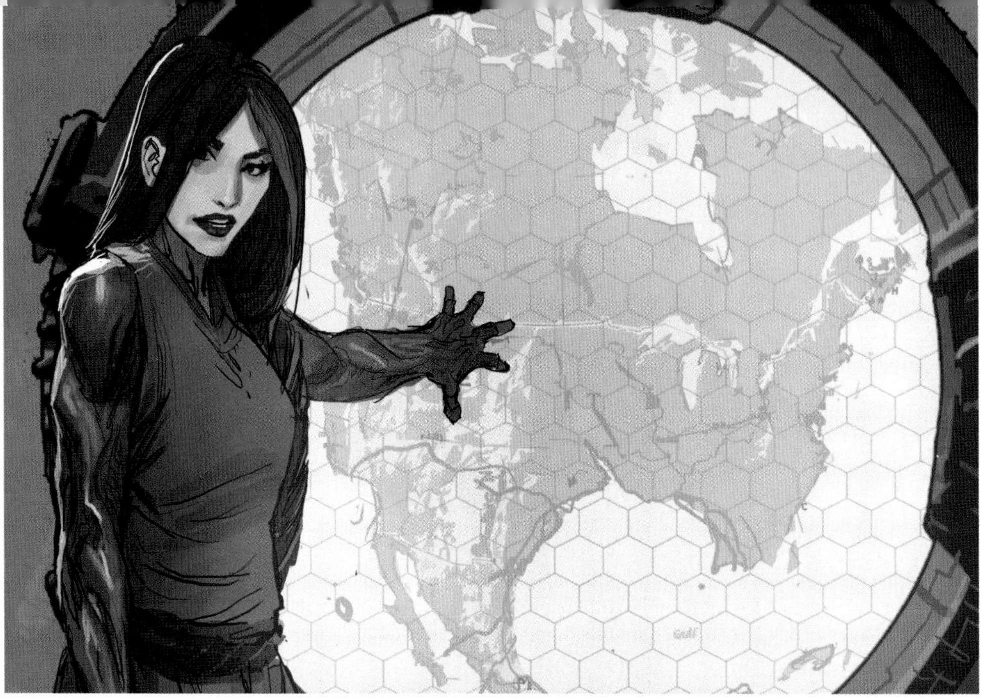

would not having to worry about dying affect your behavior?

stantially one would think. Realistically, these scientific advances will only be able to extremely wealthy people for the most part. Some of it will trickle down est of us, but they will keep it to themselves for the most part. They'll have to. I d upset the economic disparity if poor people started living for centuries. It wou o easy to accumulate wealth (think compound interest of a small amount over dred years). I also believe that longevity will discourage scientific advancement one thing I love about science is that every new generation of scientists proves wrong about something. If the same "geniuses" stayed in control of research fo uries, this would be stymied. People get set in their ways. Imagine extrapolatin across a thousand years. It boggles the mind.

by watching this Youtube video by physicist and notable author Dr. Michio Kak

://www.youtube.com/watch?v=ckwGUai_Vvk

that, go read these links. If you get bored skip to the next one:

//www.gizmag.com/avatar-project-2045/23454/

//motherboard.vice.com/blog/scientists-are-convinced-mind-transfer-is-the-key- ortality

//www.popsci.com/technology/article/2012-03/achieving-immortality-russian-mo s-begin-putting-human-brains-robots-and-soon

//www.gizmag.com/avatar-project-2045/23454/

//www.livescience.com/37499-immortality-by-2045-conference.html

ll that and we'll talk online or here in upcoming volumes

When I first started *Aphrodite IX* two years ago I was hoping to get in a single new volume to go along with the original Finch/Wohl one from the '90s. Now fifteen issues into this future, and another eight already planned, it has really opened up...and that doesn't include the *Cyber Force* issues! It's opened up so much that I can give you all reading this a brief heads up that next year's Talent Hunt will be all about *Aphrodite IX* and *IXth Generation*, so let that percolate for some story ideas.

ARTIFACTS AS TECHNOLOGY

"Any sufficiently advanced technology is indistinguishable from magic." -Arthur C. Clarke.

I kicked off issue three with this quote and it's this quote that got me thinking about the artifacts when I was doing the Aphrodite IX run. I always intended to include the Coin of Solomon but as I thought about it, I could use them all…and will! I don't want to give too much away, but think about the quote for a minute…and then think about the Artifacts. Fun stuff!

JAPANESE WITCHBLADE

You might note that the Witchblade in the flaschbacks is Japanese. This is intended as a nod to the anime, although it's not the same character. If you've never checked it out, you should watch it. Gonzo and Funimation did a great job and I'm proud to have produced that show.

WITCHBLADE
FUNIMATION

That's all for *Science Class*!
Send me your thoughts or questions on my social media (I don't mind long posts on my Facebook wall. I read them all, I don't read the IMs there though, so post it to the wall).

Carpe Diem,

Matt Hawkins

http://www.facebook.com/selfloathingnarcissist | @topcowmatt

When Russ Dobler wrote the following article, I asked him if I could run it. I'm not always right and appreciate it when people correct me. I do update scripts for trades, reprints, etc. Authenticity and accuracy are important to me!

-Matt Hawkins

REALITY CHECK: THE SCIENCE OF IXTH GENERATION: HIDDEN FILES

Physicist and Top Cow Productions president, Matt Hawkins, wants you to take seriously the cyborg science of his property mash-up series, IXth Generation. So much so that last week he published IXth Generation: Hidden Files #1, an issue that devotes about half its real estate to describing the various locales of this particular vision of the future – one where ruling elites govern realms of mechanical citizens – and the rest to an analysis of the science that makes it possible. But does he have an artificial limb to stand on?

Normally I'd say, "Who cares? It's fiction; it's fun." As I pointed out in AiPT's very first Reality Check column, despite being a big-time science guy, I don't usually feel the need to reconcile real science with science fiction. I'm willing to overlook a dubious premise if it makes for a neat story. Fantasy isn't reality.

But since Hawkins went to the deliberate trouble of trying to bridge that gap, I feel like we have to look at the ideas a little more critically. In this case I say, "In for a penny, in for pound"!

LET'S GET THIS OUT OF THE WAY

IXth Generation hinges on humanity achieving immortality, or at least a greatly increased lifespan. Hawkins pays lip service to cryonics – the freezing of the body and/or brain to be (one hopes!) reanimated at a later date – but dismisses it somewhat curtly. I'll skip it as well, as I've already outlined a lot of the problems with that idea.

Let's also gloss over the moral and philosophical implications of human immortality. I mean, resources aren't infinite. We already have an overpopulation problem. And social revolution doesn't usually happen until the fogeys die off, so we might be stuck with intractable racism. Ya know, more than we already are.

Before we finally get to feasibility, we should briefly touch on practicality. Even if creating real-life cyborgs is *possible*, when push comes to shove, would we actually do it? Hawkins cites the Moon landing as an example of technology playing catch-up to planning, but Apollo might function as a very different parable.

As Chris Edwards points out in his book *Spiritual Snake Oil*, we got to the Moon really quickly, but haven't done jack all that's new in the 46 years since then. Aviation kind of peaked at that level of complexity, and instead of taking day trips to the Sea of Tranquility, as plenty of people once predicted, we all settled into simple jet flights instead.

"Exponential growth can slow, stop or recede very quickly if the energy cost is too much," Edwards says in the book.

According to the technology research group Gartner, these things tend to follow a pretty identifiable "hype cycle." People get really excited about an emerging technology, thinking it will solve all the world's problems. Then we realize how hard it is to work with, at which point people go the other way and think the whole thing is worthless. It's not until years later that we start to figure out the real uses, and a more realistic "plateau of productivity" is reached.

Take a look on the figure at where "Hybrid Cloud Computing" will likely be in two to five years. Makes sense for it to be on the pessimistic downslope, as some of the bloom is already coming off that rose. Gartner places "Human Augmentation" squarely on the upslope, where it will likely reside for more than 10 years. As critics like to say, our merger with robotics is only a decade away, and it always will be.

expectations
Internet of Things
Natural-Language Question Answering
Wearable User Interfaces
Consumer 3D Printing
Cryptocurrencies
Complex-Event Processing
Big Data
In-Memory Database Management Systems
Content Analytics
Hybrid Cloud Computing
Gamification
Augmented Reality
Machine-to-Machine Communication Services
Mobile Health Monitoring
Cloud Computing
NFC
Virtual Reality
In-Memory Analytics
Gesture Control
Activity Streams
Enterprise 3D Printing
3D Scanners
Consumer Telematics
Speech Recognition
Speech-to-Speech Translation
Autonomous Vehicles
Smart Advisors
Data Science
Prescriptive Analytics
Neurobusiness
Biochips
Affective Computing
Smart Robots
3D Bioprinting Systems
Volumetric and Holographic Displays
Software-Defined Anything
Quantum Computing
Human Augmentation
Brain-Computer Interface
Quantified Self
Connected Home
Virtual Personal Assistants
Digital Security
Bioacoustic Sensing
Smart Workspace
As of July 2014
Innovation Trigger
Peak of Inflated Expectations
Trough of Disillusionment
Slope of Enlightenment
Plateau of Productivity
time
Plateau will be reached in:
less than 2 years
2 to 5 years
5 to 10 years
more than 10 years
obsolete before plateau

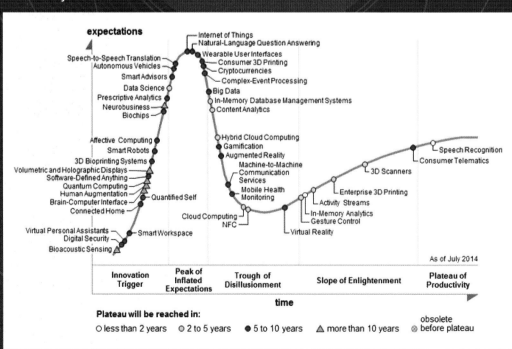

PUT YOUR BRAIN IN A ROBOT BODY

That's if it can work at all. Hawkins bases his future cyberfolks on the Avatar Project of media mogul Dmitry Itskov. Itskov believes he'll be able to download human consciousness into an artificial brain within 15 years, although he seems to have no clue how to do it. But hey, space race technology was up to the challenge, right? So why not?

Like getting your grandmother to not clutch her purse when a black man walks by, some problems may just be intractable. You can't travel through space faster than the speed of light. You can't forecast the weather more than two weeks in advance. And it's really hard to reproduce something as complex as the human brain.

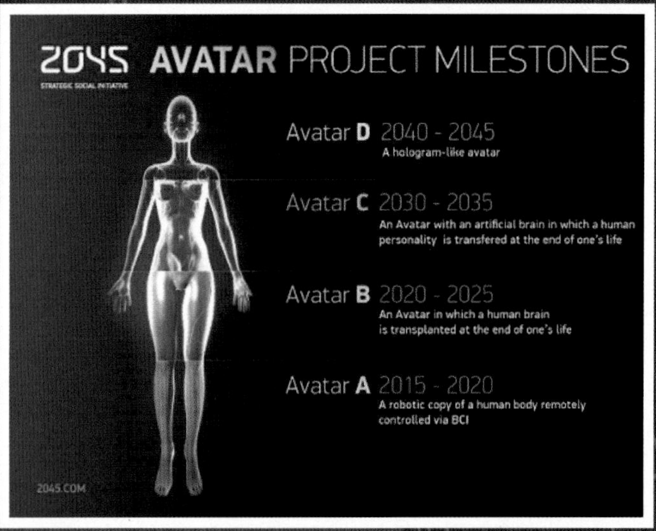
2045 AVATAR PROJECT MILESTONES
STRATEGIC SOCIAL INITIATIVE
Avatar D 2040 - 2045
A hologram-like avatar
Avatar C 2030 - 2035
An Avatar with an artificial brain in which a human personality is transfered at the end of one's life
Avatar B 2020 - 2025
An Avatar in which a human brain is transplanted at the end of one's life
Avatar A 2015 - 2020
A robotic copy of a human body remotely controlled via BCI
2045.COM

"What exactly is our basis for calculating the processing – I mean, I don't even know what the processing power of a neuron is," says former *Scientific American* editor-in-chief, John Rennie. "We only have to be a little bit wrong about some of the neuroscience, and all those calculations fly out the window."

Unfortunately, Hawkins is more than a little bit wrong when he says that "memories are recorded similarly to how we record information on a [computer] chip." Despite a recent, widely misinterpreted study that likens the nervous system of a human being to that of a sea slug, it's pretty well agreed that information isn't stored within a neuron itself, but in the synapses – that is, the gaps – BETWEEN neurons. That's an important distinction, as then you're trying to model not just a simple structure, but a sea of ever-changing chemicals and electric potentials.

That's why neuroscientist Daniel Korostyshevsky doesn't think you'll ever truly be able to put "you" into something else.

"I doubt it for the simple reason that we would have to understand the microenvironment of every synapse," he says. To really recreate a person, the "programmer" would have to know – at every one of the frontal lobe's trillions of synapses – how quickly neurotransmitters move through the gap, which ones are present, how much each uploads and releases, etc., etc.

"All that affects our behavior, our moods," Korostyshevsky says. "We would need to understand that in networks, we would need to understand that on an individual synapse level.

"At this point, there's no technology I can conceive of that could give us this knowledge," he says.

CYBER CRIME

One of the good things about models, though, is that they don't have to operate exactly like the thing they're modeling. If the human brain turns out to be modular, and not a general purpose tool with all functionality spread out over the whole thing, it would be able easier to simulate, limiting the amount of processing power needed.

But then, as Hawkins is right to ask, is that really "you"? Rennie imagines a greedy, A.I. pod person trying to convince its creator of just what it is.

"I'm conscious. I'm John Rennie. That's me in a box. Give me all those assets."

Talk about identity theft.

-Russ Dobler

CREATOR BIOGRAPHIES

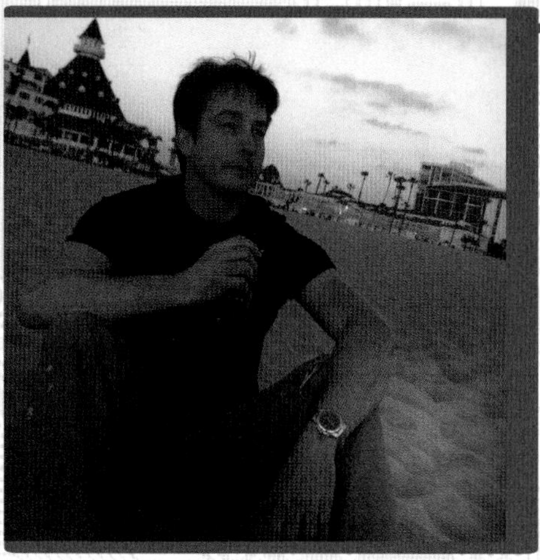

MATT HAWKINS

A veteran of the initial Image Comics launch, Matt started his career in comic book publishing in 1993 and has been working with Image as a creator, writer, and executive for over twenty years. President/COO of Top Cow since 1998, Matt has created and written over thirty new franchises for Top Cow and Image including *Think Tank*, *Necromancer*, *VICE*, *Lady Pendragon*, *Aphrodite IX* as well as handling the company's business affairs.

STJEPAN SEJIC

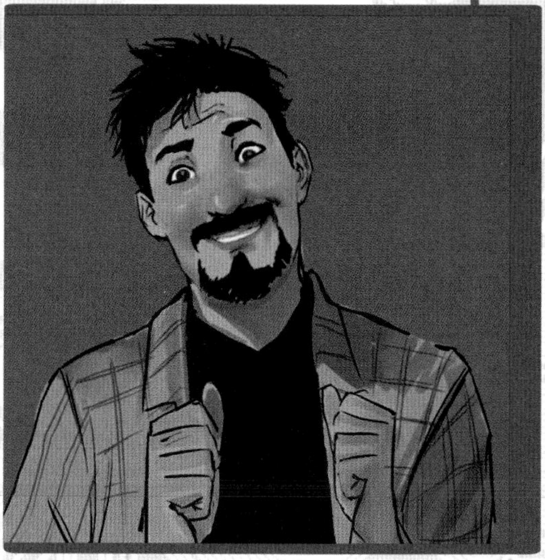

Stjepan Sejic is the "Croatian Sensation" who has worked on almost all Top Cow's major Universe titles since joining the company as one of their star artists. In addition to the longest run a single artist has ever completed on *Witchblade*, Stjepan has several of his own comic series in development both through Top Cow and online through his Deviant Art page. *Ravine*, *Death Vigil*, and *Sunstone* name a few with others in the works.

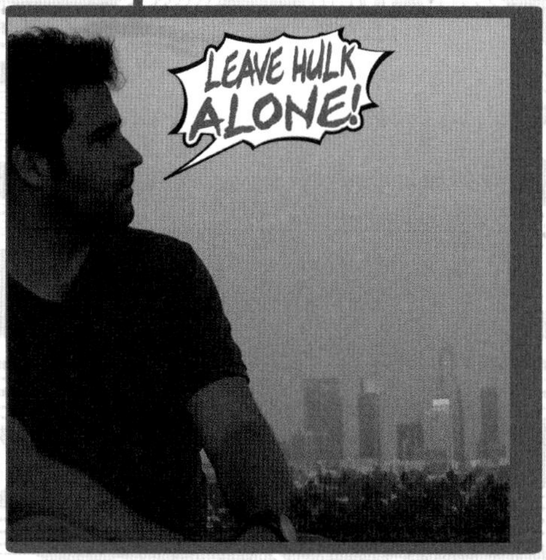
LEAVE HULK ALONE!

TROY PETERI

Starting his career at Comicraft, Troy Peteri lettered titles such as *Iron Man*, *Wolverine*, and *Amazing Spider-Man*, among many others. His career hit a bump in the road known as CrossGen Comics, but that's neither here nor there. Thankfully, he met a number of great creators there, which led to him lettering roughly 97% of all Top Cow titles since 2005.

In addition to Top Cow, he currently letters comics from multiple publishers and websites, such as Image Comics, Dynamite, and Archaia. He (along with co-creator Dave Lanphear) is currently writing (and lettering) *77 Hero Plaza*, a webcomic of his own creation for www.Thrillbent.com. (Once again, www.Thrillbent.com.) He's still bitter about no longer lettering *The Darkness* and wants it back on stands immediately.

ISSUE #1 PREVIEW

STJEPAN SEJIC

creator

STJEPAN SEJIC

story & art

Published by Image Comics, Inc. Office of Publication. 2001 Center Street, Sixth Floor, Berkeley, CA 94704. Death Vigil™ 2015 Stjepan Sejic. All rights reserved. "Death Vigil," the Death Vigil logos, and the likenesses of all featured characters herein are registered trademarks of Stjepan Sejic. Any resemblance to actual persons (living or dead), event, institutions, or locales, without satiric intent is coincidental. No portion of this publication may be reproduced or transmitted, in any form or by any means, without the express written permission of Stjepan Sejic.

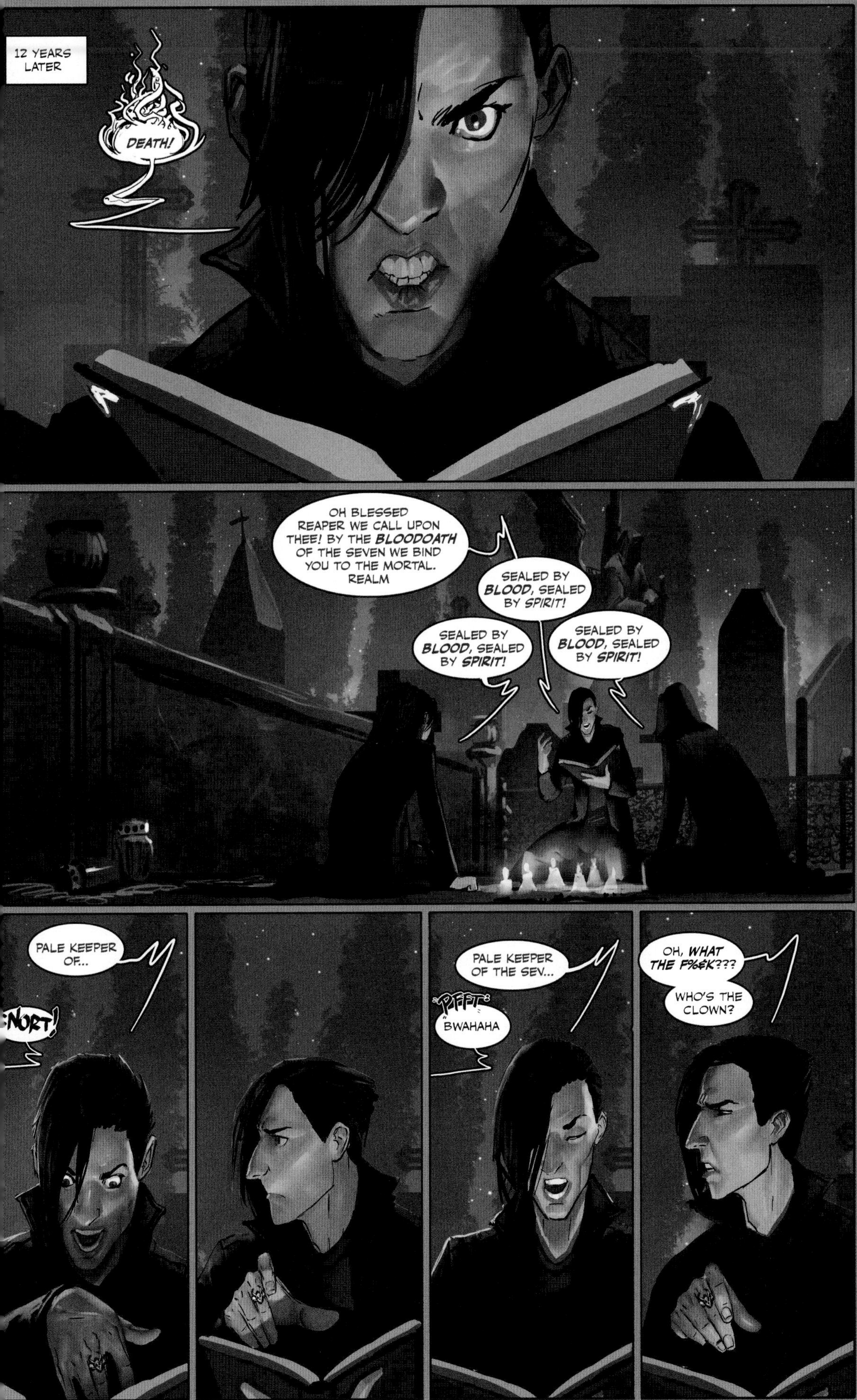
12 YEARS LATER
DEATH!
OH BLESSED REAPER WE CALL UPON THEE! BY THE BLOODOATH OF THE SEVEN WE BIND YOU TO THE MORTAL. REALM
SEALED BY BLOOD, SEALED BY SPIRIT!
SEALED BY BLOOD, SEALED BY SPIRIT!
SEALED BY BLOOD, SEALED BY SPIRIT!
PALE KEEPER OF...
NORT!
PALE KEEPER OF THE SEV...
PFFT
BWAHAHA
OH, WHAT THE F%&K???
WHO'S THE CLOWN?

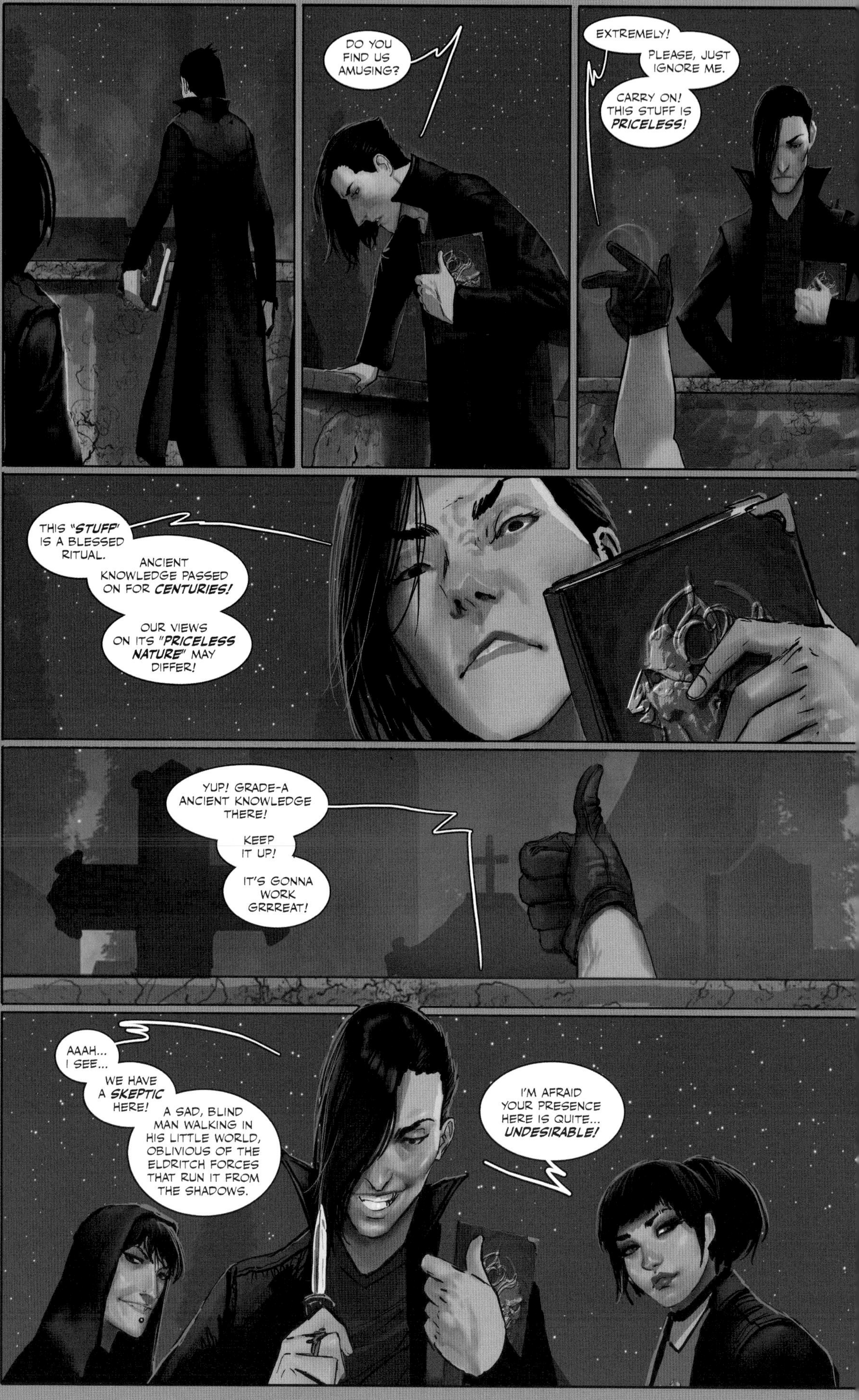
DO YOU FIND US AMUSING?
EXTREMELY!
PLEASE, JUST IGNORE ME.
CARRY ON! THIS STUFF IS PRICELESS!
THIS "STUFF" IS A BLESSED RITUAL.
ANCIENT KNOWLEDGE PASSED ON FOR CENTURIES!
OUR VIEWS ON ITS "PRICELESS NATURE" MAY DIFFER!
YUP! GRADE-A ANCIENT KNOWLEDGE THERE!
KEEP IT UP!
IT'S GONNA WORK GRRREAT!
AAAH... I SEE...
WE HAVE A SKEPTIC HERE!
A SAD, BLIND MAN WALKING IN HIS LITTLE WORLD, OBLIVIOUS OF THE ELDRITCH FORCES THAT RUN IT FROM THE SHADOWS.
I'M AFRAID YOUR PRESENCE HERE IS QUITE... UNDESIRABLE!

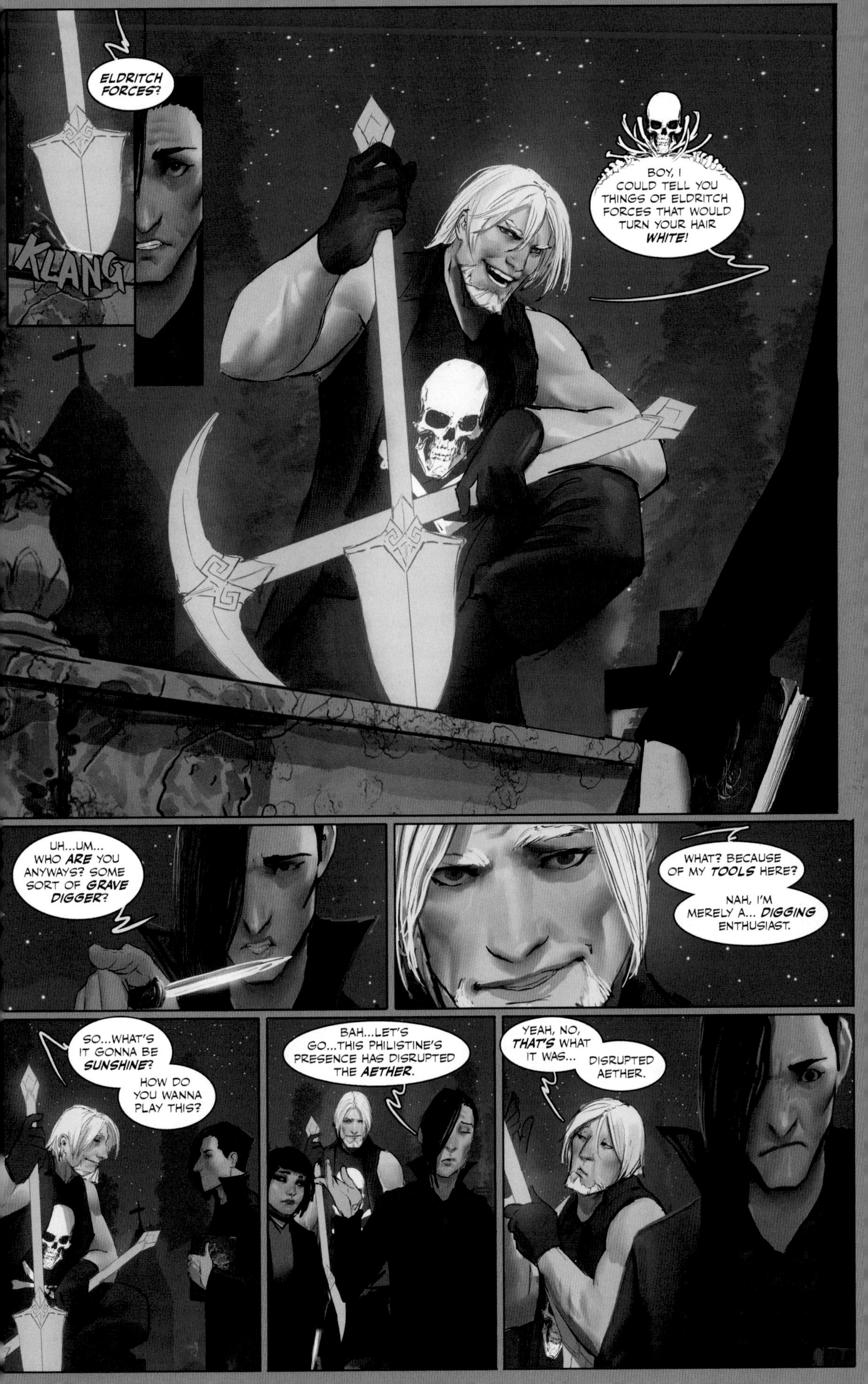
ELDRITCH FORCES?
KLANG
BOY, I COULD TELL YOU THINGS OF ELDRITCH FORCES THAT WOULD TURN YOUR HAIR WHITE!
UH...UM... WHO ARE YOU ANYWAYS? SOME SORT OF GRAVE DIGGER?
WHAT? BECAUSE OF MY TOOLS HERE?
NAH, I'M MERELY A... DIGGING ENTHUSIAST.
SO...WHAT'S IT GONNA BE SUNSHINE?
HOW DO YOU WANNA PLAY THIS?
BAH...LET'S GO...THIS PHILISTINE'S PRESENCE HAS DISRUPTED THE AETHER.
YEAH, NO, THAT'S WHAT IT WAS...
DISRUPTED AETHER.

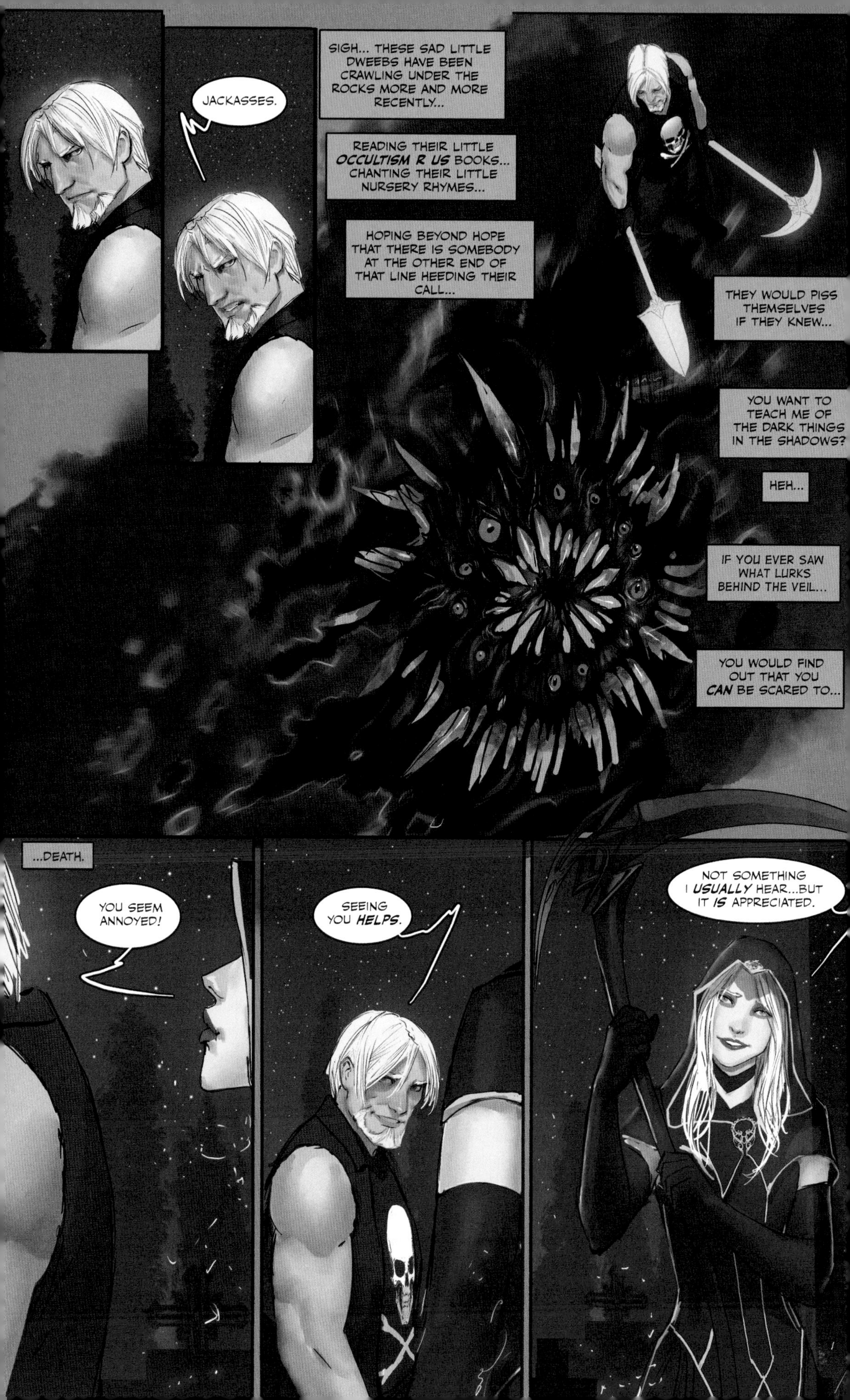
JACKASSES.
SIGH... THESE SAD LITTLE DWEEBS HAVE BEEN CRAWLING UNDER THE ROCKS MORE AND MORE RECENTLY...
READING THEIR LITTLE OCCULTISM R US BOOKS... CHANTING THEIR LITTLE NURSERY RHYMES...
HOPING BEYOND HOPE THAT THERE IS SOMEBODY AT THE OTHER END OF THAT LINE HEEDING THEIR CALL...
THEY WOULD PISS THEMSELVES IF THEY KNEW...
YOU WANT TO TEACH ME OF THE DARK THINGS IN THE SHADOWS?
HEH...
IF YOU EVER SAW WHAT LURKS BEHIND THE VEIL...
YOU WOULD FIND OUT THAT YOU CAN BE SCARED TO...
...DEATH.
YOU SEEM ANNOYED!
SEEING YOU HELPS.
NOT SOMETHING I USUALLY HEAR...BUT IT IS APPRECIATED.

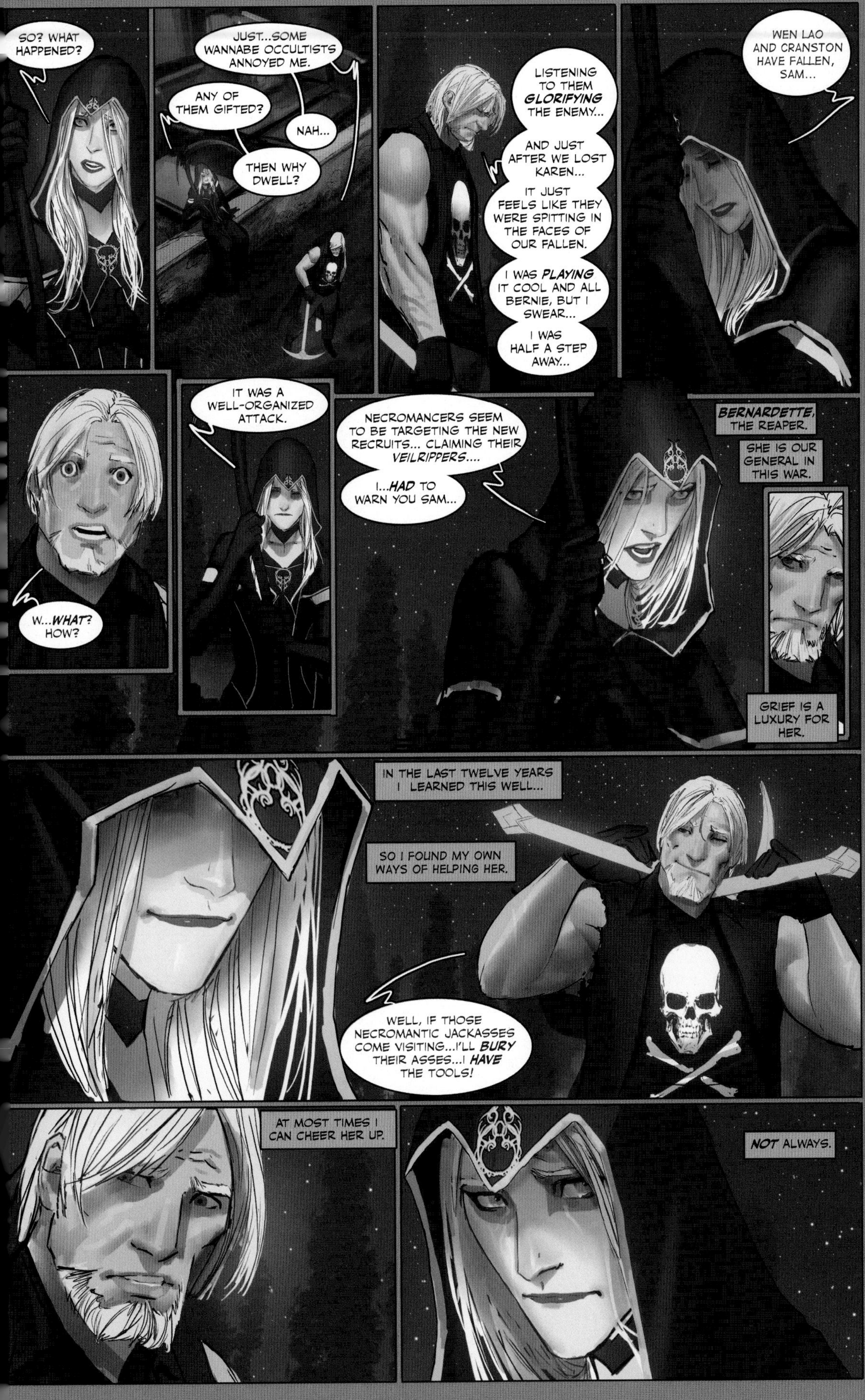
SO? WHAT HAPPENED?
JUST...SOME WANNABE OCCULTISTS ANNOYED ME.
ANY OF THEM GIFTED?
NAH...
THEN WHY DWELL?
LISTENING TO THEM GLORIFYING THE ENEMY...
AND JUST AFTER WE LOST KAREN...
IT JUST FEELS LIKE THEY WERE SPITTING IN THE FACES OF OUR FALLEN.
I WAS PLAYING IT COOL AND ALL BERNIE, BUT I SWEAR...
I WAS HALF A STEP AWAY...
WEN LAO AND CRANSTON HAVE FALLEN, SAM...
W...WHAT? HOW?
IT WAS A WELL-ORGANIZED ATTACK.
NECROMANCERS SEEM TO BE TARGETING THE NEW RECRUITS... CLAIMING THEIR VEILRIPPERS....
I...HAD TO WARN YOU SAM...
BERNARDETTE, THE REAPER.
SHE IS OUR GENERAL IN THIS WAR.
GRIEF IS A LUXURY FOR HER.
IN THE LAST TWELVE YEARS I LEARNED THIS WELL...
SO I FOUND MY OWN WAYS OF HELPING HER.
WELL, IF THOSE NECROMANTIC JACKASSES COME VISITING...I'LL BURY THEIR ASSES...I HAVE THE TOOLS!
AT MOST TIMES I CAN CHEER HER UP.
NOT ALWAYS.

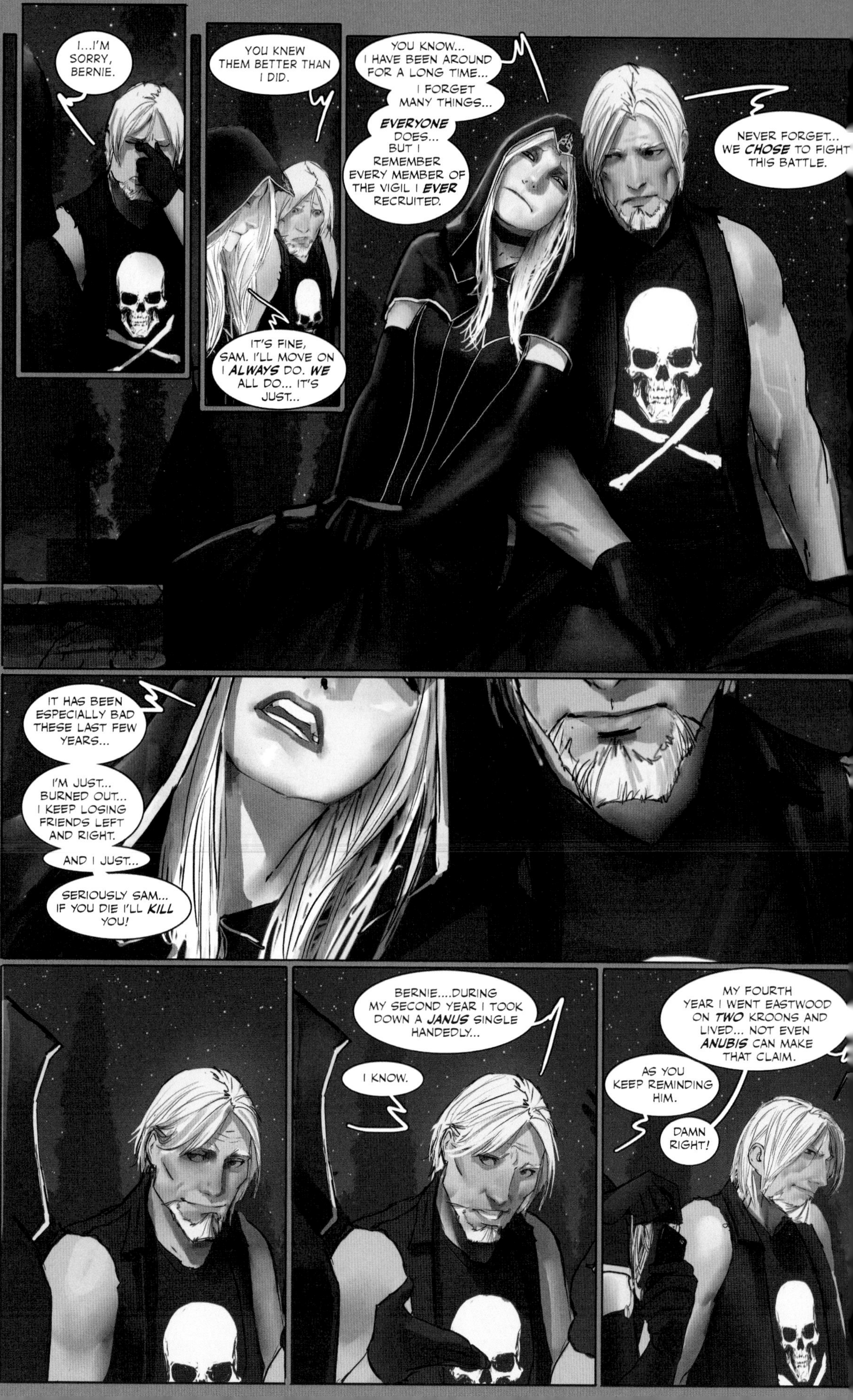
I...I'M SORRY, BERNIE.
YOU KNEW THEM BETTER THAN I DID.
IT'S FINE, SAM. I'LL MOVE ON I ALWAYS DO. WE ALL DO... IT'S JUST...
YOU KNOW... I HAVE BEEN AROUND FOR A LONG TIME...
I FORGET MANY THINGS...
EVERYONE DOES... BUT I REMEMBER EVERY MEMBER OF THE VIGIL I EVER RECRUITED.
NEVER FORGET... WE CHOSE TO FIGHT THIS BATTLE.
IT HAS BEEN ESPECIALLY BAD THESE LAST FEW YEARS...
I'M JUST... BURNED OUT... I KEEP LOSING FRIENDS LEFT AND RIGHT.
AND I JUST...
SERIOUSLY SAM... IF YOU DIE I'LL KILL YOU!
BERNIE....DURING MY SECOND YEAR I TOOK DOWN A JANUS SINGLE HANDEDLY...
I KNOW.
MY FOURTH YEAR I WENT EASTWOOD ON TWO KROONS AND LIVED... NOT EVEN ANUBIS CAN MAKE THAT CLAIM.
AS YOU KEEP REMINDING HIM.
DAMN RIGHT!

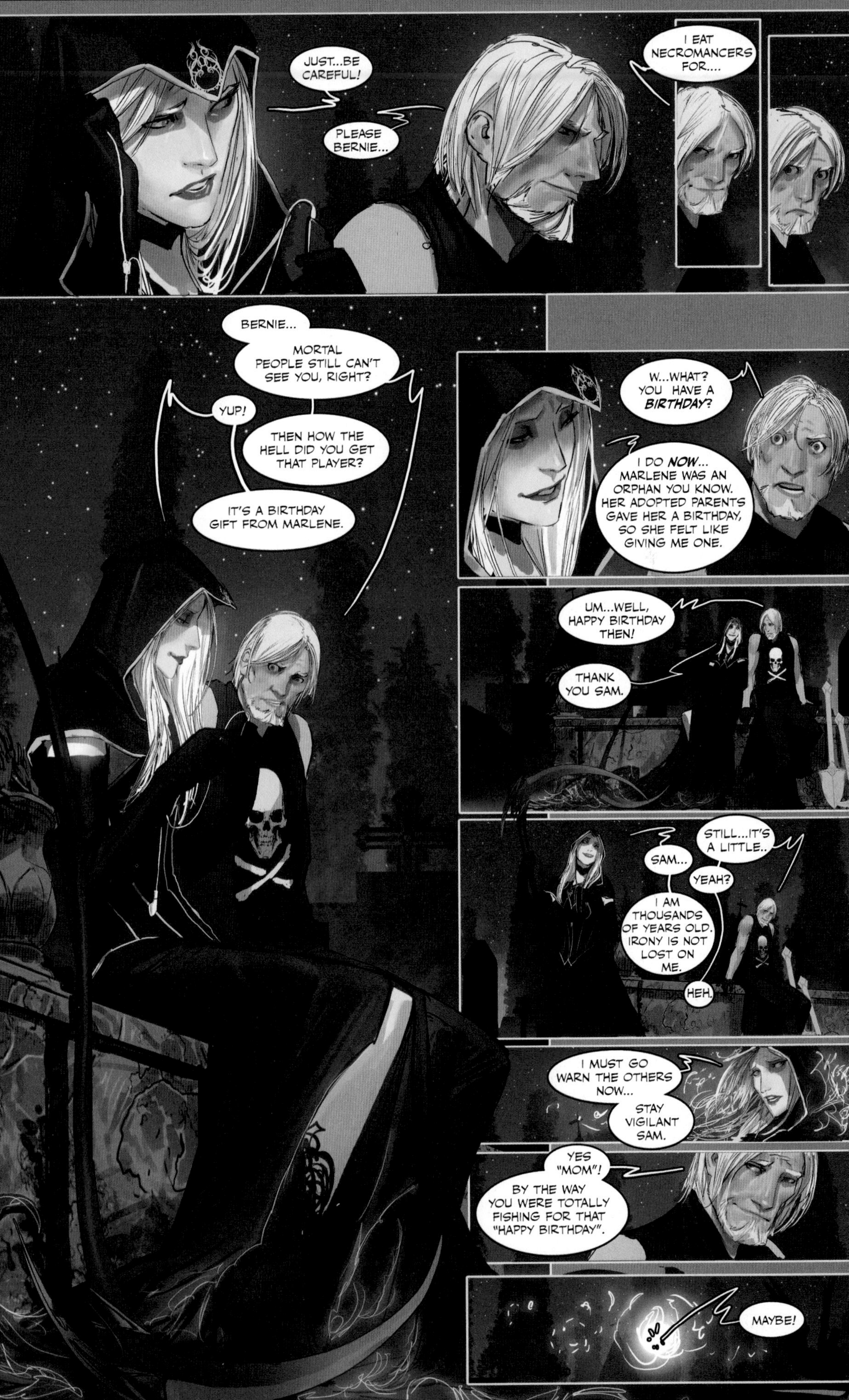
JUST...BE CAREFUL!
PLEASE BERNIE...
I EAT NECROMANCERS FOR....
BERNIE...
MORTAL PEOPLE STILL CAN'T SEE YOU, RIGHT?
YUP!
THEN HOW THE HELL DID YOU GET THAT PLAYER?
IT'S A BIRTHDAY GIFT FROM MARLENE.
W...WHAT? YOU HAVE A BIRTHDAY?
I DO NOW... MARLENE WAS AN ORPHAN YOU KNOW. HER ADOPTED PARENTS GAVE HER A BIRTHDAY, SO SHE FELT LIKE GIVING ME ONE.
UM...WELL, HAPPY BIRTHDAY THEN!
THANK YOU SAM.
STILL...IT'S A LITTLE..
SAM...
YEAH?
I AM THOUSANDS OF YEARS OLD. IRONY IS NOT LOST ON ME.
HEH.
I MUST GO WARN THE OTHERS NOW...
STAY VIGILANT SAM.
YES "MOM"!
BY THE WAY YOU WERE TOTALLY FISHING FOR THAT "HAPPY BIRTHDAY".
MAYBE!

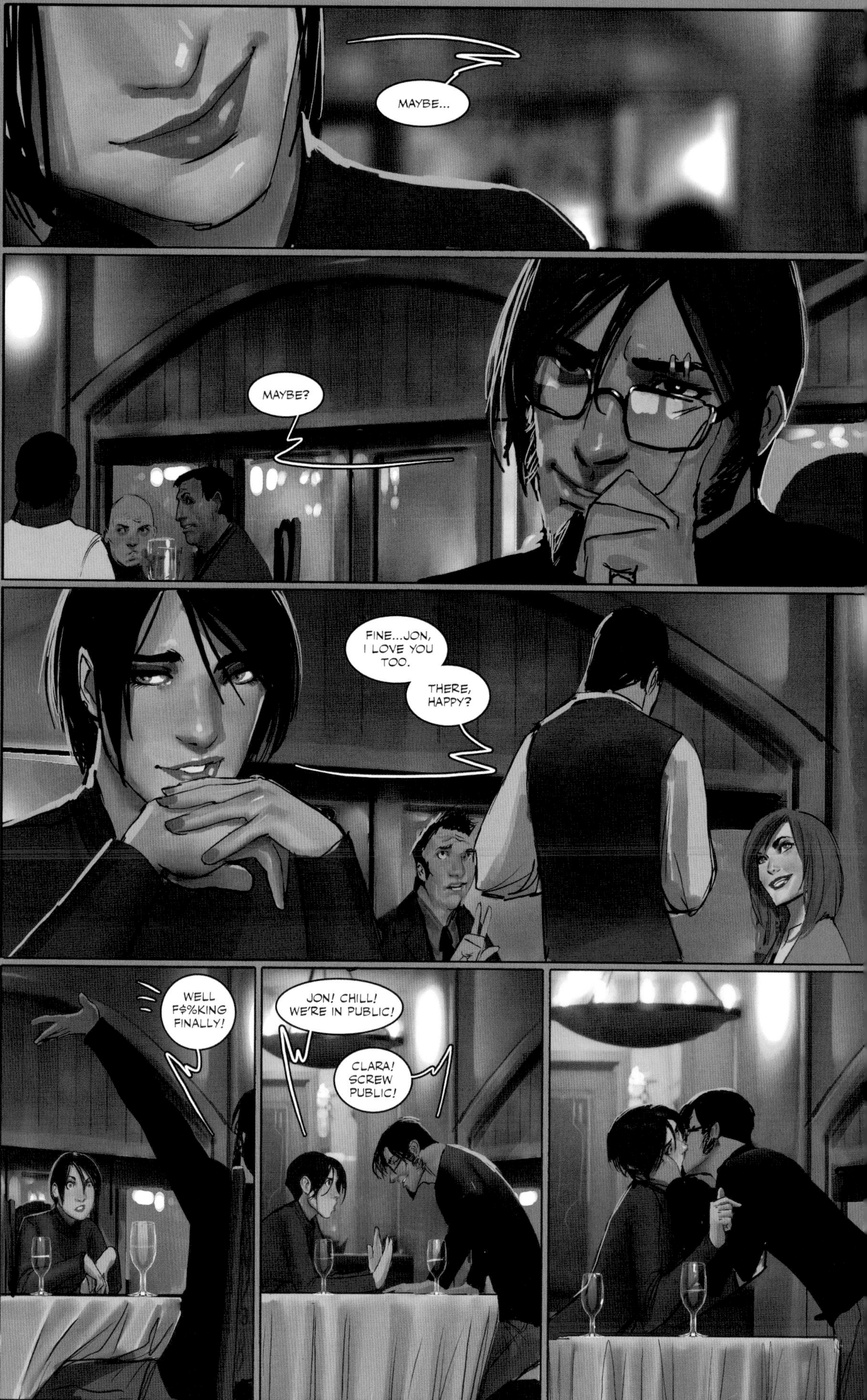
MAYBE...
MAYBE?
FINE...JON, I LOVE YOU TOO.
THERE, HAPPY?
WELL F$%KING FINALLY!
JON! CHILL! WE'RE IN PUBLIC!
CLARA! SCREW PUBLIC!

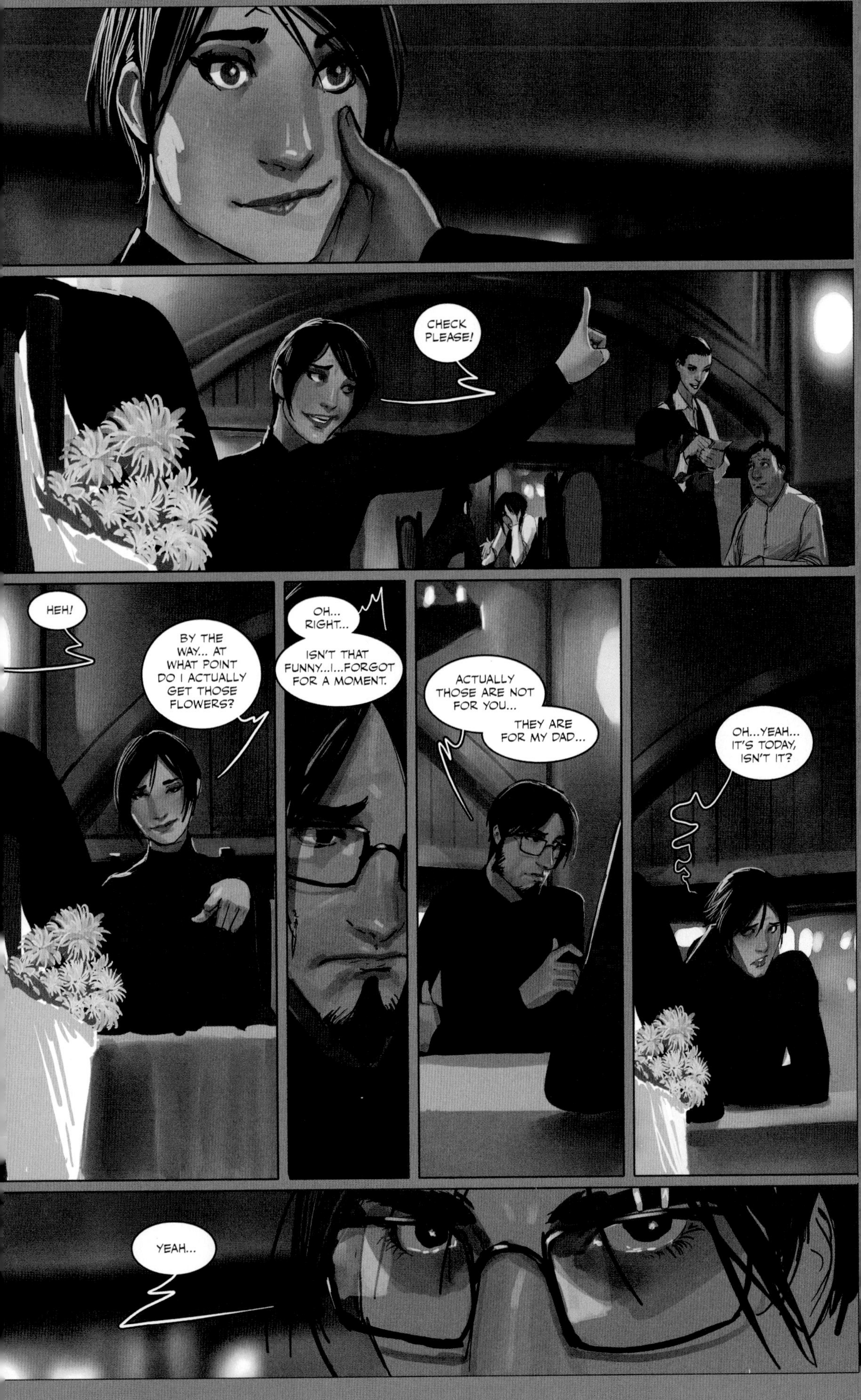

CHECK PLEASE!
HEH!
BY THE WAY... AT WHAT POINT DO I ACTUALLY GET THOSE FLOWERS?
OH... RIGHT...
ISN'T THAT FUNNY...I...FORGOT FOR A MOMENT.
ACTUALLY THOSE ARE NOT FOR YOU...
THEY ARE FOR MY DAD...
OH...YEAH... IT'S TODAY, ISN'T IT?
YEAH...

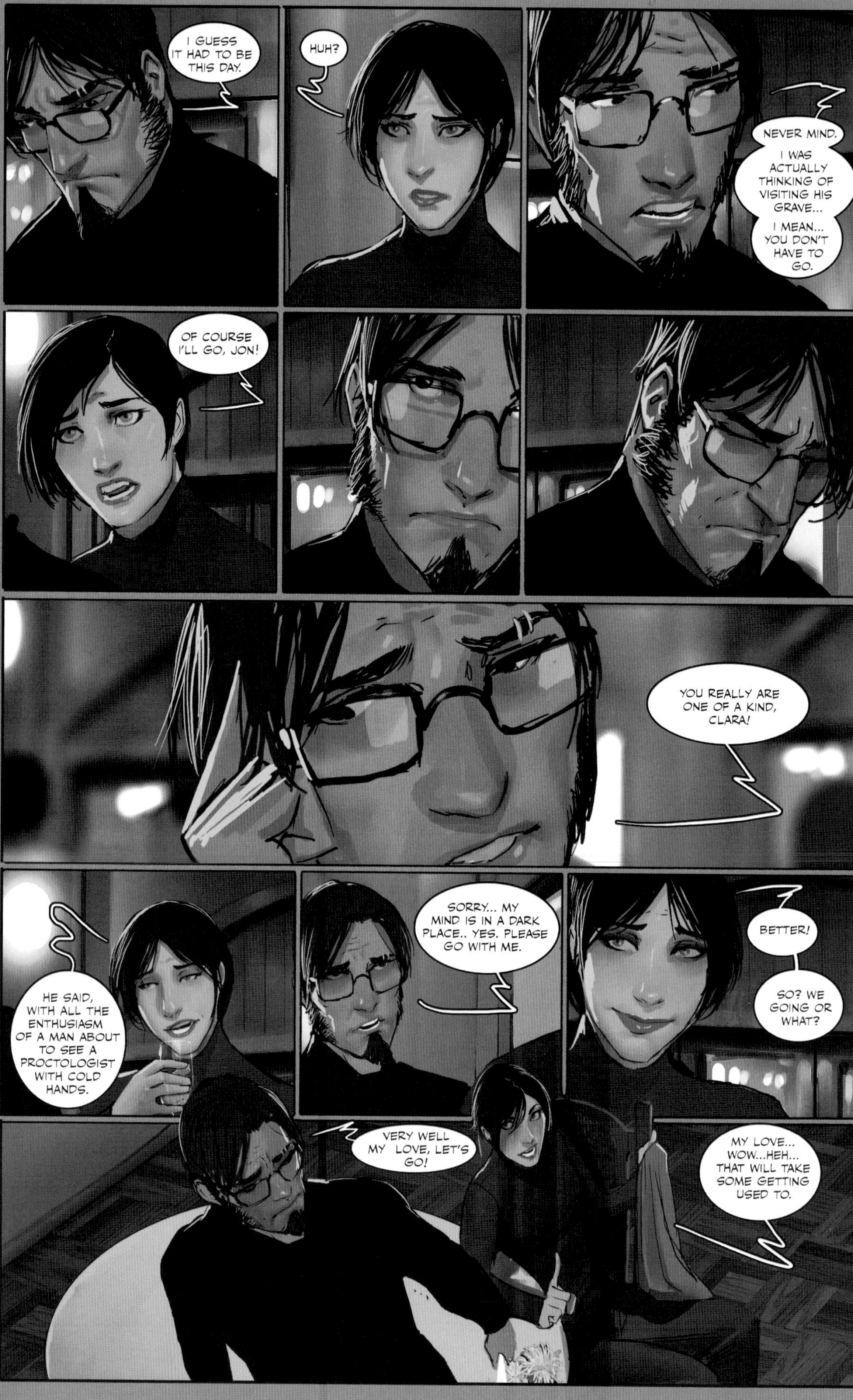
I GUESS IT HAD TO BE THIS DAY.
HUH?
NEVER MIND.
I WAS ACTUALLY THINKING OF VISITING HIS GRAVE...
I MEAN... YOU DON'T HAVE TO GO.
OF COURSE I'LL GO, JON!
YOU REALLY ARE ONE OF A KIND, CLARA!
HE SAID, WITH ALL THE ENTHUSIASM OF A MAN ABOUT TO SEE A PROCTOLOGIST WITH COLD HANDS.
SORRY... MY MIND IS IN A DARK PLACE.. YES. PLEASE GO WITH ME.
BETTER!
SO? WE GOING OR WHAT?
VERY WELL MY LOVE, LET'S GO!
MY LOVE... WOW...HEH... THAT WILL TAKE SOME GETTING USED TO.

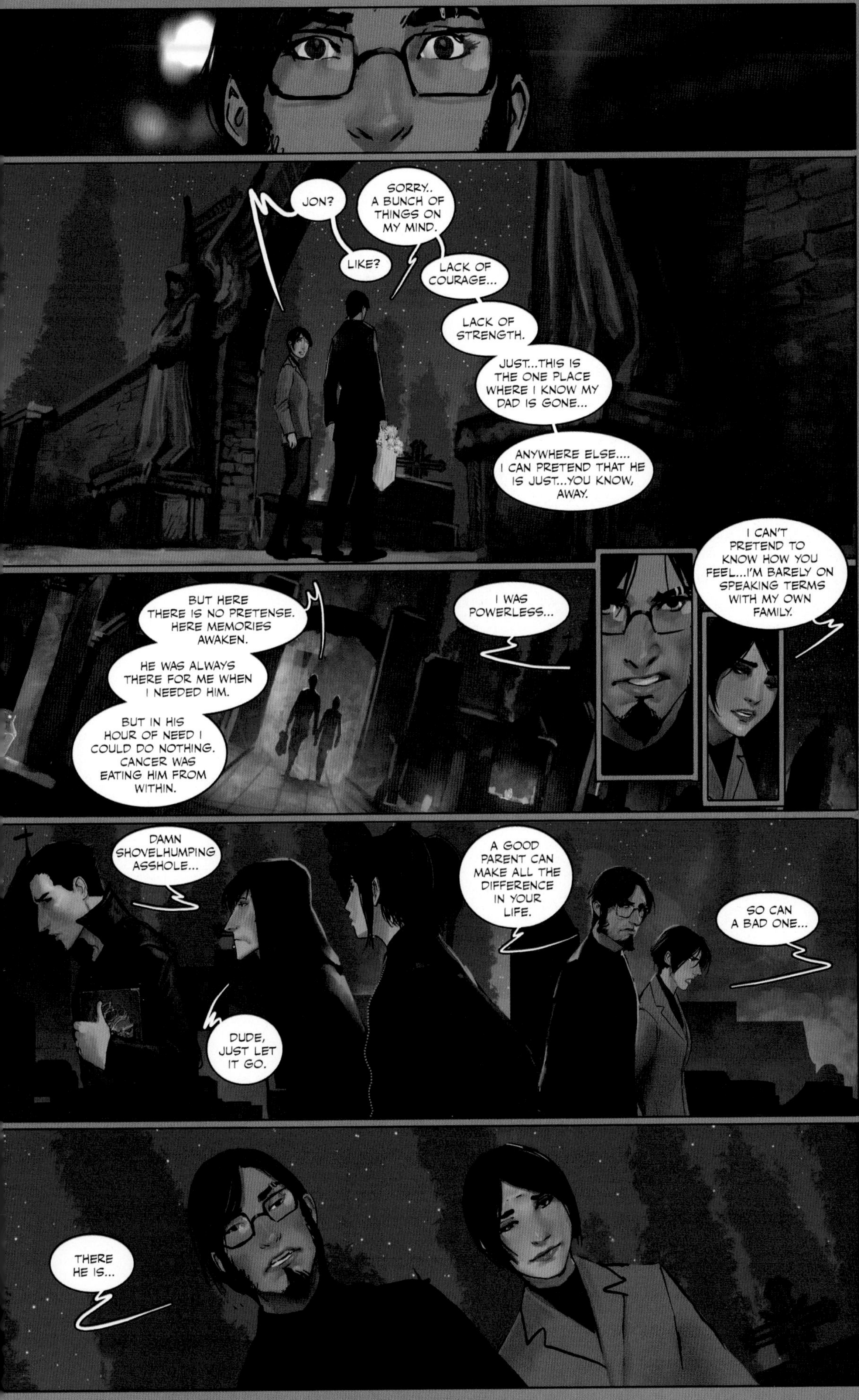
JON?
SORRY.. A BUNCH OF THINGS ON MY MIND.
LIKE?
LACK OF COURAGE...
LACK OF STRENGTH.
JUST...THIS IS THE ONE PLACE WHERE I KNOW MY DAD IS GONE...
ANYWHERE ELSE.... I CAN PRETEND THAT HE IS JUST...YOU KNOW, AWAY.
BUT HERE THERE IS NO PRETENSE. HERE MEMORIES AWAKEN.
HE WAS ALWAYS THERE FOR ME WHEN I NEEDED HIM.
BUT IN HIS HOUR OF NEED I COULD DO NOTHING. CANCER WAS EATING HIM FROM WITHIN.
I WAS POWERLESS...
I CAN'T PRETEND TO KNOW HOW YOU FEEL...I'M BARELY ON SPEAKING TERMS WITH MY OWN FAMILY.
DAMN SHOVELHUMPING ASSHOLE...
DUDE, JUST LET IT GO.
A GOOD PARENT CAN MAKE ALL THE DIFFERENCE IN YOUR LIFE.
SO CAN A BAD ONE...
THERE HE IS...

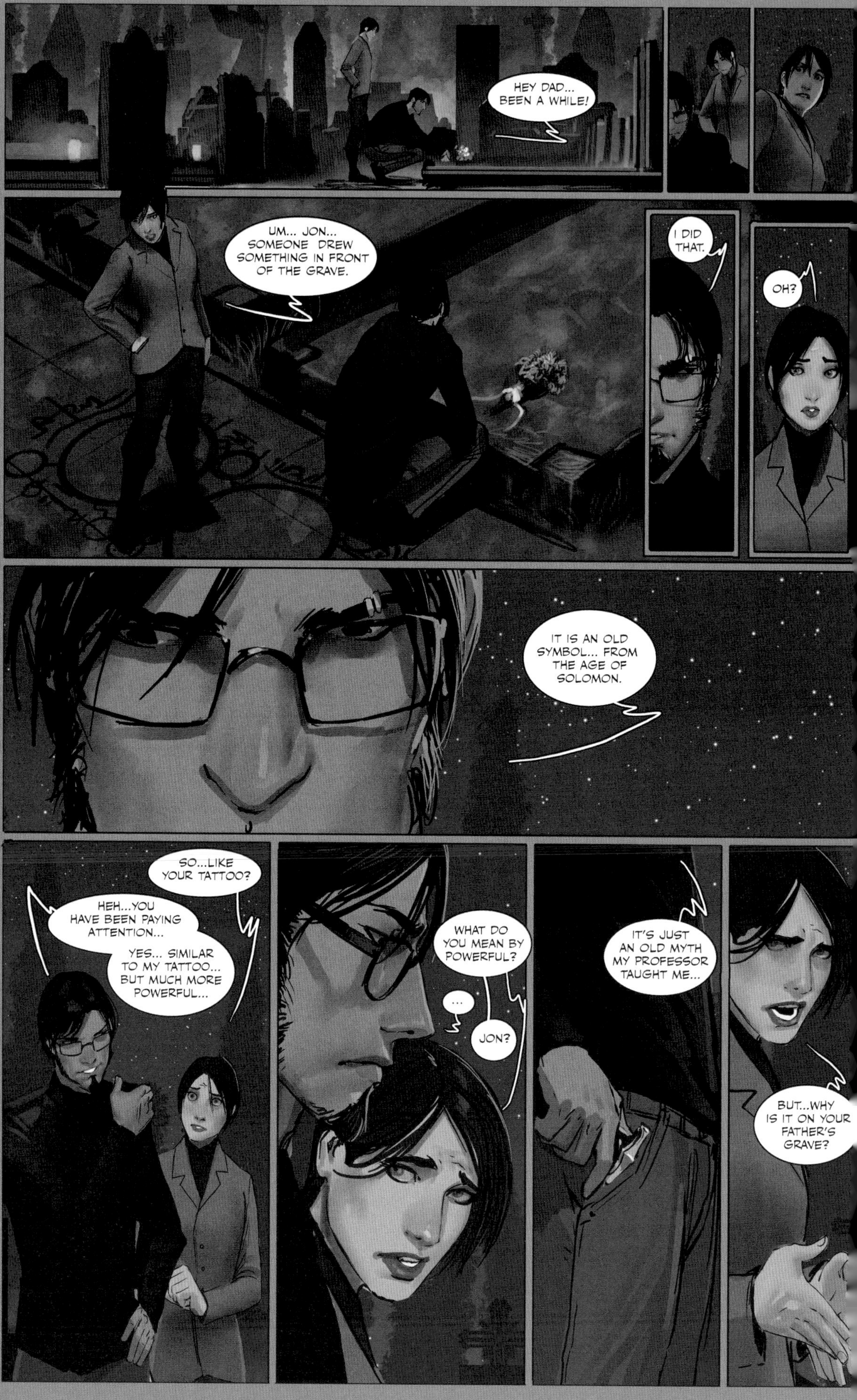
HEY DAD... BEEN A WHILE!
UM... JON... SOMEONE DREW SOMETHING IN FRONT OF THE GRAVE.
I DID THAT.
OH?
IT IS AN OLD SYMBOL... FROM THE AGE OF SOLOMON.
SO...LIKE YOUR TATTOO?
HEH...YOU HAVE BEEN PAYING ATTENTION...
YES... SIMILAR TO MY TATTOO... BUT MUCH MORE POWERFUL...
WHAT DO YOU MEAN BY POWERFUL?
...
JON?
IT'S JUST AN OLD MYTH MY PROFESSOR TAUGHT ME...
BUT...WHY IS IT ON YOUR FATHER'S GRAVE?

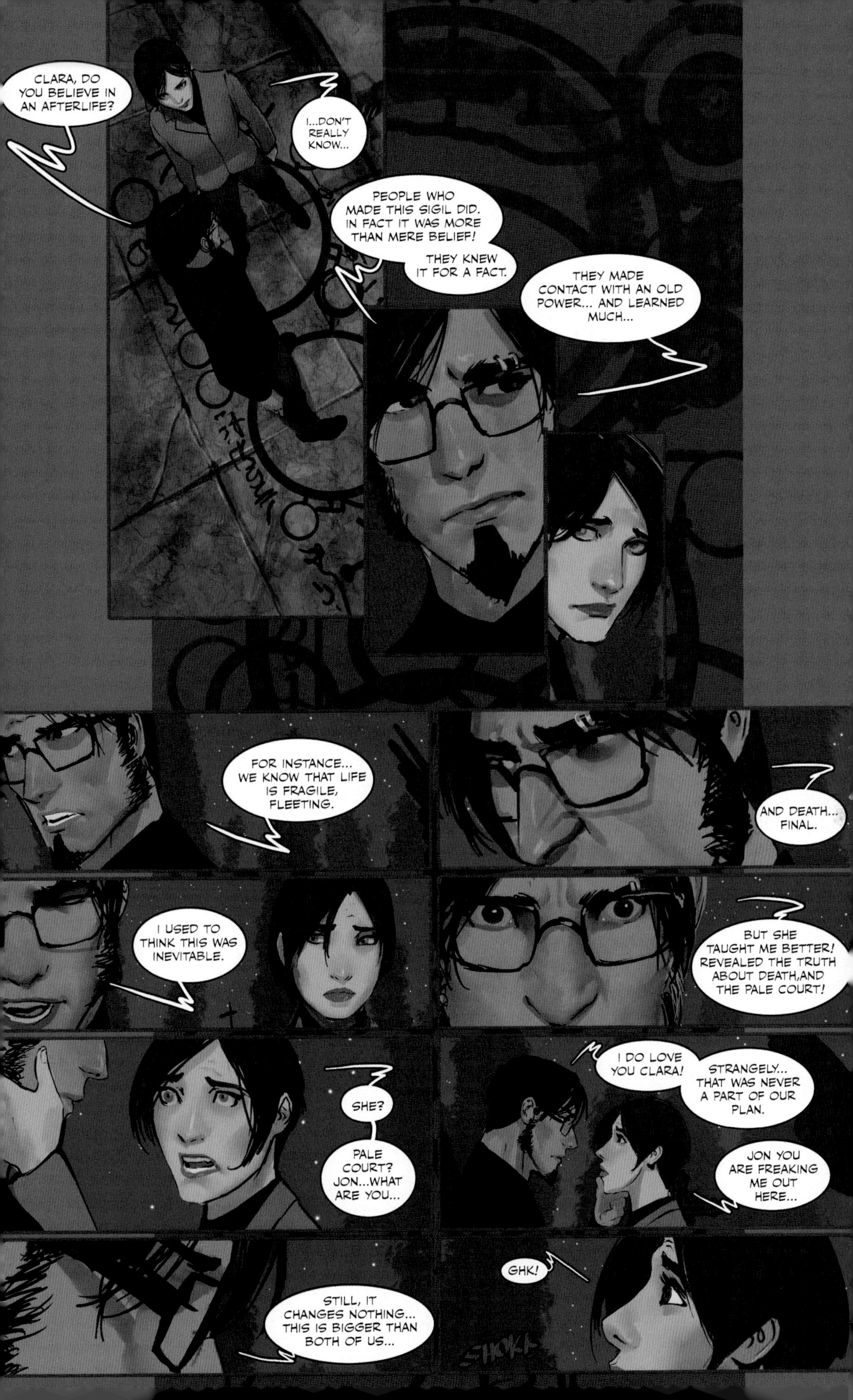
CLARA, DO YOU BELIEVE IN AN AFTERLIFE?
I...DON'T REALLY KNOW...
PEOPLE WHO MADE THIS SIGIL DID. IN FACT IT WAS MORE THAN MERE BELIEF!
THEY KNEW IT FOR A FACT.
THEY MADE CONTACT WITH AN OLD POWER... AND LEARNED MUCH...
FOR INSTANCE... WE KNOW THAT LIFE IS FRAGILE, FLEETING.
AND DEATH... FINAL.
I USED TO THINK THIS WAS INEVITABLE.
BUT SHE TAUGHT ME BETTER! REVEALED THE TRUTH ABOUT DEATH,AND THE PALE COURT!
SHE?
PALE COURT? JON...WHAT ARE YOU...
I DO LOVE YOU CLARA!
STRANGELY... THAT WAS NEVER A PART OF OUR PLAN.
JON YOU ARE FREAKING ME OUT HERE...
STILL, IT CHANGES NOTHING... THIS IS BIGGER THAN BOTH OF US...
GHK!
SHOKK

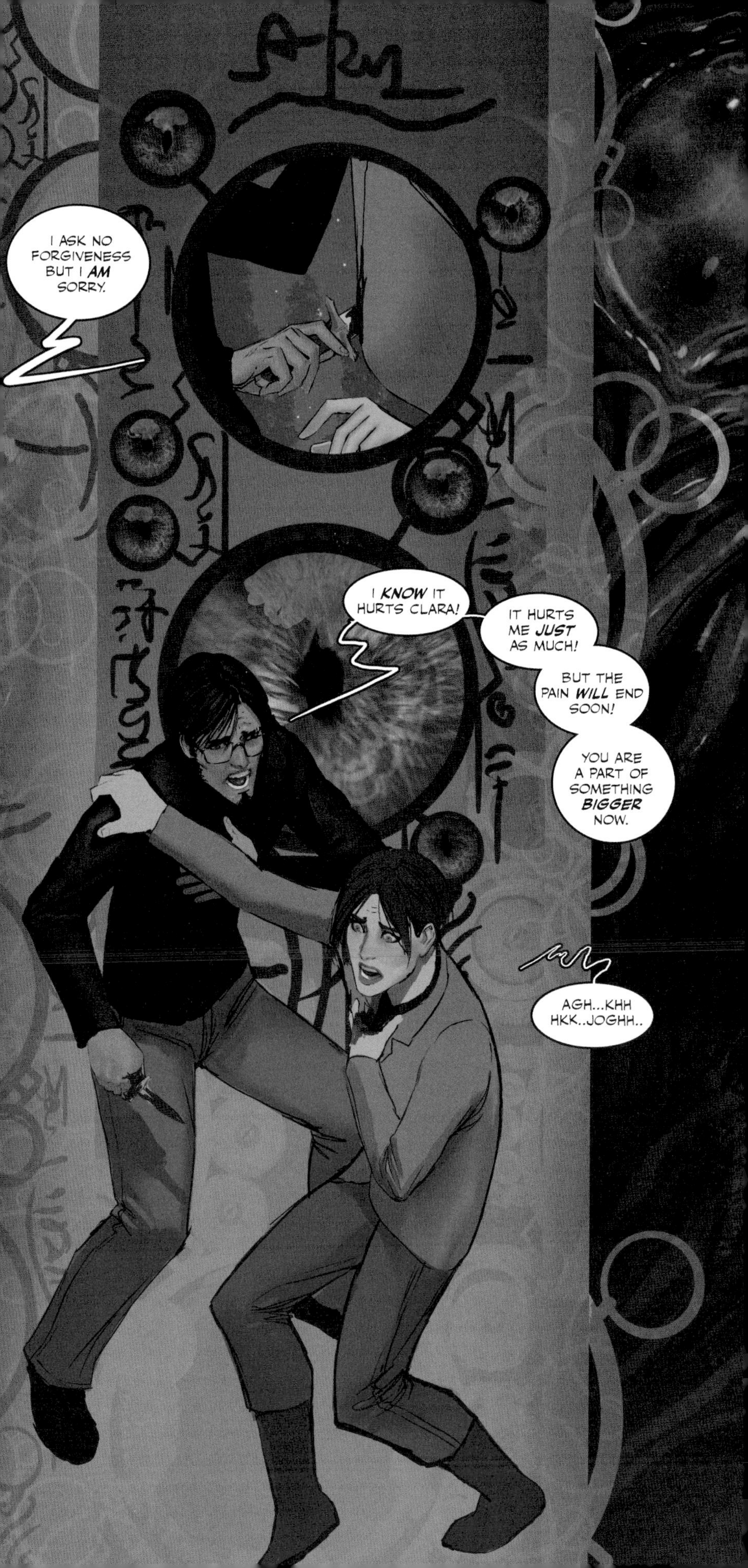
I ASK NO FORGIVENESS BUT I *AM* SORRY.
I *KNOW* IT HURTS CLARA!
IT HURTS ME *JUST* AS MUCH!
BUT THE PAIN *WILL* END SOON!
YOU ARE A PART OF SOMETHING *BIGGER* NOW.
AGH...KHH HKK..JOGHH..

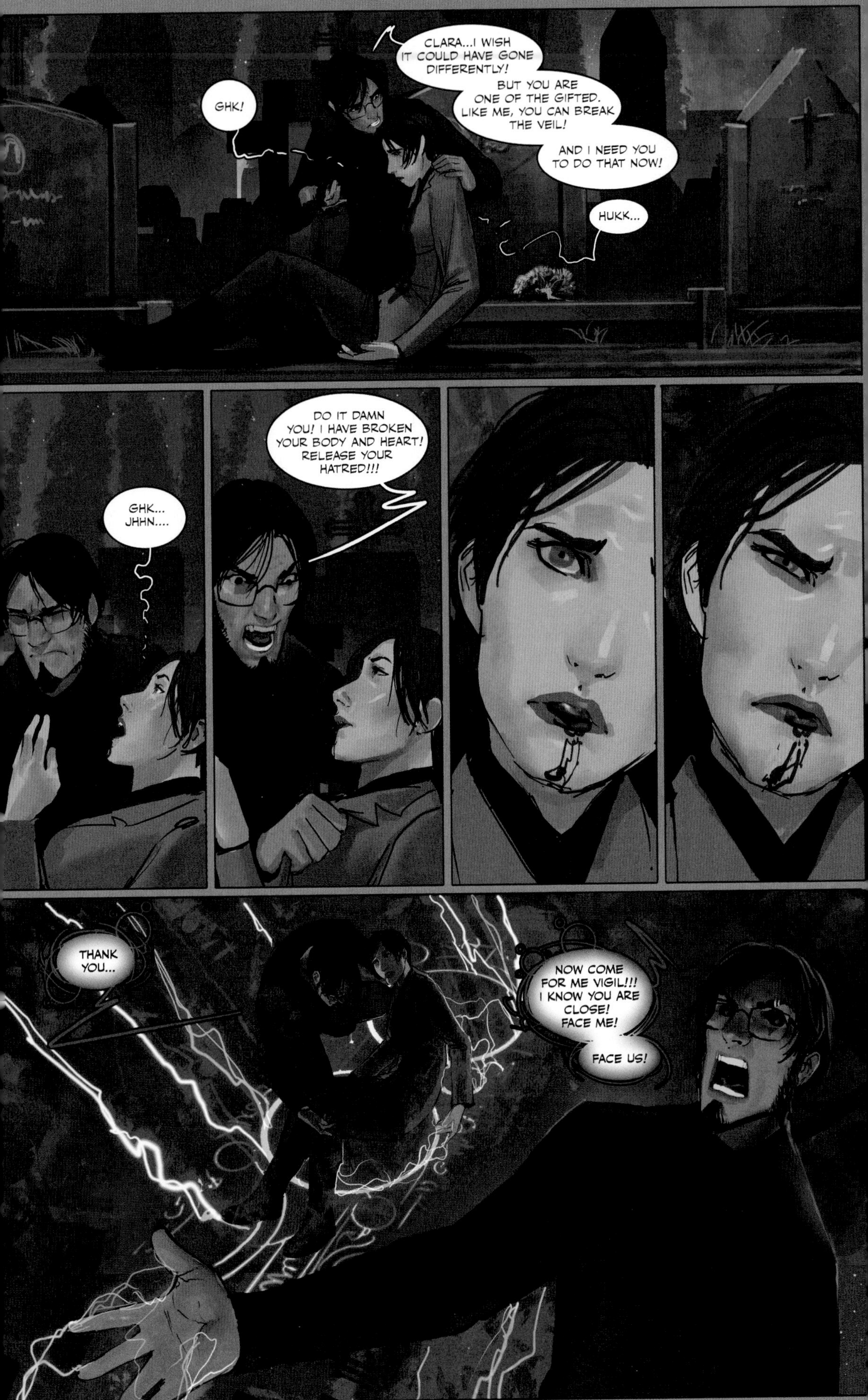
GHK!
CLARA...I WISH IT COULD HAVE GONE DIFFERENTLY!
BUT YOU ARE ONE OF THE GIFTED. LIKE ME, YOU CAN BREAK THE VEIL!
AND I NEED YOU TO DO THAT NOW!
HUKK...
GHK... JHHN....
DO IT DAMN YOU! I HAVE BROKEN YOUR BODY AND HEART! RELEASE YOUR HATRED!!!
THANK YOU...
NOW COME FOR ME VIGIL!!! I KNOW YOU ARE CLOSE! FACE ME!
FACE US!

COVER GALLERY

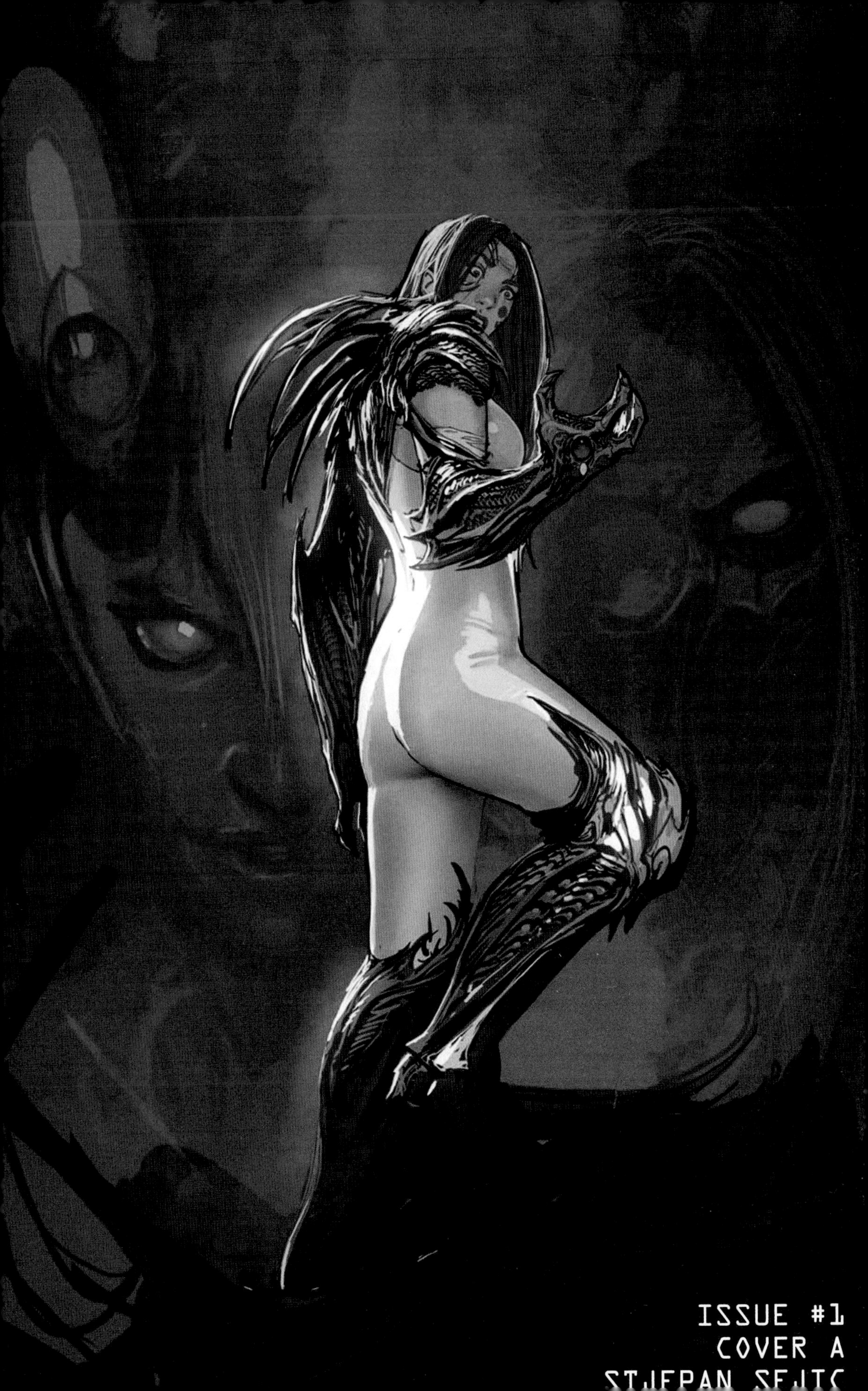

ISSUE #1
COVER A
STJEPAN SEJIC

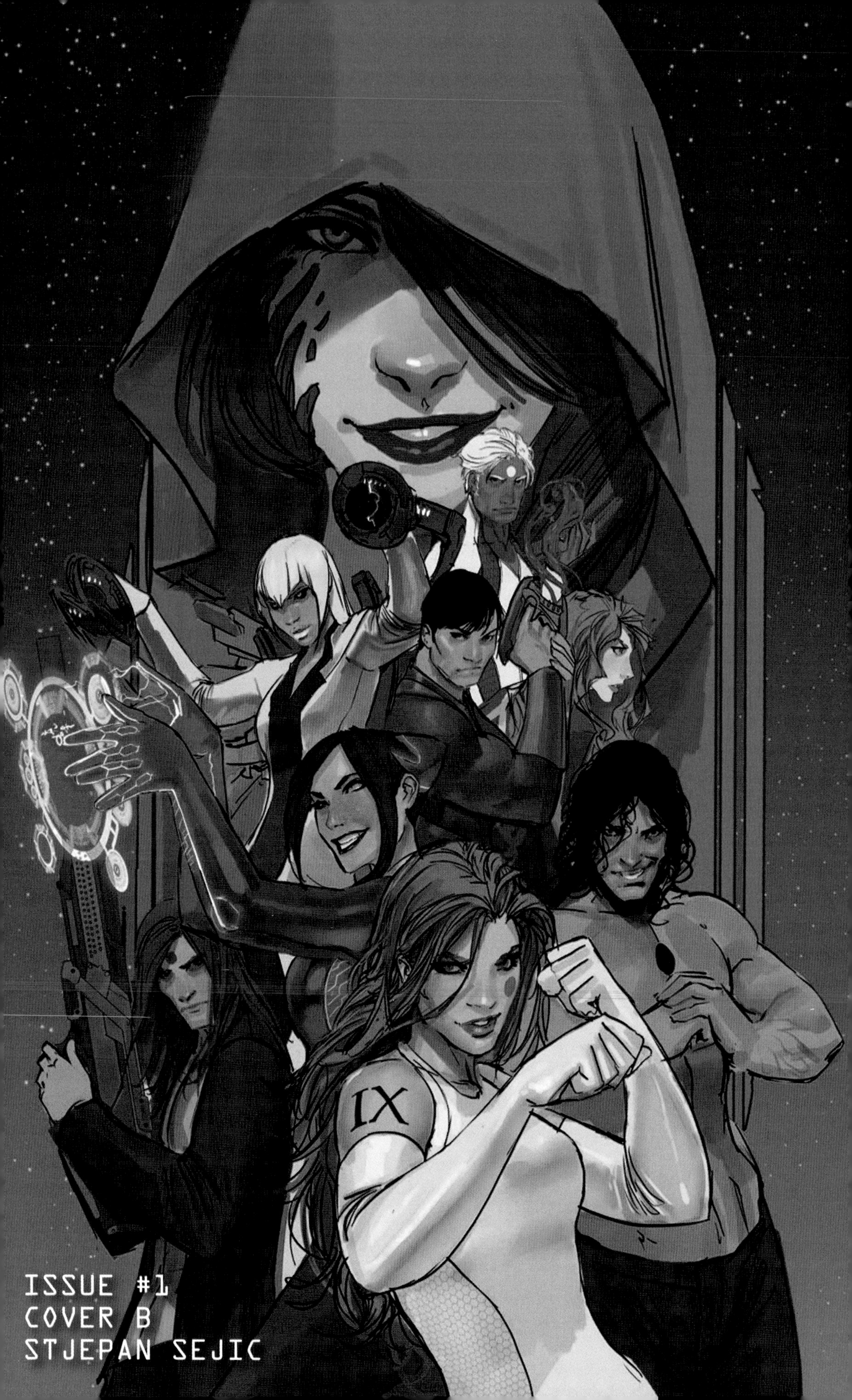
ISSUE #1
COVER B
STJEPAN SEJIC

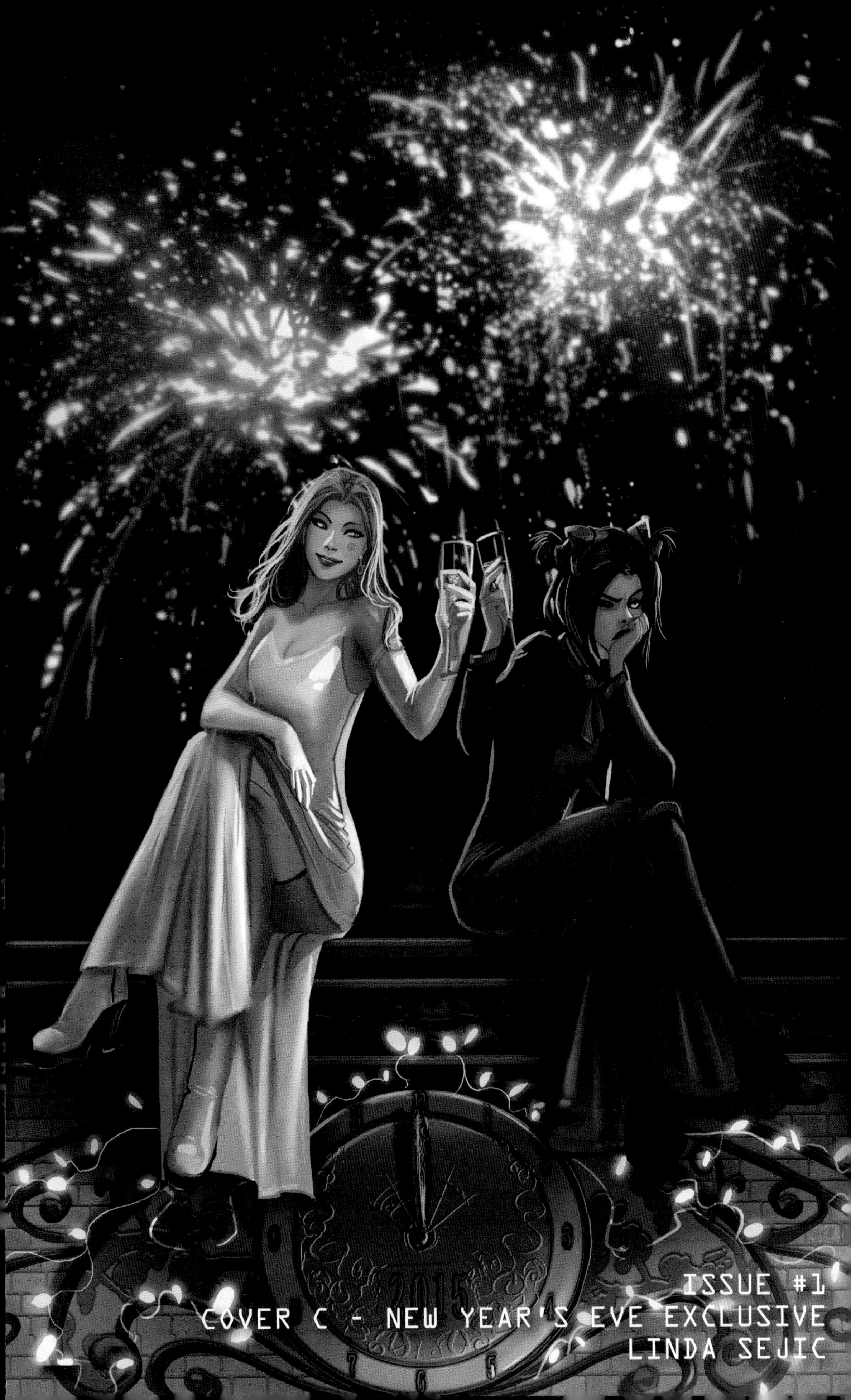
ISSUE #1
COVER C - NEW YEAR'S EVE EXCLUSIVE
LINDA SEJIC

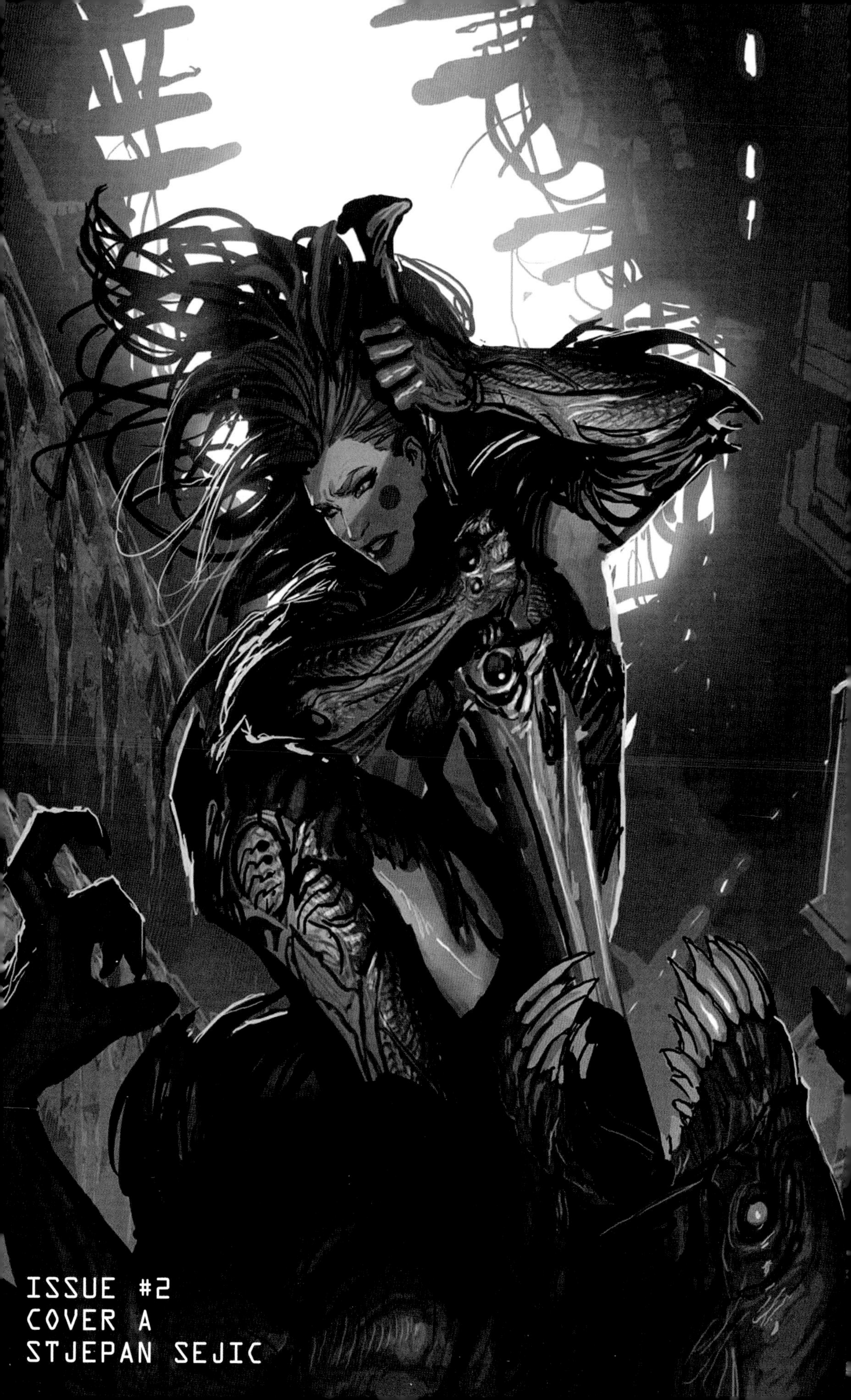

ISSUE #2
COVER A
STJEPAN SEJIC

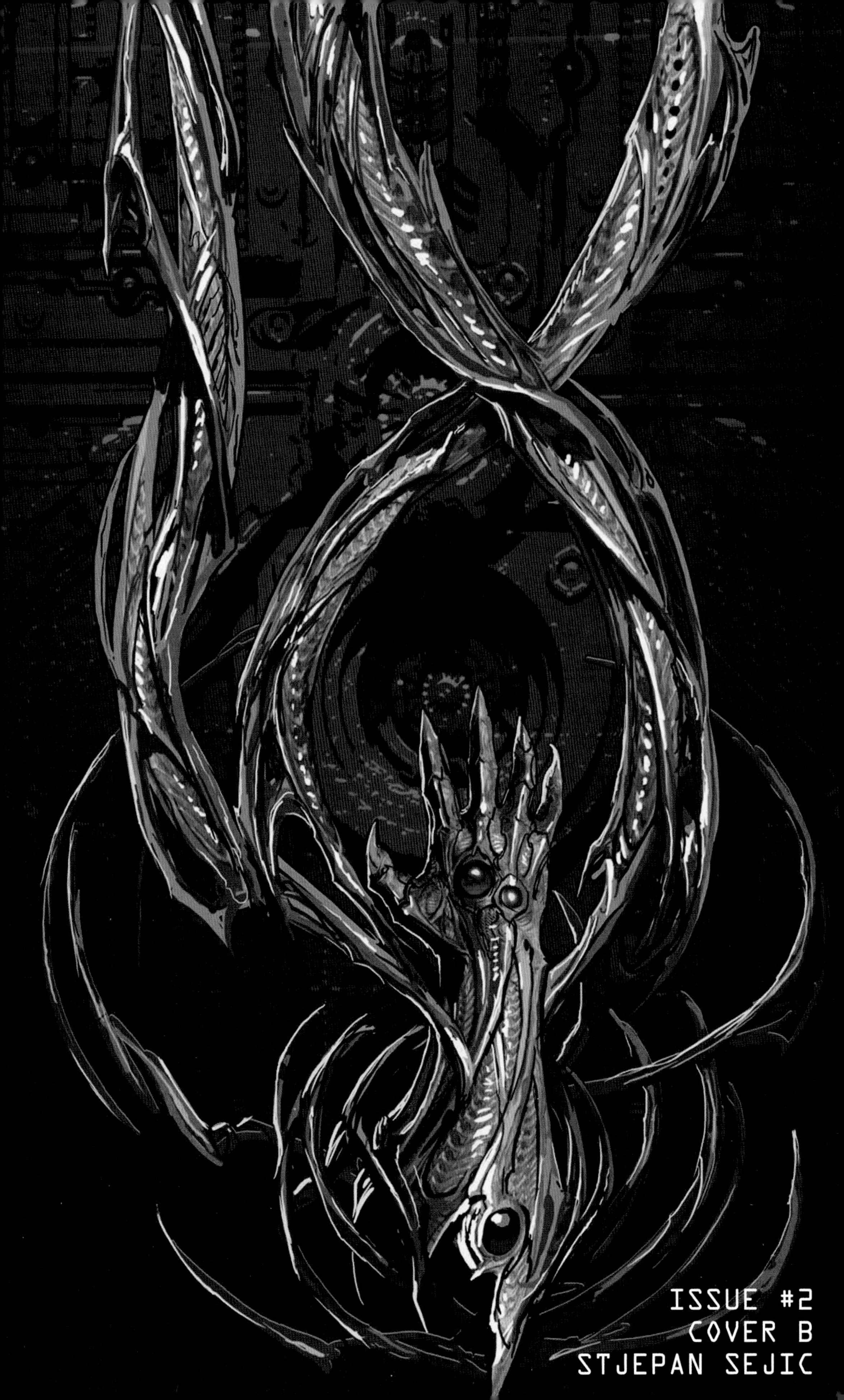
ISSUE #2
COVER B
STJEPAN SEJIC

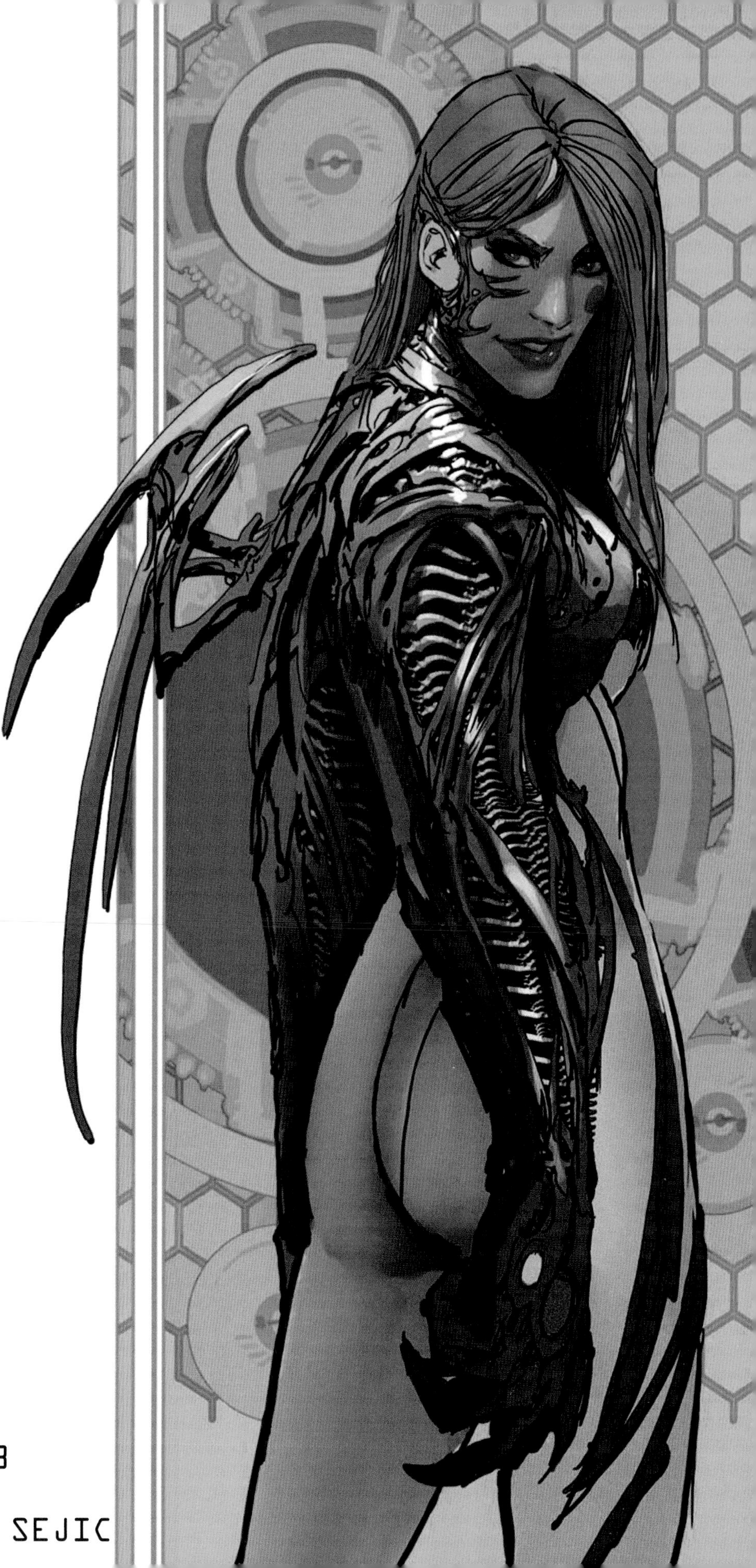

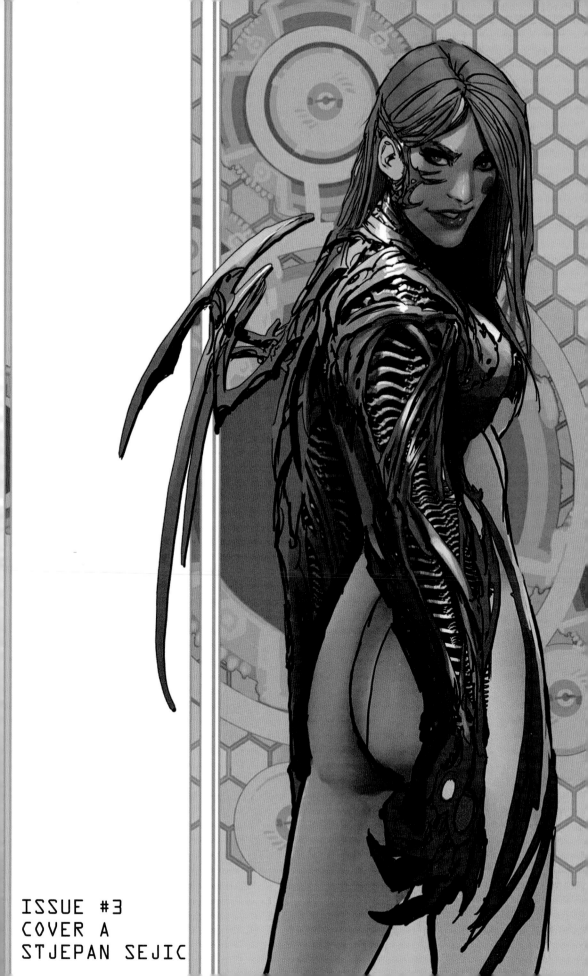

ISSUE #3
COVER A
STJEPAN SEJIC

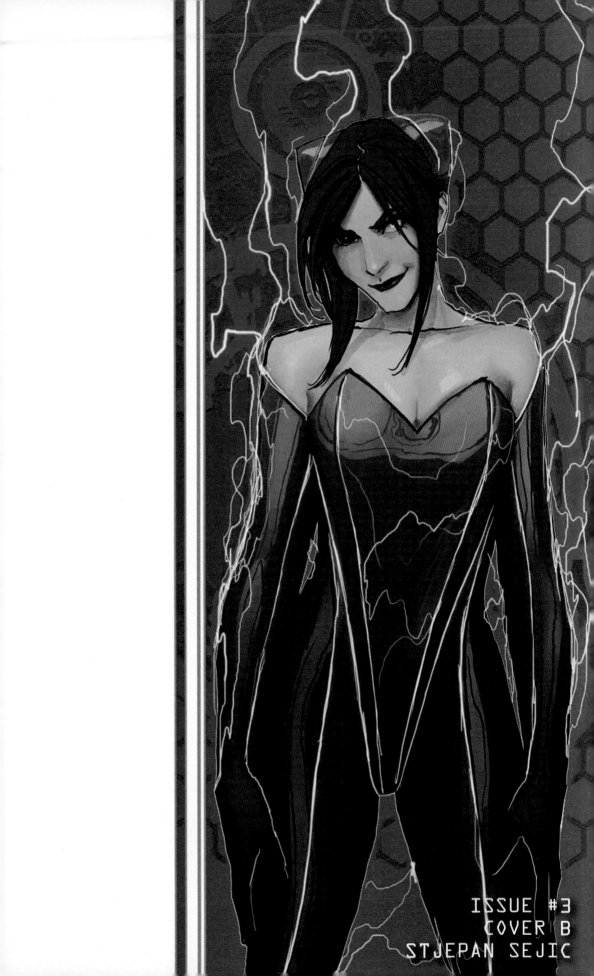

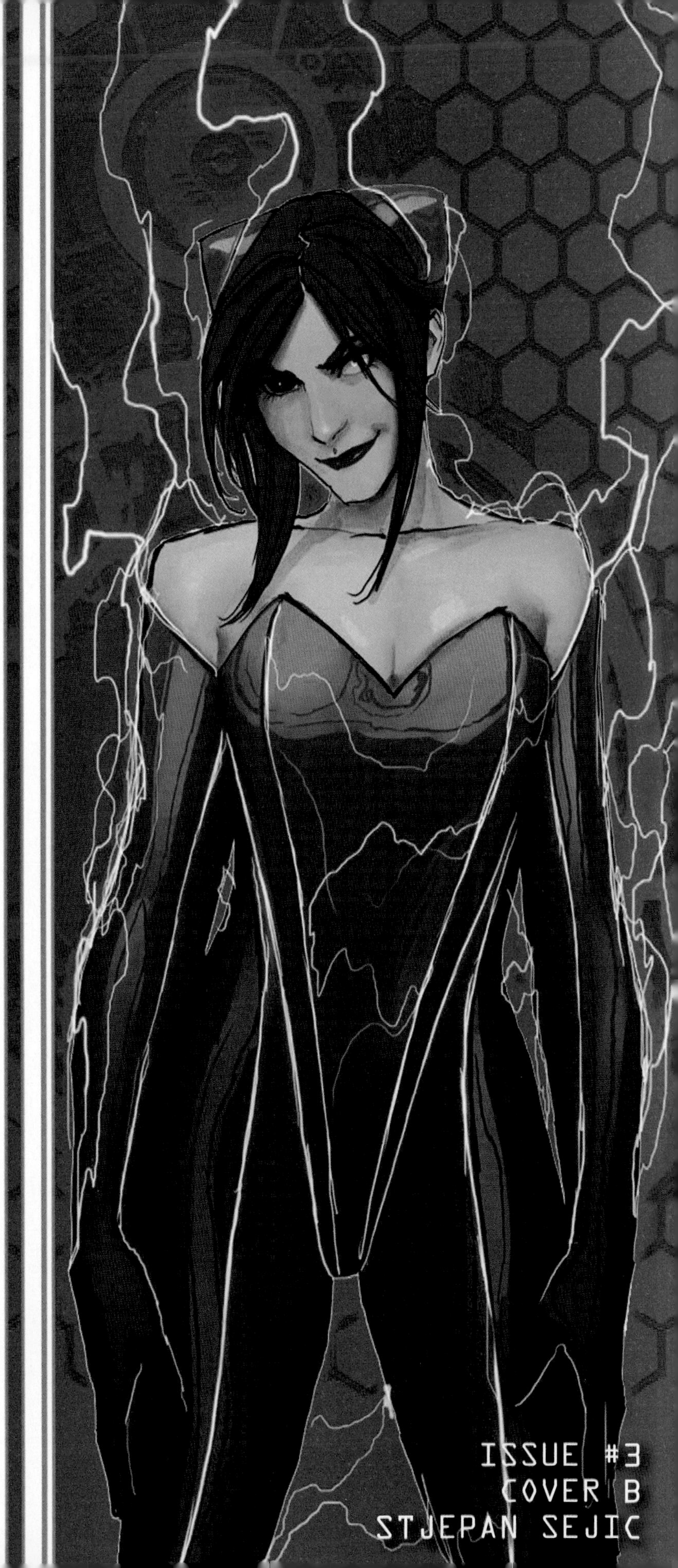
ISSUE #3
COVER B
STJEPAN SEJIC

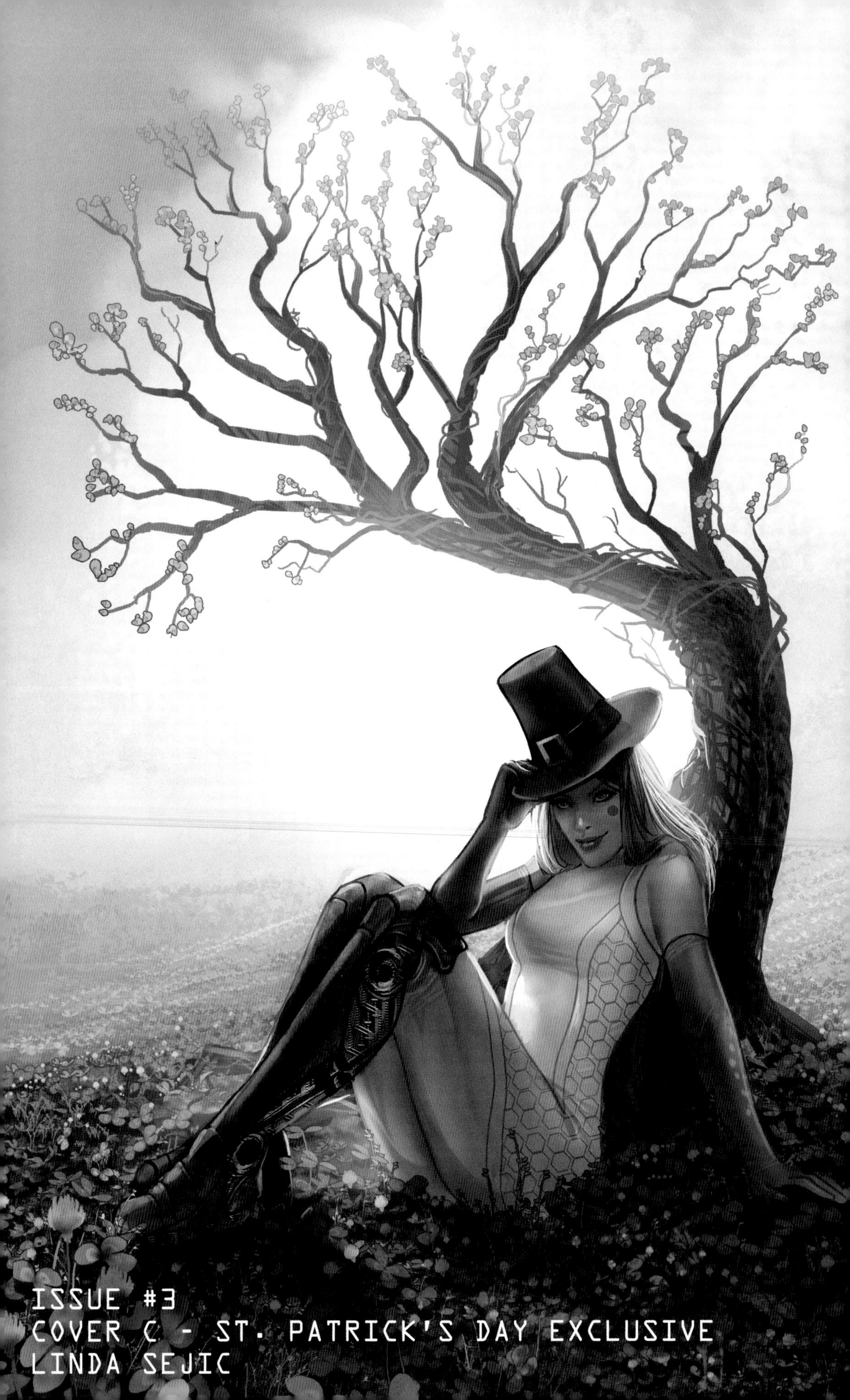

ISSUE #3
COVER C - ST. PATRICK'S DAY EXCLUSIVE
LINDA SEJIC

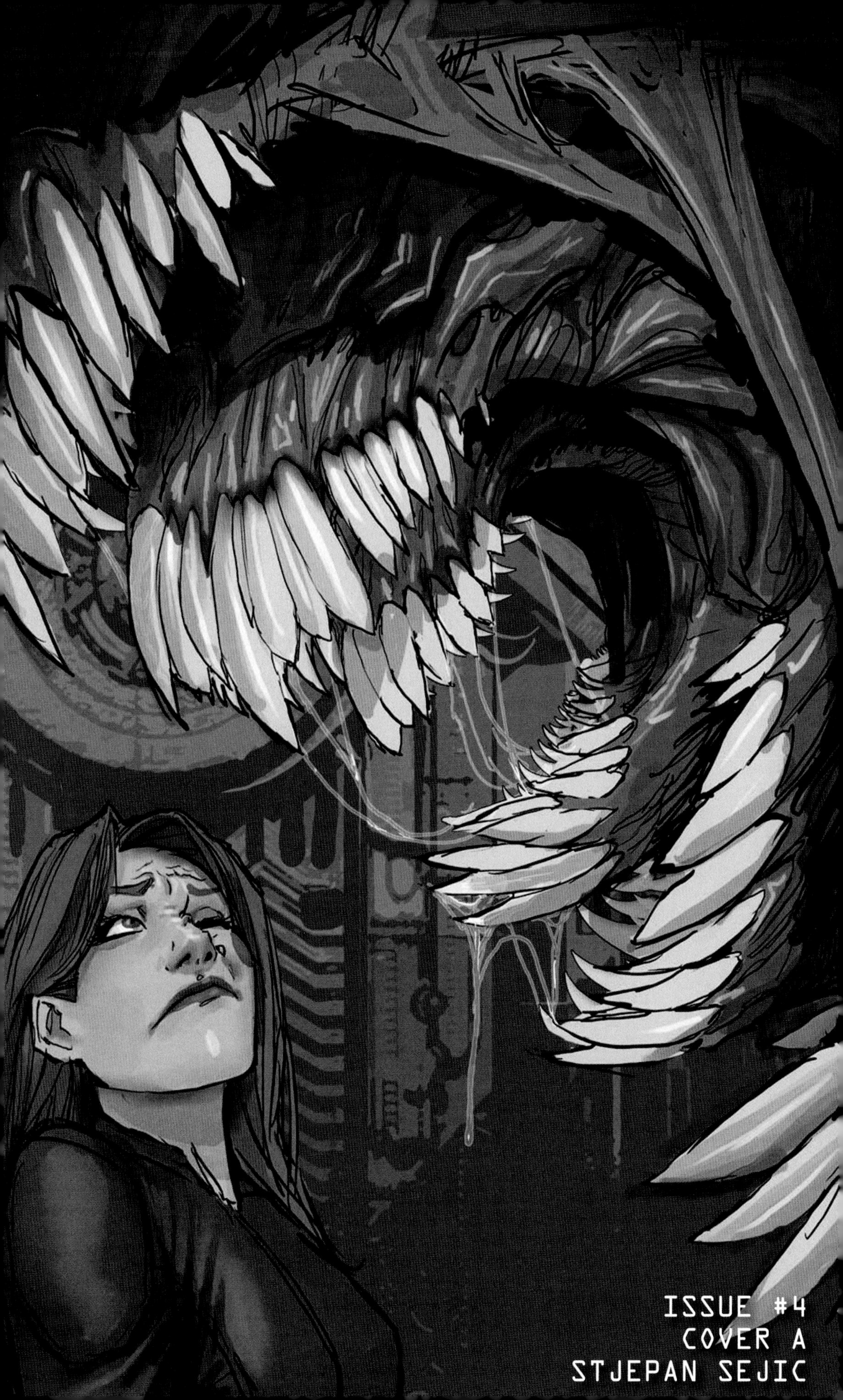
ISSUE #4
COVER A
STJEPAN SEJIC

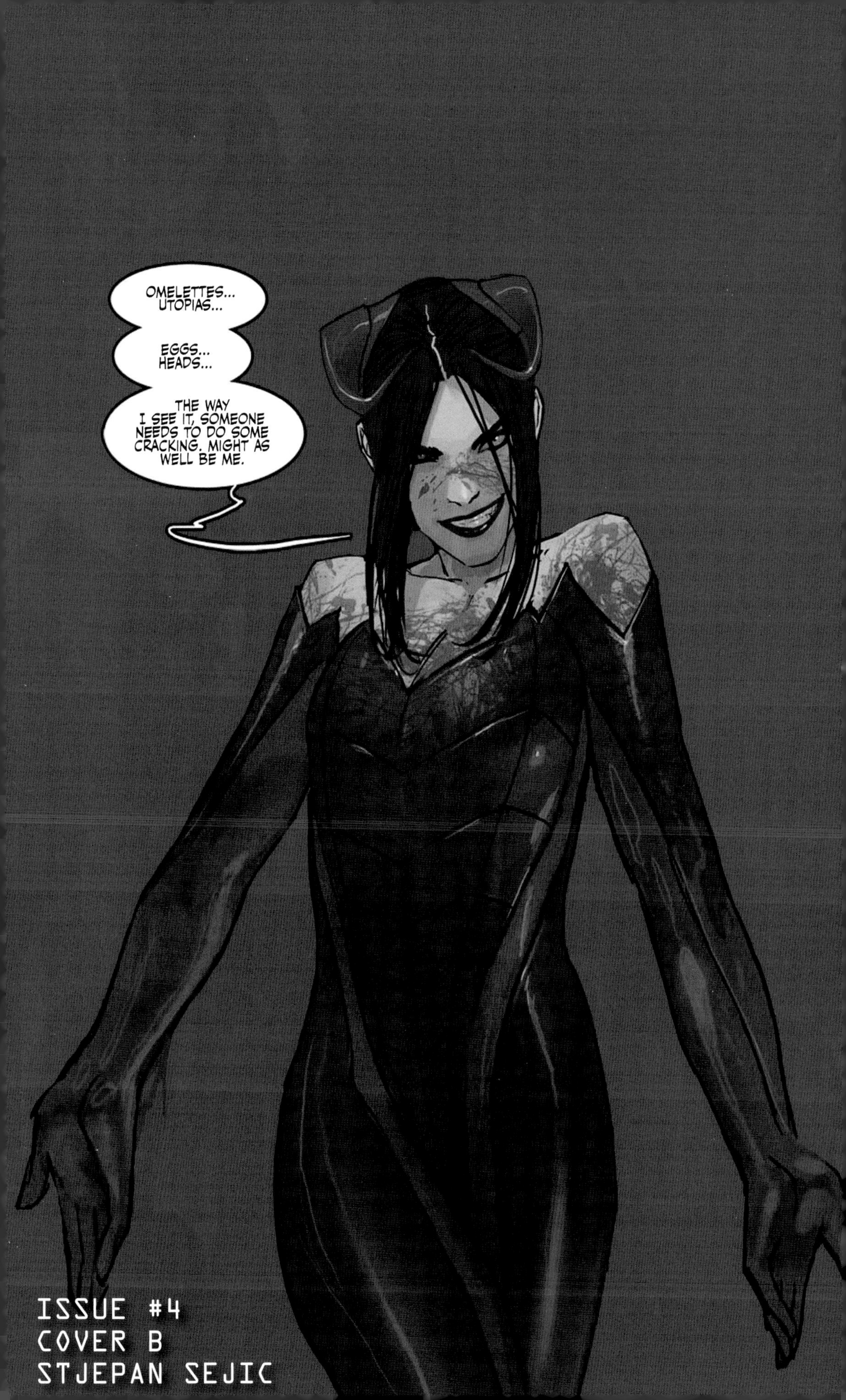
OMELETTES... UTOPIAS...
EGGS... HEADS...
THE WAY I SEE IT, SOMEONE NEEDS TO DO SOME CRACKING. MIGHT AS WELL BE ME.

ISSUE #4
COVER B
STJEPAN SEJIC

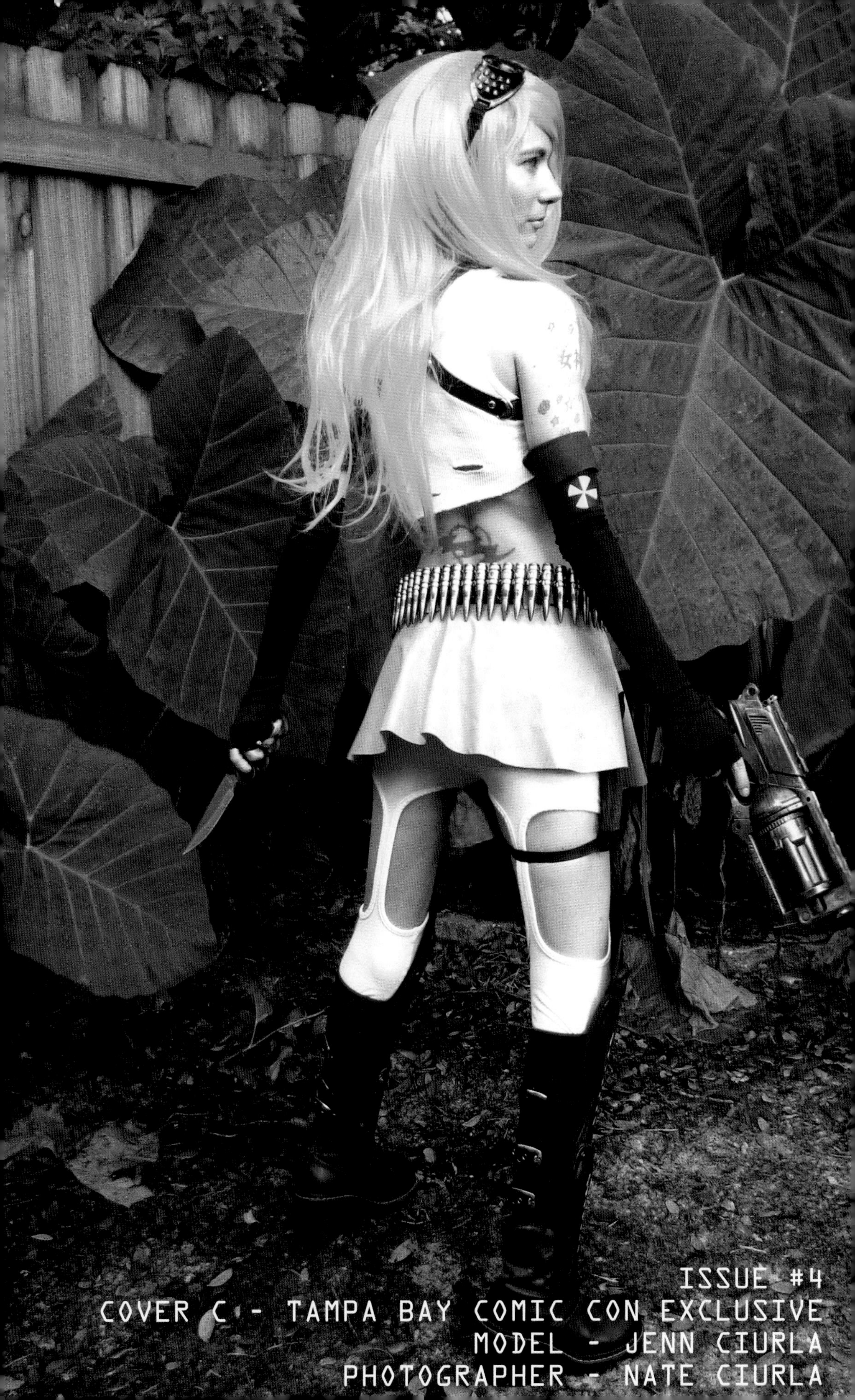

ISSUE #4
COVER C - TAMPA BAY COMIC CON EXCLUSIVE
MODEL - JENN CIURLA
PHOTOGRAPHER - NATE CIURLA

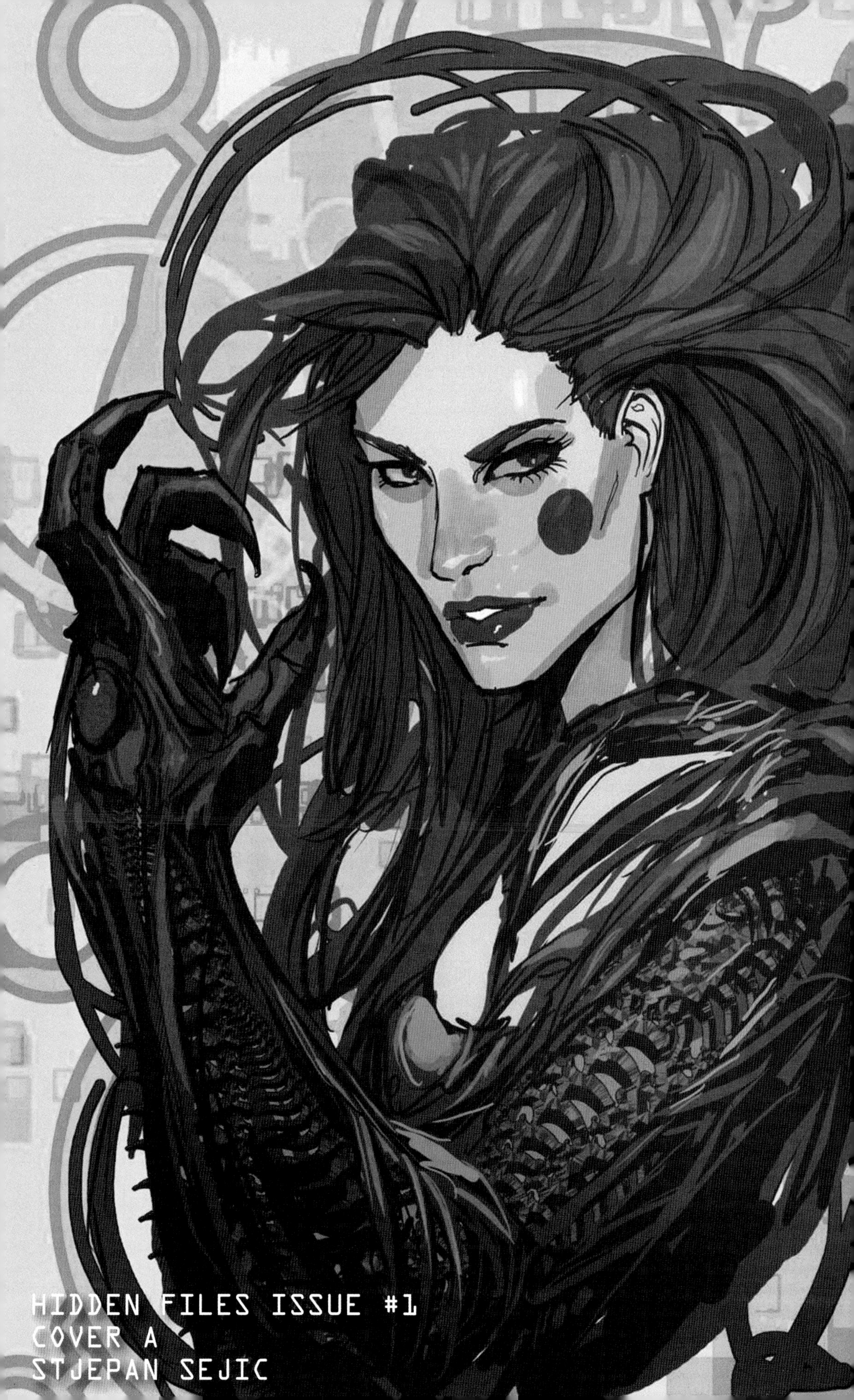

HIDDEN FILES ISSUE #1
COVER A
STJEPAN SEJIC

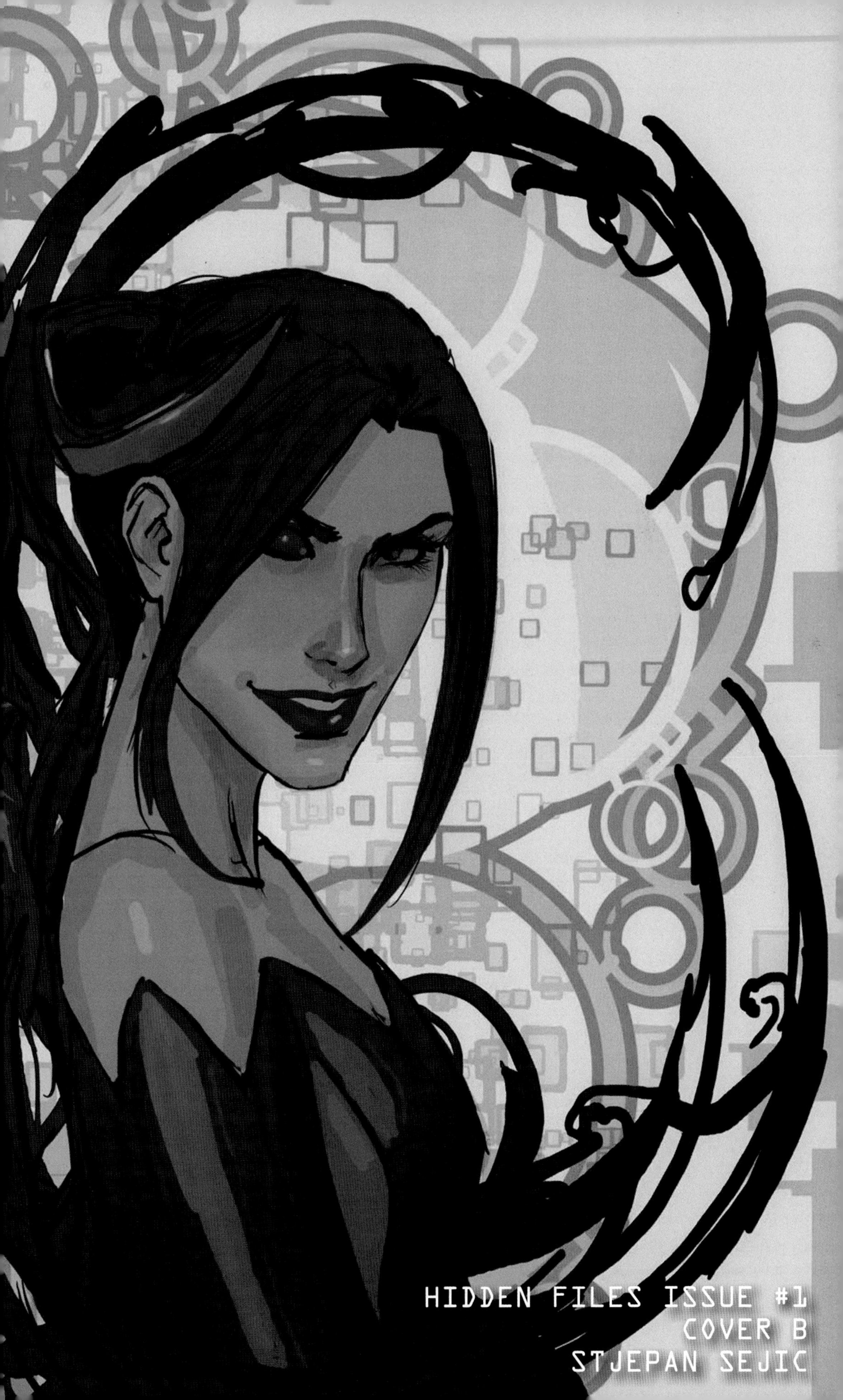
HIDDEN FILES ISSUE #1
COVER B
STJEPAN SEJIC

The Top Cow essentials checklist:

Aphrodite IX: The Complete Series
(ISBN: 978-1-63215-368-5)

Rising Stars Compendium
(ISBN: 978-1-63215-246-6)

Artifacts Origins: First Born
(ISBN: 978-1-60706-506-7)

Sunstone, Volume 1
(ISBN: 978-1-63215-212-1)

Broken Trinity, Volume 1
(ISBN: 978-1-60706-051-2)

Think Tank, Volume 1
(ISBN: 978-1-60706-660-6)

Cyber Force: Rebirth, Volume 1
(ISBN: 978-1-60706-671-2)

Wanted
(ISBN: 978-1-58240-497-4)

The Darkness: Accursed, Volume 1
(ISBN: 978-1-58240-958-0)

Wildfire, Volume 1
(ISBN: 978-1-63215-024-0)

The Darkness: Rebirth, Volume 1
(ISBN: 978-1-60706-585-2)

Witchblade: Redemption, Volume 1
(ISBN: 978-1-60706-193-9)

Impaler, Volume 1
(ISBN: 978-1-58240-757-9)

Witchblade: Rebirth, Volume 1
(ISBN: 978-1-60706-532-6)

Postal, Volume 1
(ISBN: 978-1-63215-342-5)

Witchblade: Borne Again, Volume 1
(ISBN: 978-1-63215-025-7)

For more ISBN and ordering information on our latest collections go to:
www.topcow.com
Ask your retailer about our catalogue of collected editions,
digests, and hard covers or check the listings at:
Barnes and Noble, Amazon.com,
and other fine retailers.

To find your nearest comic shop go to:
www.comicshoplocator.com